Once Upon A Time In Berbice

Malcolm Alves

Once Upon A Time In Berbice

Written by Malcolm Alves

For my cousins in Berbice:

Neville Taylor, Keith, Colin, Terry and
William Myers, Brian, Oswald,
Adrian, Patsy, Andrea, Joanie,
Belinda, Judy and Leslain Alves

Once Upon A Time In Berbice

ISBN:

First Printed – January 2008

Published by Lulu Publishers www.lulu.com
Visit our website at
www.unitedstatesofthewestindies.com
for availability of this book and others by this author.

Cover design by Mal.
Edited by Godfrey Wray

Printed in the United States of America
By Lulu Publishers.

Once Upon A Time In Berbice

Chapter One

My older sister Reena who was a year younger than my seventeen-year-old brother Sunil and five years older than I was, woke me up and as usual I was not pleased. It was never easy for me to get up in the morning, especially when it was a school day. I wiped my weary eyes and drowsily looked around for my younger sister Sondra. The pale yellow glow of the kerosene lamp in the kitchen filtered in and dimly illuminated the little bedroom where four of us children slept on a double sponge mattress spread side by side on a low wooden frame.

We did have a gas lamp but my mother did not light it in the mornings because she did not want the harsh yellow-green light to wake us too early. My stepfather went to work at around four in the morning. He drove a truck for the sugar estate at Rosignol which was some twenty miles to the east.

All four of us children attended the Seaview Primary school and had to take the bus every morning. My mother usually woke Reena first and she was responsible for waking the rest of us. She depended on me to wake Sondra. Actually, her name was supposed to be Sandra but at the registration office my mother had put a little too much English on the pronunciation and the faithful clerk wrote it the way she heard it.

I shook Sondra violently and called her harshly. Sunil was already up and I could hear the commotion in the pig pen at the back of the little shack we lived in. It was his job to feed the pigs.

I sat up in bed and immediately knew that disaster had struck. We never slept in pajamas simply because we had none. The poorest in condition of the shredded old hand-me-downs we got from time to time from Sister Girdharry came in handy as sleeping clothes. Now I could feel mine was wet at the entire front and I immediately knew that I had wet the bed again. My mother had been threatening to tie a crappaud by the bed to stop me and Sondra from wetting the bed so often and I dreaded that she might one day carry out that promise. I quickly looked for a way to blame the "crime" on someone else. Sondra was sleeping next to me on one side and Reena had slept on the other side. Both Reena and Sunil had apparently given up on the bed-peeing idea a long time ago and obviously thought I should leave that to Sondra. But for some reason my body would not let go of the practice.

I sat there trying to think of how to pin the crime on a very drowsy Sondra. I pretended to be rousing her again and felt the front of her old dress to see if she had accompanied me in swamping away the bed. No such luck. She was as dry as can be. She rolled over and was going back to sleep again. She was always hard to awaken in the mornings. I held her gently by the arm so that she would not awaken and rolled her onto the wet part of the bed where I had done my damage. She remained there but I realized she would not get soaked enough to convince them she was the one who wet the bed that morning. I would have to add some help.

After I was done squirting the evidence on Sondra, I took off my wet pants quickly and concealed it way under the bed frame. Then I dived into the big cartoon box behind the door and quickly located another pants. I pulled them on and went out into the kitchen, leaving Sondra asleep on the bed.

My mother was stabbing at something in the black and battered frying pan over the unsteady flickering blue and orange flame of the two-hole kerosene oil stove. It was sizzling noisily, steaming and spitting quite a bit. The kitchen reeked of frying fish and oil. Reena was leaning out the kitchen window and over the old enamel kitchen sink noisily washing wares.

Once Upon A Time In Berbice

I took the old galvanize bucket by the door and stepped outside into the cool morning air. It was still dark but I could see the streaks of pink in the eastern sky. I had to full up the barrel by the kitchen sink with water from the trench some thirty yards away and to the back of the yard. The tarred barrels to the side of the house that caught rain water from off the roof held water that we used for cooking and drinking.

I stepped on the wooden planks that lay on top of the soggy track all the way down to the trench. The noise from the crickets and frogs were dying down now that the day was dawning. The sound of birds whistling was becoming more dominant. I could see the lamp light on in my friend Majeed's house across the trench and on the other side of the bisi-bisi covered savanna.

It was my chore to water the plants; the greens and other vegetables that littered the little kitchen garden bordering both sides of the board walk-way to the trench. I had to complete that in the afternoon before turning in to bed.

I reached down to the trench and bent at the waist and knees to scoop the bucket into the dark water. I strained a bit as I straightened up then lifted the bucket onto my head. It was easier for me to carry it that way. I really preferred to carry two buckets at a time in my hands but Reena was using the bucket in the kitchen. One bucket was inconvenient to carry in the hand because I had to lean over to the opposite side of the hand carrying the bucket to prevent the bucket from grazing against my leg. I walked carefully up the wooden planks and to the barrel by the kitchen. I took the bucket off my head and emptied it into the barrel with a loud splash. Then I returned to the trench to refill the bucket.

It was while emptying the bucket into the barrel for the third time that I heard my mother quarreling with Sondra for peeing the bed, and then I heard the licks start flying and Sondra started wailing. Oh well, better she than me.

Chapter One

After another six trips, the barrel was full and my job was finished. I took off my "sleeping pants" and headed back to the trench again to bathe. We all bathed down by the trench. My stepfather bathed at night or very early in the morning. My mother bathed at night. Reena used to bathe in the morning after day break or there about like the rest of us, but since she began wearing those white things with the cups in front and the straps at the back, she began bathing very early in the morning when it was still dark.

My stepfather had made a little cubicle with zinc sheets out in the yard and we all used to bathe there. But since on two occasions we came across two snakes - though harmless - all of us abandoned this bathroom and bathed in the open near to the trench.

The spot on which we bathed was a little down stream from where we dipped water to fill the barrel. I got there and picked up the cut butter pan we used to dip water. On a piece of zinc nearby was a piece of soap that we all used. I dipped the pan into the water and shivered in anticipation of the cool water running over my bare skin. I poured the water onto my head and let it run down my shoulders then down the rest of my body. This usually got rid of whatever sleep might have been left in me.

In another five minutes I was running friskily up the planks back to the house.

"Sondra, give me meh towel," I yelled as I hopped restlessly on the tattered mat by the door to the kitchen.

"Go and bring the boys' towel and give Milo," I heard my mother yell to Sondra.

She came to the door, all snot and tears, and threw the towel at me. By the looks of her I knew Mammy gave it to her good. Sondra probably didn't even know she hadn't really wet the bed. I wasn't sorry for her a bit. She usually got away with a lot at home because she was the youngest.

I gingerly dried my skin with the towel that I shared with Sunil. I ran into the bedroom and threw the towel onto the

4

wooden clothes horse there. I went over into Mammy's room and rubbed some powder on my chest and spread it under my arms and other places. Then I took the coconut oil off the ledge against the wooden wall and threw some into the palm of one hand. I rubbed my palms together then bent down and rubbed the oil all over my legs and arms. I listened to locate Mammy and Reena. They were still in the kitchen. I located the little fancy bottle of perfume on Mammy's vanity case and threw a little in my hand then rubbed it on my chest. I corked the bottle again and went into the little room in front that we called the living room. It was even smaller than Mammy's bedroom.

On the back and seat of the only chair in the living room, an old battered settee that Mr. Parkinson from up the road had given to my stepfather, Mammy had spread our school clothes. Each of us had only one suit of school uniform. Usually before she went to bed Mammy could be heard ironing with the two heavy irons which had to be heated on the kerosene oil stove. She also did ironing for the Parkinsons.

"Milo, take out that mattress to sun. Don't leave it in there to stink-up the place," said Mammy.

"Mammy, I have on me school clothes," I said since I knew she would not want me to risk damaging my clothes when carrying out the sponges.

"He lie, he ain't put on nothing yet," said 'big mouth' Reena.

"Milo, get you'self in there and take out dem mattress," Mammy shouted. "And if you pass out here in your school clothes you' getting it."

I stomped into the bedroom to let all at hand know that I was mad at this chore. I dragged all the bedding off the bed in a pile, then picked up one of the sponges. It reeked of pee; the fresh and the stale, along with the sour of perspiration. The sun could only do so much and no more.

5

Chapter One

As I came through the kitchen with the mattress I shot Reena a nasty look. Were it not for her running off at the mouth Mammy would probably have let Sunil carry out the mattress. I went out the back door and around the side of the house where the sun would be for the first part of the day. I knew the spot well. I had enough practice. Usually when I brought out the mattress I am in tears since it would be just after a spanking. But Sondra took that for me already.

As I lay out the first sponge on some blacksage bramble placed there for that purpose I looked around farther to the east and across the public road. Chandra Ramnaught lived in the house across there. She had the same mouth problem as Reena and found it profitable to talk about the frequency of my bed-wetting - which she could have counted by the number of times I brought out the mattress - with the others in my class. I did not find that funny.

I returned inside again and brought out the other one. As I passed through the kitchen Sondra was coming in from bathing at the back.

"Next time you pee up the bed I go tie a crappaud on you' foot," I muttered to her.

" Mammy!" she bawled. I knew she did not like that.

I smiled then went around the side of the house. I placed the second sponge beside the first. I straightened up and, out of habit more than anything else, looked across the road for Chandra. She was standing there by her gate with a milk jug in her hands and staring in my direction. I scowled and lowered my hands to cover my privates. Then I scooted back inside.

"Is what smell so?" Reena said as I went through the kitchen.

"Smell how?" Sunil said. He was in the house and going out back to bathe. He had on his blue buckta - a sort of underwear - and the towel I had just used over a shoulder.

"Somebody have on perfume," Reena said. I kept going, hopefully out of the range of Reena 'Pinocchio.'

"Come here Milo," said Mammy. I halted. I knew I should have put on my school clothes first to cover some of the scent. I had made two trips past them and thought I was safe since they did not smell anything. Then I realized that the stench of the sponges would have overpowered any perfume.

My mother came up to me while she dried her strong dark hands on her dirty apron. For a minute I thought I was being approached by a sniffer dog, for she had her nostrils flared and was sniffing loudly. By the time she was up to me I knew I was in for it.

"You been thiefing my perfume again!"

"No Mammy," I lied stupidly.

"Go and bring the belt," she said. By the time I turned for our bedroom Sondra was already trotting out with belt in hand.

After I stopped hollering I went into the living room and put on my school clothes. I could still feel the angry burning on my buttocks. That Reena would have to be dealt with. I could not think of anything then but I knew by the end of the day I would come up with something. I had tried doing something with the belt before but it had backfired. I had thrown it in the trench at the back one day only to have Sunil find it five days later and return it to Mammy. He didn't get licks anymore, so he didn't care about the belt being in the house. When Mammy wanted to punish him she refused to give him cinema money. The soaking of the belt for those five days seemed to have cured the leather in it somewhat and it seemed to sting more than it did before.

I sat at the table and drank my "sweet broom" tea and ate my bakes and peanut butter. Mammy was now packing

Chapter One

the four-sectioned lunch container which Sunil carried to school for all of us.

After I was through eating I went outside with a cup and my toothbrush and made much of brushing my teeth so that Mammy wouldn't send me back to do it again.

By a quarter to seven we were all standing at the roadside waiting for the bus. The bus usually came just after seven. If we missed that bus it is not likely we would get another until somewhere after eight. Most of the buses coming from Rosignol were running express to Mahaica or Georgetown at that time of the morning. After then the buses would be crowded with workers who were going in to work for eight o'clock.

While we were standing there my mother was looking through the window during one of her very few breaks.

"Sunil, don't forget to buy the kerosene oil," she called out. "You have the money?"

"Yes Mom," said Sunil. He thought he was too big to be calling her "Mammy" in public so he called her "mom." He had tried calling her by her first name once but the slap she registered to his jaw put an end to that idea.

Chandra came out of her gate with her red and white uniform looking all new and stiff with starch. Her hair was combed with a little thatch spilled over on her forehead and the rest combed back and plaited in two at the back all the way down to her shoulders. There was one red ribbon at the end of each of the plaits. That was her hairstyle every day. I used to think her mother only had one page of a hair styling book.

She came across the road with her cute plastic book bag slung across a shoulder. I wished the bus was passing now. She said "hi" to Reena and gave me one of those "I-know-what-you-did" looks. I sucked my teeth and looked up the road in the opposite direction. I could see my friend Majeed from next door, coming out of the dam leading from his house at the back to the road. He came up the

8

road in that slow shuffling way of his. Except for Chandra, none of us had book bags. We all held our books in our hands. Sondra was in Big Infant and, instead of a book, carried a slate bordered with a wooden frame.

"Look what I get yesterday," Majeed said when he came up to me. He dug into his bulging pants pocket and came up with a shining tagga which was actually one of those square washers used on the wooden poles supporting the electric cables. We used it to play tagga - a game similar to marbles.

"Where you get it from?" I asked and looked at the thing with genuine surprise.

"Me uncle give me last night when he stopped by we," he said as he threw his head back proudly and brushed a lock of hair from his forehead. Majeed's uncle drove a bus. My uncle was something called an accountant. Whatever that was he didn't get washers at work. When I grew up I wanted to be a bus driver.

Majeed and I were close. We were both in our second year in the same class; second standard. We had also been repeaters in the last class. We both had a passion for tagga and slingshots. And we both hated girls, except for Mala. We both thought Mala was the prettiest girl in our class. As a matter-of-fact, she was the prettiest in the whole school.

The bus came shortly after. It had been picking up school children all along the coast and we all had to stand by the time it got to us. I recognized most of the children from our school in their red and white uniforms, including a bunch from my class. I gave them the "cold shoulder" before they gave it to me. They looked upon me and Majeed as if we were aliens because we couldn't spell words like "this", "that" and "when."

I tucked in my shirt properly and tried to look more decent. I had spied Mala at the back. She usually got a drop to school in her daddy's rice truck as it went by school on its way to Mahaicony. When the truck did not go that way she used the bus. She was talking with Cindy Fiffe, her best friend. I nudged Majeed as I eyed Mala. He looked in the same direction and smiled broadly at her. He had one of those round faces and full eyes. His teeth were small and spaced and his big jaws made his smile look goofy. Mala didn't pay attention to us. So we stood there waiting for her to make us happy with at least a glance.

The bus was approaching the village with the police station and we forgot about Mala for a while. Bhahandas Teelockdharry Jainarinesingh lived in this village. We called him Dracula. He was a stocky Indian lad with broad drooping shoulders and long arms with big hands dangling at the end. He thought Dracula was a cute name, which was the kind of intelligence that got him kept back in our class - much to our displeasure - for a record third time. Mrs. Seecharran, our class teacher, referred to him as "our resident student." Dracula was a full-out bully. He squeezed, choked, knuckled, and pummeled us for minor reasons such as looking at Mala. He knew that we liked Mala and for some strange reason thought Mala was fond of boys who looked like gorillas and had fangs for teeth. He figured if we stopped goggling at Mala then she would have a chance to notice and admire him. So anytime we were in the vicinity of Mala we were entitled to a knuckle each or a half-nelson if we were lucky.

Apart from the fact that Dracula was dead from the teeth upward the only advantage that we had was that he had all that bulk to carry around, the result being he could not run well, at least not enough to catch us. The problem was that most of the time we were in close quarters with him and if we did run today he would catch us tomorrow.

I remembered Ms. Seepersaud telling Miss Griffith, "...The dunce ones are never absent." This held true for Dracula - and come to think of it, it also held true for me and Majeed. As the bus came up to a group of students at the side of the road he stood out like a sore toe. He had his three books - two exercise books that had more dog ears than a congested city kennel, and a text book that was used primarily for resting his lunch when he sat on the playfield to eat at midday. He wore the same formerly white shirt with its seven curry and two jamoon stains. His pants showed signs of expansion at the sides, and buttocks caused by the stress and strain from the expanding bulk enclosed. He stood there gaping at the windows, apparently looking for Mala. Instead he made eye contact with us. He smiled; at least he thought he did. To us it was more like that little grimace Dracula does before he jumps on a well-blooded neck. I could feel my head aching already and my throat muscles began flexing as though preparing for the choke hold.

They all came on the bus and I tried to stay to the front to distance myself from Mala. On came Dracula. He had his tall lunch carrier in one hand and his books in the other. I began to smile at him, thinking his hands were filled and he couldn't hurt us. He continued grinning, passed an armpit - that smelled slightly better than my mattress - over my head and the next thing I knew I was in the midst of a half-nelson. He squeezed while Majeed patiently awaited his turn. I pretended to gag and I could see his lunch carrier right before me. I took aim and planted a solid kick at it while gagging loudly as if I was suffocating. My foot connected solidly with the container and I winced a bit. The pain was drowned out by the satisfaction of seeing his lunch canister bang against the metal cover of the engine by the driver. Curry crab spilled all over the steps of the bus and anyone who was in the vicinity.

Dracula let go of my neck in surprise and I dropped to the floor grabbing my throat and gasping, pretending to be in great distress.

"Is what the hell..." began the middle-aged driver.

"He was choking him," Majeed quickly pointed out and stabbed an accusing finger at Dracula.

"What the hell you choking the li'l boy for!" shouted the irate driver.

"He always doing it," said Majeed. "He does choke we for nothing."

"He was troubling me," Dracula mumbled.

"You just come on the bus. I didn't see that boy tell you nothing," said the driver. " I ain't want no rats on meh bus. Clean up that mess." He reached under his driver's seat then threw a dirty rag at Dracula. The monster slowly picked up the rag from the floor and began working on "de-currying" the man's bus.

I made a quick recovery as the bus moved off. The driver continued fretting under his breath. I turned and sniggered with Majeed now that our tormentor was in trouble. Mala was looking in our direction. I gave a little wave to her and she smiled broadly. Then me and Majeed began arguing about to which of us the smile was directed.

I got a little tense as we came to the end of our three mile journey to school. I figured Dracula was going to have my hide when we came off the bus. I positioned myself close to the exit. Sunil had the passage money for all of us. He would pay behind me. As the bus came to a stop before the school I darted out and ran a good fifty yards up the road before slowing down and looking back. Majeed was running away from the bus and toward me. There was no Dracula in sight.

"Where he is?" I asked anxiously.

"He still in the bus mopping up curry," Majeed said.

We stood there looking to see the monster alight from the bus. More children came oozing from the bus but Bhahandas Teelockdharry Jainarinesingh did not emerge. The bus moved off again and continued west. We walked back to the school gate and asked one of our classmates what had happened to Dracula.

"He ain't finish wiping up the bus so the driver say when he finish he go let him out. He carry him up the road," said the boy.

Me and Majeed cracked up with joy when we realized that Dracula would have to leg it back to school from wherever the driver dropped him.

"Let we go for Hector," Majeed said and we headed up the road past the school. We walked slowly over a wooden bridge over a trench by the roadside and down a long dam. Hector lived nearly two hundred yards down this dam.

When we got to his house which was very much like mine, and called for him, his mother announced that Hector had just got out of bed. We waited in front of his yard on the dam. Majeed took out his tagga and made a few practice throws. I took a turn at it and silently cursed my uncle for being stupid enough for being an accountant when being a bus driver was there for the taking.

Hector came out half-hour later with biscuit crumbs all over his mouth and his crotch wide open.

"Aye, your 'cake shop' open boy," Majeed said and laughed. Hector smiled sheepishly and was looking at the open crotch of his pants as though he didn't know what to do. He turned back and ran into the house.

"Mammy," we could hear him shout. "Where the safety pin to pin up me crotch?"

We slowly headed down the dam back toward the public road and the school. The exciting adventure of Dracula and the Curry-Crab fiasco was related to Hector with full dramatization. Hector didn't enjoy it so much, probably because he was thinking of what Dracula was going to do to us in return. I planned to eat my lunch early. Dracula was not going to rob me of my lunch that day.

As we came over the wooden bridge across the trench we saw children rushing for the gate. To our horror we realized it must have been eight o'clock. Sometimes, depending on which way the wind was blowing, we couldn't hear the school bell from the dam.

Other children galloped over the bridge and dashed madly up the road toward the school gate. As they got there it was swung shut before them. Two of the bigger boys from the forms were bringing out the desk over which we boys would have to reach for us to be caned. The fourth standard teacher who we all called Spanky behind his back, stood behind the gate smiling cunningly. He was slowly tapping the wild cane on the open palm of a hand and had the general air of a rooster at a cockroach convention. The gentleman was probably sizing up the little bottoms he would soon be smoking into. Not mine if I could help it.

I turned up the road away from the school and Majeed and Hector followed. It was not likely that he would see us. I led them into a nearby dry goods shop.

Five minutes later we were with the little crowd of students that had accumulated at the gate. Spanky had rolled up his sleeves and was now flexing his muscles. We made our faces appropriately distressed to match the expressions on the faces of the other students.

Spanky began asking the first in line why she was late. The girl mumbled something and got two lashes in her hand for her troubles. She wept loudly and held her paining hand as she walked slowly up the steps and into school. The children in school were goggling at us and laughing and making faces. I did not like them one bit even though I did the same thing when I was early.

The second in line was a lad named Tyrone who was always late.

"And why are you late?" asked Spanky who looked at the lad with bored eyes as though he knew a lie was about to be served up. Tyrone did not disappoint him.

"Sir, me grandmother dead yesterday Sir," said Tyrone with eyes cast downward as though weighted down by grief. From personal experience I knew his eyes were down casted because that was the best place to have them look when constructing a lie. It helped with the concentration.

"Tyrone, your grandmother dead again? I went to her funeral last year," said Spanky.

"Is the other grandmother Sir," Tyrone said.

"The other one died before you were born," Spanky said patiently.

"Not she Sir, the next one," said Tyrone. Now that was stupid. Even Dracula wouldn't have made a mistake like that when lying.

"How many grandmothers you have boy?" asked Spanky.

"Three sir. And we spend all night last night digging the grave. Is now we finish sir," Tyrone verbally galloped to a finish and from his voice I guessed he thought he ended up on a pretty strong note.

"The one that dead before you were born was your father's mother, right?" said Spanky.

"Yes Sir."

"And the one that dead last year was who?"

"Meh mother' mother Sir," Tyrone said with a glow.

"And the one that dead last night was..." Spanky left that unanswered for him to finish. Tyrone's face dropped. It took him this long for him to realize his mistake.

Instead of finishing the sentence Tyrone reached for the edge of the desk to take his lashes.

"Tyrone, you're getting the usual two for being late, then one for lying, and another two for telling a stupid lie," said Spanky.

While Spanky was working away on Tyrone Majeed nudged me. I looked around and following his direction, looked up the road. Dracula was lumbering in from where ever the bus driver had dropped him off.

Chapter One

Tyrone straightened up after he got his dose. He did not shed a tear. I guessed he had been getting it so often he was immune to licks by now.

Seven out of the following nine students got their licks; the girls in their hands, the boys on the seat of their pants. Two got off without a spanking because Spanky thought their stories were true. I thought they were lying through their teeth. If Burnham came up then and said he was late because he was the Prime Minister I would have thought he was lying. As long as he wasn't going to get licks he was lying as far as I was concerned.

It was Dracula's turn. He had come in behind everybody but as was his custom, he had pushed his way to the front of our little gathering.

"Yes Mister Jainarinesingh, what's your excuse?" asked Spanky.

"Sir I had to clean up the bus sir," Dracula said in that low bully voice of his. Having spent a lifetime telling lies he had trouble making the truth sound convincing.

"What bus. Your father buy a bus?"

"No Sir."

"So what bus you' talking about. Boy, get your lie straight before you reach here."

"Sir, you can ask them sir," Dracula said and indicated the gathering behind him.

"This boy had to clean any bus?" asked Spanky.

"No Sir," chorused the gathering. Actually, they were being honest in their answer because they did not know about the incident on the bus.

"Bend over Mr. Jainarinesingh."

"Sir you can ask them two. They were on the bus," he protested his innocence and pointed out me and Majeed.

"You boys know about this?" asked Spanky. That would be the day when I let the likes of Dracula get off from a licking. I shook my head vigorously in the negative and Majeed followed my lead. Dracula gave us a poisonous look; the kind that would turn a horse blue.

"I thought as much. Bend Mr. Jainarinesingh," said Spanky.

Dracula bent over and took his licks without protest. He was accustomed to not winning disputes when teachers were involved. He didn't cry. He never cried. He walked off into school with his two exercise books and text book. When Spanky wasn't looking he showed us a powerful fist, indicating what was going to happen when he caught up with us.

Four students later I stepped up to Spanky.

"What's your excuse young Teekasingh?" he asked. Now, if I didn't lie he would suspect something. I dug into my archives of lies and fished out an old one.

"Sir, we cow dead," I said lamely.

"When is the funeral," he said and looked like he was resting and catching a second wind more than being interested in me and my dead cow.

"Look," he announced as though as an afterthought to all awaiting his/her turn. "The next person that have something that dead for them going to get two extra lashes."

With that announcement I guessed most of them out there had to re-invent their lies.

"Bend Teekasingh," said Spanky. I reached for the end of the desk.

The first lash landed with a resounding whopping sound. I felt next to nothing, but I grimaced as though he was creating havoc on my behind. The second stroke was even tamer than the first. I figured Spanky must be tiring. I straightened up and squinted heavily as if on the verge of tears. I gathered my books and moved away slowly from the desk and toward the school. I wanted to laugh. The newspaper I had stuffed in my pants had done its job.

I looked over a shoulder as Majeed stepped up, mumbled something, and bent over the desk.

Chapter One

Whop! Bop! I stopped smiling. The sound was totally wrong. I heard Spanky mumble something about the quality of pants cloth. He reached over and pulled at Majeed's pants. The Chronicle newspaper fell out onto the ground. I turned and continued toward the school. Too bad for Majeed. Just as I was about to put some pep in my step I heard Spanky's voice again.

"Come here Young Teekasingh. Both of you buy pants cloth from the same store? Come let me check that pants!"

I dejectedly made my way back to Spanky. I had warned Majeed that was too much newspaper. He wanted to be on the safe side and used the whole Sunday Chronicle papers. As I approached Spanky I could see Hector in the gathering behind the gate trying to get rid of his newspaper.

When we did get into our classroom we were in tears. From the back of the class Dracula took one look at us and started guffawing. For a moment I wished he would bite himself to death with those vampire teeth of his. I dried my eyes quickly and glanced around to the front and side of the class to see if Mala had seen me crying. She wasn't looking my way. I went to my seat at the back of the class but on the side away from Dracula. Most of us repeaters were deposited at the back of the classroom so that the teacher would not be bothered often. My seat was in the same column with Mala's. We all sat on long wooded benches with long desks before us. Each bench seated about four or five students. There were two columns of benches in our class and about four rows. The entire back row was christened "dunce section" by everyone. This held true in each classroom except the infants.

I sat to the end of my bench, right next to the left wall and windows. Hector sat to my right, then Majeed was on his right. Next to Majeed was a tall awkward bespectacled lad we called Blinky. Charlie Valentine sat next to Blinky. Charlie was a kind of celebrity. He was an excellent batsman in cricket, even at his young age. The teachers always came for him when our school had to play another school.

Next to Charlie was a lad we called Goofy. He had these large teeth that he always forgot to enclose in his mouth. The lad just seemed incapable of tucking in those front teeth. When it came to school work Goofy made the whole row look smart. Goofy would probably bring second-to-last in a Little Infant class test. But when it came to playing tagga nobody could touch him. Not even the bigger boys could play better. Down to the end of the other bench was Dracula.

Our teacher, Mrs. Seecharran, was a little woman who had a little too much energy for our liking. Unlike most of the other teachers who usually left "dunce sections" alone, she liked to stray away from the table and come at the back. This was very disturbing to us. It curtailed many a comic-book sketching and reading session.

She didn't wear glasses which I found to be unusual for a teacher. I used to think she wasn't really a teacher but was some kind of prison warden who was lending a helping hand in the school. She was always neat in her pleated skirt and white blouse with the elaborate lace in front. Her long shiny black hair was always combed backward and coiled in a bun at the back of her head. She always wore high heeled shoes but had perfected the art of approaching silently in them by walking on her toes. We didn't like that either. Hector said she liked to drink but I'm not sure that was true. He had said that after she had given him a few across the behind. Cindy once mentioned something about Mrs. Seecharran's husband. *She actually had a husband?*

Mrs. Seecharran was still attending to the register. I chucked my books below the desk. I looked across at the others. Majeed was now finishing up with his crying. Hector was fidgeting with his notebook. He was trying to position one book so that he could discreetly peep at the tables at the back. We all knew that Mrs. Seecharran would begin with the tables. Charlie was just sitting there slumped in his seat. Goofy had his tagga in one hand and was rubbing residue of dirt off it with the thumb of the other hand.

Mrs. Seecharran got up and wrote "Mathematics" on the chalkboard. I knew it was that because the word she wrote began with an "M" and it was too early for Music. At her direction we began reciting our time tables beginning with "two-times" tables. It resounded around the classroom in a loud chorus.

" ... two fives ten, two sixes twelve, two sevens fourteen, two eights are sixteen..." and on we went. Most of us in "dunce section" were repeating the "two fives" and "two sixes" but the answer we mumbled mainly because, for the most part, our answers did not correspond with each other, much less with that of the class.

On we went to three times tables, then four. By this time Mrs. Seecharran was back to her table and fixing up the laced table cloth that covered it, and the books and vase and flowers some girl had brought her that morning. The girls always brought flowers for her. Hector tried that once but he got his tail licked twice that day anyway. Once Dracula had brought some flowers he had picked by the roadside and Mrs. Seecharran looked visibly shaken. I never understood why she was.

Now that her attention was elsewhere I took the opportunity to goof-off. I looked away through the window and onto the public road. A bus sped past and headed west in the direction of Georgetown some fifty miles away. Then a gas truck passed. I nudged Hector in the side.

"Guess what going to pass next," I said.

"Where, so or so?" he asked and indicated east then west.

"So," I said and indicated west.

"A truck," he said.

"A bus," said Majeed who had tuned in to us.

"I say a car," I said.

We were on to seven times tables now. A donkey cart came rolling by to the west.

"Awe shucks, I wanted to say that," said Hector.

"Alright, alright. What coming next," I said.

"A' oil truck," said Majeed.

"A donkey cart," said Hector.

"How much donkey cart it go have running on one road," I fretted with Hector.

"I still say a car," I said and we all looked out the windows to keep watch on the road.

We turned in front to pay attention for they had got to ten times tables. This was fun for us because it was easy.

"Ten ones ten, ten twos twenty, ten threes thirty..." we yelled and the chorus picked up speed like a train. " Ten elevens one ten, ten twelves one twenty!"

Then we all took a deep breath. Eleven times tables was even more fun because the chorus was fantastic.

"ELEVEN ones... ELEVEN twos... ELEVEN threes..." We in "dunce section" didn't care about the answer, just that loud, explosive, exhaled "eeeeleven." When that was done so was our interest. The others continued with the twelve times tables.

"Boy, nothing ain't running on this road this morning?" I asked impatiently as we directed our attention through the window and onto the road again.

"Maybe it had an accident up the road," said Majeed.

Whop! Whap! Whop! I felt the last lash across the shoulder blades. I straightened up as the sting seemed to soak into my skin. Majeed and Hector were also writhing in pain.

"There is going to be another accident back here if you all don't pay attention," said Mrs. Seecharran from behind us.

21

Chapter One

There it was again. As soon as we had pinned her down to the front of the class and took our eyes off her, she sneaked around behind and ambushed us.

"Alright everybody, hold it." Mrs. Seecharran remained standing at the back as the class stopped and looked around.

"Everybody in the back row stand up," she said. The "dunce section" stood. The rest of the class looked around at us with these amused grins on their faces. It was as though an entertainment section was on stage. All of the others were probably thinking that the combined brains of us standing there did not measure up to half of that of any one of them.

"Alright, let's start at the end," said Mrs. Seecharran. I looked around to see which of the ends she indicated.

"What is eleven times four," she said. " Milo?"

I stood there looking up at the roof of the classroom as though in deep thought. "Dammit, didn't we clean this roof two Fridays ago as punishment? Dem spiders gone and make a royal mess up there again. If they think I was going to jump up there again to clean..."

"Next!" Mrs. Seecharran's voice broke my line of thought. I bit my lips and made a facial expression as if I was on the verge of an answer when she moved on to the next student.

"Yes Milo? You got the answer now?" said Miss.

"Miss..." I paused and looked around desperately for a clue on the faces upturned before me. I saw Chandra mouthing an answer to me.

"Miss Seventeen," I said positively.

When the class finished laughing it was Hector's turn. Miss had gone around to the front of the class now.

"Miss Forty-four," said Hector. The class cheered frantically, indicating that Hector was correct for once. For a minute I was shocked out of my wits. Then I realized he was peeping at the answer under the desk.

"Very good Hector. I see you've been studying," said Miss. " Okay. What is eleven sevens. Majeed?"

Majeed squinted and tried to see the little writing on the book that Hector still had exposed.

"Miss he cheating," said a girl named Drupatie who sat in the row in front of us. " He' looking at he book under the desk."

"Bring the book Majeed," said Miss.

"Miss I ain't have no book..." Majeed began and trailed away when he realized it was useless. He took up his book so that Hector would not get in trouble and went to the table with it.

Miss continued with the quest to get the answer to eleven times seven from the rest of "dunce section" and got the following answers: seventeen, one twenty one, (silence), twenty, thirty-four, (silence), forty-four, and from Dracula, exactly one hundred.

With the exception of Hector, we were all marched up to the table and got two lashes in the hand for our lottery-like answers. I took my lashes like a man, mainly because Mala was right in front there watching us. We went back to our seats at the back. A donkey cart was passing again toward the west. Hector was right after all. They must be having a donkey cart convention up the road.

For the next fifteen minutes we were supposed to do some problems Miss had put on the chalkboard. We had some breathing room to fool around at the back because Miss had taken out her radio and was listening to cricket. If there is one thing she liked more than spanking us it was cricket. She was mad about the game and a fanatic when it came to the West Indies. The West Indies team was playing in England. I wished I could hear how Rohan Kanhai, Wes Hall, Charlie Griffith, Basil Butcher, Gary Sobers, and the rest of the boys were doing.

We switched to Reading after another thirty minutes. The cricketers had gone in to lunch or tea or something.

Chapter One

We took out our West Indian Reader text book. We were on page fifty-something. I could pick my way to page six so far. We were going to do a new story that day. Miss let us read by columns. My column read the first paragraph pretty well with no contribution from us in the back even though you couldn't know that by looking at us.

Then it was the next column to read. So we continued taking turns. When the class was down to the last paragraph Miss had a brain wave; what she considered to be a good idea. She was afflicted with one of these from time to time.

"All of you in the back row stand up. You're going to read the last paragraph," she said.

The class began giggling in anticipation of some humor. 'Dunce Section' was going to read. It was 'silly hour' again. We all stood and fidgeted with our reading books. A few of us were now looking for the right page.

"Well?" said Miss.

The story so far was about this spider named Anancy and something about him going to an island named Bird Cherry Island.

"Well?" said Chandra Ramnauth, imitating the teacher.

I gave her the "dead eye." I had not forgotten her giving me the wrong answer to that sum and making me look like a fool in front of Mala.

"Anansi..." I began, for I noticed the first word began with the letter 'a.' The others in 'Dunce section' chorused "Anansi" as they followed my lead. The class erupted in laughter.

"That word is 'after' Fooly-The-Fifth," said Drupatie.

"Oh, I'm on the wrong page," I said quickly and pretended to change the page.

"You' on the right page. You can't read," said Drupatie and she laughed.

"I can read yuh mother," I said under my breath.

"What? Wha' he say there?" Drupatie said to the girl next to her with a frown. She was all for telling Miss on me. Thank God she didn't hear me well.

"Listen," Miss said with a frown. "You boys are in Standard Three and you don't know how to read? When you-all going to take this reading seriously. What you-all intend doing when you-all grow up, eh? Milo? What you want to be when you grow up?"

"I go be a bus driver Miss," I said this proudly for I wanted her to know that I did not have to learn to read to be what I wanted to be.

"A bus driver. You intend driving to Georgetown or New Amsterdam?" she asked.

"Yes Miss," I said brightly.

"Well, unless they have streets with only names like Rat Street and Cat Street, you won't be able to know the names of the streets if you can't read, will you?"

The children laughed again.

"And do you know you will have to do a written test before you get your license?" she asked. I shook my head in the negative. This was news to me. There seemed to be a test stuck in everywhere to hinder us non-readers. Maybe I'll just be a dragline operator. I won't have to know the names of streets.

"And what you want to be Hector?"

"Miss, a doctor," said Hector.

"Doctors have to read books and charts Hector, so I suggest you get started with your reading now."

"Hummm! Me ain't want he operating on me," said Cindy. "He might cut open me head when my chart say 'belly.'"

Even Mrs. Seecharran had a laugh at this remark.

"And you Majeed?"

"A bus driver, Miss."

"Well, I can see you and Milo would be having the same problems. Egbert, what are you going to be when you grow up?"

Blinky batted his eyelids a couple of times as was his habit.

"Miss, a secret agent." Well that killed us all. Blinky as a secret agent! He couldn't even keep regular eye contact with a door and he was going to be like James Bond. Secret agent Blinky - double 'O' zero.

"Secret agents have to know how to read," Miss said patiently. "Charlie?"

"A West Indian cricketer Miss," Charlie said proudly.

"You intend signing autographs?" said Miss.

"Eh?" said Charlie with a frown.

"Autographs, when you have to sign things for people."

"I can write my name Miss."

"Autograph is more than writing your name sometimes," she said.

She continued up the row and just when you thought you knew these boys they up and told you what they wanted to be when they grew up and they seemed like strangers. We had sitting at the back a future lawyer, an astronaut, a cinema door man, an estate truck driver, something called an engineer, a barber, a bicycle repair man, a fireman, two policemen, and a train driver. Then she came to Dracula.

"And what do you want to be Mr. Jainarinesingh?" asked Miss. The teachers seemed to have this tendency to address him like an adult. Maybe his size had that effect on them.

"I go be a teacher," he said in that bully voice of his. Now that floored us all. Dracula as a teacher. We all laughed heartily.

"Boy, you couldn't even teach them plants outside," said Drupatie.

"I can write though," he said. Now it was true that when Dracula did write anything it was extremely neat if one ignored the spelling. Miss gave him one of those strange thoughtful looks.

The bell rang to signal that it was lunch time. Miss Seepersaud had us stand then we said prayers. After that we started leaving the classroom for lunch. Some of the girls gathered around in groups and began taking out their lunch containers. I hurried out of the classroom before Dracula could get hold of me. I looked back and saw him reaching a paw out for an unsuspecting Majeed. I ran all the way up the stairs to Sunil's classroom.

I met him standing on the corridor smiling from ear to ear with a girl named Dolly Shivnarine. Dolly was good-looking, though not as pretty as Mala. She had that little thatch of hair spilling down over the top of her forehead - just like the ladies on the Indian movie posters - and the rest was combed back and plait in one. She had a mole in the middle of her forehead. She looked like a big girl.

" Hi Dolly," I said boldly. She looked at me and smiled. I wished I could say the same for Sunil. He looked at me like he would at a tick on one of our pigs.

Sunil and Dolly

Chapter One

"What you want," he mumbled out of the side of his mouth then smiled at Dolly again.

"My lunch, Stupid." I knew he wasn't going to slap me in front of Dolly so I could afford to take liberties with him now. He laughed and turned into the classroom for my lunch. I stood there looking up into Dolly's face. She threw her head back like those ladies did in the Indian movies. She began humming that tune from the movie "Sholay" which happened to be one of my favorite songs.

"You like my brother?" I asked.

"He tell you that?" she said with a smile.

Sunil came back just then. He knew better than to leave Dolly alone with me.

"What you' waiting for now?" Sunil said impatiently.

"My bus passage for this afternoon, Stupid," I said again. He frowned crossly and dug into his pockets then gave me my passage. Reena came up to us at that moment for her lunch. She had two of her friends with her. I didn't tell her anything. I was still mad at her for the spanking she made me get that morning.

I went downstairs and after looking around to see if the area was Dracula-free I ran out of the school compound and up the road to the concrete *koka* where me and my friends normally meet to eat our lunches.

The usual group was there. There was Blinky with his bowl of cook-up, Goofy with his fish and bread, a lad named Kerwin who was in class with us last year, Rai from First standard, and Sleepy Thomas who was in our class and sat in the second row. Hector had gone home for lunch. Charlie, as usual, was already on the playfield playing cricket. Majeed was just finishing up crying as he wiped the tears from his eyes. He had just survived another mauling by Dracula. I unveiled my fish, gravy, and rice lunch. Some of us swapped parts of our lunches with each other. I shared mine with Majeed since Dracula had taken away a good portion of Majeed's curry fish.

It was after lunch that I noticed something in Sleepy's saucepan that looked like chocolate.

"Oh skites boy!" I exclaimed. "He got chocolate and ain't even telling we."

"Gimme piece nuh," Majeed said immediately as I quickly dipped a hand into the saucepan and scooped up the unwrapped chocolate.

"No!" exclaimed Sleepy and grabbed unsuccessfully for it.

"It ain't chocolate. Is a thing me aunty bring from England to clean out your inside."

"He only saying that because he ain't want fuh give we none," I said and unwrapped the stuff to reveal four fegs of what seemed to me to be brown chocolate. But it was kind of different. It was lighter than chocolate and didn't have that chocolate smell. I looked at the thing for a while and tried to decide if I should eat a piece.

"It good to eat or what?" I asked.

"You does use it like senna or salts. It does send you to the latrine," said Sleepy.

"Ohh!" said Rai. " It name brook lacks. It taste just like chocolate but is not chocolate. It does send you to the toilet. It worse than senna."

I was getting disenchanted with the thing by now. I knew what senna did to a person and if this thing was worse than that I wanted no part of it.

"Then why you bring it to school?" I asked Sleepy.

"I just want to show you all it," he said.

"Alyuh want?" I asked the others and waved it at them. Nobody wanted to take the chance.

I was about to give it back to Sleepy when it dawned on me that I would be passing up a golden opportunity.

"I guh use it," I said with a crafty smile.

"You guh eat it?" asked Sleepy.

"Naw. Alyuh don't come. Just watch me," I said.

Chapter One

Three minutes later I was sauntering gaily onto the playfield just before a group of boys; one of whom was Dracula. I saw him out of the side of my eyes and pretended that I didn't see him. I walked on seemingly without a care in the world, and apparently munching on my chocolate. In reality I was getting tense in anticipation of the impending mugging.

He set eyes on me and for a few seconds seemed not to believe his good fortune. He let go the neck of a suffering Fourth Standard lad and sneaked up behind me. He grabbed me around the neck and confiscated my "chocolate."

"How long you go run for?" he said and with one smooth action, downed the whole four segments into his mouth. He threw me onto the ground and knuckled me twice on the head. I lay on the ground and bawled. Dracula stood over me and looked away toward the cricket game while he licked the bit of "chocolate" left on his fingers. When he thought of somewhere else to be he simply stepped off and left me there crying on the ground.

That knuckle on the head really hurt but I was going to have my laugh after that. I slowly got up and made sure my clothes were not damaged. My mother would kill me if they were. I wiped the tears from my eyes and looked toward the koker to see if the boys were looking. They were. I waved to them.

When they came down to the playfield I told Kerwin to go bring his notebook and pencil from his classroom. When he came back I left the tagga game that was in progress and sat down on the grass with him.

"I want you write a letter for me," I said. He looked at me as if Dracula had given me brain damage.

"Write a letter to who?" he asked. Then he smiled cunningly. " To a girl?"

"Yea, just write what I tell you. 'Dear Reena.'"

"Reena? But that ain't your sister?"

"Just write the letter boy."

Kerwin stuck his tongue out of his mouth like he did when he concentrated and began to write.

"How you spell 'Reena?'" he said.

"How I go know," I said irritably. He opened his mouth to argue but changed his mind when he seemed to remember that there was no relationship between me and spelling.

"'I want to tell you how much I like you this afternoon behind school,'" I continued. " 'I love you.'" I waited for him to catch up.

" Who name to write at the bottom?" asked Kerwin.

" Write Harry," I said smugly. Kerwin wrote as I asked.

I knew Reena liked Harry Kissoon. I heard her talking about him with Chandra when they were at home. Harry was in the same class with Sunil.

After Kerwin tore the page out of his book I folded it like a letter and had Kerwin write "to Reena Teekasingh" on it. I got up and looked around the playfield. Harry was playing cricket with the other boys on the pitch in the middle of the field. I knew Reena would be in her classroom gossiping with the other girls.

" Go give this to Reena in Form Two," I said to Rai as I pulled him away from the tagga game. "Don't tell her I give you. Tell her Harry that playing cricket out there send it." I indicated where Harry was. Off ran Rai. I returned to the tagga game.

It was one O'clock and recess was over. We lined up to return to our classes. When we got back in our classroom Miss Seepersaud had us prepare for General Knowledge. As we prepared I looked across to Dracula. He was his usual leering, menacing self.

"Aye Majeed, ask Sleepy if he sure that thing wasn't chocolate," I said.

Chapter One

Word came down the row from Sleepy that he was sure it wasn't chocolate. I looked again at Dracula but he remained unperturbed.

We were doing the names of the young ones of animals. Hector nudged me in the side and directed my attention to Majeed. Majeed motioned in the direction of Dracula. I craned my neck to get a better view of my tormentor.

His eyes were wide open apparently in surprise and he was leaning slightly forward with his arms across his belly. Suddenly we were engulfed by a powerful stench. Dracula must have managed to squeeze off what we called a "silent assassin." We covered our noses. Miss Seepersaud was asking questions like what a young dog was called. We started giggling at the back and peeping with pleasure at Dracula who was now obviously in distress.

" Milo," said Mrs. Seepersaud.

I looked around with a start. What did she want now. The whole class - except for Dracula, of course - was staring at me. She must have asked a question but I had not a clue what it was. If I asked her what the question was she would know I wasn't paying attention. I looked at the others in my row but they seemed to be more unaware of the situation than I was. The expressions on the faces of the others in class gave me the impression that it must have been an easy question; like what was a young dog called.

" Well?" said Mrs. Seepersaud.

" Pup, miss." They laughed their heads off while Miss looked at me as though I was deliberately being rude.

" Next," said Miss. Hector stood up and looked up at the roof.

" A Kitten?"

" Next!" She went down the row and got answers like lamb, sheep, alligator, pup again, and Goofy finally gave her "mouse."

" Yaah! A young pig is called a mouse!" exclaimed Drupatie.

Once Upon A Time In Berbice

Just when Mrs. Seepersaud was getting ready to flex her cane there was a terrible sound like the ripping of a bed sheet coming from the back of the class. For a few seconds, no one laughed simply because we did not know what it was. When the scent hit us we were too choked to laugh. Our hands flew up to our noses. It smelled like some kind of addled ancient curry with something gone very wrong with it.

Dracula was crouched over his desk. He was sweating like a pig on market day. The lads sitting next to him suddenly drifted away from his area. Mrs. Seepersaud looked flabbergasted and seemed unable to make anything of the situation.

"Jainarinesingh, what's the matter with you. Are you ill?" she finally asked.

Dracula opened his mouth to answer but instead another fart ripped out of his bulk.

"Go to the toilet boy," said Mrs. Seepersaud with some degree of irritation.

Dracula was reluctant to get up. When he did we could see the brown wet stain that spread over the seat of his pants. The smell was terrible. He waddled out of the classroom as quickly as he could. We howled with laughter while some of us tried to open the windows wider. Because of the distraction with Dracula we got off from a spanking for our errant answers. My only regret was that Sleepy did not have anymore of that chocolate stuff for me to slip to Chandra. Droopatie could do with a piece too.

Our next subject was Art. That was my subject. I was considered to be something of a wizard by my classmates when it came to art. Today we were required to draw a vase with flowers the teacher put on a desk in front of the class. This was boring stuff for me. I was surprised at the unrecognizable doodles some people put down on paper for art. And they were the ones who usually got high marks in class. Dunce Section was somewhere else in the classroom

Chapter One

when it came to art. I made it a point to go around to Drupatie and Chandra to laugh at their feeble attempts.

Mala came by for me to help her with her work. She stood beside me while I expertly sketched the vase then worked away at the flowers. From time to time I glanced at her small tapered fingers as her right hand rested on my desk. Above the residue of Dracula's stench I could smell the coconut oil and powder on her skin.

She went back toward her seat to see what Cindy wanted. I quickly turned over her paper and wrote as best as I could spell, " I love you." Then I continued working on her vase. She soon returned and picked up her finished work. She smiled her approval at me and I felt all warm and aglow. Majeed just sat there staring at her longingly.

It was sometime after returning to her seat that she noticed the writing behind her art sheet. I could see her trying to make out what it was. She erased it and my heart sank. Actually what I had written was 'I luve yuo.' Maybe she couldn't read all that well.

Some time before dismissal Dracula was brought back to the classroom. He gathered up his two exercise books and the text book and he was sent home. The whole school saw the brown caked back of his trousers and knew he had messed in his pants. He was looking as sick as a hog when we last saw him. Thank God Sleepy stopped me from eating that thing.

As we filed out of the building after dismissal Sunil came up to me. He wanted to borrow my bus passage which I had got from him at lunch time. I was shocked. He did not tell me this but he had spent most of the kerosene oil money buying snacks for Dolly who he was trying to impress. Now he wanted my bus passage to make up for the kerosene oil money.

"What you do with the kerosene oil money?" I asked cockily.

"It lost. Look, you giving me the money or not," he said irritably.

"And how me guh reach home?"

"You can walk home."

"Why *you* don't walk home?"

"Mom want the kerosene oil early."

"You didn't think about that when you been blasting it out in the shop on Dolly." I wasn't going to give him an easy time.

"If you give me the passage I go water the plants for you," he said.

"For three days."

"Alright, just give me the money."

As I thought about digging more concessions out of him I saw Harry Kissoon heading for the gate. I already knew Dolly was in the teachers' staff room. I took out my bus passage and gave it to Sunil who grinned his appreciation at me.

I pushed my way through the exiting students and tapped Harry on the back when I got up to him.

"You are Harry Kissoon?" I said, pretending not to know him. He nodded.

"A girl name Dolly tell me to tell you that she is waiting for you behind school," I said and ran back toward the school.

When I looked back I could see he was wide-eyed with excitement and was moving slowly back toward the building as if in a dream. I hid by the steps of the school. He walked around toward the back of the building and I discreetly followed him. He stopped abruptly, whipped out a comb and vigorously combed his straight black hair. He put some spit on the tips of his fingers and daubed at his eyebrows and premature mustache. Then he went around the building. I ran to the corner of the building and peeped around.

Chapter One

It was pretty private behind the building since it faced the back where there was nothing but bush. Reena was standing there with her hands behind her back and smiling from ear to ear trying to look pretty. I could see Harry slow down as he approached her and looked around to locate Dolly. I saw Reena give him some kind of note and for a minute I thought it was the note I had given him. But then he began reading it and it must have been a longer note than the one I had sent to her. Then it occurred to me that Reena must have written him a love note of her own. I could have died laughing. I didn't hear what he said but from his gesticulations and the ugly scowl on his face I could tell he was being nasty to her. She started crying. He tore up the note, sucked his teeth and walked away.

I ran around to the front of the school so that Harry could not see me. He went out of the school compound and I could tell he was mad. I waited for Reena to come around from the back. I wished she would hurry up. There was a group of boys who were walking home in my direction though not as far. I wanted to catch up with them.

When she finally came around the building she was still crying though not as much as before. I came out behind her.

"What happen Reena," I said. She was startled. She really didn't expect to see me in school after everyone had left. She turned her face from me.

"I have a headache," she said.

"Is Harry give you a headache?" I said maliciously.

She stopped and turned to me. I could see she was trying to figure out what I had to do with what had just happened. She narrowed her eyes and glared at me as it dawned on her that I had something to do with the note she got.

"I go tell Mammy that you been meeting boys behind school and you did writing them love letters," I said and began running out toward the road.

"Milo!" she said in anger. I knew she couldn't do anything about what I did. What was she going to tell Mammy.

I ran and caught up with the boys from my class. One of the boys had a bicycle and he was pushing the bicycle while walking with us. As we talked and laughed while we headed home I suddenly remembered a couple of the boys who were laughing at us in dunce section and wouldn't mouth the answer to questions to us.

One of them, Roy Ramdatt, was particularly stingy with his answers. I grabbed his books from his hands and managed to get three out of four. I ran ahead and down by the trench. I held his books over the water and threatened to drop them in if he came any closer to me. They all stood obediently on the road looking at me and waiting for me to call the shots.

I reminded him about the incidents in class.

"I have a good mind drop them books right now," I said as if I were angry.

"No!" said Roy. I knew he would get a cut tail if he took his books home wet, especially when it didn't rain.

"Alyuh dance for me while I think about what to do with them books," I said. Roy started a fancy Indian dance and desperately pleaded with the others to do the same. Four of them joined in and the other two couldn't care less if Roy got licks. They were laughing.

For the next fifteen minutes I made them dance, slap each other, play boxing, kiss each other, and walk like girls. Eventually I got tired of this. I was about to give up the terrorist act when I saw a hire car coming up the road.

"Alyuh stop that car. Stop that car boy. I going home," I said.

Roy jumped to the task. He stretched out his hand and the car came to a stop. They stood there looking stupid while the driver waited impatiently.

Chapter One

"They always doing that stupidness Mister," I said from the trench. "They' always stopping cars and they know they ain't have no money. Is every afternoon they does do it."

The man cursed them then angrily drove off. The rest of us laughed our heads off. Eventually, I returned Roy's books to him. When they reached their homes I convinced the boy with the bicycle to drop me home.

When I got home I got a cut tail right away. My mother had found my wet pants under the matress and had realized that Sondra's clothes had urine at the back but the front was dry. She had put two and two together and concluded correctly what I had done. I ate my lunch in tears.

After eating I went up the road where the boys played tagga. We played until the sun went down. I didn't have to rush home to water the plants. Sunil would take care of that for me. I stayed and chatted with Majeed and the others until close to seven O' clock when "Doctor Paul" was coming over the radio.

I went home and immediately got another cut tail. The plants were not watered. I complained bitterly that Sunil had promised to water them for me in exchange for my lunch money because he had spent the kerosene oil money on his girlfriend. Sunil simply denied everything and I got a few more lashes for lying on Sunil.

I marched out the back door to water the plants in the dark. I was going to fix that Sunil on the morrow.

When I finally finished watering the plants it was pretty late. I went back into the house. Sondra was already in bed. Reena was crying and Mammy was rubbing her down with Limacol because she thought she was coming down with something. I knew she was just heartbroken.

I put on the pants I had on that morning and dived into bed. Mammy soon left and went over to her room. I could hear Reena sobbing quietly. I knew she would think twice before she got me in trouble again. Besides, she knew I could tell Mammy what really happened.

Once Upon A Time In Berbice

I soon drifted off to sleep. Suddenly I found myself running with the other boys from dunce section out on the sea shore. We were dragging Dracula by the toes toward the water. Mala was standing by some trees cheering us on. We reached the water and dragged Dracula deeper as we tried our best to drown him. We were at it for some time but every time we thought we had him under he changed into a vampire bat and flew up. We had to pull him down again. Then he changed into the monster we knew and we tried all over again to drown him.

I suddenly felt the urge to urinate. I did not want to come out of the water to do it because Dracula might get away. I began urinating in the water and it felt really good. Then I suddenly realized it was very wet. I continued peeing in the water.

Suddenly I woke up. It was a dream. But I still felt the wetness. I got to my knees with a start and felt myself. I had wet the bed again.

Chapter Two

Chapter Two

The next day was Saturday and I woke up just after nine. I could hear Reena talking with Chandra Ramnauth somewhere behind the house. The pigs were grunting contentedly in their pens which meant that Sunil had already fed them. I got up and changed from my wet pants. Sondra was up already and out of the room.

I yawned off the remaining sleep left in me and stumbled out of the bedroom and into the kitchen. I got my toothbrush from the enamel cup by the sink, daubed some toothpaste on it and brushed my teeth right there by the sink which hung over the kitchen window to the back. I could see my stepfather Haroon sitting on a crate across from the pig pen. He had a piece of mirror positioned in the crook of a branch of the fivefinger tree and was shaving with a comb and razor blade. His entire chin and cheeks were lathered up with soap suds.

Haroon was shorter than my mother and stocky. He had married my mother two years before. He was from somewhere on the West Bank of Demerara. As far as I knew he had no children of his own and we had never had any of his relatives visit us here where he had met my mother when he had come to work at Blairmont Estate, just past Rosignol by the Berbice River, and on the opposite side from New Amsterdam. I didn't have much contact with him for he always seemed to be at work driving one of the estate trucks which picked up workers along the coast. On Saturdays he still worked although for only part of the day.

On Sundays he was off. Like most of the men along the coast he drank but not often. He was never drunk nor loud; at least not around us. When he was home he spent a lot of time down by the shop in the village playing cards with the men there. The only time me and Reena spent time with him was when he took us for a ride on the truck. Most times he was up before us and came in after us.

He had probably dropped Mammy off at the market at Rosignol and would return for her in the afternoon. I looked around the kitchen and found the peanut butter and bread and chocolate tea left for me. The latter was cold. I wasn't about to go drinking cold tea that early in the morning. I went outside and to the back of the house where Reena was.

"Reena, me tea cold," I said. She and Chandra had heard me coming and had stopped talking. They both looked my way with poisonous glances. She drew her teeth loudly and turned back to Chandra. I could see she wasn't about to forget about my prank on the previous day.

"You pissed the bed today?" Chandra asked with a smirk. I was about to tell her whose bed I pissed when I realized Reena would be glad to have something to complain on me about when Mammy came home. Instead, I drew my teeth and turned back inside. I had no choice but to drink the cold tea with the peanut butter sandwich.

Haroon returned just after two that afternoon with my mother. I went out after Reena to help bring in the bags of groceries Mammy had bought. By the time the goods were unloaded my stepfather was off again in the truck. Sunil was nowhere to be seen. Mammy stood up in the hot sun talking across the street to the hairstylist, Chandra's mother.

As soon as we got the bags in the kitchen I began digging in them for the little paper bag of sweets my mother usually bought us. Reena tried to stop me from looking and I pushed her aside. No sooner had I done that when I felt two slaps to the sides of my face. I wailed and grabbed my face as though she had torn it off. Mammy broke off her conversation with Chandra's mother but took her time in coming to see what all the fuss was about.

"Mammy, he digging in the bags looking for sweets and he know he got to wait 'till you come. And he pushing me

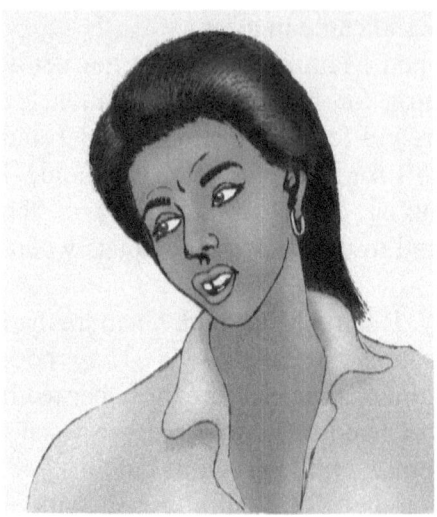
Mammy

down when I try to stop him," Reena said as she got her complaint in first.

"She slap me up!" I bawled.

"She shoulda slap your head off. Since when I teach you to push girls. Besides she's your big sister. You do what she say," Mammy said in a matter-of-fact manner.

"But she ain't got no right slapping me up," I insisted.

"If you push her you ask for it," Mammy said as she began unpacking the goods. "Besides, you shouldn't be eating sweets. You see them boils on your foot that won't go away?" She was referring to a couple of mosquito bumps I had on my lower legs.

I didn't say anything. Reena was looking at me with a smirk. I knew she was getting back at me for the previous day in school. I figured we were even now. I sat down on the steps, still pretending to be hurt. I kept my eyes on them to see when they were going to fish out the bag of sweets. As they emptied the bags and put the things away in the little wooden safe and on the shelves, Mammy was telling Reena about whom she ran into in the market. Mammy was the one who finally took out the sweets and she put the little bag into a big Milo tin on the shelf where they are usually kept. That meant none for me today. It was no use crying for it either, for the result would be negative; it had been tried before.

Once Upon A Time In Berbice

With nothing to be gained from hanging around the kitchen except more work I slipped off the steps and headed out the yard for Majeed's yard.

Sunday morning after I brought out the mattress to sun-out Majeed came running up the road and he was well dressed. He wore the big goofy grin on his face.

"We going New Amsterdam," he announced. I had gone there once with Mammy but I barely remembered anything about it since I was only two.

"What you going for?" I asked.

"We going by Shanta. We coming back tomorrow night." Shanta was his big sister who had married a few years before and lived in New Amsterdam.

"So you not going school tomorrow?" I asked in dismay. I had no intention of facing Dracula alone on the morrow. I figured the Brooklacks would have run its course by now and Dracula would be out for blood, provided he figured out who was behind his diarrhea crisis.

"Naw, I ain't coming school till Tuesday or Wednesday," he said happily.

Immediately I thought of concocting an illness so that I wouldn't have to go to school on the morrow but, unless I'm down with a fever, Mammy wouldn't fall for it. Besides, if she does she's likely to feed me senna and salts and a lot of ghastly tasting things to get me better. It was not worth it.

Just then Majeed's mother called him to help with the little grip and three little bags she had at the foot of their stairs.

"Good luck with Dracula tomorrow," he said as he brushed a lock of hair from before his eyes and grinned. He turned and ran up the road toward his mother. I definitely was not looking forward to school that week.

Chapter Two

Monday morning began with a spanking for me again for wetting the bed. It was raining heavily. After some hesitation I went out in the rain to bathe at the back. While bathing I looked over at Majeed's house and could only see one light on. Only Majeed's father was home with them gone to New Amsterdam.

After having tea and having finished dressing in my school uniform, I was hoping that the rain would come down even heavier so that Mammy might think of keeping us home. But just as we got our books and lunches together the downpour simmered to a drizzle. The bus came up the road on schedule and I climbed aboard behind Reena, Sondra, Chandra and Sunil. My usual scan of the bus for Mala was unsuccessful which made me even more depressed. She probably was traveling to school on their rice truck that morning. The bus moved off and I made my way toward the back where I might be out of Dracula's reach.

As the bus came to a halt in the village with the police station I peered outside for Dracula in the little group of school children crowding the door of the bus. But he was nowhere in sight. Maybe he was still sick with diarrhea from Friday. I began to feel a whole lot better when the bus moved off without him. It might not be such a bad day after all with Dracula absent.

After we alighted from the bus I went up the dam to Hector's house and he came right out. We weren't going to face Spanky that morning. We got into class and my day was even brighter when I saw Mala standing with a group of girls by the chalkboard. They were talking about their clothes or some other girl talk.

The bell rang soon after and we stood for prayers. After we were seated again Mrs. Seecharran attended to the register while me and Hector looked through the window and mocked the children as they came in after getting their lashes from Spanky at the gate. Then, to my horror, in rolled Dracula. He didn't look any different than he did last week. If anything the Brooklacks seemed to have added more bulk on him. Maybe some of the air was still left in him.

By the time we began reciting the time tables word came down Dunce Section that Dracula wanted to know where Majeed was. After a while we learned that he thought it was Majeed's curry fish that did him in on Friday. He seemed to have forgotten consuming the "chocolate." None of us was about to educate him about the source of his diarrhea. I passed word down the row hinting that Majeed's mother usually mixed senna in his food to clean Majeed out. Dracula seemed to have bought it and I supposed I was off the hook. The thing was, because of how this played out, I was in a vulnerable position with my friends. I had to be careful not to offend any of them since they could threaten to set Dracula right about what had really happened. But for the moment, I was fine with the way things were.

By the time we were up to ten times tables me and Hector were already into our "what passing next on the main road" game. Then we heard a siren and saw an ambulance race east up the road toward Rosignol. Then about five minutes after a fire engine raced that way. We guessed there must have been a major accident or fire down that way. By the time we were in the middle of doing math a policeman drove into the school compound. Shortly after a teacher from upstairs came into our classroom in a hurry and told Mrs. Seecharran something. She immediately got up and hurried out after the teacher. I could see her standing with three other teachers outside the classroom door. They were talking in a very animated way. Something was happening and I guessed it had something to do with the policeman coming. The rest of the class was deathly quiet. We looked at each other wondering what the problem was. Hector said maybe Mrs. Seecharran's house was on fire.   But with the fire engine and ambulance coming from Georgetown direction they had to be coming from Mahaica which meant it was something more serious than my teacher's house burning down.

The policeman drove out of the compound and up the road in the direction in which the fire engine and ambulance had gone. Mrs. Seecharran was still outside and now there were four teachers there speaking very excitedly. She came back in the classroom and quickly gathered up her handbag, noisily blew her nose then left in a hurry. I guessed she was crying. The headmaster, Mr. Moriah, came in to take our class. We saw our teacher hurrying out the school yard and toward the public road. After a while a hire car stopped and she got in.   They headed in the direction of Rosignol. It was then rumored around class that Mr. Seecharran worked at Blairmont estate and someone had heard Blairmont being mentioned.

The headmaster didn't inform us of anything. He was in and out of the classroom. After a time the school bell rang. We weren't sure why because it was too early for the morning break. The headmaster came back and told us we were getting an early recess. We shuffled outside with the other classes but not many were in the mood for playing since we were curious about what was going on.

Some of the children were saying that, from what they overheard from the teachers, something bad had happened at Blairmont estate. I wanted to know if it was an accident with a truck but they seemed to think it was something at the estate itself. I was a little relieved since my stepfather drove a truck and didn't really work on the estate itself.

The morning break was extended or so it seemed to me. When the bell did ring we returned to class with the same air of alarm and expectancy hovering over us all. It was while we were preparing for reading that a bus coming from the direction of Rosignol, stopped before the school.

Several adults got out which was unusual for that time of day. And to my surprise my mother was among them.

My heart skipped a beat. What was my mother doing here in the middle of the day? Did it have something to do with the accident at Blairmont or did I do something that had to do with the school. I thought quickly about the things I had done for the past week that would warrant my mother coming to the school. She hadn't said anything about me doing anything bad over the weekend.

For a moment I wondered if Reena had had the nerves to tell her what had happened between her and Harry Kissoon and the role I had played in it. If so why would Mammy wait until today in school to tackle that problem. Then it occurred to me that she might have come to school to confront Harry Kissoon about what he had done. A small sweat had broken out on my forehead. But I could do nothing but wait.

A teacher came in class to the principal. They went by the door and spoke in hushed tones. Three parents had come up to the door by then; my mother being one of them. I could hear my heart beating. The headmaster told me, Goofy and Chandra to pack our books and go with our parents. I did as I was told. I had no idea what was happening.

When I went out of the classroom Reena, Sondra and Sunil were already there with their bags and lunches. Mammy had this distraught look on her face and immediately turned to leave with us in tow. Reena and Sunil looked baffled so it was no use me asking them anything. By the time we got to the road the other parents were coming out of the school compound too.

Chapter Three

Mammy kept looking up the road to the west toward Georgetown to see if any hire car or bus was coming. Nothing was.

She turned and looked the other way. I could see her eyes were swamped.

"Mammy what happening?" Reena asked in an unusually high frightened voice as she started crying. Mammy looked at us and I could see the tears beginning to run down her smooth brown oval face.

"Something happen to Haroon at the estate," she said in a surprisingly calm voice. "Something happen to Haroon and some other workers."

"The truck run in a trench?" Sunil asked anxiously.

"No, not the truck. They say is at the estate itself," she said.

"But he don't work on the estate itself," I said.

"I know. I know. He only supposed to be driving the truck," she said in a strained voice and more tears came. Then Sondra started to cry too even though I didn't think she understood what was happening.

By now the others had reached us and they were all crying. Mammy dried her eyes and looked up the road. Some cars were coming. We got into the car as another one pulled up for the other families. The driver was talking his head off about what he had learned. According to the driver the accident had something to do with the tower collapsing and workers couldn't breathe. Ten people were dead in all and about twenty in hospital. It was all confusing to me.

Just then an ambulance came racing up the road towards us. It flew by with sirens wailing and lights flashing.

"That mean they carrying somebody to Georgetown hospital," said the driver. I knew Fort Wellington Hospital was back east where we were heading and a whole lot closer to Blairmont. But if injuries were serious enough they took the patient to the hospital in Georgetown.

Mammy stopped the car at our home. I was surprised we weren't heading for Blairmont. Chandra and her mother also came out. Mammy told us to go in the house while she stood up and talked with Chandra's mother for a while. I walked in the house slowly behind Reena who had Sondra by the hand, and Sunil. Reena had stopped crying but her eyes were still moist.

Mammy came in after a few minutes and told us that Chandra's mother would keep an eye on us from across the road and that she was going down to Blairmont. She took Sondra with her without changing her from her school uniform.

As soon as she left Sunil went out and toward the shop in the village. He said he was going to find out what happened. Reena went inside and changed into her home clothes then started busying herself in the kitchen. Mammy had apparently begun preparing the midday meal when she got the news. So Reena continued with the preparation.

I sat in the kitchen feeling depressed. Majeed wasn't around and the other boys in the village were in school. I looked up at Reena as she started mixing flour to make roti.

Reena was slightly shorter than my mother at five feet six inches or thereabout. To me she was pretty plain looking but you couldn't find a feature on her to taunt her about, except maybe her backside. I had heard people comment before that, for a coolie girl her behind was too big and some wondered if she had black in her. They said the same thing about Mammy. Although the girls in Sunil's class were older than Reena, her behind was noticeably bigger than theirs.

"You think something happen to Haroon?" I asked her.

Chapter Three

"Why you think Mammy bring we home from school," she said a little irritated. She was frowning and I could see she was worried.

"You think he dead?" I asked.

"I dunno. But it serious," she said and stopped mixing the dough. She wiped her forehead with the back of a hand then looked at me with the same worried look. "You ever stop to think what go happen to we if Haroon dead?"

"No," I answered then went into deep thought. I hadn't thought about it at all. Haroon was practically the only breadwinner in the home with Mammy doing a little here and there to help out. But if Haroon was gone how were we going to make out.

"Aunt Doogoo might want we go live with her in New Amsterdam," Reena continued thinking aloud. I knew whenever Aunt Doogoo came by she was always trying to talk Mammy into moving in with her in New Amsterdam. Apparently she had a big house there and could afford to have us live with her. But Haroon was always against it even though his workplace was just a launch ride away. Many workers at Blairmont estate lived in New Amsterdam and there was a special steady launch service for them.

I must admit that, although life here was Alright, the prospect of going to live in New Amsterdam excited me.

"You want to go live in New Amsterdam?" I asked Reena.

"Not at Aunt Doogoo," Reena said. "She only want marry off people as soon as they leave school."

Now I knew why she wouldn't like that. If I knew anything about Aunt Doogoo it was that, next to Mammy moving to New Amsterdam, her favorite topic was marrying off her girls. She was already talking to Mammy about finding a suitable boy for Reena but Mammy didn't seem too keen on the idea.

Sunil came in just then. He seemed troubled by whatever news he had got from the shop.

"What they say happen?" Reena asked anxiously. Sunil sat down slowly as though he was tired.

"They say some workers were cleaning inside some kind of tower that hold bagass or something," he began.

"Wha' is bagass?" Reena wanted to know.

"I dunno. Something to do with the cane leftovers when they boiling it to make molasses," Sunil said.

"And wha' happen, they drown?" I asked.

"Shut up," said Reena and waited impatiently for Sunil to continue.

"They say about six of them climb down and when they reach the bottom like some kinda poisonous gas get stir up when they walked on the trash and thing at the bottom. Some start collapsing after they breathe it in and some make a rush for the ladder to come up back. But like the gas start rising and they start fall back in," Sunil continued somberly. Reena's eyes began watering again.

"So the men who were on top starting hollering and some climb down to help get the men out. And some other men who were outside run in to help. Haroon was one of them and Chandra' father was already inside."

"But the car man say the tower fall down on them," I said.

"No tower ain't fall down on nobody. Is inside the tower it happen," said Sunil.

"So wha' happen to Haroon?" I asked.

"They don't know who dead and who they drag out still alive," Sunil said.

Reena daubed at her eyes with her shirt sleeve and continued with the dough.

"They take some of them to hospital and they still trying to get out the rest," Sunil concluded. "It come over the radio at the shop too."

"Reena say we might go live New Amsterdam if something happen to Haroon," I said.

Chapter Three

"With Aunty Doogoo?" he said and looked at her. Reena nodded. Despite the sad situation I could see Sunil's eyes light up.

I went and sat in front and waited for Mammy to come. After a while I got bored and dropped to sleep.

I awoke to strange voices in the house. I sat up in the chair and looked around. Aunty Doogoo had arrived with Mammy. She had brought two of her daughters with her. They were in their late teens or early twenties and a little shorter than Reena, a lot fairer and were well dressed in pastel colored full length dresses. They had their hair styled like the actresses on the Indian movie posters.

Aunt Doogoo was about Mammy's height but fairer. She looked taller because she was kind of plump compared with Mammy's slimmer frame. She must have been in her early fifties and had a serious gaunt face with a *sindoor* in the middle of her forehead signifying her Hindu faith. She had a gold tooth somewhere to the front of her mouth which glistened as she spoke. She was also attired in a pastel colored dress which was constructed with much more material than those of her daughters. From what I knew, she had two older daughters who lived somewhere in Canada.

Mammy took her into her bedroom while Reena served a snack to the two girls who smiled politely at her. Sondra stood staring at the girls as though they were goddesses. Sunil was sitting in the kitchen ogling them although they were our cousins. I got up and went past them without saying anything as they smiled at me. One asked Reena something and they began a conversation. I went into the kitchen.

"Wha' happening?" I asked Sunil.

"Haroon is one of them that dead," he said matter-of-factly. I waited for him to continue but he seemed more interested in his cousins.

"Wha' happen to Chandra' father?" I asked hoping to pry more news from him.

"He at Fort Wellington Hospital. He ain't wake up yet," said Sunil in a sort of distracted way. I heard Mammy crying inside and Aunty Doogoo trying to calm her down. Just then Reena came back to the kitchen and burst into tears. Sunil promptly got up and went outside. Reena sat down on the chair Sunil had just left and leaned forward with her face buried in her hands on her lap as she cried loudly. Mammy wasn't doing much better inside either. The two girls looked at each other with sad faces then got up and came to Reena. One of them bent down and put her arms around Reena who continued crying. I got up and went outside.

The sun was out and the grass around was glistening from the rain drops. Apparently rain had fallen again while I was asleep. Sunil was leaning against the side of the house. He quickly daubed at his eyes when he heard me coming and walked off out of the yard and up the road. A bus stopped before our house and several passengers got off. Three came into our yard and two went across the street to Chandra's house. Mrs. Parkinson from up the road came into our yard behind the people.

"You' mammy come home?" one of the women asked.

"She inside," I said.

As they came past me one of them tussled my hair affectionately.

"Is he li'l boy this?" the woman asked another.

"No, them is Yvette's children before him," replied the other.

I continued out to the road. I was thinking of heading down by the shop where Sunil probably had gone when Majeed came running up the road from his house. He was still well dressed so I supposed he had just come back from New Amsterdam.

Chapter Three

"I thought you ain't coming back 'till tonight," I said as he slowed to a walk.

"You ain't hear wha' happen?" he said excitedly.

"In New Amsterdam?"

"At Blairmont you fool," he said. "That is why we come back so early. Mammy thought Daddy was in it too but he meet we at Rosignol stelling when we come across in Torani."

"They say Haroon is one of them that dead at Blairmont," I said.

"Yea, so Daddy say. They carry Chandra' father to Georgetown hospital."

"Georgetown? I thought was Fort Wellington," I said.

"Naw, they carry him there first but he in a bad way. They had to carry him Georgetown," Majeed said as though his news was from the horse's mouth.

By evening the house was crowded with sympathizers from the village and beyond. The men from the village brought and set up tables outside and domino games were in progress. Aunty Doogoo took her two daughters to the ferry stelling at Rosignol to return to New Amsterdam and she came back to the house to stay with Mammy. Majeed and his family came over and Chandra's mother left her to stay with us while she traveled to Georgetown to see about her husband.

Things were a bit livelier at the house that night with the men playing dominoes, draughts, and cards outside and rum being gobbled freely under the glare from two dazzling gas lamps hung on poles in the yard, the women cooking and talking in the house and us children playing around the yard. I could tell Mammy was not her usual self or she would have been out there playing draughts, a game she loved and for which she had a talent. A few of Reena's friends and their parents had stopped by and hung around for a while. Mala's father came but he did not bring Mala. I was wondering why he even bothered to come at all.

From what I understood, most of the other six men who died were from New Amsterdam and Rosignol area. One was from Bushlot and Haroon was the only one from our area who had died.

Mammy seemed to be okay again but the other women from the neighborhood were doing most of the work in the kitchen. Sunil was playing dominoes with the men out front.

By midnight most of the people had left. The children were all gone with their parents. The owners of the lamps took them home but the tables were left out front.

When I went inside Chandra was already asleep on Mammy's bed. She and Mammy and Aunt Doogoo were going to sleep there. I went into our room, changed my clothes and lay down next to Sondra who was already asleep. Sunil was on the other side of me, and Reena who was still in the kitchen, usually slept next to Sondra and against the wall.

Sunil was staring up to the zinc roof. He was toying with a piece of grass or something in his mouth and had one foot up by his romp and the other leg crossed over the knee of that leg. His hands were behind his head and he appeared to be in deep thought. Although it was late I wasn't sleepy; maybe because I had slept earlier.

Reena put out the kerosene lamp in the kitchen and came in the bedroom. The light from the lamp in Mammy's room spilled over the top of the wall separating the two rooms to the roof of our room. Reena went in the corner where she had her clothes hung up on a few nails in the wall there. She lifted her dress over her head and took it off then hung it on another nail. Then she loosed off the straps behind her and removed the thing with the cups that big girls and women wear. She kept her back to us. She pulled her sleeping dress over her head and let it fall over her dark maturing body before coming in bed beside Sondra.

We could hear Aunty Doogoo and Mammy talking next door but we couldn't make out what they were saying. From time to time we could hear them laugh. I supposed they were talking sister things about when they were growing up.

"You think we going live with Aunty Doogoo?" I asked.

"I dunno," said Sunil. "You sure Aunty Doogoo want us to go live at she?"

"That is what Aunty Doogoo say," said Reena.

"When we going?" I asked.

"They ain't even bury Haroon yet and you want know when we moving," Reena said with some irritation.

"So we going New Amsterdam to live," Sunil said and seemed pleased.

"That is what Aunty Doogoo want," said Reena.

"What if Mammy don't want go?" I said.

"Mammy never say she didn't want go, only Haroon," said Reena.

"I hope we going," said Sunil.

"Why?" asked Reena.

"Well, it ain't have work to do here when I finish school except at the estate and me ain't want work there," Sunil said. "New Amsterdam have more opportunities."

"Reena frighten Aunty Doogoo marrid she off if we go live at she in New Amsterdam," I said.

"Shhh! She might hear we," said Reena.

"That not so bad," said Sunil.

"You're a boy so you can talk," Reena said reproachfully.

"You rather get marrid off to a boy over here or in New Amsterdam where you can go cinema?" said Sunil.

"They can marry you off to a boy living anywhere out of New Amsterdam. It don't have to be a boy from there," argued Reena. " Remember Savitri?"

Once Upon A Time In Berbice

I remembered Savitri. She was from the village. She had finished school three years ago and her parents immediately married her off to a boy from somewhere named Letterkenny on the Corentyne. She came back once sometime last year to visit and already had two children.

"You don't want dress up and look nice like Lea and Indira?" asked Sunil.

"Who's Lea and Indira?" I asked.

"Your two hoity-toity cousins," said Reena.

"Oh, they're pretty," I said.

"Yea, you can dress up pretty like them and smell nice too instead of smelling like you been in the kitchen whole day," said Sunil.

"Is because of ayo make I in the kitchen whole day," Reena said.

"Well when we go live at Aunt Doogoo you won't have to be in the kitchen whole day," said Sunil.

"Yes, just before they marrid me off," said Reena.

I was getting tired of her bad talking going to live in New Amsterdam.

"Who go want marry you though," I said aloud.

"Shut up you fool. She go hear," Reena urged and pointed to the next room where they were still in conversation.

"Harry Kissoon was asking about you," said Sunil. My ears perked up. Was this the same Harry Kissoon that cussed out Reena last week? Reena didn't say anything.

"What he asking you?" I asked.

"Nothing. He just want know about Reena," said Sunil. Reena drew her teeth and turned her back to us.

"Me ain't like he," she said bitterly.

"I know he like Dolly Shivnarine in my class but like now he interested in you," said Sunil. I didn't know if he knew something and was toying with Reena or if what he said was true. Reena was silent for a while.

Chapter Three

"What he ask you?" she said, just when I was going to ask a question.

"He want know what kinda nice things you like eat," Sunil said. Silence again. Reena turned again facing us.

"And what you say?" she asked.

"I tell him ask you," Sunil said.

"When was that?" I asked, for this seemed an about turn for Harry, judging from how angry he was when he met Reena behind school just last Friday.

"That ain't your business. Go to sleep," said Reena.

"This morning before all this start happening," said Sunil. Reena was silent again. "Imagine that. Haroon wake up good good this morning and tonight he done dead," Sunil said thoughtfully.

"If Aunty Doogoo make a match for you to marry Harry Kissoon you would like that?" I asked Reena to bring the conversation back to what I was interested in.

"Boy shut up," said Reena. Sunil chuckled.

"Reena Kissoon. That ain't sound too bad," Sunil said and laughed.

"Maybe Aunty Doogoo go arrange for you to marry Dolly," I said to Sunil.

"Dolly? Naw, I won't marry a girl like that," Sunil said and I could see he was enjoying this.

"Wha' wrong with Dolly?" said Reena.

"Yea, I thought you like her," I said.

"Naw, she ain't go make a good wife," Sunil drawled. "She interested in too much boys."

"You mean she don't like you enough," I said.

"Oh she like me alright. But she ain't me type."

"If she ain't your type why you spend out all the kerosene money fattening she up?" I said. I had had enough of this denial game these two were playing.

"What?" Reena said. Apparently she didn't know anything about this.

"He spend out Mammy' kerosene oil money buying snack for Dolly and had to ask me for me passage money Friday to make up the oil money," I explained.

"Boy that is just a li'l favor I do her to get what I want from she," said Sunil.

"What you want from she?" I asked.

"You too small boy. You will learn later," Sunil said and laughed.

"All ayo is the same thing," said Reena and sucked her teeth again. I wasn't sure what she meant by that.

"I ain't spending no money just to get a kiss from no girl," I said.

"A kiss?" Sunil said and laughed. "I get that everyday from Dolly."

"Then what else you want?" I said.

"Milo shut up," said Reena.

"Why you think Harry want buy things for Reena?" said Sunil.

"Nothing like Harry can touch me," Reena said angrily then sucked-her-teeth. "Why he don't go to Dolly for that."

"He say Dolly batty too flat," said Sunil.

"So why he run round behind school to meet she then?" I said.

"Milo shut up. You talk too damn much," Reena said harshly.

"Meet who behind school," Sunil said and I could see I had his attention.

"I thought you say she nuh good enough for you," I said.

"What make you think Harry want anything from me?" asked Reena.

"Why else he asking about you then," said Sunil. Reena was silent. "You better get smart girl. You getting big and getting woman parts. You think I ain't see how Mr. Ramdat does look at you?"

Mr. Ramdat was a tall skinny teacher just out of Training College who taught the class next to Reena's.

Chapter Three

"How he does look at me?" said Reena. I wasn't sure if she was playing ignorant and already knew Mr. Ramjit was eying her up, or if she really had no idea. For me it's the first I was hearing of this.

"You play you stupid," said Sunil. "And I go tell Mammy to make your skirt longer."

It was true Reena was growing out of her skirt. While most of the other girls' skirts were down to their knees or below, Reena's was approaching the territory of the new mini skirt style. Much of her legs showed under her uniform and she had to be careful to keep her knees together when she sat down and prevent her skirt from riding too far up.

Reena drew her teeth again and turned away from us.

"What is that about Dolly and Harry behind school?" Sunil asked.

"Ayo hush up. I want sleep," said Reena and squirmed in her bedding like she was settling down to sleep.

"Harry get a note from a girl that like he to meet he behind school but he thought it was Dolly," I said quietly.

"So he went behind school after school over and was vex when he see wasn't Dolly." Sunil laughed at this bit of news.

"That good for he," said Sunil. "He always go on like he is the star boy in the class."

"Ah tell you ah don't like Harry Kissoon and I didn't write he no love note. And you Milo, you mouth like duck batty; it run too damn much," Reena retorted.

"Is you he meet behind school?" Sunil was putting two and two together. "Oh, so now Harry realize he miss a' opportunity with you so he trying to get a second chance."

"He ain't miss nothing. I just wanted to talk to him," said Reena.

"I hope you know what you doing," said Sunil.

"Who go like big nose Harry," said Reena and drew her teeth. She turned her back to us again.

Once Upon A Time In Berbice

Outside the wind had picked up and I could hear the rain starting to drizzle. The frogs and night insects were loud outside as though it were the middle of the rainy season. I could hear the loose zinc on the roof rattling in the wind. Mammy and Aunty Doogoo had stopped talking and had put out the lamp. They had probably fallen asleep by now. The wind blew stronger and I could hear the rain beating down on the zinc roofs of the houses in the neighborhood as it came our way. Sunil started breathing heavily and I knew he had fallen asleep.

"Reena?" I said.

"What?" she said.

"Ah sorry," I said. She turned in bed and I supposed she was looking in my direction. "I shouldn't ah done that to you Friday," I continued. She turned again, probably back to the wall.

"Go to sleep Milo," she said.

The rain came down heavily and the noise it made on the zinc roof drowned out anything else she might have said. I yawned and began drifting off to sleep.

Chapter Four

A week later most of our things were packed in cartoon boxes and ready for the estate truck which was due in two days to come and take everything along with us to the ferry then over to New Amsterdam. The funeral was held two days after the accident and Aunty Doogoo came back with all three of her girls this time. The third daughter was dark like Reena. Nearly the whole village turned out for the burial at the little cemetery out by the foreshore. No relative turned up for Haroon. Mammy didn't know any of his people nor did she know exactly where on West Demerara he was from. Many of our friends from school and their parents had turned up as well as some teachers; including the headmaster Mr. Moriah, my teacher Mrs. Seecherran, Sondra's teacher Ms. June, and Mr. Ramdat. Mrs. Seecharran's husband was not in the accident as she had feared.

From my class Hector, Goofy, Droopatie and Mala showed up with their parents. I didn't get to talk with Mala. Reena's close friends who had visited the house that first night were there again with their parents. Some of Sunil's classmates were there too but Dolly Shivnarine wasn't. Harry Kissoon showed up well dressed in black and white but Reena pretended he didn't exist.

After the funeral some of them came over to the house but Mala left with the truckload of people her parents had transported, heading east. Aunty Doogoo stayed the night with her three daughters who slept on Mammy's bed. They kept to themselves most of the time they were there. Mammy slept with Aunty Doogoo on a floor bed she made in the living room.

Apparently Mammy had already made the decision to move to New Amsterdam. Aunty Doogoo and her daughters returned the next day to make final preparations to accommodate us.

For the rest of the week we were busy packing and burning things Mammy thought we shouldn't take with us or were too shabby to give away. A butcher came by and bought all of our pigs. Reena said if we stayed Mammy would be reminded of Haroon too much so she was in a hurry to move. None of us went to school all week even though my Common Entrance exam was coming up. Mammy didn't worry about me being disrupted at home with all the activities and not studying because I was failing everything at school anyway. I guess she had resigned herself to believing I was just not good at book work. None of us seemed to be, although Reena was good at mathematics.

From what I overheard, Mammy was due some money from the Estate since Haroon died on the job, more or less. Chandra's mother was behind her to make sure she got it. The estate was helping us out by making a truck available for us to move.

On Monday morning Mammy made me dress for school since it was Common Entrance morning. Sunil, Reena and Sondra stayed home. I went out with my school lunch to the side of the road and waited for the bus with Chandra. She wasn't her usual mocking self, maybe because she knew it was probably my last day at school. She was writing the Common Entrance exam too, so maybe that had something to do with it. Or it could simply be that Reena wasn't out there to stop me from slapping her up if she did.

Majeed's mother had him catch the earlier bus so he won't be late for his exams. Maybe she hadn't seen his report card in years since she actually thought he had a shot at passing it.

The bus took us to school without much happening on the way although Dracula was on it. By the time I got in school Majeed and Hector were already there. Everybody was outside the classrooms since they had removed the screens and combined three classrooms together and rearranged the benches so that all faced forward. We were buzzing with tension and expectancy; well, at least they were.

As I stood there with Hector and Majeed I saw Arnold Teekasingh strutting his ultra chubby self around, rolling from group to group with the air of a rooster that already had top prize under its wing. He was a sure shot for acing the exams. He was in the other Standard Four; the one for the bright students. He was fair and round like all three little piggies rolled in one, and wore these big round spectacles which looked like they ought to carry wipers like the car windshields did. They made him look even smarter. Usually, if he wasn't reading something he was either always eating something or looking for something to eat.

I remembered I had one of the three Cadbury chocolate bars someone had given Mammy when they all had come for the funeral. I strolled over to Arnold.

"Arnold, let we make a deal," I said as I took a fat arm and steered him away from the sugar cake stall he seemed to be aiming for.

"I shan't be giving you any answers in the exams," he announced in his very British accent which had afflicted him since he went with his family to England for an eighteen day holiday three years earlier.

"Shut you' ass and come over here," I said harshly, already getting mad that he had to blurt out what I wanted to cook up.

"Unhand me, you ruffian," he said and offered some resistance.

"You want chocolate or not," I said. His resistance subsided.

"Where's the chocolate?" he asked when we were away from the others. I dived into my lunch canister and showed him the brand new unopened bar of Cadbury chocolate.

His eyes gleamed at the sight of it. Tiny beads of sweat appeared on his upper lip. Chocolate was very expensive and quite a rare treat for us children. He looked at me suspiciously.

"How do I know you didn't just wrap something uneatable in chocolate wrapper," he said. So I removed the outer paper then unwrapped the top part of the silver paper to unveil the first three fegs of deep brown chocolate. They had nuts in them. Arnold licked his lips then looked at me with his greedy piggy eyes. I knew I had him where I wanted him.

"How am I going to give you answers when there are teachers patrolling the room," he said.

"You not giving me answers. You doing the test for me," I said.

"You must be off your rockers!" he exclaimed.

I tore off the first three fegs of chocolate and gave him two. He savored them one by one and licked his fat fingers while I explained.

"You're smart enough to do this test two times, right? So all you have to do is do the test and write my number on it instead of yours, then I'll give you my blank paper and you can do the test for yourself. You'll be done in no time," I explained.

"And how am I going to know your number?"

"I'll show you it," I said then showed him how I will use my fingers to signal to him what my number is.

"How do you know we'll be close enough to exchange papers?" he asked. He really asked some good questions but I had thought it out after I realized that, the previous year when I had written and failed the exam, they had seated us alphabetically. With Arnold and me having the same last names we should be pretty close if not right next to each other.

"What would be the signal?" he asked.

"Clear your throat or cough," I said quickly.

Arnold looked around then back at the chocolate I still held in my hand.

"I desire an advance on this venture," he announced pompously.

"Wha' you mean," I said and peered at him suspiciously.

"Gimme piece more." Damn, the boy was bright, using all them fancy words.

"Uh-uh. Naw. When you eat out all right now you could always change your mind when we get in there. You done eat three already and …"

"Two," he interrupted. " You ate one."

"Alright, you done eat two. If everything go right you will get half of it when we come out the exam."

"Half? All of it or nothing," he demanded.

"Why you li'l…." I thought.

I was debating whether or not I should choke the fat little pig when I realized I would be throttling the goose that was about to lay me a golden egg. I restrained myself.

"The whole thing?" I said incredulously.

"The whole thing," he repeated with a sense that he had me where he wanted me. He was right. I had no choice.

"Alright, the whole thing," I agreed. Who's to say I would keep my part of the bargain when that time came.

We filed into the exam room and I could barely recognize part of it as being my own classroom. With the rooms joined together it looked like one long classroom with benches arranged in neat rows. Our names were called and we were escorted to our seats. Although there were some of our teachers present there were a lot of other teachers, probably from other schools. Mrs. Seecharran and other Common entrance teachers at our school were not allowed to be there. Like the others I placed my pencils, sharpener, and eraser down on the desk before me and waited quietly for further instructions.

Once Upon A Time In Berbice

Just as I had expected, Arnold was seated right behind me. There was no need to signal my number to him. It was written in bright chalk mark right on my desk. Each student had his or her number on the desk. If I just moved to one side I knew Arnold could see mine.

When all the papers were shared out we were told to note the time on the clock on the wall in front and we were told to begin. I looked at the first three Mathematics sums then pretended to be in deep thought, working through and marking my multiple choice answers. Arnold was mumbling to himself as he buzzed through the problems, trying to finish early so he could get his own done. After ten minutes I peeked through the crook of an arm to see how he was doing. He was toiling away feverishly and beads of perspiration were nestled on his forehead, nose and by his temples; which wasn't saying much since a similar effect was observed when he first caught sight of my chocolate.

I started marking a few answers since the teachers were coming around and might suspect something if they saw my paper completely blank. Even though all the work was to be done in pencil I made mine light so that Arnold could easily erase them when he got my paper.

After what seemed like forever but was actually just over an hour Arnold stopped buzzing and cleared his throat. I dropped my pencil and paper then bent down to pick them up. He did the same and we exchanged papers before we surfaced again. A teacher started heading up our row, inspecting her way towards us. I put my head down and inspected the paper. The idiot! He had his own number on the paper. I quickly erased it and replaced it with mine. I began checking over, which was what the teacher found me doing when she swung by us.

Arnold started swearing in the Queen's English when he realized he had to erase my pencil marks. I shrugged. That was his problem. I glanced across the classroom. Majeed was looking up at the roof as though in deep thought. I knew from experience that he was thinking of anything but the work before him. I made eye contact with Goofy who apparently was making the same visual survey of the room as I was. I saw Mala sharpening her pencil. When she was done she blew the remaining shaving out of the sharpener and we made eye contact. She smiled then put her head down again in concentration. This was a very good morning for me.

When it was ten thirty a bell rang and one of the teachers said "time up" and "pencils down." I heard Arnold started crying behind me. I glanced back and saw him lying over his papers with his chubby shoulders jerking as he cried. Apparently he was nowhere near finished. The teachers reminded us to make sure our numbers were written on our sheets and that they were correct. Then they came around and picked up all the papers.

When we were given the signal to leave we crowded out the doors and flooded the corridors. Arnold had bolted out first. I met Majeed and Hector just outside the classroom. Most of the other students were excitedly telling each other how well they had done or which problems had given them trouble. Majeed gave me the thumbs up when he saw me. I wondered what the hell that meant; that he'd completed shading all the answers or he thought he got one right.

"How was it?" Majeed asked.

"How was what?" Hector asked.

" I did Alright," I said. " I think ah pass this time."

"Me too," Majeed said.

"When ayo moving to New Amsterdam?" Hector asked.

"Tomorrow," I said.

"So today is your last day in school?" asked Hector.

"I think so," I said. Hector looked depressed.

We continued up the corridor then out into the school yard.

"We ain't go see you at all at all?" Hector asked in dismay.

"I dunno. Maybe when we come back over here to visit," I said. I was getting sad too. Until then it hadn't dawned on me that I would no longer be seeing Hector and Majeed on a daily basis; maybe not at all after that day. I saw Arnold over by the gate motioning vigorously to me. I strolled over there after telling Majeed and Hector to wait for me.

"Our deal is off," Arnold announced.

"You breaking the deal? That mean no more chocolate," I said clarifying things. I was well aware that we still had English and General Knowledge sections of the test to complete.

"There just isn't enough time to do it twice," he said. I was already cracking open my lunch canister to bring out my bargaining chip again.

"You wrote down the answers before we exchanged papers?" I asked.

"What do you mean?"

"After you did the first paper you didn't write down the number and the letter for the answer so you won't have to work it all over again when you got the second paper?" I explained. He looked blank for a few seconds.

"Good Grief! What a fool I am!" he exclaimed and knocked his forehead with the palm of a hand. I wished he had told me that needed doing, for I would have gladly obliged him. I broke off three fegs of chocolate and gave it to him.

"Same thing this afternoon and you get the rest," I said and put away the other half of the chocolate.

"The deal is on again," he announced and waddled away from me. If he had a tail I'm sure it would've been twitching merrily as he slurped up my chocolate.

I met with the usual bunch of boys down by the playfield. At first they were talking about the test but the topic soon changed to more interesting things like sports and who was about to fight who and for what. By eleven we were back at our seats and ready for the English portion of the exam.

I ran the same scheme with Arnold and it took him so long to complete the English test that I was wondering if he was doubling back on our deal. Eventually I got the signal and we swapped papers. When the time was up Arnold was distraught again for time had again run out on him.

We were all ushered out of the classroom for it was lunch time. We had to return at one O' clock for the third and last part of the exam, General Knowledge. Again Arnold requested a conference with me by the gate.

"I'm afraid this is not going to work. There just isn't enough time to do two papers," he complained.

"But the last part is just General Knowledge," I pointed out.

"I already failed to complete the first two sections so I think it would be unwise on my part to take a risk at not completing the third part too," he said. By then I had broken out the chocolate treat again and was preparing to pay down another three-feg installment.

"Alright, what about if you do my own second and give me back before time up. That way you can make sure your section finish," I said. I figured if this lad was as brilliant as the teachers claimed, I should still cross the passing line even if he didn't finish the General Intelligence section.

I surrendered the second-to-last installment of chocolate to Arnold and it was quickly consumed.

"Listen for my signal," said Arnold and hurried away to attend to his lunch.

When I was sure he was gone I broke off a feg of chocolate and ate one. There were only two left. I began putting it away and turned to head for the playfield to eat my lunch when I felt someone grab my chocolate from my grasp and knuckled me on the head.

Once Upon A Time In Berbice

I fell to the ground but managed to hold my lunch canister aloft. Dracula stood over me and was already unwrapping the chocolate. He gobbled down both remaining fegs, looked me over as though deciding if any more chocolate was on my person, then he walked off licking his fingers. Apparently the goon had not learned his lesson. And there I was thinking, "Where's a slab of Brooklacks when you really needed it."

I got up slowly and dusted myself off before heading out by the culvert with the other boys.. We ate our lunches with the boys focusing on me more than anyone else and making a big thing of that day being my last day. Those who went to New Amsterdam before were describing what the town was like to me and what I should expect.

When we were lined up again to return for the final session of the exam I saw Mala some distance down the line. I left my position in the line and headed back to her. When I got up to her she was eating something.

"Mala, today is me last day you know," I said.

"Last day for what?" she said innocently.

"I going New Amsterdam to live."

"I thought that was 'till August holiday time," she said.

"Naw, we moving tomorrow."

"Alright," she said. I wasn't sure what I was expecting.

"Alright, " I said and began to walk off then turned back to her on an impulse.

"I can see you after school this afternoon?" I said.

"For what?" she asked. My mind blanked out for a few seconds.

"Uhh, is a secret," I said. I turned and walked off before she could ask me another mind-stalling question.

I rejoined the line and didn't look back. In fifteen minutes we were ready to begin General Intelligence. There was a lot of reading to do before answering the questions and I wasn't equipped to wallow through all of that. I waited for Arnold's signal. When it did come I did

Chapter Four

the paper-fall-on-the-floor act and switched papers. Although the teachers on duty were getting tired of walking around and checking on us, we didn't want them finding me without an answer sheet.

As soon as I got Arnold's paper I changed the number again. I was thinking of just keeping the paper and ignoring Arnold's signal when time was up and not switch back the papers. But I wasn't sure Arnold would not throw a fit and reveal our little scheme to the teachers. So when it was about five minutes before time up we switched papers again. I wrote my number on it then looked to see if he had finished. There were close to twenty not completed so I ran down the list with my pencil and marked off answers using the "eenie, meenie, minie, moe" method.

At last we were dismissed after all the papers were collected. Some parents had come in to meet their children after the exams. I guess they were anxious to know how well they had done. I supposed they were the parents of the bright kids. I couldn't see Mammy rolling in here anxious to know how I had done.

Of course both of Arnold's parents were there to greet him. I saw this as an opportunity to spirit myself away since I no longer had the last installment due to him. As he rushed out to greet them I dived behind the crowd and headed for the door at the far end of school. I hid by the stairs where I could keep him in sight. Mrs. Seecharran and other Standard Four teachers had come down to greet the students and Arnold's parents were talking to one of them. From my hiding place I saw Majeed and Hector looking around for me then they began drifting towards the stairs by the exit amongst the other students.

By now Arnold realized I was out of sight and began looking frantically for me. He left his parents talking with his teacher and began bustling amongst the crowd looking for me. I stayed by the stairs until I saw him go down the steps at the other end of the corridor and out of sight. I ran higher up to the top of the stairs and looked through the opening where I could see the students streaming out to the school gate and beside the road. Arnold continued his search for me and began talking to Majeed and Hector; most likely asking for me. They must have told him something in the negative because he continued his search.

A bus had pulled up before the school heading east. Children were boarding the bus and I could see Arnold getting more frantic. The bus pulled off. Other children were on foot; some heading east and some heading west up the road. A couple of hire cars stopped, loaded up and pulled off. As the crowd got thinner I spied Mala standing by the gate. My heart skipped a beat.

She was actually waiting for me. I wanted to jump up and run out there right then. Usually she would have been on that bus that left but the fact that she was still by the gate and her friends were gone told me she was waiting for me. Just then Arnold's parents headed out to the gate where he was standing dejectedly; probably cussing me off in perfect English for scooting with the chocolate and leaving him with a mouthful of spit. His parents weren't fat like he was but boy were they walking slowly. I left my place of hiding and ran downstairs and down the corridor to the stairs at the exit of the building.

When I got to the steps I pulled up and peered out to locate Arnold and his parents. A bus pulled up just then heading east. Some more children got in and Mala hurried from the gate across the road and into the bus. There was no way I could have caught that bus even if I immediately left my place of hiding. The bus left and I felt a sadness overcome me. I wondered if that was the last I would ever see of my beautiful Mala.

As I waited for Arnold and family to depart it dawned on me that, but for three fegs of chocolate, I had missed out on a chance to have a brief farewell with the girl I had loved for the last three years. I realized I was being greedier than Arnold was.

I had to wait another twenty minutes before I saw the last of Arnold. By the time I got out to catch a bus all the students were gone. Majeed and Hector were long gone. When the bus came I climbed aboard and it pulled off. I looked at my soon to be "old school" and wished I could come to school again tomorrow.

Chapter Five

By midday of the day we moved, we were in the truck at the Rosignol ferry stelling waiting for the ferry boat M.V. Torani to take us over to New Amsterdam, our new hometown. Mammy, Reena and Sondra were riding in the cabin of the truck with the driver while me and Sunil were riding in the tray with our meager belongings. I was sad and excited at the same time. A feeling of deep sadness had overcome me as the truck had pulled off from our soon to be old house. It was the house in which I was born. It was the village I had known all my life. We were leaving everything and everyone I had ever known for a new beginning in a new location.

Looking at Sunil and how happy he was lifted my spirits a bit. It would be exciting to live in a big town like New Amsterdam if what my friends had told me about it was true. Reena didn't seem too excited about it and was probably worried about Aunty Doogoo's reputation and passion for match-making. Mammy didn't show any excitement one way or the other but she must have been happy to leave a village in which she had just buried husband number two.

Our truck was the second in a line of five trucks on the left side of the stelling. On the right side there was a line of just over a dozen cars. The stelling had a high roof which also covered the section behind a high wire fence which looked like the passenger area. People were coming in, buying tickets at a booth and entering another area after surrendering their tickets. There were long benches in there for people to sit on. Below the whole roof the floor was covered with thick planks and I could hear the waves of the river lapping beneath. Apparently the stelling was built a little way out over the river. Toward the river was a gangway which loped gently down toward the light brown water of the Berbice River.

I could see over the wooden wall beyond the cars where there was a small tributary from the river running back parallel to the road to the stelling. Beyond that was a canefield. Sunil had shown me the tower in the distance beyond the canefield and said that was Blairmont Estate where the accident had happened. It seemed a mile away but was probably much more than that.

The ferry was coming. New Amsterdam stelling was on the other side of the mile wide river and maybe three miles downriver. Looking northward I could see the river widened to a larger expanse of water. They said that was the Atlantic Ocean out there. Imagine that; the same Atlantic Ocean Mrs. Seecharran had talked about and had shown us on a map. Across the river from us there was just bush all the way along the bank of the river until you can barely see the stelling and buildings behind that which was where the town of New Amsterdam was located. Then more bush and what looked like another stelling. More bush followed, then way down river where the two banks appear to meet but was actually a bend in the river, was a big factory which I later learned was the Reynolds Bauxite company.

The M.V. Torani looked bigger as it got nearer to the stelling. I could see trucks and cars on the lower deck and people standing on the balcony upstairs. For a minute I thought it was going to come straight into and ram the stelling. It slowed as it got nearer. Then it drifted just past the stelling and I could hear a clinging of some kind of communication bells. She drifted to a stop just beyond the stelling with her engines at the back kicking up water which appeared to be lighter than the river water. Ropes were tossed onto the platform at the back and front and caught by workers. These thin ropes were tied to huge fat ropes which were dropped into the river. Using the thinner ropes the men pulled the stout ropes out of the water and placed them around huge anvil like anchors on the platform. Then sailors on the ferry began working on tightening up the fat ropes from that end. Slowly the ferry boat drifted closer to the stelling and backward until her lower doorway was in line with the gangway below. The heavy metal door was lowered onto the gangway and secured by the sailors then the two doors on the sides of the boat on the upper flat were opened to the elevated passenger gangways up there.

People poured out downstairs before the first car was directed out of the boat. Other people were coming out upstairs then down the stairs on the passenger side. The stelling was suddenly busy and bustling with activity. Verndors were busy, hire car drivers were soliciting passengers going to Georgetown or anywhere between, and the directors of traffic out of the boat were shouting instructions. People were climbing aboard colorful buses waiting beyond the stelling.

I watched all of this with excitement. This was all new to me. I was actually at the starting point of all those vehicles that sped past our house and school during the day. As the vehicles noisily came up the gangway from the ferry they drove out of the stelling then up the road on the beginning of their sixty-seven mile journey to Georgetown. Some cars stopped to pick up their passengers before speeding off. On the passenger side some incoming passengers were greeting outgoing passengers.

Eventually all the passengers from upstairs had disembarked. The passengers from the seated section on our left began climbing the stairs and boarding the ferry on the upper flat. The trucks were now directed out of the ferry on the lower level. The big ferry rocked gently every time a truck rolled off the boat and onto the gangway.

After the last truck had labored its way up the gangplank and had driven out of the stelling a sailor signaled the first truck in our line to enter the ferry. The engine of our truck roared to life. When it was our turn the truck slowly drove toward the gangway then down the gradual descent and onto the boat. I was excited and frightened at the same time. After maneuvering back and forth we were finally parked up against the back wall of the ferry next to the truck that had been first in line. I stood up to watch the other vehicles being directed onto the boat and into parking positions. When the last car was in position a whistle was blown and people with carts and other heavy hand-held items came down the gangway and into the boat. I could hear the metallic doors on the upper floor slam shut. After the last person came onto the boat below the whistle was blown again and the big metal door was slowly pulled up from the gangway.

The big ropes attaching the boat began going slack as the sailors onboard release more rope. The men on the platform then removed the heavy ropes from the metal "anvil" and the ropes, under their own weight, slid off the platform and dropped with loud splashes into the river to be pulled up by the sailors.

The rattling sound that was audible but not noticed before, suddenly stopped. I thought it was all a part of the engine noise but now I could hear the deep drone of the engines. There were some little noises like cables being pulled and bells ringing then I heard the engines rev up and it appeared as though the stelling was moving backward. After a minute I realized it was the boat that was moving forward. We moved past the stelling as though heading out to the ocean then the ferry began turning slowly toward mid river then started heading south.

Sunil began climbing off the truck. When I asked he said he was going upstairs and if I wanted to come. I carefully climbed down after him. He jumped up on the step to the cabin and told Mammy we were going upstairs for some fresh air. Reena decided she wanted to come with us since she wanted to use the toilet.

Once Upon A Time In Berbice

Sunil led us through a passage way in the back wall. We passed a doorway which apparently led downward to the engine room since the sound of the engine was very loud in there. Beyond this led to the back of the boat where some people were sitting on some stacked eight by four feet wooden frames that functioned as seats. I could see the clearer looking water kicked up by the double propellers. We climbed short metal steps into the upper floor of the ferry. There were more wooden platform seats with people there looking out on the river. We went through another doorway into the boat. I guess we were directly above the trucks on the lower deck at that point. There was a shop in the front section and most of the space was occupied by rows of long wooden seats back to back along the length of the boat. People seated on them faced the sides of the boat. I could see the four closed metal doors which allowed passengers to disembark when opened.

Sunil led us toward the front of the boat. In the front walls were the two entrances of the bathrooms labeled "Men" and "Women." Reena headed in the women's but was soon out with her nose cringed up in revolt. She told us she had changed her mind.

We followed Sunil out onto the front deck where I had seen people standing when the ferry was approaching the stelling. It was breezier out there and quiet. We couldn't hear the engines. There was not a seat in sight. We looked out and down the river where New Amsterdam awaited us. I looked around at the other people. Most of them were well dressed, especially the women and children. A few vendors came around hawking peanuts, sweets or cigarettes. We stood leaned against the rails like many others out there.

"This river big boy," I said.

"Is not the biggest river though," Reena said.

"Who say so?" I challenged.

Chapter Five

"You duncy, you ain't know Essequibo river bigger than this?" Sunil said.

"How big that is so?" I wondered in awe.

"Where you think the Titanic sink?" said Sunil.

"You mad? Titanic ain't sink there boy," Reena said then laughed.

"Where it sink then?" said Sunil.

"In some ocean, but I bet you it ain't sink in no Essequibo river," Reena said.

"So is on this boat all them cars does be coming," I said in awe. " All of them going New Amsterdam?"

"I guess so," Reena said.

"Maybe they going Corentyne," Sunil said.

"Where Corentyne is?" I asked.

"Somewhere past New Amsterdam," said Sunil.

We were distracted by a moderately fat Portuguese man shuffling his way past the seated passengers with a tin cup in one hand. He was dressed in khaki pants pulled very high up with striped white and orange shirt buttoned down to the wrists. The clothes were wrinkled and slightly soiled but everything was well tucked in with a robust leather belt holding the fort at the waist. Stuck on his head was what looked like a well used hat and his unshaven face had a permanent smile and the general affable expression of a child. People seemed amused as they watched him waddle his way around.

"Dario, what you doing on this boat?" a lady asked. "You went down to Georgetown?"

" My name is Dario Gomes," the man said in a soft voice and seemed oblivious to the question posed by the woman who by now had fished out her purse from her bag and was reaching into it.

"You went to town to get a wife?" she continued. The other people seated around were laughing. She dropped a few coins into his cup.

"My name is Dario Gomes," he repeated.

Once Upon A Time In Berbice

"Aye Dario, why ayo don't stay in the Mental instead of bothering people out here," said a sailor who had come from within the passenger section inside and went toward the stairs leading to the lower deck. The man showed no sign of having heard him. The sailor disappeared down the stairs.

Reena and Sunil stared at the man.

"What is the Mental?" I asked Reena quietly.

"The Mental Asylum, the Mad House," she whispered.

We stared at the man. We all knew that the only mental asylum in the country was in New Amsterdam but this was the first time we were actually seeing a mad man. Had the sailor not said anything we would not have known he was mad even though he did appear childish in his expressions. I wasn't sure what to expect from him; maybe he would suddenly go berserk and attack everyone. But the other people around seemed to know he was a madman but they seemed anything but afraid.

The man continued circulating among the passengers on the deck and received coins in his cup from many. Then he shuffled off inside the boat again. We returned our attention to the river.

The ferry was closer to the other side of the river now. We could see a tributary wide enough for the ferry to travel up but we glided right past it. The New Amsterdam Stelling came closer but the ferry seemed to be drifting past it instead of straight to it. We passed a good six hundred yards away from the stelling. For a moment I thought the captain had fallen asleep or was drunk. Then I heard pulled cables rustling and bells ringing. We couldn't hear the engines. The ferry then began making a wide turn toward the shoreline then toward the stelling. After a while it slowed down and slowly drifted closer to the platform of the stelling where the whole trick with the small and big ropes was repeated by the men on the stelling and the sailors on board.

Chapter Five

Me and Reena were urging Sunil to return to the truck below but he said we had time since all the cars had to come out first before the truck could move. It made sense. We peered over the side rails as people on deck began getting up and moving inside the ferry towards the doors on that side. When the large ferry settled in its final position the heavy door below clanged open and was lowered onto the gangway of the platform. Then the two doors on top dropped open. Me and Reena were anxious and were going to leave with or without Sunil.

By the time we got downstairs and back on the truck there was much noise with the vehicles roaring to life and people shouting to each other. Some men who I later learned were taxi drivers, were standing to the edge of the stelling beckoning to passengers in the boat. The sailors began directing the cars out of the ferry. By the time it was the trucks' turn to exit, most of the outgoing passengers were gone.

Our truck labored up the gangway and onto the wooden platform which rumbled beneath the its weight. Then we came out from beneath the roof of the stelling and onto the stelling road. We were in New Amsterdam at last.

Once Upon A Time In Berbice

Chapter Six

New Amsterdam was about a mile long and half mile wide. Its length was in a north to south direction along the east bank of the Berbice river. To the north was the Canje Creek next to which was the Mental Hospital complex which included several buildings and a lovely well kept cricket ground. A main highway came over a swing bridge across the Canje Creek and ran south right through the town. This was Main street, more commonly called Main Road.

As this road wound past the Mental Hospital complex going south, the first street ran across Main Street and continued east for about four hundred yards before turning south and more or less parallel to Main Street. This continued southward and was called Backdam. After running the length of the town for about a mile and a half Backdam swung right and reunited with Main street.

If you came off the Canje Bridge and turned right on the same cross road, instead of left toward Backdam, that road turned left after eighty yards and continued south and just about parallel with Main Road to form Water Street. This street ran the length of the town and reunited with Main Street at the same point as Backdam.

Throughout the town there were cross streets joining Main Street to Waterstreet and Backdam. Most streets ran right through from Backdam to Waterside but a few of them ran only between Backdam and Main Street. Most of these short streets carried the title Alley or Lane behind their names. From north to south all the streets had names until you got to Philadelphia Street, popularly called Highbridge. After that point was a section of the town called Stanleytown. The streets were then numbered beginning with Lot Thirty-one and the numbers increased all the way to the last street before the three main north to south streets merged.

Chapter Six

On the eastern side of Backdam and south of Highbridge were two housing schemes known simply as First Scheme and Second Scheme. Between First Scheme and Second Scheme was a large ground.   The big burial ground occupied the entire area from Lot 31 to Lot 36 on the Waterside and extended another lot farther on the backdam side of the Main Road.

I was amazed. There were more buildings than I had ever seen before, and so close to each other. The truck stopped at the junction of the Stelling Road and Water Street. To our left was the Post Office and just to our right was a huge high white building with wooden louver windows which were closed and very high. Sunil was pointing to it excitedly. He said it was a cinema. There were billboards outside and large posters advertising various shows. I could recognize one as a war movie and the others were westerns.   Then there was a board advertising two Indian movies.

As the truck turned right I could see the front of the cinema was on Water Street. There were more posters in glass cases and vendor's stalls cluttering the sides of the wide entrance. On either side to the front were two shops. Apparently a show was in progress since there weren't many patrons crowding the entrance.

As the truck moved past the cinema I noticed a wide and open area with a gas station and what seemed like a bus park. There were about six buses there with two lined up on the street itself just before the cinema, ready to leave. One was gray with the name "Her Highness" stylishly painted on its side, and the other was a fancy green bus named "Duke of Kent." Sunil said these buses traveled up the Corentyne.

We turned left down St. Ann Street. The few pedestrians down the street stopped and stepped way off the street to make way for the big truck. We got up to the head of the street then the truck turned right onto big, bright, busy Main Street. To my surprise there on our left was another cinema, though not as huge as the one we had seen by the stelling road. I later learned that the one by the stelling was The Globe and this smaller one was Gaiety; both owned by a Chinese businessman named Ho Young. There were more posters on bill boards in front along with the days and showing times. But this cinema had the windows open and no shows were on at the time.

The truck turned left down Theatre Alley, the street beside the cinema. The truck drove extra slowly as the street was very narrow and was littered with pot holes. The truck came to a halt before a two storied light blue house which was somewhere just past the middle of the street and closer to Backdam.

I was at least expecting a mini welcoming party at the house. Instead, there was a little crowd of about eight to ten people with their attention on a black woman across the street from us who was berating and attempting to spank a big girl who was in school uniform – white blouse and brown skirt. The girl appeared a little older than Reena. The girl was protesting and cowering while at the same time retreating into the open yard which was partly encircled with tenement shacks. The mini crowd was laughing while the woman continued striking out at the girl with a strop of some kind and cussing her out. Apparently, the girl was supposed to be in school, with it being just after two in the afternoon, but was seen in the botanical gardens with a boyfriend by someone who knew her mother. The mother was told and went there, caught her and brought her home.

The truck driver blew the horn twice. We got down from the tray of the truck and Reena, Mammy and Sondra cautiously disembarked from the cabin. Aunt Doogoo came hurrying out along with the third daughter that had visited us when Haroon had died. The two fair ones were apparently not at home. A man in his early twenties who

Chapter Six

was introduced to us as our cousin Dil, came out slowly from the yard toward the truck. He wore a baseball cap, vest, and short pants. Apparently he was awakened from an afternoon nap. Aunty Doogoo got a few of the men standing around to help us unload our things from the truck and take them inside.

By three O'clock most of our things were in the house and some in the shed at the back. The lower flat of the house was elevated just a foot or so off the ground and had a wooden floor. As we entered the front door there were two rooms on the right; the second seemed to have been added very recently and cut into the space for the dining room. The kitchen was added to this floor beyond the dining room. From the dining room there was a stair leading to the upper floor. There were four bedrooms up there; a large one and three smaller ones. Doogoo and her husband Inchan slept in the large room almost over the kitchen. The two "queens," Indira and Lea slept in the one next to Doogoo's. Next to the "queens' chamber" was Nanni's room in which Seelochanie also slept. Nanni was Mammy and Doogoo's mother. Next to this and facing the street was the room in which Dil and his brother Raj slept, but was now vacated for Mammy, Reena and Sondra. Apparently Raj and Dil were to sleep in the second little room downstairs. Next to this was the new addition in which me and Sunil were to live. Mammy's new room had her wardrobe, a clothes horse and a big spring bed. They also had Mammy's vanity case with its mirror, and drawers for their clothes. Reena seemed happy with the new living arrangements for them.

Me and Sunil had two separate beds which were fiber mattresses mounted on wooden frames. Instead of nails on the walls we had a clothes horse on which to hang up our clothes.

Once Upon A Time In Berbice

The bathroom and latrine were beside the house against the fence, with the former being just behind a high enclosed shed which was a kind of store room below and wood and lumber stored above. The latrine had a roof but the bathroom didn't. The walls of the open bathroom were high and partly behind the shed so you couldn't see into the top from an upstairs window, unless you were in upper part of the shed where the wood was stored.

Our yard was separated from the next yard on that side by a high zinc fence. To the back of the yard was a wire mesh fence, then a gutter which ran parallel to Theatre Alley, then another fence and the back of the house in the next street, Church Street.

Dil got dressed and went out the yard just after three. Aunty Doogoo boasted that Dil worked at the Gaiety cinema and he was the projector operator. I didn't know what a projector was until Sunil told me it was that machine that make the ticking sound and showed the film when they had film show in our village. We then looked on Dil as though he had the keys to heaven.

Sunil told Mammy he was going out on the road and Mammy told him to take me with him. He surprised me by not objecting. I was about to head out barefooted when Aunty Doogoo objected and insisted that we couldn't go out barefoot. She made me put on my school yachting shoes.

We went out to the head of the street by the cinema. By then the Main Street was filled with school children in different color uniforms. Some wore blue shirts and khaki pants. Others had light blue or gray shirts. I even saw some boys with red shirts and some girls in pink plaid dresses.

There were many people in front of the cinema including vendors. People were dressed up and talking excitedly while others bought tickets and walked up through the front entrance. Most of the casually dressed males were purchasing tickets from a little booth to the side then walking all the way along the side of the building to the entrance at the other end of the building.

Sunil took me south down Main street. He walked as if he knew the town but I knew he hadn't a clue since he hadn't come to New Amsterdam for years. We walked in the hot afternoon sun past streets with names like Trinity Street, Coopers Lane, New Street and Lad Lane. When we reached the big Catholic Church at St. John Street we turned left down that street. Unlike Theatre Alley this street was pitched with tar and gravel. The large church on the left side was joined to another building that was even bigger. There were many school children in this street and only girls in brown uniforms were playing in the yard or on the steps of the building. This building was joined by an old dilapidated wooden tunnel to another smaller building. There were many boys in blue shirts and khaki pants with their books in their hands and some playing in the yard.

After the Boys School building was a worn out playground and a large metal tank, probably a water vat. Then the street slanted upward to the Backdam road. It was breezy out there.

We went out on the Backdam and turned left heading back towards Theatre Alley. We walked behind other school children who were going in that direction. There were many children in light blue shirts and blouses coming in the opposite direction. Others wore gray and some in red. There were bigger children coming up the Backdam from the northern side of town, riding on bicycles. They were dressed in navy blue pleated skirts and white blouses.

It was much breezier and cooler out on the Backdam. There was mostly just savannah on the right side. About eight hundred yards beyond this area was a dam and more houses behind there. I later learned that over there was called Cow Dam.

When we got back to the house Lea and Indira had come home from Commercial School. They were sitting at the breakfast table eating when we came in. Their sister Seelochanie who everybody called "See" was busy in the kitchen. Raj came in just after we did. He was an electrician and worked with the Electricity Company. He usually rode around with two other workers in the Electricity truck.

Raj went upstairs and took Sunil with him. I went to my room and took off my school yachtings shoes. When I came out again Reena and Mammy were downstairs and Doogoo was pointing them to the table. See appeared to be doing all of the work in the kitchen. She brought out food for me, Reena and Mammy. Indira and Lea had gone upstairs, I supposed to change. As we ate I excitedly told Reena and Mammy where we had gone and what we saw. Doogoo called down Raj and Sunil to eat. They came down and See gave Raj his food in his hand. Sunil came to the table. Raj went to the back door and sat with his food in his lap and his legs on the short steps.

After we ate Doogoo told See to take Reena for a walk to show her around. I asked Mammy and she said I could go with her. Raj had changed into a striped yellow and black t-shirt and black trunks. He had on rubber slippers and over a shoulder he had a pair of dirty football boots with socks stuffed in them. He told Mammy he was taking Sunil with him.

When the three of us left the yard it was almost five O'clock. I had put on my school yachtings again. Reena had changed into a yellow top and her red school skirt. See was dark like Reena and about the same height although she was three years older. She wore a full length plaid dress and thick rubber slippers. Her hair was long and straight, reaching down to her shoulder blades. She had it combed back in one with a rubber band bunching it together. She seemed friendly and was eager to take us out.

We walked in the same direction to Main street as I had with Sunil earlier. As we passed Gaiety we could hear the

89

action from the movie being shown. See turned right up Main street instead of left. The street was busy as usual with many workers in uniform riding or walking home. A few buses passed by going south; one a green bus named "Duke of York," then a red one named "Tourist Deluxe." A blue bus also went by. See said the blue ones went to a different area named Canje. The only bus that went in the opposite direction was a short orange bus named "Round-the-Town." See explained that this bus ran, as the name suggested, around the town; the entire length of Main Street, then turned for Water Street just before it reached the Gardens, then all the way down Water Street until that street met Main Street at the southern end of town.

We continued walking past shops and other business places on either side of the street. On we went, past Charlotte Street, Coburg Street where See said the Police Station was on the Waterside half, Wapping Lane, then King street where Main Road took a slight turn to the left. We continued walking until we reached a cross street named Vryheid Road. There was a "No Entry" sign on the Main Street here where traffic only came down toward us. See said the big church to the right was Scotts Church. Then she was explaining something about the big black patch on the roof by the steeple which was as a result of a thunderbolt falling there during a thunderstorm and burning its way right through the building. As interesting as this sounded, my attention was only half there. For I was more interested in what looked like swings and a playground on the left behind the high trimmed hedge which served as a fence.

"That is somebody yard over there?" I asked. I could hear children playing and screaming behind the hedge.

"That is the gardens. Is there we going," See said.

We crossed the street carefully, for vehicles were traveling very fast down this one way street. See said those vehicles were coming from Canje or Corentyne.

Once Upon A Time In Berbice

When we went into the gardens my eyes lit up. There were four swings – one was broken – a slide, seesaw, a big rusty cannon, and something with a horizontal wheel with steel cables connected to the top of the pole which passed through the center of this iron wheel. The center of the wheel rested on a ledge about four feet up the center pole. Some children were pushing the wheel to the right and as it turned the five cables wound around the pole and the wheel raised off the ledge. When the children released it a few held on to the wheel which rotated to the left and down to the ledge, then up again. Then it changed direction and spun down again and this was repeated until the energy was spent.

See and Reena sat on one of several benches positioned around this area. I went over to the swings and waited there for a turn. As soon as a little boy jumped off one of the swings I swooped in and stuck my bottom on the wooden seat leaving another girl frowning angrily at me for beating her out of her turn at the swing.

The three of us – another boy and a girl – swung as high as we could, competing with each other. When the swing went forward and upward I could see over the high hedged fence and onto the road where the traffic raced down from Canje and the Corentyne. I was at it for some time when Reena called me off the swing and told me they were going. I reluctantly came off while other children scrambled for the swing.

See and Reena walked up one of the neat passageways in the gardens. There were many smaller trees bristling with colorful flowers and huge trees towering like canopies over the gardens. The path wound past more benches and a pond. There were couples standing around in shaded areas talking secretively and hugging each other. See and Reena sat down again on a bench positioned where the path went around a small pond. The pond was almost covered with lilies and with the biggest leaves I'd ever seen just sitting there on the water like boats.. Each leaf was large enough for me to lie on and had upturn edges like a flat bottomed bowl. See said they were Victoria Regia and they were supposed to be famous. There was a frog on one of them. I picked up a small stone and threw in its direction. The stone skated off the water then onto another leaf and remained there. The frog was not impressed. I was looking around for a bigger stone when Reena suddenly slapped at her lower leg. See said something about us going back home before "sandfly come down."

We returned home walking the same route we had taken to go to the gardens. The street lights had come on and a few boys hanging around at the street corners whistled at See and Reena as we went by. One boy offered me ten cents to talk to Reena. I was about to take up the offer when Reena dragged me away. See was amused.

By the time we returned, the street lights were turned on and the vendors in front of the cinema had their flambos burning. When we turned into the yard Inchan, Aunty Doogoo's husband, was standing by the gate chatting with two other men under the light from the "lantern post" outside. He was a wiry short quiet looking man with sad eyes. We said "good afternoon" to them then went into the yard.

When we went into the house Aunty Doogoo was busy with something in the kitchen and immediately started fretting with See about her forgetting to do some chore before she went out. Lea was adjusting the big radio on the cabinet in the dining room. It was playing Indian music but wasn't quite on the station. As she adjusted it the radio seemed to be catching a Spanish station. With nothing else to do I went back into our room. Sunil hadn't come back as yet with Raj. I lay on the clean cream sheet and cotton stuffed pillow. This was much more comfortable than our floor bed back in the village. The room was semi lit by the light from the florescent lamp in the dining room. I closed my eyes and took in the sounds of my new neighborhood.

Apart from the Indian music fading in and out from the radio as Lea toyed with the tuning dial, I could hear Indira talking through the window upstairs to somebody next door. I could hear the three men outside when they laughed or exclaimed something loudly. I wished the house was nearer to the head of the street so I could hear the movie showing at the cinema. I could hear children squealing as they played somewhere down the street and in the Yard across the street. There were the intermittent sounds of water splashing as someone emptied a basin, or some child being called by a parent, or a car rumbling down the street as it maneuvered its way past and over the potholes, or a noisy bicycle being ridden down the street.

I must have dozed off because when I opened my eyes again it was bright in the room. Sunil had turned on the light which was a naked bulb hanging near the ceiling. I hadn't even noticed it before.

"Alyuh come back already?" he said as he sat on his bed and took off his yachtings.

"Where you all been?" I asked.

"We been by the mental ground. Raj been and play football," Sunil said.

"Mental ground?"

"That is by the Mad House."

"Them mad man chase alyuh?" I asked excitedly.

"No, you stupid or what. The really mad ones does be lock up in them other buildings. Is only the Alright ones does be outside," Sunil explained.

"Well if they alright why they still there?"

"They got to go for medicine or something."

"So they still mad then," I pointed out.

"I didn't go to check on no mad man; just to watch the football."

"Who win?"

"Raj side win. Wasn't really a match. They just pick two sides and play. Raj nearly score a goal. Plenty people know he man."

"Where Mental Ground is?" I asked.

"Is way up so going up Main Road," he said and pointed in the direction from which we had just come.

"Oh yea? We went up that side to the Gardens."

"Well is past there going up more," he said. "Is who bicycle in the dining room?"

" I ain't see no bicycle there," I said.

"Go see for yourself," he said.

I got up and looked in the dining room and there was a Big Ben bicycle leaning against the wall by the back door. I returned to the room.

"Must be Aunty Doogoo' husband bike," I said.

"He must be does ride to work," Sunil said. "I got to get some picture to put on this wall."

He was looking around at the bare wooden walls of our room. Sondra and Reena came downstairs just then and stopped by our room. Reena came in and sat on my bed while Sondra went back upstairs. We started talking about what we had seen on our first day. We continued talking until Doogoo came downstairs and changed the radio station to listen the "Death Announcements." By then her husband had come in and gone upstairs to their room. By eleven O'clock we were all in our beds. The light in the dining room was left on for Dil when he came in which was usually just after midnight when the eight-thirty show was over.

Although my bed was more comfortable, I had trouble dropping to sleep again. I wondered how the day went for Hector and Majeed. With me gone I wondered who Dracula was feasting on. I smiled when I realized that Majeed would have returned to school that same day, not realizing that Dracula had him in mind as the guilty party in his diarrhea episode. Poor Majeed. At least Dracula wouldn't be taking away his meals anymore now that the monster believed it was laced with senna or salts. I wondered if Mala missed me and if Arnold was still looking for me to get his last installment of chocolate.

Thinking of school I wondered if Mammy was going to bother sending me to school, seeing just a couple weeks were left before school closed. I had already written my Common Entrance Exams and this was the idle time for children in Common Entrance Class. This was Reena's last year for school so I guessed she wasn't going back.

On the bright side there was a whole town to explore and I was yet to have my first experience with going to the cinema. I could see life was going to be pretty exciting for me here.

Chapter Seven

Chapter Seven

"Wake up boy," I heard a feminine voice say and it wasn't that of Reena nor Mammy. I sat up slowly and rubbed my eyes sleepily. It was See. She wore a full length, badly rumpled cream dress with little orange and white flowers. I supposed it was her "house" dress. The waist line was very high as though for a pregnant person but I could see her belly was flat under it. Her long, black, shiny hair was combed back and tied at her shoulders by a rubber band. She was tidying up things in the room. Sunil wasn't there.

"Where Sunil?" I asked.

"Sunil gone with Doogoo to get a work," See said without looking at me.

"Where dat?" I said.

"Come on, get up. Too much questions boy. Come drink your tea. You got to go out too," she said.

"Go out where?"

"You coming with me to carry Nanny by the shoemaker shop," she said as she straightened from what she was doing. " From now on that go be your job every day."

"Every day? Is how much bruck-up shoes she got so," I thought aloud.

See's face broke into a wide grin then she threw her head back and laughed heartily, revealing lilly white teeth which contrasted with her dark complexion. "She ain't going for no shoes."

"Then what she got to go there for?"

"Get-up and I go tell you everything when we ready," she said. I was about to get out of bed when I realized it was wet. I froze and looked anxiously at her to see if she had noticed. She had.

"You pee the bed," she stated and smiled.

"I ain't pee no bed," I defended and remained seated on the evidence.

"Then the roof and the floor upstairs must be leaking make the bed wet," she said and laughed. "Don't worry. Reena done tell me you piss-up the bed already. Come carry out the wet things at the back to dry," she said then left the room.

Trust "big mouth" Reena the prophet to tell everybody about my nocturnal leakage. I'd have to teach her another lesson. Two things were in my favor this time where carrying out my wet things was concerned. I didn't have to take out the whole mattress which was covered in plastic, just the sheets. And there was no Chandra across the street to witness my embarrassment since the yard was enclosed with a high fence by the street preventing anyone from seeing in.

By the time I went for tea Reena was downstairs at the table. The "Royal Twins" were nowhere to be seen. They were probably off to Commercial School already. Reena and See were talking about something to do with the day's chores. Apparently Reena had offered to help See in the kitchen and See was telling her what she could do while she was out with me. Reena had to cut up and season fish that was already lying on a wooden chopping board on the kitchen counter.

"How long you go take to come back?" asked Reena.

"Not long. I just going and carry them there and come back. The shoemaker shop ain't far; is just 'round the corner and up the road," said See. "Ah sure he can find he way back without getting lost." This she said while looking at me. "Your brother want know how much bruck-up shoes Nanny have make she got to go shoemaker every day," she said and laughed. Reena looked at me with a disapproving frown.

"Why she got to go every day?" she asked See.

Chapter Seven

"She and the shoemaker' father-in-law grew up together up Corentyne. They does talk every day since everybody else they grew up with dead out already," See explained, which, in the first place, she could very well have done for me when I had asked.

After we ate See showed us where the bathroom and latrine were in the yard. The bathroom was behind the wood shed at the back and the latrine was a little farther across and against the side fence. Me and Reena went out with See to the bathroom. We both had our towels. It was wooden with a bucket and pipe within the enclosure. The floor was concrete and slanting slightly backward so that the water drained into a small gutter running out to the bigger gutter behind the yard. I was wondering why they had a low pipe instead of running it all the way up for an overhead shower like I'd seen in some Big Shot houses, when See explained that the water pump station was all the way across town and the water pressure wasn't strong enough to deliver water that high.

It was clean inside with two water worn boards on the concrete to stand on. There was an empty galvanized bucket with a plastic bowl sitting under the pipe.

See left us and went back to the kitchen. Reena decided to bathe first and I could see she was nervous about this new bathroom with its roofless enclosure even though the sides and doors appeared to be secure.

"Go wait by the steps 'till I done bathe," she said. I drew my teeth and withdrew by the steps. I could see the door and one side of the bathroom from where I sat. The side walls were only boarded up to the height of her shoulders. I guessed she was nervous about that too but then nobody outside of the yard could see in the backyard much less in the bathroom.

She hung her towel over the wall then I could see her pulling her dress over her head and she threw that over the wall too. Then came her other under things and I heard the water running in the bucket.

After ten minutes Reena emerged from the bathroom fully dressed and the towel over a shoulder.

"You had to take so long?" I complained when she came by me. " The water warm?" I asked.

"Go find out for yourself," she said over a shoulder and rushed into the house.

I went in, secured the door on the inside with a wooden latch then undressed after turning on the tap to full the bucket. The water was surprisingly warm. I dipped the bowl into the water and poured it over my head. The warm water ran through my hair, down my face and over my body. It felt really good and I repeated this about a dozen times before going to the worn Lux soap sitting on a wooden ledge. I was in that bathroom on that first day for closer to half an hour before coming out after See called to tell me she was ready.

After I was finished drying my skin I realized I had only my peed sleeping pants, having forgotten to bring a clean one with me to the bathroom. I wrapped the towel around myself and scooted into the house with the pants in a hand.

When I went to my room there was a clean pants and t-shirt laid out on the bed for me. I guessed Reena must have pressed and put them there. I dressed and slipped on my school boots then went to the kitchen to find See.

"See waiting for you outside," Reena said. She had already began preparing the fish.

I left and went out the front but See wasn't there yet. I stood by the open gate and stared into the tenement yard across the street. These were rows of low wooden shacks in a square "U" shape, all joined together and standing on short three foot supports. The main doors were on the inside of the "U" and the kitchen sinks hung out the back walls.

Chapter Seven

It must have been well after nine because there were no school children in sight. One and two grown-ups were milling about the yard; some coming from or going to the assembly of zinc partitions beside the U-shaped tenements which were likely the bathrooms and latrines.

A woman in her early thirties hurriedly slip-slopped her way in her rubber slippers into the yard. She looked like she had dressed hastily, with her zipper half way up the back of her dark green skirt and her yellow tube top threatening to surrender to the pressure of her ample breasts even though the latter were harnessed somewhat by a stubborn black brassiere. Her long kinky hair was unkempt with a yellow plastic comb stuck in the crown. She had something wrapped in a paper bag stuck in the waist to the back of her skirt. Just when my attention was waning where she was concerned I heard her angrily shout out to one of the closed shacks.

" Richie, climb off that heifer and open this blasted door lemme murder she!" bawled the woman. Heads began to turn in her direction as the others in the yard were attracted to her announcement.

"Richie, ah say to open the friggin' door before ah kick it ass down," she threatened.

Other wooden shutters were thrown open and heads popped out to see what was afoot. Some came out to their doors even though they were only half dressed.

"Richie!"

"Jean, is wha' noise you making so early in the morning waking up people," came a male voice from within the shack as the person stirred. At the same time I heard tumbling in the house.

"Is nine o' clock. Open the blasted door!" Jean demanded and punctuated that with a violent kick on the wooden door. Surprisingly, the door stayed put. She must have hurt her "kicking" foot because she didn't stand on it after that. Somebody dropped out of the kitchen window at the back of that shack and the wooden kitchen sink followed her. I think the lady's intention was to lower herself gingerly but quietly out of the window and sneak away unseen by the rowdy Jean who could not have seen this from her position at the front door. Instead, with the kitchen sink not constructed to withstand the weight of a pressure cooker accompanied by half dozen of so pots, much less a thick, well figured, ample bosomed woman of twenty-five, the sink inevitably gave way and the woman was deposited into the slush where the dishwater gathered below.

If anything, Jean was not deficient in her hearing and she quickly abandoned her evil intentions where the front door was concerned and focused on what she rightly guessed was an attempt at a quick getaway. She ran down the short steps keeping most of her weight on her "non-kicking" leg and stooped to peer under the low house. She must have seen the lady trying to gather herself in the mud behind the building. She then ran around to the front past me then around to the back of the shacks where the woman was now getting up and gathering her senses.

"You blasted good-for-nothing whore!" screeched Jean as she rushed toward the woman. "As soon as you think I out of town you run up here to sleep with he!"

A little crowd of tenants and other neighbors down the street had gathered by then and were laughing at the guilty woman's misfortune. The lady stood up in the mud by the broken kitchen sink. She had a dress in her right hand but it was all muddied now. She was attired only in panties, a half slip and brassiere.

"Keep you' ass away from me if you know what good for you!" she threatened Jean who stopped short of the mud puddle in which the woman stood.

"Come out the mud, you sow, and ah go teach you a lesson this morning," Jean threatened.

Chapter Seven

"Richie! Come and talk to this crazy woman before I cut she tail!" the woman shouted over a shoulder.

"Cut me tail? You li'l slut you…" Jean quickly pulled the paper bag out of the waistband of her dress and charged the woman in the mud.

The woman began falling backward as Jean whipped out a knife from the paper bag and raised it in the air to stab downward at the woman. The woman caught the hand with the weapon and they both fell into the mud again, rolling and grunting as they kicked, scratched and fought. Some of the women in the crowd were shouting for the men to go stop the fight. Some of the men agreed it should be done but they were ogling the women with glee and nobody lifted a finger. Richie, the object of this "fight card," stood bare chested and in short pants behind the crowd, grinning proudly and not too concerned about the outcome of the fight.

"Richie, you stand up there with you li'l ugly self and Jean looking to stab up the girl?" one woman complained. " Go and stop them nuh."

"I ain't going in no mud to stop no fight," Richie drawled.

"But wait, is this li'l ugly ducklin' they fighting over?" said a woman who had stopped on her bicycle, probably on her way to work. She laughed loudly. "Some women ain't got no shame," she said and sucked-her-teeth loudly as she rode off.

All this time Richie just stood up there grinning proudly.

"Oh lawd, oh lawd, ah dead! She done stab me up!" bawled Jean as she scrambled her way out of the mud and away from the woman. She was clutching at her left side and there was blood on her fingers. The woman now had Jean's knife and she took her time walking out of the mud behind the retreating and terrified Jean.

"Ah tell you don't mess with me but you won't listen!" the woman panted.

Once Upon A Time In Berbice

"Help! Murder! Ah dying here man! Somebody help me!" bawled Jean. Some women ran to her aid.

Just then See came out the yard leading Nanny. The latter was a small gnarled figure dressed in a sari of pastel colors. She had a thick gold bangle around each ankle and several around her bony wrists. She was bare footed. She wore dark sunshades to hide her gray, flexed, blind right eye and the ogling near-blind left. See led her by the right hand and she had a white walking stick in the left.

"Is wha' happen over there?" See asked.

"Two girls fighting over that man there," Reena said behind me just as I was about to describe the whole affair to See. I didn't notice she was even out here and in one hand she still had the knife with which she was cleaning the fish.

"Dem ah fight over there again?" Nanny said, then made disapproving sounds with her mouth.

By now the women had taken Jean into custody and rushed her to one of the bathrooms to wash her off. The other contestant had discarded the knife and was heading toward another bathroom. I wanted to see more but See said we had to go.

"Nanny, this is Milo, Aunty Yvette' li'l boy. He go be carrying you to the shoemaker from now on," See said as she led her up the street toward Backdam with me in tow.

"Come hold the lady hand nuh boy."

Nanny slowly turned her head in my direction although I doubt she could see anything. See laughed when she saw my reluctance to hold Nanny's hand.

"When you bringing her back you go have to hold she hand just like I holding it now," See said and continued leading Granny out of the street.

We went up to the Backdam and turned right   I must admit for an old stooping woman Granny was making good pace as she shuffled gingerly between See and her walking stick while I strolled reluctantly behind. After just over five minutes of walking I began wondering how far away this shoemaker shop was when they turned onto a wooden bridge that led to a one flat wooden shack with a dilapidated verandah in front.

An old man who very much reminded me of that Gandhi character I had seen in photographs, was sitting in a rocking chair. His glasses looked to be made by the same people who made Arnold's but they were a little smaller. He wore a light colored *dhoti* and a big rumpled shirt.

The door to the inside of the house was open and I could see at least two people in there.

"Mornin' Uncle," See said. "Ah bring Nanny to see you."

See led Granny to a Berbice chair which was next to the rocking chair in which sat "Gandhi" and, after feeling about the front of the chair Nanny eased herself into it. She and the old man greeted each other in what was probably Hindi. See went into the shop and I followed her. There was a counter just inside the door behind which was a dark complexioned middle aged man with a moustache, goaty beard and short cropped hair plastered to his skull. He had on an apron and was doing something with an implement to a high-heeled shoe.

"Sooklal Morning," See greeted him. The man nodded as he looked at See and smiled. He had two small tacks held between his lips and I supposed that was why he couldn't answer. His eyes were smiling and he glanced quickly at the girl who had her back to us before flirting with See again.

"Don't say nothing before you swallow dem tacks," See said and laughed. "Chandra, you working here or what. Wha' you doing here so early."

"I just helping out. He ain't giving me a cent for this," the girl said as she turned to face us.

"Ah wonder wha' he giving you then for you to be here so early," See said and laughed. The girl looked at See in a mocked disapproving manner.

"Don't go putting ideas in this man head, eh?" she said. She was about the same age as See but was fair skinned, had large clear eyes with thick eye lashes, and a black mole high on her left cheek. Her hair was long and wispy and plaited in two at the back. She wore a greenish shirt and red skirt which stopped at her knees. She was now looking at me.

"This is me cousin. They just move over here from across the river," See explained after seeing where the girl had her attention. "I gone. Milo go take Nanny home when she ready."

With that See walked out of the shop, said something to the old people out in the verandah and was gone. I stood uncomfortably in the shop while Soooklal and Chandra attended to the business of repairing shoes. I looked around the shop and realized there were shoes everywhere. Behind the piles of shoes and other equipment was another room which I supposed was where Sooklal lived.

"Where you all used to live?" Chandra asked. Her voice was husky for a girl's but I didn't suppose she drank, although I wouldn't put it past her.

"At West Berbice," I said.

"Which part?" she asked.

I hadn't a clue what the name of our village over there was so I told her what I knew.

"Hopetown," I said without batting an eyelid.

"I been there already," she said. "How come I didn't see you there?"

My brain froze like it did with Mala that midday. I didn't even know she knew Hopetown. But before I could answer she broke out laughing.

"Ah just joking boy," she said. Sooklal was grinning.

"So how come ayo move?"

"Me father dead in a' accident," I said.

" Car knock he down?" she asked.

" No, was a' accident at Blairmont estate."

"Oh, your father dead in that?" she said and sounded genuinely sorry. Sooklal looked up from his work at me. I nodded. I didn't know that accident was so well known.

Chandra

I was getting tired of the questioning and figured it would have been better had I been in a police station instead of a shoemaker shop. She seemed ready to ask some more. If this questioning came around to me and my school work I was going to clear that counter and bash her with one of those high heeled shoes in the pile over there. I figured I'd be better off with the two old people outside. So I started easing myself out the door. I didn't know if they noticed my departure and chose to ignore me. But they both continued with what they were doing and the next thing I knew I was outside in the verandah. Nanny was telling the old man about the fracas in the neighboring yard that morning in English with a few Hindi words thrown in. She finished off with a caustic criticism about Doogoo renting out her place to "nigger yard black people." That was when I knew Doogoo owned the row of tenement houses across from her house.

This reminded me of the fracas down the street and I thought of running back to see how it all ended. The old people didn't notice me and I supposed I could run back and still come back for Nanny in time. I walked briskly at first then began running down the road back to Theater Alley.

Once Upon A Time In Berbice

When I got back to the tenement yard the crowd had long gone. There was no sign of Jean nor the gladiator woman. People were going about their daily chores and business in the yard and down the street.

" Aye boy, gimme a hand to carry these things up the road nuh," said a boy about my age who was struggling with two baskets and another bag. The second boy had his hands full too and there were two more bags on the wooden steps to the shack next to Richie's. I wasn't in a hurry to return for Nanny so I had nothing to lose. I grabbed the other two bags.

"How far ah got to carry it?" I asked.

"Is just up the road. Not far," said the taller of the two and grinned at the other boy.

"Where you living?" asked the taller one.

"Coco, wha' you asking the man he business for," said the shorter one.

"Spanner, Alyuh don't walk so fast. Wait for me," screeched a portly and very fair woman who carried two more bags.

"Yes Miss Olga," said the shorter boy.

"I living over there," I said and indicated Doogoo's yard with limited facial gesture.

"You is Doogoo them family? How come?" asked Coco.

" Is me aunty," I said.

The boys looked at each other knowingly but made no further comment. We walked up to the Backdam and turned away from the direction of the shoemaker shop. We walked for another couple hundred yards then turned right on a bridge over the wide backdam trench which was covered with some kind of lily plants. I could see a big L-shaped school just like my old school on the West Coast.

"Which school is that?" I asked.

"That is Vryman's boy," Coco said.

"That is your school?" I asked.

Chapter Seven

"Sometimes," Coco said and they both laughed.

They turned into the school yard and put the bags down by a vendor's stand. Miss Olga arrived just behind us and paused for a minute to catch her breath. Coco and Spanner began assembling the rest of the stall, taking out a stool and trays and helped Miss Olga to lay out her goods. In ten minutes the trays were well arranged with things like sugar cakes, black pudding, red cake, jam slice, pine tarts, cheese straw, mittai, manbug, barra, bullseye and hard white sweets, stretcher, and more confectionaries than I could remember. The air was rich with the smell of all these goodies.

As payment for our labor we were allowed to choose one item. I chose the red cake. Coco chose two cuts of black pudding and Spanner went for the jam slice. I guessed she usually set up every morning just before the children got their first recess.

I left with the two boys who said they were passing by the cinema to see what was on for the week. We walked up Charlotte Street to get to the Main Road then walked down to Gaiety. There were mostly the same posters that I had seen out there the previous day. Coco and Spanner had seen some of the movies on display and were talking about what had happened in them. Then they decided to walk over to the Globe cinema on Water Street. I tagged along, forgetting about Nanny at the shoemaker's.

Globe was the cinema I had seen at the junction of the stelling road and Water street when we had come on the truck. Standing in front of it now it seemed much bigger than before. It was definitely bigger than Gaiety. There were more posters here too and many more inside by the stairs that went up into the cinema. The shop to the left side had many people standing around with a group of old men listening to cricket commentary coming from a green speaker box like a young jukebox, parked by the entrance.

Once Upon A Time In Berbice

After staring around at the posters and being captivated by all the new sights, sounds, and smells around me, the boys said they were going down by the stelling. I told them I had to go somewhere to pick up someone. They said they'll see me later.

I walked past the bus park next to the cinema and stopped to stare at the brand new motor car and fancy things in the showcase of a big store called Bookers. I didn't know how long I was staring there but I eventually moved along farther down Water street. There were so many things to see and I stared at them all.

Eventually I came to a big market with a large car park across the street next to Lallman's Store. I was tempted to go in but it looked so large and busy I decided to leave it for another day. The street across from the market which I supposed would take me back to Main Road then Backdam was just as busy as the market. It was named "Pitt Street" but I couldn't make out the name. With so many stores and things to see it took me quite a while to get to Main street. By then I supposed I was behind schedule where Nanny was concerned so I continued across on Pitt Street to the Backdam. I turned right and began looking for Sooklall's shoemaker shop but couldn't find it. After a while I got to the street with the school yard and the huge empty tank. Boys in blue shirts and khaki pants were playing in the big open school yard.

I turned back, for I realized I hadn't passed here with See to bring Nanny, so I should've turned left out of Pitt Street instead of right. I retraced my steps back to Pitt Street and continued up the Backdam until I got to Sooklall's shop.

"Gandhi" was still in the verandah but there was no Nanny. His glasses seemed to glisten angrily as he swore something in Hindi then mumbled if is only now I came back.

"I couldn't find me way back," I said.

Chapter Seven

"The boy new here. Is how alyuh expect him to know he way around," Sooklal said from behind the counter.

"Nanny gone?" I asked. The old man swore in Hindi again.

"Chandra carry she home already boy," Sooklall said. I didn't know what else to say. I turned and walked down the wooden bridge with the old man swearing at me.

Now I was wondering what kind of trouble I was in, abandoning Nanny on my first morning out. Maybe they might think sending me with her was a bad idea in the first place and that would let me out of this unpleasant chore. On the other hand, there was no way escaping a cut tail from Mammy for mislaying Nanny so soon.

I headed home dejectedly, making up and discarding lies as I went along. I was still in deep creative thought when I turned down Theater Alley. Sunil was by the gate and my eyes grew wide with excitement. He was sitting on what looked like a new bicycle. But it wasn't an ordinary bicycle. It had a big metal tray in front with a big empty cartoon box sitting there. Under the cross bar was a metal panel painted black with the words "Bassit's Grocery" painted in yellow.

Sunil was sitting braced against the gate and had one foot cocked up on the bar. He had his head cocked to one side and was talking with Chandra. He was in full flirt mode. Whatever they were talking about Chandra seemed to be enjoying the conversation.

I ignored her and examined the bicycle in awe. When I rang the bell noisily it seemed to break Sunil's concentration and he slapped my hand off the bell.

"Boy take your nasty hands off me bicycle and have some manners. You ain't see big people talking here?" he said in a voice deeper than his usual. Then he continued talking with Chandra who then said she had to leave. He asked her where she was going and she indicated up the Main Road. He offered her a drop and she laughed, looked at him for a while then told him when she got out the street. They left with her walking and he riding slowly beside her, still chatting his head off.

I looked across to the tenement yard again but there were no children there. I slowly made my way into our yard but didn't go in the house. I didn't want to run into Mammy for that would surely mean a beating which I was determined to postpone as long as possible.

I walked past the front of the house in the little space between the house and the front fence. Then I tip toed along the side of the house by the open yard, past the door and scooted into the big shed. I closed the door behind me. It had no lock, just a latch. There was lumber piled up against the wall and an upper portion with lighter shorter pieces of board. There was a wooden ladder leading to the upper portion. The whole place was poorly lit with sunlight barely seeping through the spaces between the loosely boarded walls. The roof was covered with zinc. I climbed up to the upper portion and walked carefully on the shorter pieces of board. Immediately I thought of finding a suitable piece to make a cricket bat. But most of the pieces seemed to be more than six feet long. I figured I'll have to get one cut somehow before making the bat.

Just when I was thinking that this was an excellent hiding place when a flogging was due I heard footsteps outside. I froze. I wondered if anyone had seen me come in here. The person was humming a tune and was wearing rubber slippers. I could hear the slip-slopping all the way past the shed then I heard the bathroom door was opened then slammed shut. I breathed a sigh of relief. At least I was still safe. I figured it wasn't Reena since she had had her bath already and Mammy wasn't home. The Royal Ones were at Commercial School and Doogoo had been out all morning. Although Dil was probably at home I doubt he could hum a tune in such a feminine voice.

Chapter Seven

On came the tap and I could hear the water noisily pour into the metal bucket. I quietly got on all fours and slowly crept my way to the wall overlooking the bathroom. From there I peeped down and was surprised I could see right into the bathroom without being detected. It was See.

She had already taken off her dress and now she reached behind her and unsnapped the straps to her cream brassiere. They swung free and she hung it over the wall. I got my first view of a live pair of breasts other than Reena's. Then she slid out of her half slip and threw that over the wall. She continued humming as she reached down and slipped off her panties. I had no idea hair grew on those parts of the body. Within the next twenty minutes I saw a lot of things for the first time.

Chapter Eight

I stayed in my new found perch until I got hungry. By then I saw school children going home for lunch. I quietly climbed down and retraced my steps back to the front of the house. There were many children coming down the street and even more on the Backdam with uniforms of various colors. I slipped into the house. Dil was coming from the kitchen with a plate of food.

"Where' your brother," he said.

"I ain't know. He gone out on a goods bicycle," I said.

"He get work already," Dil commented with some surprise. "Must be Doogoo put he up to that. Alyuh come around by the cinema this afternoon let me show you around," he said while chewing. He sat down by the back door to the yard. I was too excited to say anything.

"Come eat your food," See called from the kitchen. I went into the kitchen and washed my hands, being careful not to make eye contact with See. Now that I had seen her naked I felt a bit bashful and awkward looking her in the face for fear of my expression giving me away.

I took the plate of fish stew with rice and went to the table. While eating I stole glances at See. She was now wearing a faded blue skirt and plaid shirt but all I could see were all those smooth bumps and curves I had seen earlier.

That afternoon Mammy came home and took me and Sondra up the Backdam, past Sooklall's and the Boys school and beyond. I had never come this far before.

"Where we going Mammy?" I asked.

"We going by your Aunty Nalini in the Scheme," she said.

We continued walking for half an hour. The streets and houses on our right gave way to a large cemetery. On the left was a swampy grassy area with blacksage bush then a footpath winding beside a housing scheme with mostly small, low one flat bouses. Mammy led us up this short cut and turned through the second street. We walked all the way across and turned into the yard of a two storied white house with an old swing in the front yard. She knocked on the door and after a while Aunty Nalini opened it. She was shorter and older than Mammy but you can see the resemblance. She erupted with joy at seeing us and hugged mammy. Then she picked up Sondra and we all went into the house.

It was fancy with a lot of rich looking things around the room. The wooden floor was shiny and polished. There was a big orange rug on which sat an expensive looking center table. To one side of the room was a very tall Grandfather clock with its swinging pendulum. In another corner stood what I later learned was a radiogram. There was a large radio by a Berbice chair. Over the windows were brownish colored curtains.

Aunty Nalini was fair like Lea and wore a long multicolored dress. Her hair was cut short at the neck and she wore large gold earings. When we all sat down in the large soft chairs in the drawing room Aunty Nalini told Mammy how sorry she was about Haroon dying and said she had just gone to Trinidad for a two week trip. She had wanted to return immediately to help out with things but her husband Keith told her it wasn't a good idea. Mammy said she understood and things worked out for the better. Then Mammy asked about the girls and Aunty Nalini said that they weren't home from work yet.

Aunty Nalini gave us sweet drink and cake to eat then had me and Sondra look at the fish in a tank in the dining room while she and Mammy went in the kitchen and talked privately. Sondra seemed to like it here and after an hour or so we left without Sondra. Mammy told Aunty Nalini that she would send Sunil with Sondra's clothes that evening. Sondra didn't seem to mind us leaving her there. I had no idea then that this was the beginning of Sondra living with Aunty Nalini.

Once Upon A Time In Berbice

We made our way back to the Backdam then cut across to the main road then to Water Street and eventually to the big market I had seen earlier. We bought fish and meat then walked all the way back home. By the time we returned, school was dismissed for the day. I changed into my house clothes on Mammy's insistence then came out of the room again. So far there was no mention of the Nanny incident that morning.

One of the Royal Ones came in from the bathroom and I realized I missed another opportunity in the wood shed. I went out by the gate to look over in the tenement yard where I had seen some boys playing cricket when I had come in with Mammy. The zinc wicket was still standing there in the middle of the yard but the boys were behind the shack searching in the bushes there. I supposed someone had struck the ball over there. I went over and joined the search.

There were about six boys there among whom were Spanner and Coco. The others gave me the once over and continued the search. Just when I was about to ask what was the color of the ball we were looking for I noticed a lanky boy with chopped up hair with a blue sponge ball in hand.

"Why alyuh can't play with that ball instead of looking for another one?" I asked him.

"It ain't the ball that lost, is the bat," Coco said without breaking his search.

"The bat?" I was puzzled.

"This clown think he is Kanhai and gone hooking; and he can't even hold he damn bat good," said another boy with a slingshot around his neck. He had indicated Spanner was the culprit. Spanner looked away sheepishly then continued the search. After another five minutes the bat was located, washed and the game continued.

Chapter Eight

During the course of the afternoon I got to know the rest of the boys. Spanner and Coco lived in the tenement yard and so did Moppa and Tillam. Squingee lived farther up the street and Chinee Roy often got away from his residence from the next street where his father ran Choose Bookstore. Dillip was short for his age and I was told that, because of his little moustache, he was the only one of the boys who could get into the cinema when shows were for "Adults Only."

During the rest of the week I also got to know some of the other neighbors. Coco and Spanner gave me detailed descriptions of their life stories.

One of the tenants was a middle aged man they called Kisskadee. He was tall, with lots of unkempt hair on his small head, had fair pock marked skin and a pretty broad mouth on such a narrow featured face. Coco told me the man was once a celebrity around town. He was what Coco called a professional whistler who was very much in demand at variety concerts at the town hall and cinemas and had often opened for visiting calypsonians like The Mighty Sparrow and Roaring Lion. Whistling was pretty popular then, with composers like Ennio Morricone using whistling in their western movie scores. From "For A Few Dollars More" onward you couldn't find a western without whistling and Italian westerns were the biggest crowd drawers.

"So why he stop whistling?" I asked.

"Somatie cuff he on he mouth and frill it up one Boxing Day when they had a fight," Coco said. "Since then he ain't whistling right again and he had to retire he lips."

I might have thought Coco was joking had I not seen this Somatie. She was a heafty woman who worked with the gutter cleaning crew of the town council. Years of pushing filth up the concrete drains with a long handled hard bristled broom had toned the muscles of those hefty arms and she must have packed a pretty good punch to knock the music out of Kisskadee's lips for good. The thing I couldn't understand was that he still lived with her.

One day I noticed a very pretty girl in her twenties come out of one of the shacks on the other side of the "U" from Richie. She was of Amerindian decent, average height, spotless olive skin and long thick dark shiny hair. She wore no make up. The first time I saw her I was standing by the gate and she caught me staring at her. She smiled with dimples sinking into her round cheeks and she winked at me. She wore a navy blue uniform of some kind and high heeled shoes. Her curly hair was brushed back at the sides and held in place by some plastic comb-like things, with a tatch of curly hair spilling over in front and onto her smooth forehead. She had even untrimmed eyebrows and long eyelashes.

According to Coco, her name was Alice but everyone called her Bucky. She was originally from up the Berbice River but had won a scholarship in her younger days to come to high school in town. She spent all her high school days in the same shack in which she now lived, and was successful at her exams. She now worked at Barkley's Bank on Waterstreet. Back then she had lived with an old retired teacher named Mrs. Parkinson. When this lady passed away two years after Bucky had passed her O'level exams, her bigger brother Lucky came down to live with her. He operated a dragline by the Canje bridge that lifted heavy metal and material to make cargo boats for Cipriani. I liked her. He was way too quiet for me to form an opinion about him.

One afternoon I was playing cricket down the street with the boys when Moppa slugged the ball high and mightily. The ball sailed over the street, hit a coconut tree and landed in a well fenced yard three houses away from mine. From the boys' reaction you would think it was the death of the ball. They were mad at Moppa until they saw me running in the direction of the yard to go retrieve the ball. They followed uncertainly. I pulled up short at the gate. There was no dog that I could see and none barked. I tried to open the gate but it was actually padlocked.

"Come go around this side," Tillam said quietly. He led me around to the side of the galvanized fence where there was a hole under the fence. I noticed he was making no move to go in.

"Why you ain't goin' in?" I asked.

" I too big to go in man. Hurry up," he said. That made sense since he was quite a bigger lad than I was.

"Who living here?" I asked.

"Aww, is just Mr. Christian," said Tillam.

"He's a church man?"

"You going for the ball or to go do Jehovah Witness work," he said irritably.

Bucky

I ducked through the hole and raised up on the other side of the fence amongst rows of neatly planted tomatoes and other vegetables. The other boys were standing on the street trying to spot the ball, or, come to think of it, Mr. Christian. I looked around for a dog but there was still no sign of any. After carefully moving around the garden I finally spotted the ball nestled between two potted plants. I carefully picked my way across and retrieved it.

"Look out!" The boys shouted from the street as I straightened up. I wasn't sure what to look out for but the urgency with which the warning came communicated to me some immediate action was required. Like the hare in the story that awoke to find the time and tortoise gone, I raced across the garden toward my hole in the fence. I heard the "woop-woop-woop" sound of a missile spinning through the air and closing fast on my person. In desperation I ducked and plunged headlong at the hole under the fence. There was a loud explosion as the sizable staff Mr. Christian had pelted at me collided violently with the zinc fence under which I had just dove and was now gathering myself on the other side. Tillam was nowhere in sight. I scrambled to my feet and galloped after the boys who were laughing and beating a speedy retreat back to the tenement yard.

When I got there I still had the ball in hand. I was steaming mad at them. Now I knew why they didn't even think of going in that yard for the ball. They knew what this Christian fellow was capable of and they let me go right in there. They were all collapsed on the ground laughing their heads off. Some of the grown ups were outside and found it funny too. I didn't think it was funny at all. Then I noticed the entire front of my shirt was covered with the dirt and grass skid marks from my escape and I had the taste of grass in my mouth. I began spitting. They laughed even more. I was thinking of picking out someone to charge and beat up but I did not know these boys well enough to know who was "beat-up-able."

"What happen boy, they set you up, nuh?" Bucky said from her door. Lucky was sitting on the steps below her eating a mango and grinning.

"Come let me wash off your face boy," she said. She had on a big tee shirt and a three quarter blue-dock pants with her thick orange-brown legs looking as smooth as ever. I went to the steps by Lucky and Bucky came out with a wet rag and began wiping my face. Forget about Mala. This girl was the prettiest thing I'd ever seen. She was even prettier close up.   She smelled of coconut oil and some other sweet scent.

"What's your name?" she said while daubing at my face.

"Milo," I murmured.

"That's your real name?" she asked.

"Yes."

"And you just move down the street?"

"Yes."

"Well Milo, careful with these boys and don't let them set you up; especially that Tillam. If he tell you walk, run."

My anger had dissipated once I was in proximity of Bucky. She finished off wiping my face and went back in the kitchen. I stood there staring at her. She came back to the door.

"You Alright now?" she asked with some concern.

"Yes Miss …." I didn't want to call her Bucky. It just didn't seem dignified enough for a lady this pretty.

"Is Alright, you can call me Bucky," she said and smiled with those dimples sinking in her smooth brown cheeks again.   I swore then that if this girl didn't get married before I got big I was going to do it myself.

I came down the steps and the boys started whistling and hooting because Miss Bucky had attended to me. The game was at a halt since I still had the ball in hand.

"Man, that was so funny," Dillip said and they started laughing again.

"Oh yea?" I said feeling the anger returning. Then an idea occurred to me.

"Lemme see how funny it is," I said and scooted out of the yard, across the street and into my yard with the ball in my possession. They were so surprised that they were now getting up to come after me. Lucky, Bucky and some other grown ups in the yard were laughing at this turn of events for the boys. I ran into the house and straight to my room. I took off the dirty shirt and looked at my face in the mirror. Miss Bucky had done a good job of cleaning my face but when I opened my mouth I still had a blade of grass stuck in my teeth. My lips were sore too.

"Milo, some boys at the gate calling for you," Reena called from upstairs.

I came out to the door with my bath towel around my neck and the ball in hand.

Tillam, Dillip, and Coco

"Aye Milo, we sorry man. We should'a tell you about Mr. Christian," said Coco.

"We sorry man, give we the ball nuh man," pleaded Dillip.

"Oh, now you sorry," I chided them.

"We ain't go do it again man," said Spanner.

"Alyuh promise?" I said.

"Promise," a few of them said.

"I ain't hear everybody say they sorry," I said. I was going to make them suffer.

"Milo give dem boys their ball and stop playing the ass," Reena shouted from the front window upstairs.

"We sorry, and we won't let it happen again," more of them voiced.

"I ain't hear Tillam saying nothing," I pointed out.

"Tillam, tell the man you sorry nuh man, let we get the ball," pleaded Dillip. Chinee Roy found it funny and was laughing through this whole exercise. Meanwhile, Tillam was not bowing to this blackmail. He sucked his teeth and folded his arms stubbornly.

"Man just give we the blasted ball!" Spanner shouted impatiently.

I looked at the ball then back at them.

"You know what, the ball lil dirty. I going and bathe and I go bathe it same time," I said and turned away from them while they swore at me.

When I came back from the bathroom they were gone from the gate.

That night Sunil filled my ears about the adventurous job Doogoo had got him. From what he said he had to get in to the shop by Nicolay Street by ten O'clock. People ordered goods in a little notebook and he had to get the goods each person listed then pack them in a cartoon box. He then put this box in the big cartoon in the tray of his bike and took the goods to the address stated under the name in the book. The goods were already paid for so all he had to do was double check each item when he got to the person's home to make sure everything was delivered. If the shop didn't have the item a check mark was placed beside the item and it was delivered when it came in. Earlier in the week he had Raj draw up a map of the streets of New Amsterdam by name.   Stanleytown was easy since the streets were numbered.

He was lying down with his foot up against the wall and a matchstick in his mouth.

"What about Chandra?" I asked. He smiled and switched the matchstick to the other side of his mouth.

"She like me," he said.

"Because a girl talk to you mean she like you?" I asked.

"Most of the time," he said.

"Then Miss Alice like me then," I thought aloud.

"Who's Miss Alice?" Sunil asked.

"She live across the street in the Yard. She's the prettiest girl I ever saw."

"I ain't know no Miss Alice. How much years she in?" he wanted to know.

"She too big for you," I snapped.

"Then she too big for you too," he pointed out.

"Well she like me anyway," I said.

"Tomorrow ah got to make a delivery in a place name Vryheid," Sunil said and consulted the hand drawn map of the town. "This is for a lady that came in with a pretty daughter today. Where the hell is Vryheid. I ain't seeing it on this map."

"Dil say we was to come around by the cinema to watch a show this week," I said.

"Oh yea," Sunil said, looking up from his map. " Maybe this weekend I might carry Chandra to see a picture," he bragged.

I had enough of this Chandra talk. Just when I was thinking about leaving and going up to Mammy's room Reena peeped in at us then came in and sat on my bed. She looked tired.

"Wha' happen to you now," Sunil said.

"What you think," she said. " You working, so you all right."

Chapter Eight

"Yep. And ah getting pay this Saturday too," said Sunil. I made a mental note to be nice to him until Sunday.

"When alyuh starting out to school?" he asked arrogantly.

"You' backside shoulda been in school too," Reena said.

"Naw, I done with school. I is a working man now," Sunil said snootily.

"I hope we starting next week. I bored already," Reena said.

"Bored? In a' exciting town like this? If you still been over the river you woulda been slaving in the kitchen whole day," Sunil pointed out.

"And wha' you think I been doing whole day here," Reena retorted. " Besides..." she paused and peeped out the door before continuing. "... Besides is more mouths to feed here so is more work."

I began to sympathize with her. Poor Reena. Moving here definitely wasn't a bed of roses for her. Now that she was here it seemed Doogoo wanted her in the kitchen with See; possibly to replace See when she found a suitable husband for her. After that, all she had to look forward to was an arranged marriage to someone she did not know.

"Wha' happen with you and Nanny today?" she asked me. I opened my mouth but couldn't think of anything to say. "You lucky See making excuse for you or you woulda done get your tail cut long time."

" What he do to Nanny?" Sunil asked.

"He supposed to bring she back from somewhere and he went and stray and never went back for the lady," Reena explained.

" I went back yes," I argued.

"Yea, but is when you went back, after Chandra done bring she home," Reena said. " Ah had a good mind to tell Mammy." I had no comment to that.

"Wha' See say?" I asked.

"See say she forget to tell you to go back for her," Reena explained.

"See said that?" I said. "Then she **did** forget to tell me."

"You know she damn well tell you bring Nanny home," Reena said. My sympathy for her had evaporated. "And what you had them boys down the street begging for?" she wanted to know.

"That is my business," I said and rolled over in bed to sleep.

"So Sondra go stay with Aunty Nalini?" Sunil asked.

"It look so. Nobody go have the time to look her here. Besides with she here peeing the bed it go be too much. Aunty Nalini say she got an extra room over at she and she seem to like over there anway," Reena explained.

She left shortly after and Sunil rambled on about his day and his plans for Chandra.

On Friday morning I deliberately woke up late so I would not encounter the boys down the street. I was about to go take my bath when I heard shouting on the street.

"Inside! Letter!" shouted a sonorous male voice. I peeped out the front door and saw a tall, thin, gangly fellow with glasses sitting on a noisy Velosolex motor cycle. He had on some kind of uniform and a bag with letters hung with a broad strap over one shoulder.

"Somebody go collect letters from the postman," See called from the kitchen.

I took a chance and walked out to the gate with no shoes nor shirt on, for if Doogoo saw me go out there like that she would throw a tantrum.

The post boy was in his early twenties and looked pretty strange with his long legs and nervous hands. He was a fellow with quite a pronounced nose, large eyes under his small glasses, and a baseball cap pulled down over a mop of long wild hair.

"Who is you?" he asked when I got out there.

"Who is **you**?" I countered.

"I is the postman," he said and indicated his uniform as proof.

"And I is the new letter collector for this house," I announced.

"I don't know you so I can't give you no letter," he said.

"I don't know you either but I go take the letter anyway."

"What you name," he said.

"What is **your** name," I shot back at him.

"I is Bertie Bhagwandin," he announced then caught himself. "What I tellin' you all this for."

"You giving me the letters or not. Me water in me bathtub getting cold," I said impatiently.

"Well you better go bathe quick..." he caught himself again. "Your bathrub!" He threw his head back and laughed. "You is a funny li'l so-and-so. Go and call somebody that live here."

"What I doing with bath towel and no shirt on and in this yard if I ain't living here," I said.

"You sure?"

" I live here boy. Just give me the letters," I said. I liked this fellow. He seemed pretty gullible. I was already thinking how I could get him to put me on that motorbike.

Suddenly, his mouth dropped open in awe and his glasses slipped a notch down his large nose. I was just wondering what I had said to occasion this reaction when I heard footsteps coming up behind me and realized that was where his attention lay.

"Good morning," Reena said as she came up to the postman. "Milo, go inside before Aunty Doogoo see you out here like this."

I ignored her. Bertie's Adam's Apple bobbed as he swallowed and cleared his throat.

" 'Morning Miss," he managed then cleared his throat again. "Ahh...." he began but words failed him. He stretched forth half dozen letters to her and she took them. She seemed oblivious to his reaction to her.

"Thanks," Reena said and turned away as she sifted through the letters and looked at the names. She was attired in one of her old school skirts and a cream blouse and her hair was just brushed back with her fingers. I could not figure what a boy saw in Reena, except her backside. But this fellow was flabbergasted just seeing her from the front.

"You satisfied?" I said.

"Eh?" Bertie emerged from his trance. He looked blankly at me then back to the front door through which Reena had disappeared.

"Um, she live here?" he asked and his mind still seemed to be somewhere else.

"You ain't know if she living here but you give she all them letters, and you couln't give me," I said sulkily.

"She live here for truth?" he asked excitedly.

"Yea, and I live here too. That is me sister, so don't go getting ideas," I said.

Bertie grinned, put his bike in gear then rode slowly down the street to the next house after glancing toward the front door again. I turned to the bathroom thinking how I could exploit this new situation with this boy with a motorcycle, liking Reena.

That day turned out to be a busy one. Mammy began taking in washing and her first batch came that day. I had to run to the shop out on the main road several times for her to buy Zex washing soap, bleach and Blue. On my second trip I ran into Coco. Seemed like this lad was allergic to school. I decided it was better to surrender the cricket ball early to Coco and dissipate the wrath of the boys by afternoon. On my next trip out I gave Coco the ball.

Between going to the shop I had to help Mammy and Reena hang out clothes in the backyard. At one point we had to pick them all up because of a short shower, then hang them all out again. I began thinking I was better off going to school and wondered when Mammy was going to take me to a new school.

That afternoon I cautiously joined the boys and was surprised they had all but forgotten my little stunt of blackmailing them into apologizing. They still laughed about my escape from Mr. Christian.

We played cricket for the rest of the afternoon even though Reena called me several times. I ignored her. Some of the grown ups in the yard joined the game. Of them Lucky was the most annoying to face at the wicket. He had this uncanny ability of turning the ball either way with the same bowling action. I wasn't that great a batsman like Charlie Valentine from my old school was. But I usually lasted through four or five overs at a wicket. With the ball in Lucky's hands I didn't get through one over that afternoon.

When it got too dark for cricket Coco and some of the boys said they were going out by the cinema to see what new posters were up. I went out there with them instead of going straight home. New posters were up on most of the boards.

When we got out there the usual crowd was milling around the bevy of vendors parked before the cinema and along the entrance. We could hear a car chase of some kind being played inside the cinema. We walked into the yard and to the poster boards.

"Oh core! 'The Good, The Bad, and The Ugly' showing this weekend," Spanner announced excitedly and pointed to a colorful poster with three dangerous looking gunmen and a cannon over the title of the movie.

"I see that already," Coco said, " But ah want see it again."

"It showing with 'Ace High.' That is with Eli Wallach too," Spanner said. "I coming Sunday to see this boy."

"Is only Sunday it showing?" I asked.

"It opening tomorrow night. It go show 'till Tuesday," Spanner explained.

I wondered if Dil could carry me to see it. I was also interested in drawing the poster.

"What they does do with the poster after the movie done show?" I asked.

"I dunno. They does tear it off I think," Coco said. I made a mental note to ask Dil to get me this poster.

After a while we headed back up the street with Coco and Spanner arguing whether Clint Eastwood or Lee Van Cleef was faster on the draw. When I got to our house Raj was at the gate talking to a brown skinned girl in braids. They were standing close up like they were boyfriend and girlfriend. Reena was taking a plastic jug with water

Raj

upstairs when I went in and she told me Mammy calling me. I went upstairs to their room where I met mammy pressing the clothes she had washed that day.

"Where you been whole afternoon. Ent Reena tell you I calling you since afternoon?" she said angrily.

"No Mammy," I lied. Reena was about to open her mouth and object.

"I hear when she call you so don't lie," Mammy said. Reena smiled with satisfaction. " Gimme that belt Reena."

Dammit! I had escaped a licking after the Nanny fiasco and now I was catching it for this? I couldn't believe I was getting my first flogging at my new home for such a minor infraction.

Chapter Eight

After the flogging I stifled my cries and went downstairs quietly. Indira and Lea giggled as they passed me on the steps on their way up. I did not like these two. If they got on my second-to-last nerve again I would have to think up a scheme for them.

Later that night me, Sunil and Reena were talking in our room when a loud argument broke out between Doogoo and Raj. It had something to do with the girl I had seen standing at the gate with Raj. As Reena later explained it, Doogoo was mad at Raj for not following tradition and settling for a marriage she had proposed to arrange with what she called a suitable girl from up the East Bank. Doogoo did not like the idea of Raj going around with Rachael, a black girl. Although Doogoo didn't actually say it what she said implied it. Raj was arguing bitterly that he was Guyanese, not Coolie and nobody was going to tell him who he could or could not have for a girlfriend or wife. Doogoo then turned to her husband Inchan for support but all Inchan told Raj was that he should listen to his mother. Eventually Raj went out again and in reply to Doogoo accusing him of running off behind Rachael again he said he was going down by Rachael to spend the night. We didn't know if he was joking. Doogoo eventually went in to Mammy to gain a sympathetic ear.

Chapter Nine

Saturday arrived and to my surprise I saw Moppa and his mother, dressed in church clothes, apparently going to church. I thought they got the days of the week mixed up but then See told me that some people went to church on Saturday instead of Sunday since they were strictly following what the bible said. After I had my bath my first chore was to go with See to carry the clothes Mammy had washed, pressed, and packed neatly in two cartoon boxes, to the owners who lived in Cooper's Lane. I was to go with See for her to show me where the people lived.

I put the bigger of the two cartoon boxes on my head while See already had hers in hand. We headed up the Backdam toward the Shoemaker's.

"Why you lie for me yesterday?" I asked.

"I lied for you? About what?" See asked pleasantly.

"About me going and leave Nanny."

"You mean I didn't forget to tell you to take her back home?" she said in mocked surprise and looked at me with amused eyes. I made no comment.

"Besides, Aunty Yvette woulda cut your tail if she find out. So you owe me one."

I supposed I did. We mercifully turned down the same street with the shoemaker shop and stopped at the gate to the house right after the shop. See called at the gate and a big bosomed negro lady came to the gate. It was a white house with a big yard. There was a dog asleep outside of a little dog house under a mango tree. He seemed uninterested in any security work at this time of day.

See greeted the lady and explained that I would be bringing the washing from now on. The lady opened the cartoon boxes and briefly examined the clothes. She grunted with satisfaction as she briefly went through each box.

Chapter Nine

Movement upstairs caught my eyes. There was a brown skinned girl about my age peeping over the verandah. She had her hair in fine plaits hanging down the sides of her head and spilling over her forehead. She stared at me without saying anything and I stared right back at her.

Eventually the woman reached into her bosom and fished out a little blue purse. She took out a small roll of bills, counted out some and gave it to See. Then she gave me ten cents. We thanked her and we left for the Backdam again.

As we headed up the Backdam toward Theater Alley See said she had to make a stop. We turned right on a road that took us just on the other side of the lily covered Backdam trench and to a large two storied concrete building which See said was the DC building.

There were a lot of people in offices waiting with uniformed men and women behind desks and typewriters. We climbed the stairs and See looked in the second office where there weren't many people on our side of the counter but about half dozen people at desks behind the counter. She greeted a man sitting at the nearest desk and asked for someone named Alicia. The man turned and asked the others where Alicia had gone and someone else said she went to the duplicating room. See thanked him and we went back downstairs and down to the end of the corridor.

She knocked and went in the room. I followed her. The room was noisy with two inky machines rolling and a lot of paper about. There were about four men in there, a big lady with glasses and a brown skinned girl in her early twenties. The girl's face lit up when she saw See and she came to the door. They stepped outside.

"This is your cousin Milo," See told the girl and motioned to me. "This is Aunt Yvette li'l boy."

"Milo!" the girl said and seemed excited. "I am your cousin Alicia, but you won't hear your Aunty Doogoo say that."

132

"Alicia!" See chided her. "How you go tell the boy that."

"See, you know if your mother know you does come here to see me she would cut your tail," she said and laughed.

"Girl, I stop getting that since I was twelve," See said.

"Well you ain't too far from twelve."

" I is a big woman, girl."

"Oh? And wha' make you a big woman Missy," Alicia said and put a hand to her hip waiting for an explanation. She had some papers in the other hand.

I looked at her afro hair and wondered how she was related to me. She wore the same uniform like the others and was taller than See.

"You' sister staying by us. She's a sweetheart," Alicia said and beamed at me.

One of the male workers stuck his head out the door and gave Alicia some more papers. He wore the same color uniform and sported a low afro and budding moustache, with a stubble of hair under his chin. He looked See over and smiled.

"What you looking at," See said boldly.

" I like looking at nice things," the boy said with a smile.

"This nice thing could cost you boy," Alicia said.

"I don't mind. She worth it," the boy said and grinned.

"How much I worth to you?" See said gamely.

"Hummm," the boy said and put a thoughtful hand to his chin and tugged at strands of hair there.

"Christopher!" the big lady with the glasses called from within the room. The boy pulled his head back in the room to attend to his work.

I looked at See and wondered what made her so attractive to this boy. She wasn't a bad looking girl, with her dark smooth skin and small mouth, large expressive eyes and long thick jet black hair. But she was no "eye brow raiser" either. She was only attired in a green, yellow and white plaid dress. It had a waist band but she wore no belt. I knew what I saw in the bathroom but from looking at her one couldn't tell her breast were that full nor that she was much thicker than she appeared. Her dress went down below her knees and her dark legs were clean and oiled. On her feet were a pair of orange rubber slippers.

"You interested?" Alicia said with a mischievous smile.

"Interested in what?" See said and did a poor job of pretending ignorance.

"You like him," Alicia announced softly and laughed.

" Now how you arrive at that?" See said.

"Then why you blushing all over," Alicia said.

"I ain't blushing," See said and turned her face away as she laughed. "I hardly know anything about he anyway, so what's there to like."

See and her cousin Alicia

"You can ask," Alicia said.

"The boy probably got a girlfriend or wife already."

"You asking or telling," Alicia said. See bit her top lip and looked away.

"Anyway, I got to go," See said and turned to go. She glanced quickly in the duplicating room again and Christopher waved discreetly at her. See blushed but didn't wave back.

"We'll talk," Alicia whispered.

We left Alicia in the DC office building and headed up the Backdam toward home.

"What happen just now is just between me, you and Alicia, right?" See said.

"Wha' happen just now?" I asked.

"Don't mention a word about me meeting Alicia to anybody."

"Alright." I said. Then as an after thought, "How come Alicia is we cousin?"

"Her mother and all of we mothers are sisters," she explained.

"Then how come she's black?"

"Her father is black Silly."

"Oh, so she dougla then," I pointed out.

"Yes Milo, she's dougla."

"But she ain't look dougla."

"Some dougla people look more black and some look more coolie, but most look mixed. Wait when you see she sister Juanita."

"Aunty Doogoo don't like black people?" I asked.

See turned to look at me. She seemed mildly surprised. Then she sighed.

"Your Aunty Doogoo hardly like anybody," See said.

"She like Mammy," I pointed out.

"Yes, she like Aunty Yvette," she said then looking away, she muttered, "… for now."

I pretended I didn't hear that last comment, for I had no idea what she meant.

"You like that boy that was talking to you?" I asked.

Chapter Nine

"Little boy, I just see the boy and talk to him, that mean I like he?" she said with some degree of annoyance. She sucked her teeth in disgust.

I was silent the rest of the way home. When we got there See went straight to the kitchen. I was about to go in the yard when I heard the unmistakable sound of the engine of a Velosolex motorcycle. My favorite postman had turned down the street. I stood by the gate with my arms folded across my chest like a sentry.

"Postman here!" he shouted as he pulled up just before me.

"So what, I turn invisible now?" I complained.

"You still visiting here boy?" he said with a goofy grin.

"Ah tell you ah living here boy," I said.

Reena came out and was about to turn back inside after seeing I was already out here.

"Miss, letters here," said Bertie. Reena came out to him.

"This boy live here?" he asked her.

"I done tell he ah living here," I pointed out.

"Yes, he live here but we thinking of putting he out," Reena said with a straight face. Bertie laughed heartily.

"I name Bertie Bhagwandin," he said and extended a hand.

"I'm Reena," she said and shook his hand. "And this is my li'l brother Milo," she said reluctantly.

"So you does really live here," the hypocrite said to me.

"Ah tell you that long time," I said.

"Nice to meet you Reena," he said and beamed affably at her.

"Nice to meet you too," Reena said with a smile.

He was about to push off.

"Any letters?" she asked with a playful smile.

"Ohh! Sorry," he said bashfully and gave her a couple of letters. "I don't know what happen to my mind."

"You lost it yesterday when you saw her the first time," I wanted to say but didn't.

"You like her?" I asked him bluntly.

"Milo!" Reena exclaimed in genuine surprise.

"Yes, I like her," he said without thinking. Reena blushed and turned to go back inside.

"Thanks Mr. Bhagwandin," she said over a shoulder.

"Call me Bertie," he said. " Hope I see you next week." She waved and went into the house.

Bertie looked all satisfied with his progress that morning and was smiling like the proverbial Chesire cat.

"If you interested in she you better be nice to me," I announced.

"I *am* nice to you," he said and seemed surprised I was implying he wasn't.

"Oh yea? Treating me like I living on the road?"

"Well you always by the gate here. I thought you was one of the boys from over there," he said innocently and indicated the Yard.

"Sure you did. Buy me a sweet drink if you really mean to be nice to me," I said.

" I working now but I can give you the money for it," he said, and to my surprise, reached into his shirt pocket. He gave me eleven cents which was the price for an I-cee soft drink.

I thanked him and was about to scoot out to the shop by the cinema when Mammy called me from the back of the house. She had taken in more washing from other people and needed help hanging out the clothes. I pocketed the eleven cents and chided myself for not going for a fifteen cent fudgicle instead of a mere eleven cent soft drink.

When Sunil came home from work that afternoon he was disappointed and had a few nasty words to say about his employer Mr. Bassit. He was looking forward to getting paid that afternoon only to be told it was the

Chapter Nine

following Saturday. It was only when Chandra stopped by the house later and he was making excuses about not being able to get her something he had promised her that I understood the real reason for his disappointment.

But Sunil's depression was short lived. For Raj told us to get ready for he was taking us to the cinema that afternoon. I was all excited. Reena wasn't going with us since she had to help Mammy with the ironing and Doogoo promised that she will go the following day with See, Indira and Lea.

By four O'clock we were ready. I looked my best while Raj was dressed casually. We started walking out our street with two of Raj's football friends but they stopped off at Gaiety cinema while Raj continued with us to Water Street. He said we were going to the Globe cinema.

When we got there the entrance was very crowded. Raj stopped here and there to talk to people he knew in the crowd, while he looked around as if expecting someone. Eventually Raj's face lit up when he spotted a brown skinned girl in braids coming up to the entrance. I recognized her as the same girl he was talking with at the gate.

"This is me cousins Sunil and Milo," Raj said and beamed at us.

"Hi, I am Rachael," she said and smiled. She had some of the biggest and whitest teeth I'd ever seen in a mouth. She wore a white pants suit with embroidery on the front. Sunil smiled and reached out his hand and she shook it. I did the same and she shook my hand too. Her hands were soft and her nails long but clean.

"She's my girlfriend," Raj said proudly.

Rachael smiled. "Alyuh going in the show too?" she asked.

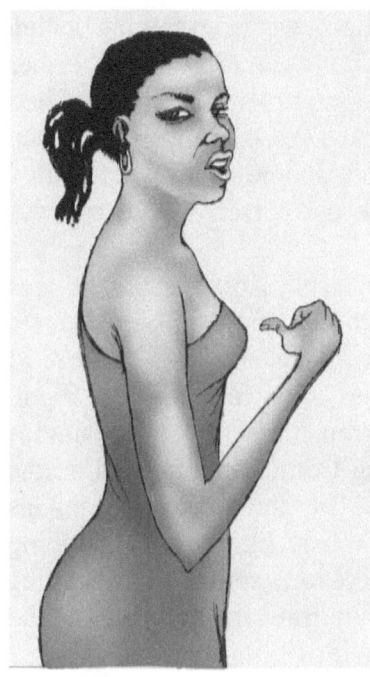

Rachael

"Yes," Sunil said excitedly.

"First time?" Rachael asked with a smile.

Both Sunil and I replied at the same time; me in the positive and he in the negative. Raj told her to wait by the ticket booth for him and that he was going to get our tickets for Pit. I'm not sure what he meant but he left her in the crowd there and led us onto the stelling road beside the cinema. There was a line gathered by a narrow passage way past a walled off area at this end of the building. In this passage was the ticket booth for the Pit section, but one wouldn't know it immediately since it was merely a hole in the wall. When we got up to the hole Raj pushed in some money and a hand gave him two tickets and some change. He gave the tickets to Sunil then told him something and left us. He went back toward the front of the cinema where he had left Rachael.

Sunil led me farther into the short, dark tunnel and we came to a narrow doorway. The people before Sunil were surrendering their tickets to a man standing there with a big stick. Sunil surrendered his ticket and we entered the cinema. There was talking and music coming from behind the huge screen which was ablazed with a car chase, then people shooting, and women screaming. As I stopped to stare someone jostled me from behind.

"Walk up nuh boy," the person grumbled. I could barely make out Sunil's orange shirt before me in the darkness. The only source of light was from the big screen for all the windows were already closed. Sunil went farther along the wall and passed rows and rows of already filled seats. Then we spotted a space on one of the wooden benches and we felt our way past people then sat. I shifted my position to see better since the person before me was partly blocking me.

After a while the changing scenes on the screen was covered with writing then the music stopped. Sunil leaned to me and explained that they were showing trailers. I nodded having no idea what he was talking about. Suddenly there were cowboys on the screen and cannons firing and red writing morphing from blood sprayed on the screen. Mixed with the noise of the guns and cannons firing was the loud pounding music like horses galloping and an instrument whining like the sound of a wailing coyote. There was an exciting murmur from the crowd and I supposed it was a popular movie.

" Is that showing?" I leaned over and asked Sunil.

"Naw, that is still trailer. I think that opening over at Gaiety this weekend," he said.

Only then did I recognize the three men I had seen on the poster boards in front of Gaiety.

"That is the Good, The Bad, and The Ugly, right?" I said excitedly.

"Yea," he said and glanced at me with some surprise.

"What showing today?" I asked.

"The Party and The Man Who Came to Kill," he said.

"The Party?" I asked and Sunil told me to hush.

I looked back at the rest of the cinema. There were more benches and people behind me. Then there was another section above the head level of the people in my section. I supposed that must be the House section where you enter from the front of the cinema. Farther behind, and higher up above house section was the Balcony section. Above this section a piercing beam of light made visible by the cigarette smoke drifting up to the roof from the three sections, played correspondingly to the action on the screen. The light came from one of several small square holes high on the wall behind Balcony. It spread outward to the width of the screen.

The Party turned out to be very funny although I couldn't follow the whole story. Then the second movie, a cowboy, came on. It had lots of action and a fat man named Sancho who was always shooting people, even his own men. At the beginning of this movie someone opened the windows along the side wall. I was surprised to see it was already dark outside.

Just before eight o' clock the starboy killed Sancho, the music started, he rode away and writing started coming up on the screen. The lights flickered on in the cinema and people started to get up from their seats. The wide side doors to the cinema were thrown open and the crowd started filing out. Music started to play and the screen went blank.

I followed Sunil but the crowd was so thick I soon lost sight of him. All of the people who were in this section of the cinema were men and boys.

I followed the crowd on to the stelling street then to the front of the cinema. Neither Raj nor Sunil were in sight. I ran into Squingee who was also in the show. We made our way through the crowd which was much larger. The crowd of people who were emerging from the cinema were interspersed with the crowd of mostly Indian patrons who were coming in to see the eight-thirty show which was an Indian movie.

Me and Squingee walked toward home retelling the movie we both had just seen. When we got to Gaiety at the head of our street we were surprised to see the magnitude of the crowd there. You could barely see the entrance of the cinema and the Pit ticket booth was the scene of a rowdy pushing, screaming and jostling crowd of men, some without shirts as they scrambled to secure tickets before show time. We even had to maneuver our way past a crowd blocking the entrance to our street.

When I got home Sunil wasn't home yet. To my surprise, Dil was. He was sitting calmly by the back door eating food from an enamel plate.

" You not working tonite Uncle Dil?" I asked. He nodded.

"But is a whole crowd fighting to get in the cinema," I pointed out.

"I is the projectionist, not a referee," he said and seemed amused.

"But the show can't start without you," I said.

"Is not time yet," he said and consulted his wrist watch.

"Raj carry we over at the Globe," I said proudly.

"They show trailer for 'The Good, Bad and the Ugly?" he asked. I nodded.

Then as an afterthought he said, "You want see it tonite?" I nodded so vigorously I nearly got whiplash.

I thought of going upstairs and asking Mammy but figured she might not want me to go since I had just come from a show already.

When Dil finished eating he washed his hands, brushed his teeth then told me to come along. I didn't even bother with dinner.

We went back up the street to the cinema. The crowd was even bigger and noisier now. Dil held me by the hand and pushed his way through the crowd and up the front steps. The doorman there barely glanced at him and let us through. We climbed the stairs and went higher and higher until we got to the Balcony section of the cinema then he climbed a shorter step to a smaller room with the square holes in the walls facing the big white screen. He knocked in a pattern and the person inside opened the door.

"Ah bring me nephew with me tonite," Dil said. The other man grunted. He was much older than Dil and had on pants and a vest. He was working a handle and spinning a reel of film from one reel to another.

The room was very warm. There were two small windows facing the street where the man was rewinding the reels. On the floor were large six sided canisters, each with the name of a movie written in red or black on white paper that was stuck to them. Three of the seven canisters were open. In each lay four or five reels of film stacked on each other. Taking up most of the space in the room were two huge machines. The main part of each machine consisted of electronic parts and big lenses pointing through two of the several square holes in the wall separating this room from the Balcony section before it. The top of each machine had a sort of stout pipe which continued through the roof above. There were two reels on each of the machines, one had no film and the other was a full reel of film. The full reel on the second machine was much larger than that on the first. There was some sort of record player off to the side with a record being played at the moment. There were stacks of other records around the player.

Dil took off his shirt and had on a vest just like the man. There were three wooden chairs in the room. The man finished rewinding the reel and placed it in one of the open canisters. He put on his shirt then asked me if I wanted to look through one of the square holes. I nodded. He placed one of the chairs by the hole and I jumped up and looked through. Then he told Dil he was going.

I could see the inside of most of the cinema from here. I could see all three seating sections and the big white screen beyond. The lights were still on and I could see the two lower sections, House and Pitt, were already full. The section nearest to us was only half full. I could hear the music loud and clear from way up here.

Dil lit up a cigarette and casually looked through the window and down at the noisy crowd outside. I continued looking through the hole and at the growing noisy crowd in the cinema.

Shortly after Dil looked at his watch and flicked his cigarette stub out the window although there was a crowd down there. He flicked a couple of switches on the wall by the record player and the lights in the cinema went out. Then he moved around to the first machine and did something. The first machine suddenly whirred to life with a very bright light being produced in one part and a strong white beam of light piercing its way through the cigarette smoke. On the screen beyond, a lion sitting in some kind of large emblem, roared twice then a trailer came on. Dil took off the needle from the record and stopped the player. Then he looked through the hole to the screen. He made some minor adjustments to the lens then he continued looking through the hole to the screen.

I watched the movie beam out of the noisy machine and materialize on the screen beyond. One trailer after another was shown. After about seven trailers the reel that had the film was almost done. Dil then went to a position between the two machines and looked through another hole in the wall. Suddenly the second projector came to life and the first one was switched off. On the screen beyond another emblem came on, faded out, then white writing across the screen then that faded to black. Suddenly we were jolted as the sound of the coyote crying music split the air and I could sense the excitement from the crowd below. The music played on with blood splattered writing whipping across the screen and an animated canon blasting the names off the screen. Eventually the music came to an end and the rugged, weather beaten face of a gunman suddenly filled the whole screen. Behind him was the whining of a coyote in the distance.

Dil had removed the full reel from the first projector and replaced it with another of six large reels stacked between the two machines. He passed the end of the film through some parts of the machine and back onto the empty reel. Then he took the reel he had removed and put it on the rewind machine by the window and began rewinding it. After completing this chore he sat by the window and lit up another cigarette. With the machine running the room had become much hotter. I continued watching the movie.

After a while Dil got up and looked through the hole again. On the screen Clint Eastwood and Eli Wallah seemed to be having a disagreement about money. Some scratches and holes flickered on the screen. Suddenly the first machine whirred to life and the second was switched off. I didn't notice any difference on the screen except the scratches and holes stopped showing up. I decided there and then this is what I wanted to do when I grew up.

In the middle of the second reel Dil asked if I didn't want to go sit in Balcony instead of standing on the box. I agreed and he directed me out of the hot projector room and into the cool balcony section with its comfortable chairs.

I fell asleep sometime during the second movie. When I awoke the lights were on and the cinema was empty. Dil had on his shirt and had woke me up. He said it was time to go and he led me down the stairs. When we got outside the streets were empty and a few of the workers at the cinema were locking up. The vendors were long gone. We made our way down the semi lit street and to our home. There was no one around. Just a few stray dogs were sniffing about the street. Even the Yard was quiet and empty.

When we got home I was hungry but there was no one in the kitchen. I went to my room. Sunil was fast asleep. I turned on the light to change my clothes. The glare awoke Sunil.

"Where you been whole night," he said drowsily.

"I just come from cinema," I said as I changed my clothes.

"What? Cinema over so long and is now you coming in?" he said in disbelief. "Mammy go kill you."

"I was with Uncle Dil at Gaiety," I said.

"You was with Dil?" he said with envy. "You saw 'Good, Bad and the Ugly?' "

"Ah huh."

"And you went up to the projector room with Uncle Dil?"

"Uh huh."

" How come he carry you?"

"I don't know. When I came home from Globe he ask me if I want go and I said yes."

"Ah shucks. And I did want to go there tonite man." He drew his teeth and turned over to sleep. "Turn off the light. I want sleep."

I turned off the light and settled down to sleep with the sound of the music of the coyote cry and galloping horses still drumming in my head.

Chapter Ten

Sunday morning after I woke and had breakfast I went up to Mammy's room. There was another set of clothing to be delivered to some people living at Highbridge. Mammy and Reena were in their room folding clothes and giggling about something.

"Is wha' happen?" I asked as I entered the room and sat on their bed beside stacks of pressed clothing.

"Close the door," Mammy said quietly and seemed very amused.

After I closed the door I came back and sat on the bed awaiting the hilarious news.

"And you not to go running your mouth off," Reena warned.

"Your Uncle Inchan came in drunk last night," Mammy said quietly and I could see she was making a herculean effort not to laugh. I was flabbergasted.

"Uncle Inchan? Aunty Doogoo' husband?" I said incredulously.

"Is how much Uncle Inchan you have," Reena said impatiently.

"He was singing and dancing and carrying on all the way home through the street," Mammy said and she and Reena could hardly contain themselves. I couldn't believe it. Quiet, soft spoken Uncle Inchan singing? And dancing! If it wasn't Mammy saying it I would not have believed it.

"Then when he reach in front of the Yard the tenants were making requests on what he' to sing and dance," Mammy continued and she and Reena began laughing hysterically again.

"Shhhhh," Mammy said when the laughter was getting out of control. "When he got to the third song he start stripping off he clothes..." They collapsed on the bed in stifled laughter. It must have been funny to see but I just

147

couldn't get over the fact that it was Uncle Inchan they were talking about.

"And what happen then?" I asked anxiously.

"That is when Aunty Doogoo rake him in and hustle he to the bathroom and throw cold water on he," Reena hurriedly concluded the story and they continued laughing hysterically.

"Why she didn't stop he earlier?" I asked.

"Doogoo was sleeping," Mammy said and got up after composing herself again. At times like these I saw the girlish side of Mammy and could have imagined what she was like growing up.

"And try not to repeat anything we talk about, hear?" she said quietly to me.

"Well I just past Uncle Inchan at the table downstairs," I said.

"How he look?" Reena asked.

"He look normal. He was holding he head," I said.

They found that funny and put their hands to their mouths to stifle the laughter.

"I wonder what he does drink," Reena said after they had stopped and continued folding and packing clothes into two cartoon boxes.

"Whatever it is, it too strong for him," Mammy said.

"I wonder if is every Saturday night he does carry on so," Reena said.

"Maybe every pay day," Mammy said. "Where Sunil?"

"He still sleeping," I said.

"Go wake he up. He got to drop you with these clothes at Highbridge," Mammy said.

Half an hour later I was on the bar of Sunil's work bike and the boxes were in the tray in front. Just when we were pushing off from our entrance the noise of children screaming from up the street by the cinema reached us. A car was slowly coming down the street and children were running behind it, touching it and screaming excitedly. It was a very shiny black Morris Minor and the irate driver was Mr. Abrams who lived at the house just before us. He was screaming at the children, warning them not to smudge up his shiny car with their nasty, grubby little hands and to stop running behind. He was well dressed and was apparently returning from church. You couldn't tell that from the words flying out of his mouth.

Across the street Bucky was waving to two ladies sitting on the steps of their shack. She was dressed in a purple dress that hugged her shapely body and her thick black hair flowed from beneath her large wide rimmed white hat. Apparently she was coming in from church. Some of the boys were doing chores for their parents about the yard and only a few men were about.

"Papers!" shouted a short dark man riding a bike like Sunil's. In the tray were stacks of newspapers. He turned into the Yard and I heard them address him as Mr. Semple. Other neighbors went over to him in the Yard to buy the Sunday newspapers.

Sunil made quick work of dropping me at a Portuguese family in Highbridge. I had the impression he was in a hurry to get somewhere even though it was Sunday and he was off work that day. The lady paid me and he rode back up the road and quickly deposited me at the gate. Then he was off again. I went upstairs and gave the money to Mammy who counted it. She gave Reena a dollar and gave me ten cents.

"How come she get a whole dollar," I said and did my best to sound wronged.

"When you start wash and press with me you will get a raise," Mammy said. Reena found it funny.

"You can take it and buy a girdle for your big batty," I said bitterly to Reena.

"Mammy!" Reena said in alarm.

Chapter Ten

"Milo stop being rude to your sister," Mammy said calmly and seemed amused.

"Rude? You hear what he say? He should get he tail cut for that," Reena complained angrily.

"Girl, that's a compliment, not a curse," Mammy said.

"How that is a compliment?" Reena asked doubtfully.

"You mean you'd rather have a flat batty like them other Coolie girls I see 'round here?" Mammy said. " You should be glad you got some shape."

"See' batty ain't flat," I pointed out, then all but bit my tongue.

"I wasn't talking about your cousins. They not so bad," Mammy said with a hint of a smile. "And you take your eye off your cousins." I was relieved at dodging that bullet.

Reena seemed appeased but still looked sourly in my direction. She and Mammy continued talking about something else and I got bored. I went downstairs. Uncle Inchan was still at the table but he was reading the day's newspaper. See and Indira were in the kitchen. It seemed as though Indira and Lea did the kitchen duties on Sundays although See was still in there and Lea was out of sight.

I heard talk of Nanny having to be taken to "Gandhi" at the shoemaker's so I slipped out the backdoor and retired to the wood shed at the back of the house. I climbed up the ladder and found a comfortable resting spot among some boards. It was quiet and peaceful up here. I could hear the birds whistling, the occasional car or motorbike driving by on our street or on the Backdam, or even on Church Street, the street before ours. I could hear different voices in kitchens of houses on Church Street. Someone was playing church music loudly on a radio.

"Where Milo is?" I heard Lea ask. I was surprised she even knew my name.

"He was just down here. See if he in his room," See said. "Daddy you want more coffee?" I didn't hear Uncle Inchan's response.

"He not there," Lea said.

"Ask Reena where he is," See said. I guessed Lea went upstairs in search of Reena. It wasn't long after that I heard Mammy calling for me. Then loud-mouth Reena joined in. I stayed put.

"He ain't home," Lea complained.

"Well you go Carry Nanny and I would hold on for you here," See said.

"Where the chopping board?" Indira asked.

"I got to bathe first," Lea said and she apparently went back upstairs. I peeped through the slits in the wall and could see Uncle Inchan at the table reading the newspaper. I could hear the pots and other utensils clink and clatter as Indira and See went about their work in the kitchen.

Just when I was thinking of slipping out of the yard and going up the road so I could safely say I didn't hear anyone calling me, I heard footsteps come out of the backdoor. I peered through the slit again. It was Dil who was attired only in loose fitting short pants. He headed across the yard to the latrine with a roll of toilet tissue in hand. Just then Lea came out in rubber slippers and a lime green towel over a shoulder.

I quietly crawled to my position at the far wall overlooking the bathroom. I lay on my belly and peered through the space between the boards on the wall. Lea went in, locked the door behind her and like See had done, disrobed and threw her discarded clothing over the wall. She was fair skinned and much more full bodied than See was. Her breasts were fuller and she was much hairier too. What arrested my attention was the red mark she had between her full breasts. Unlike See, her breasts were farther apart and between them she had a reddish mark the size and shape of a fist. It looked like someone had tried to take a red hot cow brand iron to her. At first it looked like a tattoo of some sort. But only sailors and bad men had tattoos and they were usually black or blue. This mark was

151

red. I concluded that maybe she got burned some time ago in the kitchen and it never healed.

After she was finished bathing she dried her skin then she did something strange. She put one leg up on the pipe and was examining between her legs. I wondered what she was looking for. After a minute or two she began singing and put on her under clothes, then the same dress again. She opened the bathroom and returned to the house. Dil was still laboring in the latrine so I did not feel safe leaving my hiding place.

I waited several minutes after Dil had returned to the house before coming down from the shed and scampered my way to the front of the house. Just when I was sneaking out the gate Reena spotted me from the front door.

"You Milo, you better run over at the Shoemaker shop and meet Nanny," she said. "Lea gone with she and if Mammy hear you didn't make it again you backside in hot water."

I didn't say anything. I went back inside, got my yachting boots and went out toward the Shoemaker's shop.

When I got there the old people were in the verandah yapping away and Sooklall was attending to two customers at the counter. I let the two old people know I was waiting for Nanny. Lea was nowhere to be seen.

I called to Sooklall's little brown and black mongrel lying in the grass by the side fence of the yard. The dog got up and, ignoring me, swaggered his way to the back of the yard. I followed it. The yard was big enough to play tagga back there. There were a few trees but mostly dead leaves on the ground, probably from the two large trees hanging over from the next yard where I had taken the clothes. I headed for the low cherry tree which had a few ripe red ones amongst the mostly green ones. When I got up in the tree and made myself comfortable I noticed, for the first time, the girl I had seen at the house next door. She was in her yard, just on the other side of the wire mesh fence, and sitting on one of those children bicycles with the extra two wheels for learners. She wore a pink shirt with a denim Farmer Brown over all covering most of it. Her fine plaits were speckled with plastic clips of various colors and she wore leather slippers.

"You thiefin' cherries?" she asked in a strange accent. I shook my head in the negative, being surprised by both her sudden presence and her accent.

"Then wha' you doing up there? You don't live there," she said.

"No, but that don't mean ah thiefin'," I replied.

"Wha' you name?"

"Milo. What you name?"

"Rosanne." She rode the bike in a circle. "You ain't the boy that does come with the clothes?"

"Yes. Where you mother that does collect the clothes, she ain't home?"

"That ain't me mother boy. That is Celeste. She does work for my father," she said and did another circle on the bicycle. "My mother does live in Barbados."

"You from Barbados too?" I asked.

"Yes, I born there."

"Ahhh," I thought, "that's why she talking so funny."

"You ain't got no sister or brother?" I asked.

"No, my mother got me alone. You got any?"

"Yes, I got two sisters and a brother."

"They bigger than you?"

"Yea, only one sister smaller than me. "

"Well I got two big sisters," she said and did another circle.

"I thought you say was you alone," I pointed out.

"I forgot ah had two big sisters," she said easily. This girl couldn't lie to save her life. I'll have to pick and choose what to believe from her.

"Gimme some cherry nuh," she said.

"How you go get it?" I said.

Chapter Ten

"Throw it nuh."

I shifted my position on the tree limb to throw some cherries to her. After the fifth cherry I concluded this girl might be from the island that was the fountain of West Indies Cricket but she couldn't catch squat. However, and to my surprise, she picked up the cherries that had dropped on the grass and ate them.

I climbed down from the tree with a handful of cherries and went to the fence between us where I gave her the cherries. She said thanks and stood there while she ate. As we talked some more I learned that her father was a dispenser at the New Amsterdam hospital and he used to work in Barbados. He was Guyanese and recently moved back home but his wife had a good job in Barbados and did not want to leave. So he left with Rosanne. I chose not to believe the part she told me about the Prime Minister personally begging him to come and work in Guyana and the Prime Minister of Barbados personally pleading with her mother to stay and work over there. Apparently they were that good at their jobs. That must have been one hell of a night with two heads of governments begging her parents in their living room on the same evening.

Just then Celeste came downstairs to empty the garbage in the large green drum by the gate and saw her talking to me by the fence. She ordered Rosanne upstairs. I returned to my cherry tree and picked some more cherries.

"Psssst!" I turned to see where the sound was coming from. When it came again I zeroed in on it and looked up at the windows of the bedroom of Rosanne's house. She waved at me from one of them and smiled. I showed her a cherry and motioned to her if she wanted. She motioned back to me that she did. I threatened to throw it and she stretched a hand in a catching position. I laughed silently and she did the same. Not too long after Sooklall called out to let me know Nanny was ready.

154

Once Upon A Time In Berbice

That evening while I was in my room talking with Sunil, Reena came in with my school pants and shirt. I was shocked and must have shown it.

"Yes, you going to school tomorrow," Reena announced with satisfaction and sat on my bed. Sunil chuckled.

"But how she know what color uniform I got to wear?" I wanted to know.

"Whatever school wearing red shirt is that school you going to," said Reena.

"But Vryman's don't wear red," I complained.

"Who say you going Vryman's," said Reena.

I was disappointed. I had my heart set on Vrymans since it was just across from our street and most of the boys down the street went there. Then I tried to think which school wore red shirts. I remember seeing children in red but they were coming from farther north of town where the gardens was. When I did think about it, Tillam and Squingee wore red shirts to school. At least I won't be a complete stranger.

The next morning Reena woke me early and told me Mammy said to get ready. I had to wait for Lea and Indira to finish in the bathroom before I had a turn. Uncle Inchan had gone to work already. He left at six every morning on his bicycle. Raj was now stirring and Dil was fast asleep. Doogoo was downstairs for a short time with her spectacles on. I understood from Reena that when she had them on she was counting money or doing some business having to do with money.

By eight o' clock I was back in my old school uniform and heading up the road with Mammy. She had bought a thick notebook and she brought along two of my old text books. We took the same route See had taken to take us to the Gardens. Scotts school was a one flat school house on not so high posts across from the Gardens and right next to the big Scotts Church. On the side of the school away from the church was a big play ground with long grass.

The yard was already swarming with boys in red shirts and khaki pants, and girls in red dresses and cream shirts. Mammy took me up the front steps and into what looked like a one room school house. There were benches and blackboards on both sides of us as we walked toward a stage on which stood a large desk with a chair behind and a smaller one in front. Mammy stopped briefly to talk with a teacher who was preparing her desk by one of the blackboards. She directed Mammy to a short man in a three piece suit who was by the stage area talking with another teacher.

By the time we got to him he had climbed the stairs and sat on the big chair behind the desk there. I guessed he was the headmaster. He directed Mammy to come up and sit at the table before him. I followed her.

While they talked I looked around the school. There must have been five or six classes in front of me. There was a wall behind the stage and a doorway to access that area. I guess there were other classrooms behind there.

The headmaster, Mr. Smart, asked to be excused and rang the big bell he had picked up from a corner of his cluttered table. There was noise of excitement outside as the children responded promptly to the bell. None of them came into the building. The few children who were inside hurried outside. When I peeped through the window I could see the children forming lines out there. After a while a teacher outside said something and they all quieted down. Then they came up the steps and filed in quietly and orderly, one class at a time. After they had put away their things the headmaster rang the bell and everyone stood up. At his signal they clasped their hands and closed their eyes then they began saying their morning prayers.

Once Upon A Time In Berbice

After they were seated each class began its activity for the morning, with that being calling of names from the register by the teacher.

Mammy and the headmaster continued talking. From what they said I was to be put in Standard Four since I had just finished writing Common Entrance exams. The headmaster called a dark bespectacled female teacher with a serious but kind face from a class just off to the right of the stage. He introduced her to Mammy as Mrs. Halls. He said I would be in her class. I left with her and went to her class.

The other children stared at me. I didn't see Tillam nor Squingee. She seated me between a robust girl named Cheryl Blake and a boy they called Tucksin. After ten minutes I was surprised to see Mammy was still talking to the headmaster and I was wondering what that was all about. By recess time that morning Mrs. Halls had already figured out where I stood with reading.

We left the building and went under the school during recess. I ran into Tillam and Squingee. Apparently they were in a higher class and their classroom was one of those on the other side of the wall by the stage. They took me around to some of their friends then across the street to the gardens where some of the children were already playing. The swings were all occupied.

"Come lemme show you something," Tillam said and we ran stealthily down one of the paths leading in the area where See had taken us with the benches and Victoria Regia in the ponds. We slowed down and crept under the hedges and closer to where a middle aged couple sat on a bench. The tall hedge had grown right up to the bench which was partly hidden so that anyone on the bench felt fairly concealed from anyone coming down one of the footpaths until the person got right up to the bench. However, they could be seen by anyone prowling under the hedges like we were.

Chapter Ten

Tillam put a finger to his lips to communicate the need for silence. The man was singing playfully to the woman and leaning over as if trying to nibble on her ear. She had on a full length yellow dress but the top few buttons in front were undone and he had one hand under her cream brassiere. She was blushing and looking around anxiously. We covered our mouths to stifle our giggles.

The man continued singing an Indian song and changed his position. Now he was kneeling and looking up at her. I thought he was going to ask her to marry him but then I noticed she had on a wedding ring on the hand she was now using to hurriedly pull the top of her unbuttoned dress to conceal her exposed brassiere. The man had one hand massaging the left side of her hefty hips and to my surprise, slowly ran the other hand on the inside of her thighs. She seemed just as surprised. She gasped and clamped her legs shut, trapping his hand. She looked around anxiously again but no one was in sight. The man's singing intensified as he looked up at her pleadingly with little side to side movements of his head. The woman nervously nibbled on a finger on her right hand and hesitantly opened her legs wider as he slid his hands farther up. She gasped and closed her eyes. His singing had become hoarse now.

"Wha' happening?" I asked Squingee quietly. They both turned slowly to look at me. Then Tillam showed me the finger-in-the-hole sign. I didn't ask anything else to expose my ignorance.

When I looked back at the couple the woman's yellow dress had ridden higher up, exposing her cream slip and upper part of her thick legs which were of a clearer complexion than her lower legs. The man's hand was moving in a rhythm now and the singing had stopped. He sunk his face in her bosom and she had her eyes closed and breathed heavily. Just then we heard the school bell ring.

Tillam and Squingee were disappointed as we withdrew quietly and undetected, then beat a hasty retreat to the play area, then across the street and into the school yard. On the way I had asked Tillam how he knew that was what they were going to do and he said he would show me later.

That midday when school was dismissed for breakfast me and Tillam scooted over to the gardens again to spy on the couple but they were already gone. We hurried up Main road and went home to eat. Reena was in the kitchen with See again and breakfast was ready.

After I ate I went into the Yard to wait for Tillam. Richie was sitting on his steps eating from an enamel plate. He was dressed in some kind of dark green uniform and wore an orange helmet. The woman who was stabbed in the fight over him was in his kitchen cleaning up.

Tillam came out of his shack shortly after and we went across to Spanner's. Tillam told Spanner to show him the thing. Spanner went back in the house. His mother had not come in from work yet and his big sister who was the girl that got licks for being in the Gardens the day we moved in, was heading out back to school.

Spanner came to his door and called us inside. Tillam took what looked like a small plastic binoculars and went to the open window where the light came in. Only then did I recognize it was a View Master through which you could see three dimension pictures. He looked through it and grinned.

"This is a new one? I never see this," he commented.

"Me uncle was using it last night," Spanner said. "He must be left it in."

"Lemme see?" I said.

"Wait boy," Tillam brushed me off. He pressed down on a plastic lever and part of the thing rotated.

"Oh jeese!" he exclaimed and grinned again. I had no idea what he was seeing but whatever it was he was all excited. At last the thing had apparently rotated to the first one he saw, then he gave it to me.

Chapter Ten

I got my first sex education lesson from a pornographic View Master slide Spanner's uncle had brought when he came off his ship on his break. That was when I realized what the finger-in-the-hole really meant. I also understood then that See and Lea were not abnormal in having hair on those parts of their bodies, even though the couples we were seeing were white. It then dawned on me that I would be growing hair down there when I'm old enough. Now I understood what the man was trying to do with the woman in the Gardens.

"So all marrid people does do that?" I asked Tillam on the way back to school.

"Yea, how you think everybody born," he said.

"So ent that woman in the gardens marrid? Why she don't do it with him at home instead of in the open where people can see them," I thought aloud.

"She marrid?" Tillam asked.

"Yes, she had on she marrid ring."

"Well that ain't she husband," he said matter-of-factly.

I was beginning to put two and two together.

That afternoon as soon as I went home Reena told me Mammy said to change and that we had to go back to school. It turned out that the headmaster had asked Mammy if she knew anyone interested in sweeping the school since the previous cleaner had gone to Georgetown and had not returned. After asking how much the job paid Mammy said she would take it.

So that afternoon the three of us went to the school at about four o' clock. The school was empty except for a dozen children in a classroom at the back. They were taking lessons from Mr. Anton. He was the Form Two teacher. The headmaster had left already. We started cleaning up from the front of the school with Mammy and Reena sweeping while I handled the garbage disposal. I had to take each bucket of garbage to a big drum at the side of the school by the play ground. It was not hard work but I was frustrated at not being able to go play down the street with the boys.

By the time we finished the main part of the school to the front and the stage, Mr. Anton's lessons was over. The children left and Mr. Anton began packing up to leave. He was a tall man of coffee brown complexion and was probably in his thirties. He was slim like my uncles and had a low afro and sideburns. He also sported a small moustache and goatee beard. On that day he was attired in a white polyester shirt with blue stripes, blue tie and dark gabardine pants. His shoes were black, shiny pointed tips.

"Good afternoon," he said to Mammy and Reena on seeing us waiting on him.

"Good afternoon," Mammy said tiredly and Reena smiled.

"Mr. Smart told me you're the new person on the job," he said pleasantly. "I'm Mr. Anton. You were here this morning, right?"

Mammy nodded. "I'm Yvette and this is my daughter Reena."

"Nice to meet you," he said and reached across and shook Mammy's hand then Reena's. "Mr. Smart told me to give you the keys so you can lock up when you're finished," he said and gave her a set of keys. "I'm here for lessons until four from Monday to Thursday, so I suppose we'll be seeing a lot of each other."

Mammy smiled. He took his leave shortly after and we continued cleaning the three classrooms behind there. By the time we were finished it was well after six.

When we got home Doogoo wanted to talk to Mammy about something. I went across to the yard hoping Spanner would pull out his View Master for us to watch again. But his mother and sister were home, so that idea died instantly.

While over there shooting the breeze with the boys, a fancy looking car driven by an affluent looking man who was well dressed and in a tie, pulled up before the yard. Bucky stepped out from the passenger side, closed the door then bent and told the man something through the passenger window. Then she waved and the man drove out the street and took a right turn up the Backdam.

We stood there watching wide eyed with each wondering if that was her boyfriend. Bucky came into the yard hailing to everyone in sight.

"That's the new beau?" asked one inquisitive woman from the shack before Richie's.

"You mad? That's me new boss," Bucky said. "You all full O' gossip." With that she went into her shack.

I was relieved. I wondered if she did have a boyfriend but I didn't want to bring that up with the boys at that time. I'll put that to Coco or Tillam when we were alone.

That night Reena came down to our room to bring our clean clothes. She sat on my bed. This had become a ritual now. She came down whenever me a Sunil were together in the room and we talked.

"Guess what," she said conspiringly. "Aunty Doogoo want Mammy to pay rent for us to stay here."

"That don't make sense. Ent we is family?" I said.

"Blood thicker than water," Sunil commented.

"Money thicker than blood," Reena shot back. "She complain about how much it go cost for food and boarding and how much she had to spend to prepare extra room for we," Reena explained. Sunil kept an eye on the door as we talked.

"What Mammy say," Sunil said and seemed to be taking this bit of news seriously for some reason.

"What she go say. She don't have a choice," Reena said and seemed frustrated.

"Between me and you," Sunil said and paused as he glanced through the doorway again. Then he leaned

162

forward and whispered conspiringly, "I think Aunty Doogoo got she eye on the money Mammy supposed to get from the estate for Haroon." Reena nodded.

"Maybe she see Mammy get a little money from the washing and she want that too," she commented.

Sunil produced a pack of cards and started sharing them out on the floor.

"Who tell you I want play cards," I objected. They both stared at me.

"You stupid or what," Sunil said. "We just pretending to play in case anybody pass by they go see we doing something."

I saw his point. I picked up the cards and we continued talking. From the conversation I learned that Doogoo had on her glasses that afternoon and she had a meeting at the table downstairs with three men. One was Inchan's brother, Uncle Rohit. The other was a friend of Inchan they called Rubberdog, and the third man was some kind of business associate of Doogoo's. We didn't know the full details at the time but it turned out that these four planned to pool money together to take advantage of a policy the Demerara Mutual Life Insurance was offering to bring in customers. With a prime premium paid in full, one was entitled to quite a sum if one had an accident, broke a leg or had any of a number of stated bodily harms. The four would pool their moneys to purchase a premium in Rubberdog's name. Rubberdog would then proceed to have an accident and the money they got from the insurance would be split accordingly.

At first I couldn't figure how they chose Rubberdog to be the sacrificial lamb. He was a big clumsy bearded man with a no hair on his head. He was loud and good natured, especially when drunk. Then I learned that Rubberdog had broken an arm when he fell in his house while moving pots about the floor to catch water from the leaking roof. After having his arm in plaster of paris and in a sling for six weeks, the very week the arm was taken out and pronounced healed by the doctors at New Amsterdam hospital, Rubberdog ended up in a drunken fight after drinking and broke the same arm again. This made him the most likely of the four to suffer bodily harm.

The rest of the week passed without much drama. In school two boys in my class caught my attention. Mrs. Halls was always taking away comic books from them for they were avid comic book readers. The big fat one was called Big Pinny and the smaller wiry one was called Little Pinny. Later I learned, to my amusement, that the smaller one was actually the uncle of the tubby one. It was rumored that between them they owned more comic books than Graphic Bookstore out on Charlotte Street. Big Pinny always carried a cricket bat with him but I never saw either of them playing cricket. The bat was way too narrow anyway. Squingee later explained that it wasn't for cricket but for anyone with outstanding comic books.

Little Pinny must have taken a liking to me because he often let me look at his comics during breaks when I wasn't spying on couples in the gardens with Tillam and Squingee. We went over in the gardens very often but never saw anything more than couples kissing and girls fighting off the ambitious tentacles of their boyfriends. When there was nothing exciting to see we retreated to the swings until the bell rang.

By the end of the week Little Pinny had decided to lend me five comic books. I liked the drawings in them and planned to take them home and draw from them. But before the books parted from the Pinnies, Big Pinny did the negotiations.

"You's borrowing five comic books from we, right?" he said in his surprisingly high pitched voice. I nodded.

"By next week Tuesday yuh got to give we back five comic books but they got to be five different comics. So if you know you can't ex them don't be borrowing none," he said with the air of an amateur mafioso.

"How he mean 'ex?'" I asked Little Pinny.

"Exchange them," he said.

"Exchange them where, at the Library?" I asked innocently.

They both found that funny.

"You exchange them with anybody else," squeaked Big Pinny. "See you on Tuesday." He consulted his copy of Captain America he was reading which signified the end of the conversation.

That afternoon after school I went over to the Gardens with Tillam and Squingee. We were going to play on the swings a bit before they went home. I no longer went home straight after school since I had to be back in half hour to help Mammy clean.

I wasn't sure where Squingee had gone but me and Tillam were talking about the suicidal arrangement I had been trapped into with the Pinnies.

"Let me guess," Tillam said. "One of them let you look at the comics when he reading it, right?" I nodded.

"Then he offer to lend you some, right?" I nodded again.

"That was Li'l Pinny?" The nodding continued.

"Then Big Pinny lay down the rules when they about to lend you, right?" I nodded once more, now realizing how I was sucked into their web.

"What happen if I bring back the same books?" I asked.

"You ever get lash with a cricket bat?" he asked. I swallowed deeply.

Just then Squingee came running up to us in haste.

"Guess who getting feel-up in the Gardens," he said excitedly. We both waited for an answer. Tillam scooted off in the direction of the lovers' section when he realized an answer would not be forth-coming from Squingee. I scooted after him, closely followed by Squingee.

"Come this side," Squingee called to us as we were heading to the original spot. He led us along the hedge as we went past behind the one by the bench on which we had seen the lovers on that first day. Squingee slowed to a crawl and led us under another hedge. He stealthily parted some leaves and we could see a couple sitting on a bench.

The girl was dressed in some kind of uniform which looked familiar but I couldn't recall why at that moment. She was sitting on his lap and had her head bent away from us and to his. He had one hand around her waist and the other disappeared somewhere in her blouse. She had one arm around his shoulder and was tussling his hair, but I could not see where the other was.

Suddenly they were startled. She jumped up and fumbled to button the front of her shirt. The man's glasses were knocked crooked on his face. He became busy doing nothing and seemed confused. An unshaved man in short khaki pants pulled high up on his tummy and covering his well tucked in dirty long sleeved shirt which was buttoned down to the wrists, came walking up the footpath in short quick steps with his head bowed. He seemed oblivious to what they were doing.

"Got a cigarette?" the man slurred with an obvious speech impediment.

"Get away from here, you lunatic!" the lover boy on the bench shouted. The mad man continued away from them and up the walk.

I noticed the crotch of the man sitting on the bench was unbuttoned. So that's where her other hand was. The girl began giggling. She still had her back to us. When the mad man had gone she turned and leaned over her lover with her hands on his shoulders. Only then we saw her face. I was stunned. The three of us looked at each other blankly.

Once Upon A Time In Berbice

The man straightened his glasses and pulled her into him by the waist. She leaned into him and kissed him on the mouth. He lowered his hands and roughly massaged her bare legs until the knee-length skirt began riding up her now exposed thighs. She stopped kissing him to look around briefly then carefully climbed onto the bench straddling him. He moved his hands to her blouse again and opened her shirt. While they kissed he maneuvered her brassiere below her breasts which popped right out. As he detached his lips from hers and attached them to one nipple we could see the big red mark on her chest between her breasts.

Chapter Eleven

Chapter Eleven

"Lend me a bob," I asked Coco after we were finished playing cricket that afternoon.

"Where I go get twenty-five cents from." he said.

"Wha' you go do with it?" Tillam asked.

"I saving up for something," I said.

"I could lend you twenty cents but you got to give me back," he said and reached into his pants pocket.

"Where you get money from?" Dillip wanted to know.

"I always got money boy," Tillam said and gave me two ten cent coins.

"Gimme twenty-cents too," Dillip said.

"Go ask yuh mother," Tillam replied then took off across the yard with Dillip after him.

The way I saw it, I had until Tuesday to come up with enough money to buy five comic books so I wouldn't get clobbered with a cricket bat. When I delivered clothes for Mammy that weekend I predicted twenty-five cents would be "misplaced." Then I planned to be extra nice to Reena this weekend. If she was in the mood I might get another bob from her. And I'm counting on Sunil getting paid that weekend. If things worked right I might very well be able to buy more than five comics. Problem was I didn't even know how much a comic book cost. And I wasn't about to ask the boys, for Tillam would then know why I wanted the money.

That Saturday I took Nanny to meet "Gandhi" at the Shoemakers and found myself in the backyard again. I went up in the cherry tree and made sipping sounds to attract Rosanne if she was home. After a while the blind behind one window moved then closed again. Soon after she came downstairs. I came down the tree and took a handful of cherries to her at the wire mesh fence.

Once Upon A Time In Berbice

"So how come you does be over there so steady?" she asked in her soft confidential voice and strange accent. She was dressed in blue Buffalo jeans and a pink armless t-shirt. Her hair was still in fine plaits and speckled with the plastic clips.

"I does bring a lady to visit the old man over there," I explained.

"That is his girlfriend?" she asked and laughed. I found that funny and laughed too.

"They too old. They ain't even got no teeth to kiss," I said.

"You don't need no teeth to kiss boy."

"What you know about kissing?"

"I know enough. I see it plenty times on television in Barbados."

I had no idea what this television was, for we had no TV transmission nor television sets in our country. I began to wonder if she was lying about that.

"You want a ride on my bike?" she asked.

"Yes, but how. You go pass it over the fence?"

"No, but you can come over and ride it."

"You ain't frighten you get in trouble with Celeste?" I asked.

"To hell with Celeste. Just duck under the fence and come," she said.

I was mildly surprised that such a nice, middle-class girl dropped such words. I was doubtful about this being a good move. Besides, I had already had a bad experience where ducking under fences was concerned.

"You frighten Celeste? She don't work on Saturdays anyway," she said as she walked a couple of steps along the fence to her right and pulled open the loose mesh of the fence there. I carefully ducked under then came under the house with her.

"You can't make noise. Me father sleeping," she said. I climbed on the bike and rode shakily at first before getting

169

the hang of it. We played and talked for close to half an hour before I heard Chandra calling me from the shoemaker shop. I said goodbye to Rosanne, ducked under the fence, and returned to the shop.

Chandra wasn't there before but now she was in the shop behind the counter. Nanny was still in conversation with Gandhi, so I didn't know why Chandra was calling me.

"Come go in the shop and buy a bottle of cooking oil and two box of matches," she said. I was about to ask her why she didn't go herself when I realized I would be squandering an opportunity to add to my comic book fund.

I took the money and ran up the street to the Main Road where there was a shop at almost every corner. After I made the purchase I hurried back to the shoemaker shop so that Chandra would be impressed with the timely manner in which I had done the chore.

When I came back she was in the yard at the back reaching up in the tree picking cherries. I took the cooking oil and matches there to her.

"Boy, you quick man. You went to the shop and come back already?" she marveled. I smiled and gave her the matches. Then I gave her the change.

"This is for you," she said and gave me twenty-five cents.

"A WHOLE BOB!" I thought in amazement. "From now on I can do chores for her any day."

I pocketed the twenty-five cents.

"Want to see a trick?" she said after popping two more red cherries in her mouth. I nodded.

She opened one of the boxes of matches, took one out, turned it around and held the head of the match against the side of the box with a thumb. She stooped down with her back to the road so no one can see what she was doing, then she flicked the match with her thumb. The match flew forward and flared up. It fell in the dead leaves and the flame died.

I smiled. That was a very nice trick. She showed me again then had me try it. After a few tries I got the hang of it. A movement caught my eye in the room at the back of the shop. I glanced up and saw Sooklall looking at us. He didn't say anything but promptly moved away from the window.

Chandra continued picking cherries. Then she left and went around back into the shop. To my surprise she had forgotten the box of matches we were using. I picked it up and tried the trick again. It worked every time. I heard a stir in Rosanne's yard and looked across excitedly hoping to see her. Instead, Celeste came down the stairs and took a bucket to the pipe to the side of the house. I couldn't believe a word that girl told me.

When Celeste went back upstairs I continued playing with the matches. To make it more interesting I put some dry leaves in a clump then tried to ignite them by flicking the match there. After a few tries the leaves burst into flames. I stomped the flames out and looked across to Rosanne's house to see if anyone was watching. I then built a bigger pile. When that caught afire the blaze was much bigger. I panicked and stomped furiously to control it. Sparks flew up from the leaves and after a few minor burns I eventually got it out. That was the end of that trick as far as I was concerned.

I pocketed the box of matches and returned to picking my cherries. Eventually Chandra called to tell me Nanny was ready.

That night I was lying on my bed drawing from one of the comic books when Sunil came in. He was really upset. He didn't tell me why. I figured he had not seen Chandra for the evening since she was at the shoemaker shop. It was only when Reena came down that I knew the reason for his foul mood.

"You know them blasted people only give me half me money?" he complained to Reena.

" Who?"

"Mr. Bassit nuh. He only give me half of what he supposed to give me."

"Shhhhhh!" she said to quiet him down. "He tell you why?"

"He say to ask Doogoo," Sunil said and was puzzled.

"You ask she?"

"No, I ain't see she yet,"

"Is who get the job for you?" I asked.

"Doogoo. So what," he said cautiously.

"Is you arrange how much you to get with Mr. Bassit or Doogoo?" I asked. Reena cocked her head to one side as she looked at me thoughtfully.

"Doogoo do all the talking," Sunil said and I could see he was coming around to where I was heading.

"You think she getting half of my money?" he said with slitted eyes.

"Doogoo does take goods from Bassit?" I asked.

"Yea! Yes, I does bring it meself," he said and was now seeing the light.

"So how you ain't know Doogoo must be arrange with him to keep half your money to pay for goods," I pointed out. Sunil swore and threatened to do Doogoo harm.

"That is possible yes, but that don't mean is so it happening," Reena said. "For all you know is Bassit who robbing you blind and it got nothing to do with Doogoo."

Sunil looked confused and could not make up his mind about what happened to the other half of his money.

"How much for a comic book?" I asked.

They both looked at me blankly.

"Comic book me tail. I want me money," Sunil complained.

"Where the cards?" Reena asked. Sunil looked outside quickly then produced the cards. He shared them out.

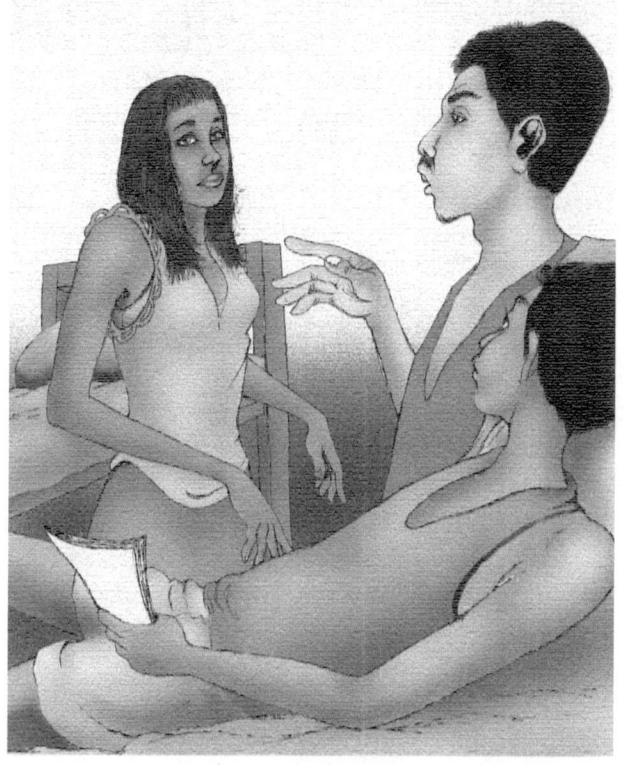

Reena, Sunil, and me

"Doogoo had on she glasses today," Reena said quietly.

"Maybe she was counting Sunil' money," I said without thinking. Sunil looked at me angrily but didn't say anything. If I was in "slapping" range of him I certainly would have felt it.

"Milo shut up," Reena said. "She had a meeting with the three fellows again. It look like Rubberdog still healthy and they don't like that. They been giving he suggestions on what he can do to become unhealthy."

Sunil found that funny.

"Then she start to complain about the girl Raj going around with," Reena continued.

"You mean Rachael?" I asked.

"Yes," Reena said. "I think is because she black."

"But See darker than she," I pointed out.

"That don't matter to Doogoo," Reena said.

"She's nice," I said.

"Yea, she pretty," Sunil commented.

"Not as pretty as Bucky though," I commented.

"Oh yea, she's beautiful," Reena agreed.

"Who is this Bucky alyuh always talking about?" Sunil said irritably.

"She live over in the Yard. She should go up for a beauty contest or something," Reena said.

"Why you don't go up for that?" I asked.

Reena looked blankly at me, trying to make up her mind whether or not I was being sarcastic. Sunil was looking at me too.

"Well, Bertie think you're pretty," I said. That caught her off guard.

"Milo shut up," she said as she blushed and looked away.

"Who's Bertie?" Sunil asked.

"He's the postboy," I said.

"How alyuh know all them people and I living right here and don't know them," Sunil complained.

"If you lift your head from under Chandra' skirt now and then you might know a lot more," Reena said bluntly.

"I ain't under nobody' skirt girl," he said and, surprisingly he wasn't mad at her for saying that. If I had said it he would have been on me in a flash.

"How much for a comic book?" I asked again.

"How we go know that," Reena said impatiently.

"Look on the cover," Sunil said. Reena reached over and took one of the comics I had before me.

"It have the price in pence," she said.

"What is pence?" I asked.

"I think is eleven cents for one of them," Sunil said.

"How much money I need to buy five comic books?" I asked.

"Fifty-five cents," Reena said easily. "You give Mammy any money?" She said to Sunil.

"I just come in. I ain't see Mammy yet," he said. "How much I should give her?"

"I don't know. Is up to you. But she working all them jobs just to mind we. And Aunty Doogoo want to take money out she hand as fast as she get it. So you should keep that in mind," she said. "Just make sure you give her more than you giving Chandra." She said and got up to leave.

"Reena, lend me twenty-five cents nuh," I said.

"To buy comic book? You must be mad. Ask the working man over there," she indicated Sunil then she left.

I looked at Sunil and he gave me that "Don't you dare" look. I didn't dare.

After Reena left and Sunil went to the latrine I counted the money I had. There was the ten cents Mammy had paid me, the twenty from Tillam, and the twenty-five from Chandra. I should have asked Reena how much that came up to. She was good at Math. But then I didn't want her knowing how much money I had. Potentially I was still counting on at least a bob from Sunil and another bob from Mammy's washing money. But I was having a change of heart where the latter was concerned. With Reena expressing how pressed for money Mammy was and how hard she was working to get it, I felt guilty taking a penny from her money. I would have to wait and see.

"Fire! Fire!" The shout was raised in the neighborhood. I jumped up and wiped my eyes clear, thinking it was a dream. But then I saw Sunil hurriedly hopping into his house pants and the shout continued outside. For a minute I thought the fire was in our house. I ran outside to see the people running out of the Yard and up to the Backdam. I could see the orange glow in the night sky in the direction of Pitt Street. Coco was among those running up the road toward the fire. I ran out behind him.

As we ran, people were saying it was Roman School on fire, but then somebody said it wasn't that far up the road. As we got nearer I could hear the fire engine wailing as it raced up the Backdam toward us. The crowd got thicker as we got nearer. People were now saying it was the shoemaker shop. We got as far as a block from Sooklall's place and I could see it was well ablaze. The fire engine pulled up before the shop and the firemen bailed out and got busy assembling their equipment. In two minutes they had water beaming out from two fire hoses and onto the burning shop.

Sooklall was on the side street in his pajamas bawling like a cow. Rumors began to spread that the old man did not get out. Some people were trying to console Sooklall to no avail. I watched the flames leap angrily up in the sky. A part of the building collapsed sending showers of sparks skyward. One woman commented that it was probably the force of the jets of water that made that part collapse and not the fire itself. Another woman was distraught, lamenting that she should have followed her mind and gone to pick up her high heeled church shoes from Sooklall that afternoon. Just then the rest of the building collapsed and more sparks rose and disappeared into the dark early morning sky.

Eventually the fire burned lower and lower and got smokier until at last, the flames ceased, leaving behind the smoldering, steamy ruins. The firemen finished dosing the fire then gave way to the policemen. By then the crowd was thinning fast for it was still hours away from morning. I didn't know where they took Sooklall. Rosanne's house was now the first house in the street. I could see their light on. She was standing with a man by her gate while five or six neighbors stood with them on the outside of the gate.

As I turned to go with Coco I saw Sunil consoling Chandra. As far as I knew she lived all the way in Pilot Street and on the waterside section. I was surprised she came all the way over here in the dead of night.

When we got back by the Yard several tenants were standing around to the front by the street, discussing what could have caused the fire. Bucky, who had pulled a raincoat over her night dress, speculated that with all those shoes piled up it only took one carelessly thrown cigarette to catch afire late at night.

Eventually everybody turned in and so did I. Sunil didn't come in until an hour later.

Sunday morning I woke up late. I hurried to finish my breakfast after hearing Coco calling for me outside. I dashed out to him before Mammy found something for me to do.

"We going and see Sooklall burn down place," Coco said. Tillam, Dillip, Spanner and Chinee Roy were waiting for us at the head of the street.

We sauntered up the Backdam where a small crowd was standing and staring at the scorched remains of the shoemaker shop. Some of them were returning home from church and had stopped to view the ruins.

We turned down the street to get a closer view. There was a huge pile of blackened wood and brown twisted zinc where the shop once stood. My cherry tree in the backyard was scorched brown and so were the other trees nearby. Even the leaves on the side of the big trees in Rosanne's yard facing Sooklall's yard, were scorched.

Looking across at Rosanne's house I could see her standing beside the same man I had seen earlier, in her verandah looking at the crowd inspecting the rubble. She gave no indication that she had seen me.

"They take out the dead man?" Chinee Roy asked.

"Who say anybody dead," Spanner said.

"Then you ain't know the old man dead in the fire last nite?" Coco said.

"Sooklall dead too?" Spanner said.

"Naw, I see he last nite," I said.

"So he ain't coming back to see if he can save some of dem shoes?" Chinee Roy asked.

"Me mother had two pairs of shoes in there," Dillip said.

"They burn up for sure. You' mother does only buy cheap plastic shoes," Tillam commented then took off down Coopers Lane before Dillip could get to him. We walked off in that direction past Rosanne's house. She did a little discreet wave with her fingers to me as I went by with the boys.

About four o'clock that afternoon Reena, Indira, and Lea were well dressed and about to head out to the cinema. Lea and Indira were dressed in colorful silky looking Indian dresses. Reena wore a full length plaid dress and had her hair pulled up on a bun. She looked like a woman.

"Wha' you all going to see?" I asked.

"Apna Desh," Indira volunteered.

"I can come?" I asked.

"No, you been already," Reena said.

"But I didn't see that picture," I protested.

"Just stop," Reena said. "You' not coming."

"I ain't want see no coolie picture anyway," I said defiantly.

"Ent you coolie too?" Lea said.

" So what. I ain't want nobody singing in me ears whole picture," I said, quoting what I had heard Raj say before.

"You ever see an Indian picture before boy?" Lea said and was very amused. They headed out the gate and up Theater Alley.

Once Upon A Time In Berbice

I went over in the Yard where the boys were crowded around something by the steps of Spanner's shack. For a moment I wondered if the view master was on display but doubted that since Bucky was sitting right nearby on her steps combing the hair of one of the little girls from a neighboring shack. There were two other girls there with her in addition to Spanner's sister sitting on their steps. I went over and was disappointed to find the boys crowded around a section of the Sunday newspaper. They were talking excitedly about new western movies that were advertised in the newspaper.

I stood on Spanner's steps next to his sister Vanessa. From here I had a clear view right over them. There was a large almost full page poster of a grinning man standing with legs apart. He held open his trench coat to reveal rows of dynamite and other explosives in the many pockets of the coat. Beside him was a stouter Mexican bandit sitting behind and firing a machine gun. The names of the two men were written large above them and what must have been the title of the movie was right across the bottom of the page. There were other smaller writings splashed across the page.

"I see that already," I said. They stopped talking and turned around slowly to look at me.

"Where the hell you see this and it ain't even open in Georgetown yet," Spanner said.

"I see the poster inside the front of Globe cinema when I went there," I said. They sighed in relief and turned back to the newspaper.

"What that picture name again?" I said.

"Duck You Sucker," said Tillam.

"You ain't see the big name write across the bottom?" Spanner said.

"He can't read," Dillip said and laughed. Bucky turned and looked right at me. It was obvious she had heard

Dillip's remark. I felt a burning shame and embarrassment engulf me.

"I can read you' mother," I said to Dillip and jumped off the steps as he got up hurriedly to attend to me. I hit the ground running and was over the road and in my yard before he could get anywhere near me.

With the Yard being out of bounds for me until Dillip cooled down, I was about to retire to my loft when Chandra pulled up by the gate. At first I guessed she stopped by to tell Nanny what had happened to Gandhi.

"Sunil home?" she said.

"He gone out," I said. She motioned for me to come.

I hesitated at first then went out there to her.

"You can keep a secret?" she said confidentially. I nodded. She looked around then walked toward the Backdam and motioned for me to follow her.

"You hear about the fire last night?" she asked when we stopped at the concrete culvert at the head of the street. I nodded.

"Don't tell anybody that we had matches in the backyard yesterday," she said. "You was playing with matches in the backyard after I left?"

I felt my whole stomach go hollow.

"No," I lied. "I ain't had no matches."

"Somebody tell me they see you playing with matches there. But don't worry, they ain't go tell nobody about it. That is we li'l secret," she said with a little smile and put an index finger on her lips to indicate silence.

"Tell Sunil I did come to him," she said and headed up the Backdam.

I stood there still in distress. I had not even thought about me having anything to do with the fire. Now that she mentioned it, it could have been started by some of the sparks caused by me trying to stomp out the little blaze I had started. That meant I was the one responsible for

180

burning down the shoemaker shop... AND I KILLED GANDHI.

My whole stomach felt queasy and I dashed toward home to get to the latrine. And just in time too, for Dillilp had just spotted me and had got up to intercept me before I got to my yard. I made it in ahead of him and headed straight through the backdoor on the other side and to the latrine. It's funny that I didn't need to go until I learned of this disappointing news. As I sat on the wooden seat of the latrine oozing liquid out the back end, I wondered what would happen to me if it was found out that I had started the fire. They would lock me up for sure. They would do even worse seeing that someone was killed in the fire. Tears came to my eyes as I realized the deep trouble I was in.

I had to begin making a conscious effort to keep my mouth shut. I was deeply indebted to Chandra. At first I wondered why she would want to do me that favor but then I realized that she was as much to blame as I was since she was the one to start playing with the matches in the yard in the first place and she was the one to show me what to do.

I wondered if I should tell Reena but decided against it. I also wondered if Chandra would tell Sunil. I hoped she could keep a secret too.

When I eventually came out of the latrine See asked me if I wanted anything to eat. That was the last thing on my mind. She was dressed to go out. She wore a knee-length orange dress speckled with yellow flowers. Her long hair was not plat but held together at the back by a plastic clasp.

"Come let we go for a walk," she said. I really didn't feel like it and told her so. "If you go you will get ten cents," she offered.

As much as I didn't feel like going anywhere I had to take care of my comic book fund.

"Where we going?" I asked as we headed out the street.

Chapter Eleven

"We going by the stelling," she said. That was fine with me. We walked out to Water street, past the Globe cinema and down the road to the ferry stelling. See said we were going for a ride on the ferry.

Torani was now coming in when we got there. As we waited for the boat to unload I saw a boy looking like Christopher waiting outside.

"Ain't that the boy from the DC office that was talking to you and we cousin?" I asked and pointed him out. See looked over there and said she didn't know. Apparently she didn't care.

When the boat began loading for the return trip to Rosignol See bought tickets at a booth and we entered through the passenger section on the upper section of the boat. We sat out on the breezy section in front. See bought me a sweet drink and two hard bulls eye sweets. Those things took forever to finish. She told me to stay there, that she was going to the toilet and come back.

I enjoyed the ride as we headed across the river. When the boat was about mid stream and See was not back yet, I figured I would do some roaming and return by the time we pulled in to Rosignol. I got up and went downstairs where the vehicles were. I maneuvered my way past the vehicles to the back of the passage way by the noisy engine then up the short stairs.

As I reached the top of the stairs I froze. A girl with long hair and wearing an orange dress, was sitting beside the same boy we had seen that looked like Christopher. I could hear See's voice too. I thought she couldn't recognize him before we boarded the ferry. They were holding hands and had their backs to me and to anyone else who passed this way. I retraced my steps and hurried back to my original position.

When the ferry reached Rosignol I watched it unload, then load again. See came back to check on me and said it must have been something she ate, that she had to go back to the toilet. Again she admonished me not to leave and I broached her for twenty-five cents for something to eat. She reluctantly surrendered it and left, as she said, for the toilet. I looked on the stelling to see if by chance Majeed,

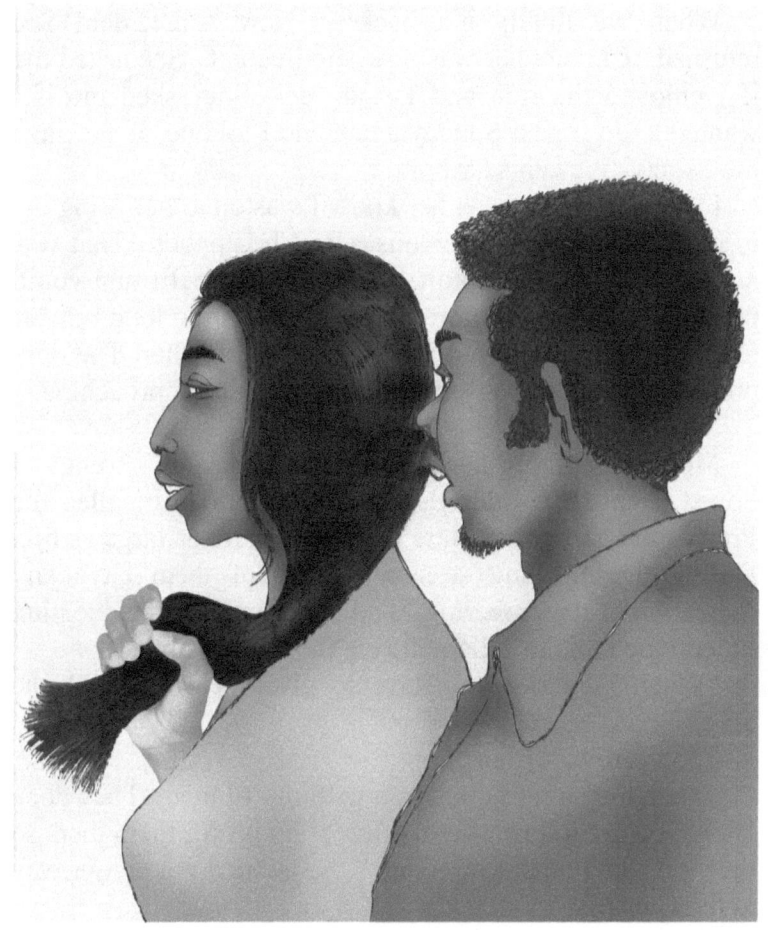

See and Christopher

Hector or anybody from my old school was about. I recognized no one.

After the ferry pulled off again and headed for New Amsterdam I sneaked away again to check up on See. She was still holding hands with Christopher. They seemed to be having a good time. I pondered whether I should surprise them and try to lift a dollar off him. He certainly wasn't in a position to refuse. But then See wouldn't trust taking me with her again. I returned to my spot.

When we finally got back to New Amsterdam See returned. Christopher was nowhere in sight. She asked me if I enjoyed the ride and I said yes. She asked me if I wanted to do it next Sunday again and I told her if she gave me twenty-five cents I would.

I was not going to let her know I was on to her using me to have this secret rendezvous with Christopher. That was a situation I could exploit for my own benefit and could potentially gain a lot more than a dollar in the long run. If she was going to use me it was going to cost her. The only problem was "Cricket-bat" Tuesday was fast approaching.

Monday morning came and back to school I went. I hoped against the odds that some illness had befallen the Pinnies but as I got in class there they were as large as life. During the morning session neither of them gave any indication of remembering I had five comic books due him. I mentioned this to Tillam during the morning break.

"When they say you have to give them back?" he asked.

"Tomorrow," I said.

"Then they ain't go tell you nothing 'til then. They done know you got to bring five different books for them then, so they ain't go bother you today," he pointed out on our way to the Gardens.

"They don't get sick or nothing?"

"Not since Little Infant," he said and looked at me, realizing how desperate I was getting. "Why you don't buy five books then. Your aunty got plenty money."

"You mad! You think me aunty go give me money to go buy comic books?"

Once Upon A Time In Berbice

"Which remind me, I go want that twenty cents I lend you," he said. I could see him thinking his twenty cents might end up in Graphic comic book shop.

"You go get it this afternoon when I go home," I said. I intended staying clear of him for the rest of the day.

That midday after I went home for breakfast I went up Charlotte Street at Graphic Book store. There were whole shelves of comic books in the last two rows of the store. I picked up a Spiderman, a Dare Devil, and a Fantastic Four and asked the cashier how much it was. He said forty-five cents. I emptied the change from my pocket on the counter and asked if that was enough. The man returned ten cents and gave me the books. Now I had to figure out how to get the other two.

I hid the books by sticking them in the back of my pants and under my shirt. When I got in school I hid them amongst my school books. I didn't want Ms. Halls seizing them or somebody begging to borrow.

That afternoon after school I hid until Tillam left, then I went over to the gardens to kill some time before Mammy and Reena came to clean up. I went by the hedges but the couples weren't doing anything exciting; just holding hands and talking.

That afternoon as I did the garbage with Mammy and Reena I thought of ways of getting two other comics before the morrow. I did find a comic book in the trash but it had no cover nor the first few pages, but because it was thick I kept it. Maybe it would be worth something.

Mr. Anton's lessons were over but he sat at his desk playing draughts with a student. Mammy was sweeping his classroom. I wondered why she didn't challenge him to a game since she was so good at it. But she totally ignored them playing and continued with her cleaning. A fund-raising idea hit me.

I stood around watching them play. After Mr. Anton beat the student he began explaining moves the student

185

could have made. Eventually the student left and Mammy was out of the room and in the main hall again.

"I bet you there is somebody in this school that can win you," I said. Mr. Anton leaned back and clasped his hands behind his head. He smiled.

"You can play?" he asked.

"No, but I bet you a dollar somebody in this school can beat you."

"And suppose they can't beat me. You have a dollar to give me?" he asked. I hadn't thought about that. He laughed, unclasped his hands, then leaned forward and narrowed his eyes. I can see he was thinking who I had in mind.

"You mean they're in the building right now?"

"Yes Sir."

"Did somebody come in the building that I don't know about?" he asked.

"No Sir."

"It's somebody I know?"

"Yes, you saw her before."

He leaned closer to me.

"Your sister can play?" he asked confidentially.

"I bet you a dollar my Mammy can beat you. But don't tell her I say so, or she mightn't want to play. If you can get her to play she will win," I promised.

He looked toward the door where Mammy had left the classroom to go back in the main part of the school with Reena.

"Tell her I want to see her about something," he said quietly.

I agreed eagerly and went in search of Mammy while he rearranged the board for a new game.

"Mammy, Mr. Anton want to see you a minute," I said when I went in to her. She looked up from what she was doing with furrowed brows.

"What you went and do?" Reena asked suspiciously.

"Nothing. He just ask to see her," I said.

Mammy wiped her hands on her skirt then went over to Mr. Anton's classroom.

"You want to see me Sir?" she said.

"Have a seat Mrs. Teekasingh," he said and adjusted his glasses.

"I'm not quite finished with the classrooms you know Sir," she said and was reluctant to sit.

"That's alright. You need to take a break anyway. Can't be work work all the time," he said and smiled.

Mammy sat down reluctantly.

"Just one game of draughts," he said indicating the game before him.

"Is Milo put you up to this?" she asked suspiciously.

"He said you were very good at it and I'm dying for some competition," he said.

"But I got work to finish Mr. Anton," she said and was preparing to get up.

"You can call me Larry. Look, if you win I'll finish the sweeping myself and you can sit down here and relax instead," he said and placed a five dollar note on the table.

"Plus, you get five dollars for your effort, win or lose," he added.

Mammy looked at him then turned to look at me but I was hiding out of her sight.

"Okay Ms. Teekersingh?" he said pleadingly.

"Call me Yvette," she said. She sighed and settled down in the chair. "Is your money."

"Your move," he said.

"No, you move first," she said.

"I'm the challenger and, ladies first" he said with a smile.

Mammy moved a piece and he countered immediately. The first combined ten moves were made in the space of just as many seconds before they slowed down to some serious thinking. Mr. Anton hunched over the board in concentration while Mammy pulled up her chair closer and crossed her legs like she does when thinking deeply.

When I went home that afternoon I had a dollar and ten cents total. I had enough to buy more than two more comic books. After I had a snack I skipped over to the Yard. Most of the boys had gone by the cinema so I went out to the Backdam. I ran into Tillam who wanted his twenty cents. I don't know what he wanted it for but he seemed bent on having it that afternoon. I would have to find change for the dollar but I didn't want him knowing I had a whole dollar. I looked down the street. Lea and Indira were coming in from Commercial school.

"What if I showed you something worth twenty cents," I said.

"What?" he asked suspiciously.

"A girl."

"You got a naked skin book?" he asked hopefully.

"Better than that," I said. He looked at me with unbelief.

"Where?" he said doubtfully.

"I go show you but you can't make no noise," I said.

I led him into my yard, around the back, and into the wood shed. Then we crept to the loft quietly. I indicated the bathroom below.

"I hope is not your Nanny coming in there you know," he whispered.

"Naw," I said. I knew Mammy and Reena had their baths since coming in. Raj was off to football, Dil was out at the cinema and Doogoo was off somewhere again, probably visiting the hospital to check if Rubberdog was admitted. That left See, Lea and Indira.

We talked quietly up there for a couple of minutes and sure enough someone came in the bathroom. It was Lea. I took turns with Tillam spying through the crack. After she had gone Tillam was so thrilled he wanted to know when we could do it again. I told him it would cost him twenty five cents. I began thinking this could be a money maker for me if I was careful.

"What is that red thing she got on she chest?" I asked.

"That is a birthmark boy," he said easily. "Some people get molds and some get birthmarks. I know a girl get a big black birthmark on half she face. She face always look like it want washing."

"So that's what that was. I thought she get burn or something," I said.

"I going and find a work somewhere else," Sunil said when we met that night in our room with Reena.

"What you find out?" Reena asked.

"Is true what Milo say. Half me salary going to pay for groceries," he complained bitterly.

"Where you go get another work?" she asked.

"I don't know. Somewhere that Doogoo ain't know about."

"Well, don't bother leave Bassit 'til you get this other job."

"Why you don't try get a job with the post office?" I asked. Reena looked at me suspiciously.

"Is not so easy," Sunil said.

"You give Mammy any money yet?" asked Reena.

"Not yet. I put all in the bank today until I get the rest Bassit owe me," he said.

"You ain't go ever see the rest," I said but he was smiling at something else.

"I see the prettiest girl in the Bank today," he marveled.

"Which Bank?" she asked.

"Barkleys Bank on the Waterside," he said.

"She was just in the bank or she work there?" I asked.

"She work there. She open my account for me," he said proudly.

Chapter Eleven

"What she name?" I asked.

"Alice something," he said. I was about to say something and Reena motioned to me to be quiet.

"What she look like?" Reena asked.

"She got long curly hair and dreamy eyes, real beautiful. I sure she prettier than that damn Bucky ayo always talking about in the Yard," he said.

"I bet you a dollar she ain't prettier than Bucky," I said.

"You ain't got no money to bet," he said.

"I bet you a dollar this girl ain't prettier than Bucky," I repeated and took out my dollar.

"Alright," he said and took out two dollars and gave one to Reena. "You hold the bet."

I gave my dollar to Reena.

"How we go know now?" he said.

"I'll show you the girl in the Yard tomorrow and then we go decide," Reena said and a snicker escaped me.

"Doogoo had another meeting today but Rubberdog didn't turn up," She continued.

"I think he know why. I got a feeling Doogoo she self would break he legs them," Sunil said.

"And I hear she talking about bringing a boy and he parents for Lea tomorrow," she said soberly.

"You mean like a marriage?" Sunil said.

"What else you think," she said.

I wondered if it was the man Lea was with in the Gardens.

"Lea know about that?" I asked.

"I don't know," Reena said.

"She better bring a boy and marrid See off," Sunil said.

"Why? Because she and Indira older?" Reena asked.

"No, but ah see See talking to a boy at DC office," Sunil said confidentially.

"You sure was she?" Reena asked.

"Yea, I was dropping goods in Vryman's scheme when I see them. And was a black boy too," he said.

"Oh jeese, Doogoo would get fits if she know that," Reena said.

"But why Doogoo want marrid off Lea first and she's the youngest?" he said.

"Who's the biggest one?" I asked.

"See and Indira older," Reena said.

"Who older, See or Indira?" I asked.

"They is twins, you jackass," Sunil said.

"Well how I supposed to know that," I complained.

"Is true," Reena commented. "They ain't nothing alike. One dark, one fair and they don't resemble."

I considered telling them what I knew about Lea in the Gardens but decided against it. Reena might tell Mammy and being Lea's aunt, Mammy would feel obligated to tell Doogoo.

Chapter Twelve

"Cricket bat" Tuesday arrived. I only had three comic books but I had the resources to get the other two. I was going to wait until the Pinnies approached me before bringing that up. But so far neither of them mentioned it. Could it be that they had forgotten about it? Not according to Tillam.

During that morning break Mr. Anton sent for me.

" Yes Sir?"

"Come here," he said and I could see something was weighing on his mind. He guided me next to an open cupboard where it was more private.

"Where Yvette...um, your mother learn to play draughts like that?" he said quietly with admiration in his eyes.

"I don't know Sir, but she was always good at it," I said honestly.

"Yes, she is good at it," he said with his thoughts far away. "Tell her I will play her again this afternoon."

"I bet you a dollar..." I began.

"Oh no, you're not getting another dollar from me," he said and laughed. He walked away and left me there. Well, that well dried up in a hurry for me.

I went home for breakfast that midday with the Pinnies still not asking me anything about the book. After breakfast I was standing in the yard by Spanner waiting for Tillam to finish eating and come out when Spanner noticed the three comic books I had tucked under my shirt. I did not leave them in school for I was not about to have them stolen, especially when that day was the deadline.

"Lemme see them?" he said. I reluctantly took them out and let him see them.

"Oh core, these brand new. I ain't read them yet," he said. "Lend me nuh."

"You mad!" I exclaimed and made an attempt to retrieve them.

"I go lend you some 'till I done read them," he pleaded and hid them behind his back.

"You ain't got no comic books," I said and tried to grab at them again.

"Come see," he said secretly. "But don't tell nobody."

I followed him into his home. He went to his bed and hoisted the fiber mattress to reveal layers of comic books spread all over the metal spring base of the bed. There must have been close to a hundred books there.

"All them books here is your own?" I marveled.

"And I got more in cardboard boxes under the bed," he boasted.

"And all this time I busin' me head to find comics and you sleeping on them?" I said with some degree of exasperation.

"I ain't know you want comic books," he said.

"Tillam know?" I asked.

"Tillam don't know I got comics," he said sheepishly.

"None of them boys know?" I asked.

"Only maybe Dillip and Chinee Roy. I does ex with Roy."

"Well, if you want borrow my three brand new ones you got to lend me five," I said. "Besides, them is old books you got here."

"Which five?" he asked. This fellow was pretty mean with his comics. I guessed that was why he had so many.

I went through the pile and selected a Spiderman, a superman, a daredevil, one Fantastic Four and a Captain America. We agreed it was a deal.

When I went back to school that midday I went straight to the Pinnies with the five books. Actually Li'l Pinny was chasing a soccer ball on the grassy ground with more than a dozen hollering boys, while Big Pinny was parked under the doungs tree reading a comic. The cricket bat was leaned against the base of the tree.

Chapter Twelve

"Big Pinny, I bring you' five comics," I said confidently. He lowered the Rawhide Kid he was reading and looked at the books I presented. He grunted approval on examining each one, signifying that he had not read them yet.

"So we even?" I said.

"We even," he said and put the books under his substantial buttocks. He continued reading.

"You want another five?" he asked.

"What you got?"

He reached into a hollow in the trunk of the tree and pulled out a stack of about fifteen comic books. I supposed that was only temporary storage while he was in that vicinity. I looked through the lot and selected three: another Spiderman, a Superman and an Archie comic.

"You can take more than that you know." I selected eight in all. "See you next Tuesday," he squeaked and went back to reading his book.

That afternoon when I went home I was eating lunch when See told me Bucky was asking for me. I was shocked. I wondered what she could have wanted with me but then I remembered the last time I was near her Dillip made an ass of me, making that remark about me not being able to read. I decided I wasn't going across to the Yard that afternoon.

I noticed Lea was home and had not gone to Commercial school that day. She looked pretty upset and instead of being in her room like she usually was, she spent most of the day downstairs moping.

I went in my room and took out three comic books. Then I took out my drawing notebook and began to draw. I had just finished one comic and was about to start the other when someone called to See. She went out to the gate and spoke with the person quietly. For a moment I wondered if Christopher had the nerve to come here to See but

194

dismissed that thought, for the voice was too feminine. See came back in and peeped in my room.

"Where Sunil?" she asked.

"He ain't come home yet," I said and went back to my drawing.

She went back out to the gate and told the person something quietly. I figured it must have been Chandra. See came back in and went to the kitchen.

Shortly after I felt the presence of someone at the doorway to my room and looked up. Bucky stood there in her uniform, patiently watching me. My eyes opened wide in surprise.

"So, you not talking to me no more?" she said quietly.

I sat up on the bed and looked at her bashfully.

"I want to talk to you about something," she said and came into the room. "I can sit down?" she said. I nodded. She came and sat on my bed. She had her thick black hair combed back and pinned at the sides. Her uniform acted like it knew it was adorning a hell of a figure. Her legs had an artificial orange-brown color which was caused by the stockings she wore. The faint scent of perfume reached me.

"Damn, this girl really is beautiful," I thought.

"Somebody rob the bank today?" I asked, having thought of nothing else to say.

"No Milo, nobody robbed the bank," she said with a smile. "But is nice to know you're concerned about my day."

I swallowed and looked down at my hands.

"Milo, remember the other day when one of the boys said you couldn't read?" she said and I could see she was struggling to find a soft way of approaching the subject.

I nodded and looked away in embarrassment.

"I know how bad you felt that day. So if I am your friend... I am your friend, right?" she said and smiled. Those dimples appeared again. I nodded and looked down at my hands again.

Chapter Twelve

"If I am your friend then I'm supposed to help you, right?" I nodded again. She lifted my chin with soft fingers. "I don't like to see you get embarrassed and I felt like knocking that boy in his head when he said that," she said.

" For true?" I said and smiled, feeling good to know that Bucky was willing to go to war for a little nobody like me.

"Honest. But then I thought I won't be there the next time someone else embarrass you about that. So then I thought, since I used to help children to read when I was back home, why not help my friend Milo," she paused to let all this sink in. " But, you have to be willing to do it. I don't want to do it if you don't want to," she said.

"But what if I still can't learn, you won't be disappointed?" I said. This was not a girl I wanted to disappoint.

"As long as you try I won't be disappointed Milo," she said.

"But all them teachers try and I still can't read," I explained.

"Sometimes is the way people explain things to you. I'm not a teacher but I did this before. You will try?" she said. I was flattered that my learning to read meant so much to her.

"Alright," I said.

"Good," she leaned back, apparently relieved. "And no more hiding from me, right?" I nodded.

"In the afternoon when you finish playing you will come over at me with a notebook and pencil and we will work a li'l bit at a time, Alright?" she said then seemed to notice my artwork.

"You drew this?" she asked. I nodded. She flipped the pages slowly as she looked at some more of my work.

"This is nice. You draw like an adult," she said. I blushed. "Lucky used to draw when he was back home."

"He don't draw no more?" I said.

"Hardly."

Just then Sunil pulled up at our door. His eyes popped out and his mouth opened and closed a couple of times like a goldfish that had suddenly found its bowl of water yanked from under it.

"Oh, sorry. I have to go," Bucky said and got up to leave.

"Thanks for coming Miss Bucky," I said.

"See you tomorrow," she said and left. He pointed after her and still couldn't say anything until she was out of the yard.

"You owe me a dollar, you jackass," I said and ran out into the street laughing before he could get hold of me.

"Let we go over the Yard to see Bucky before it too late," Reena said from the doorway of our room that evening after Sunil came in off the street.

"I tired," Sunil declared and threw himself on the bed.

"He shame. Bucky was here today," I said and laughed. Reena found it funny too.

"I still say the girl at the Bank prettier," he said stubbornly.

"Why you don't just admit you didn't know is the same Bucky you met at the Bank," Reena said.

"So the bet scrap, because ayo know all the time is the same person," he argued.

"'Scrap' me tail!" Reena said. "You are the one shouldn't ah bet since you never saw Bucky before and we did."

"How long ayo know is the same person?" asked Sunil.

"Since you say how pretty she was and she work at the bank," I said.

"Wha' she was doing here anyway," Sunil said. "And with you of all people."

"That is between me a Bucky," I said smugly.

197

"She teaching him to read and write," Reena said bluntly.

"How you know that?" I blurted out in genuine surprise.

"She done talk to Mammy about it already," Reena said.

That let a bit of the wind out of my sail.

"Aye, guess what," Reena began excitedly and looked around outside before coming quickly into the room and sitting down on my bed. "Lea had a suitor today."

" A who?" I asked.

"Aunty Doogoo bring a boy and he mother. They make a marrid match for Lea," she whispered.

"Wha' he look like?" Sunil asked.

"Very Country-ish," Reena said. "He look like he mother just haul he out the canfield and give he a shirt and pants before he come down with she."

"He tall, short, fair or what?" I asked.

"He regular like. He look nice. He got same complexion like she and he got a beard," she said.

"He's a Fullerman?" Sunil asked, referring to a Muslim man.

"You mad? Aunty Doogoo is Hindu. She rather drop dead before she let one of she daughters marry a Fullerman," Reena said.

"He father ain't come?" I asked.

"No, just he mother."

"Wha' she look like?" Sunil asked.

"She kinda fatish. Rich looking. I think they own a rice mill or something," she explained.

"They from Corentyne?" asked Sunil.

"I think so. Wherever they from Doogoo used to live there before. Besides, with them owning a rice mill is either Corentyne or Essequibo they from," Reena said.

"So what Lea do?" I asked.

"Well, Doogoo and the mother and the boy sat down in the living room and talk while See serve them refreshment. Then they bring in Lea," Reena explained.

"So she didn't go to school today?" Sunil asked.

"Naw, Doogoo keep she home to present her," said Reena. "She dress up nice in a yellow Sari."

"But she ain't look too happy when I see she just now," Sunil said.

"The boy like she?" I asked.

"I think so. First he was staring at See," Reena began.

"Maybe he thought See was the girl he go marrid," I explained.

"Well he look more than happy when they bring in Lea."

"He must be glad because Lea fair skin," Sunil observed.

"So when they go marrid?" I asked.

"I don't know," Reena said and shrugged.

"Might be as early as next month," Sunil said.

"So soon? They got to kill sheep and all that," I said.

"How long it go take to kill a sheep," said Sunil.

"Anyway, Doogoo mention Indira and the mother say she got a sister who got a suitable son. So we might get a double wedding," she said.

"Next boy she bring in here might be for you Reena," I said. Reena sucked-her-teeth in disgust.

"By the way, Doogoo say you still got to carry Nanny for a walk some afternoons," she said maliciously.

"When they burying the old man?" asked Sunil.

"They cremating he tomorrow. They got to do post mortem first," she said.

"Wha' is post mortem?" I wanted to know.

"They go cut he open to see why he dead," Sunil explained.

"They can't see he get burn up in the fire?" I asked.

"How you know somebody ain't kill he before the fire," said Sunil. "Suppose somebody kill he then burn down the place."

"We can go see them cut he open?" I asked hopefully.

"Why you go want see that," Reena said distastefully.

"Then he can't eat for a week after that. Let he go," said Sunil.

"They find out what start the fire?" Reena asked. My heart started beating so strongly I folded my arms across my chest for fear they might see how affected I was by that question and start to wondering why.

"Naw, they say maybe is cigarette or something," said Sunil.

"Doogoo say Sooklall borrow a set of money to build a new shop," Reena said.

"Is who lend he all that money?" asked Sunil.

"I don't know. They must be lend he because he go get insurance money from the fire anyway. But they does take time to give you your money," Reena speculated.

"Where you get that chain from," I asked Reena. She had leaned forward in her seated position and the thin gold chain was visible. She sat up quickly, straightened her blouse and hid the chain in the process.

"What chain?" she said with guilt written all over her face.

"You wearing a gold chain," Sunil pointed out.

"Is nothing," she said.

"Bertie giving you gifts already?" I said and laughed.

"Milo shut up," she said but was blushing.

"That is the postboy?" Sunil said.

"Yea, Bertie Bhagwandin," I said.

"Aunty Doogoo know about that?" Sunil asked.

"What that got to do with Aunty Doogoo. Besides, we does only talk," Reena said.

"If he giving you gold chain that can't be talk alone," Sunil said.

"What you think I doing other than just talking," Reena said and seemed annoyed.

"I don't know. But if I give a girl a gold chain you bet I ain't only talking with she," Sunil bragged.

"Chandra have a gold chain," I said quietly.

"Yea, but I ain't give she that," he said without thinking.

"I wonder which boy give she that," I said.

"And what she do to get it," Reena said with a smirk.

Sunil looked at us without responding.

"Is just a chain he want me to keep. He ain't give me," Reena said then took out the chain and fingered it.

"That is gold or brass," I said maliciously.

"Is gold you clown," Reena snapped.

"Mammy know?" I asked.

"She ain't must know," she said. "I gone. This room turning like a police station now with all them questions."

With that she got up and left.

"How long you notice Chandra wearing a chain?" Sunil asked thoughtfully.

"I don't know. Maybe she had it all the time," I said and settled down to do some drawing again. "Maybe is she mother give she it."

"Yea. Yes, is she aunty give she it," Sunil said and marveled. "Why I didn't think of that before."

"Why you don't ask she when you see she," I said.

"Yea, I go ask she," he said with some relief.

The following afternoon Doogoo hired a car and took Nanny and Indira somewhere up the Corentyne for "Gandhi's" cremation. They left in the morning and never returned until night. Lea left for school that morning but returned home after Doogoo left. She changed her clothes and went out again. Raj came home that midday and for the first time Alicia came in the yard to him.

During the morning break I was sitting on the silver cannon in the gardens with Tillam. Squingee had stopped at one of the vendors over in the school yard and had not come across yet.

Chapter Twelve

"So you in business with them Pinnies now," said Tillam.

"I could ex them books now so is no problem," I said.

"Once you can get the books exchanged is no problem. Just don't owe them no books. Who you exing with, Roy? 'Cause is only Roy got comic books down the street," he said.

"Yea," I said and remained tight lipped about my source.

Just then Squingee came up to us. He was sucking on a stretcher.

"Is so long you take to buy one li'l stretcher?" Tillam said. "You buy for we?"

Squingee stretched out a hand and rubbed his fingers against each other, signifying he needed money. Tillam sucked-his-teeth.

"You' cousin in the gardens again," Squingee remarked.

"Oh, is over there you been," Tillam said.

"Who?" I asked.

"Which other cousin you does see over there," Squingee said.

I left them and scooted over there. Tillam was not interested in coming. Lea sat on one of the benches with her legs crossed and one hand propping her chin. She was alone and seemed to be waiting for someone. She had on the same deep orange slinky knee-length dress she had changed into that morning. She looked at a couple some distance away locked in each other's arms. Just when I was thinking to sneak my way over there for a closer view the man who I supposed was her boyfriend, came riding up on a bicycle. He put the bicycle on the stand and she got up and kissed him on the lips. They sat down again.

"How you get away?" she asked.

"I tell them ah sick," he said with a smile. "You looking tense."

Once Upon A Time In Berbice

"Me mother bring home a boy for me to marrid yesterday," she said soberly. "We got to do something quick."

Lea

"How far away they plan the wedding?" he asked.
"Next two months time."
"I can't leave me wife so quick," he said.
She looked away and seemed frustrated.
"Well ah go just have to stop seeing you and just settle down with this boy," she said sadly.
"If you marrid to him we go still meet secretly?" he said with a smile. She turned and looked at him distastefully.
"What you take me for," she said angrily.

Chapter Twelve

"I just joking Lea. I can't let **meri mehbooba** do that," he said softly and seemed very concerned. "If you marrid this boy ah go kill meself."

She looked away unimpressed.

"Alright, give me three weeks," he said.

"Three weeks? How you go leave she in three weeks and for a whole year you couldn't do it," she said.

"Now that I realize I can lose you I'm desperate."

"Oh? So you weren't desperate before. Only for what you can get."

"Lea, don't be like that. And you know you does enjoy yourself as much as I do," he said and played with her hair. Lea blushed and looked away. "You thought about what we talked about?"

"What happen to right here like we always do?" she said and seemed in lighter spirits.

"It not private enough. I want..." He leaned into her and whispered something in an ear. She blushed and looked away.

"Today?" she said with a smile.

"We got the whole day," he said and ran one hand up and down her narrow back.

"Where we would go?" she said. He had one hand playing with the knee of her crossed leg.

"We could go up Rosehall," he said.

"Corentyne? You mad? That is where me mother gone today," she said in alarm.

"Well Canje is out," he said.

"Yea, you don't want you' wife seeing you with me," she said and pouted.

"Then let we go across the river then," he said. "Nobody know us over there."

"Suppose somebody recognize we on the ferry?" she said.

"We just walk separate so nobody would notice," he said easily. Let me drop you by the stelling road then you walk in and I'll walk in behind you," he said. "I got to stop and buy something first anyway."

" You ain't buy it yet? You ain't buying that with me standing with you. People go make conclusions."

"Alright, I go get it when you go in the stelling."

She seemed delighted with that plan. He kissed her on the lips again and they left on the bicycle.

That afternoon we stood around in the yard waiting for Chinee Roy to come with a new cricket ball. The old ball was struck into the next street and we could not find it. Roy had promised to get us another ball. While we were waiting Tillam nudged me and indicated a woman passing up the street going toward the Backdam. She was heavyset and had the biggest backside I had ever seen.

"Oh core!" I said. " That's the biggest backside in New Amsterdam."

The other boys stopped talking and looked. I should have noticed they weren't laughing. Tillam chuckled.

"You could rest two of Ms. Olga whole glass case on that backside and they won't fall off," I continued. That they found funny and guffawed uneasily.

I felt my left ear ringing before I felt the sharp slap to the left side of my face. I stumbled forward and held on to my face as I looked around for the source of this assault.

Squingee was looking at me angrily with tears welling up in his eyes. He looked like he was about to slap me again but he refrained.

"What you do that for!" I shouted.

"That is Squingee' mother, you idiot," Coco said seriously.

Tillam continued laughing.

"Slap Tillam, not me," I complained.

"I ain't say nothing 'bout he mother," Tillam pointed out.

Chapter Twelve

"No, but is you encourage me," I said, still holding on to my face which was turning numb on that side.

"You ain't know Tillam yet," Spanner said. "He go lead you in trouble then pull he self out."

I left them and went out to the head of the street. The afternoon show was on already at Gaiety. I went to the doorman by the main stairs and asked for Dil.

"What you want Dil for?" he asked.

"Is me Uncle," I said. He looked at me doubtfully but seemed to remember me with Dil before. He sent me up to Dil.

I went up the stairs to Balcony then to the door. I knocked. The man who was there the last time I was up there opened the door. I could feel the hot smoke filled air in the room.

"Dil gone out. He not here," he said above the noise of the projector and closed the door again.

I had nothing else to do so I walked in the Balcony section and sat there. There were very few people in there. Some kind of secret agent movie was on. After a while I got bored. I left and went out back to the street. Lea was now coming in.

"Doogoo come back yet?" she asked anxiously.

"No," I said as I headed down the street with her. She seemed relieved.

"Where you went?" I asked.

"Where I go everyday, to school," she said.

"In this dress?"

"We didn't have to wear uniform today," she said as she looked me full in the face. "You plan to be a policeman?"

"Eh?"

"Why you asking me all them questions."

"I just wondering what Aunty Doogoo go say if she know you went out in a dress today," I said indifferently.

"Listen you, if you mention anything to Doogoo about me wearing a dress today I go skin you li'l tail for you," she hissed at me as she poked me in the chest with a stiff finger. She had stopped to deliver this threat.

"Alright," I said without showing any reaction to the threat.

She smiled uneasily, probably realizing she had overreacted.

"Is just that people jump to the wrong conclusion when they hear certain things," she explained.

I didn't respond. She turned into our yard when she got there and I stood by the gate, undecided on whether to return to the Yard with the boys or go home. I decided to go home and get my notebook which I hid under my shirt and went over to Bucky for my new reading lessons.

That weekend Raj took me, Sunil, and Reena to see "In Like Flint" and "Fu Manchu." Half way through the second movie the whole cinema was plunged into darkness. The town was experiencing a blackout. After we waited for five minutes people started coming out of the cinema since it was getting too hot inside with the fans being off. It was beginning to seem like it was not a mere glitch in the supply but a longer interruption.

When we came out it was dark outside with the street lights all out. The only sources of light were the flambos on the stalls of the vendors in front of the cinema. The boys from the street had congregated at the head of the street, having nothing to do in the dark in the Yard. Eventually we got bored of playing in the dark and went down the street. Reena came in with Raj while Sunil remained at the head of the street, having run into Chandra. Dil had come home seeing he had nothing to do but wait for the power to return. See had lit a kerosene oil lamp downstairs and there was a smaller lamp lit upstairs. I followed the boys to the head of the street out at the

Chapter Twelve

Backdam road where we sat in the dark on the culvert over the concrete drain.

We argued about West Indies cricket and who were the best batsmen and bowlers. While this conversation was in progress there was a disturbance in the water below and behind us.

"I ain't know it had so big fish in there," Tillam remarked.

"Ah shoulda walk with me fishin' rod," Dillip said as we looked down blindly in the dark toward the black water below us. We could barely see each other much less the drain itself. As the conversation continued we heard the commotion repeated a couple of times and, judging from the sound, it sounded like some really big fishes were in that water. A car came up the Backdam toward us. As it approached the bright beam from the headlights was thrown on us.

"You nasty son-of-a...!" Spanner exclaimed and jumped up. We all jumped up and looked to where Spanner had his attention. In the glare of the headlight we caught Coco smiling sheepishly as he was in the process of pulling up his pants and withdrawing his bare buttocks from where he had it hung over the culvert and had been stooling overboard into the water below.

"A snake shoulda' crawl up your tail pipe," Squingee remarked.

"Alyuh still want go for alyuh fishing rod?" he asked and grinned. We raced away from him and up the street.

Just when we thought things couldn't get more exciting in the dark things began to lively up. We heard loud drunken singing coming from the head of the street by the cinema. We began to speculate as to who it could have been but then power came back and the street was flooded with light. Down the street came Uncle Inchan and Mr. Jacobs from across the Yard. Uncle Inchan was singing louder while he struggled to push his bicycle. Mr. Jacobs was swaying from side to side and putting one leg before the other appeared to be a major task for him.

When they got to our gap and in front of the Yard they said drunken farewells to each other. Mrs. Jacobs was complaining loudly to everyone about her husband coming home long after schedule and questioned where he was all afternoon since she was trying to reach him. There was some accusation of him seeing another woman each pay day. He explained drunkenly that he was in Dixie's Rum shop all afternoon and she accused him of lying since she was there seven o'clock to check for him and he was not there. She repeated her accusation of him probably being with some woman. She then declared that he was not going to come in her house until he had a bath.

This was a source of amusement for us since we could all see he was so drunk he could hardly stand much less undress himself for a bath. But she insisted. He mumbled something about women being "heartless" but stumbled his way toward the bathrooms at the back of the Yard. We followed him as he struggled to get to the bathrooms and began undressing. She brought the clothes into which he was to change. With Mr. Jacobs hogging all the attention there wasn't much of an audience for Uncle Inchan to perform his song and dance routine. He sulkily called it a night and stumbled into the house.

Laughter erupted in the Yard when Mr. Jacobs stripped down to his underwear. It was not his underwear at all. It was a pink ladies panty with frills around the bottom. He looked down at the thing with a puzzled expression as though he had no idea how that got on him. Mrs. Jacobs screeched at him, for she now had proof that he was with some woman and voiced the opinion that the blackout was a blessing from God to reveal his dirty deeds. Apparently he had hurriedly dressed after the blackout came. He had no idea he had put on this woman's underwear.

Chapter Twelve

Chapter Thirteen

Mr. Abrams turned down the street quietly in his shiny black Morris Minor, hoping he could crawl all the way home and avoid the, as he called them, street urchins. But some of the children spotted him and out they came, running and screaming behind the car with their hands all over it. Mr. Abrams cursed at them all the way to his yard before they dispersed. Some dashed across to the Yard where they took up residence by Ms. Olga's, hoping she would have mercy on them and throw them a morsel of one of her snacks.

Mammy had clothes to press, so she left Reena to finish that up while she took me with her to her third job. We headed to Mr. Anton's residence which was in Wapping Lane. It was a half street between Main Road and Backdam. Mr. Anton's house was a modest one-flat house which was not on posts like most other houses. It was wooden and looked very colonial, having been made in that era. The once cream paint was weathered. There was a little verandah in front. A woman in her late thirties was sitting there doing embroidery. She was cocoa brown, had an afro, and while she might have been a "looker" in her earlier days, lines of worry and fatigue now creased her oval face.

"'Morning," Mammy said to her as we went up short steps onto the verandah. I did the same. She looked at us critically and did not answer. She looked at Mammy up and down without stopping her knitting.

"You the woman Larry expect to come to clean?" she said.

"Yes," Mammy said.

"He inside," she said and returned her attention to her knitting.

Chapter Thirteen

Mammy kicked off her shoes and went in. I left my slippers with her shoes and followed her in.

"Mr. Anton?" Mammy called.

"In a minute," he answered from one of two bedrooms.

After a while he came out dressed in a rumpled gabardine pants and white T shirt. He smiled when he saw Mammy.

"Morning Yvette," he said sheepishly.

"Morning Larry," Mammy said, almost mockingly.

"You met my sister outside?" he said with a smile and seemed slightly embarrassed.

"Yes. Very friendly, unlike her brother," Mammy said sarcastically.

"Sorry about that. That's Rhonda. She don't really want me to get any help around the house. She still think she can do all that but she really can't," he said quietly.

"So, where to start," Mammy said.

My attention was wandering around the room. Although the windows were all open the room was still in semi-darkness because of all the trees in the yard and the thick curtains over the windows. There were three chairs in the small drawing room; two short ones and a settee. There was a center table with ornaments sitting on an elaborate piece of pink and white embroidery. Against the partition was a cabinet with fancy dinner wares and sitting on top were a couple of trophies. I could see the doors to two bedrooms and beyond that the kitchen was to the back.

Mammy started in the kitchen while Mr. Anton showed me where the garbage was. He said he had to go out but would soon be back. When we began working I could see there was a toilet and bathroom off the short corridor to the kitchen.

Mammy made short work of cleaning the kitchen. Then she tackled the bathroom. I took a break and went out the kitchen door into the backyard. There were clothes lines running from one tree to the other. Just by the high zinc back fence there were more trees there; one of them being a jamoon tree laden with the purple fruit. I climbed up this tree and found a comfortable seat in the fork of two branches. As I sucked the purple flesh off each jamoon I popped in my mouth, I looked around from this high vantage point. I could see over the fence and into the back of the house in the next street, Coburg street. It was a one flat house like Mr. Anton's but concrete and painted white.

That was when I heard Rhonda's voice ring out from the front.

"Aye you Harvey, if you blasted dog come in here and shit up in me yard again you coming over here to clean it," she shouted to someone.

"How you know is me dog? I see other dogs does be in you' yard," countered Harvey.

"I see you' blasted dog shitting in me yard. Nothing ain't wrong with me two eyes," she bellowed.

"My dog been home whole day yesterday," said Harvey.

" If your dog tell you that he's a damn liar just like you."

"Well do what the hell you want. It ain't me dog."

"Let me catch your dog in here again see if I don't castrate he," threatened Rhonda.

"You couldn't even catch a cold much less me dog, you one-legged witch," Harvey retorted.

"Come up here and tell me that!" Rhonda raged. "Come up here and say that to me face!"

I didn't hear anything from Harvey.

"One leg or not, I would kick your fat backside so far you would need a map to find your way back home," said Rhonda. She continued fretting while Harvey had apparently gone about his business.

I heard Mammy cautiously call me. I quickly climbed down the tree and scampered back to the kitchen. Mammy quietly told me to stay with her and not stray about the yard. I think she wanted to avoid tangling with Rhonda, seeing the latter was not too happy about us coming to clean against her wishes.

Mr. Anton came back when we were tidying up the living room. He went into both bedrooms and brought out things to wash. Mammy took them out back where there was a wash tub by the stand pipe there. He brought out scrubbing board, brush and soap then Mammy went to work. She told me I could go home and collect the clothes from Reena to carry to the people in Cooper's Lane.

I went around the side of the house and to the front, saying bye to Rhonda who ignored me.

As I went on the Backdam I ran into Chandra who was about to go down Coburg street.

"Where you coming from?" she asked.

"Nowhere," I said. "Where you going?"

"Nowhere," she said. "Where your brother?"

"Which one?" I said.

"Boy stop playing the ass with me and answer me. Where' Sunil?"

"He gone by he girlfriend," I said.

She narrowed her eyes at me then sucked her teeth.

"Tell him I go drop by this afternoon," she said.

I continued walking toward home and she remained standing there by the head of Coburg Street watching me. After a while she went down the street.

When I reached home Reena had clothes packed and ready to take for a man named Mr. Neusome. He lived in Coburg Street. It was easy to find since it was in the street before Mr. Anton's. I walked with the box on my head up the Backdam to Mr. Newsome's place. Mammy had said if he's not home to leave it by the back door to his house.

The house was a one-storied concrete flat with a well kept hedge to the front and many small trees around the house, some of them being cherry trees. It was then I saw the jamoon tree on the other side of the high zinc fence and realized that this was the house I had seen from up in the same jamoon tree. I clanged the gate twice and called for Mr. Neusome. Nobody answered. No dog barked. I opened the gate and quietly made my way to the back of the house. I thought I heard water running somewhere inside. I put the box by the backdoor and was making my way back to the front but around the other side of the house, when I spotted a window cracked open. I could still hear the water running somewhere in the house. I wondered if this man had fallen in the shower and was unconscious or something. The water was suddenly turned off. I peeked through the window and my mouth fell open.

There was a white embroidered blind on the other side of the window through which I could see. Chandra was lying on her stomach on the bed in her birthday suit, thumbing through a magazine. In my surprised state what stood out about her body were the two three inch welts she had on the upper left cheek of her buttocks. It looked like a healed cut that was inflicted with the same implement at the same time since they were symmetrical and side by side like the number "eleven."

"Somebody there?" I heard a male voice to the front of the house. I stood still by the window and did not answer. I figured if Chandra heard my voice she would recognize me. There was silence then I heard a door close. I took a peep in the window again and Mr. Newsome had come back into the room. He was a thin Portuguese man, who was probably in his late sixties. He wore a gown of some sort with baggy pants under. The sleeve of the gown was dirty with different color paint. Then I noticed he had a slender paint brush in one hand and there was a stand with what looked like a frameless picture mounted on it. But I couldn't see what was on the canvas since the back of it was facing my direction.

Chapter Thirteen

I ducked away from the window, tip-toed to the front of the yard, then climbed over the low concrete fence instead of using the gate and risk making a noise.

All the way back I replayed events in my head. No wonder she stood so long at the head of the street when I had seen her earlier that morning. She did not want me to know where she was going. I wasn't sure why she was letting this man paint her picture with her in the nude, but he must be paying her well for it.

That night Reena came into our room but Sunil was not there. He had gone out since afternoon and had not returned yet.

"What you think about Chandra?" I asked before she decided to leave.

"What you mean?" she asked and cocked her head to one side as was her habit when she was trying to figure out something.

"You like her for Sunil?"

She came and sat down on the bed.

"Well, she kinda bigger than him…" she began.

"How much years she in?"

"She about See age. She must be twenty or twenty-one."

"So why he want a girlfriend that bigger than him?"

"You should ask him," she said.

"He won't take me serious. You ask him already?"

"I ain't getting in Sunil business."

"I find she kind of strange," I said.

"What you mean strange?"

"I don't trust she. I think she does lie," I said. I was laying grounds for Reena doubting anything Chandra said in case, sometime down the road, a situation arose where it was her word against mine.

"Why you say that?" she asked cautiously.

"I think she telling Sunil a pack of lies to get money from him."

" Is funny you should say that," she said and twisted her head the other way thoughtfully.

"Why?"

"I kinda get the same feeling about her. But I just can't put me finger on what it is."

"Wha' Mammy think about Sunil running around with her?"

"Nothing much. He's a boy child so whatever he dig he self in he got to dig he way out."

I made a mental note of that, for I was also a boy child.

"You can keep a secret?" I said quietly.

"What?" she said and looked at me suspiciously. I was beginning to trust her and wondered if I could trust her with what I knew about Lea. Then I suddenly changed my mind.

"You can't tell nobody. Not even Mammy," I said.

"What's the secret?"

"You swear?"

She kissed the palm of a hand and raised it heaven ward. "I swear."

"See have a boyfriend," I whispered.

"That's it? Is about time she had one," Reena said disappointedly.

"He's a black boy name Christopher," I added.

That got her attention.

"He's black!"

"Shhhhhh! Yes, he's black."

"How you know that?" she asked suspiciously.

"She does meet him whenever she carry me out for a walk."

"Anybody else know about this?" she asked and her eyes were wide open in surprise.

"No, just See and me and now you," I said. "And we cousin Alicia."

"Alicia?" she said in surprise. "You saw Alicia? What she look like?"

"She' black," I said.

"I know that Silly. What she look like; she tall, fat, What?"

"She taller than See but brown skinned. No, she not fat," I said.

"I ain't see she since I was your age," she marveled.

"You were in New Amsterdam then?"

"No, they came by us for a day," she said. " Anyway, how Alicia know?"

"Christopher does work same place with her."

"Alright. Where she work?"

"Over at DC Office."

Reena was thoughtful for a while, then she said, "Look, if Doogoo ever find out about See and this boy don't ever mention Alicia them."

"Why?"

"Because she go think Alicia spitefully set up See with a black boy because she know how Aunty Doogoo feel about black people. They can't come here because their father black, so she go have nothing to do with them. And she don't even want people know we related to them."

"Alright."

"That's why she and Raj don't get along. Right now she mad at Mammy for leaving Sondra over there."

"When we going to see her?"

"We can get See to carry we. So See does talk with Alicia?"

"Yes, they talk like they meet steady too."

"Alright. She like this Christopher?"

"It look so."

"If Aunty Doogoo only find out she go marry See off quick quick."

That night Sunil came in well after twelve.

"Where you went so late. Mammy been asking that whole night," I lied.

"Mammy ask where I went? I is a working man. I could stay out how long I want," he said.

"You saw Chandra tonite?"

"We went cinema," he said.

"You carry Chandra cinema tonite?" I asked to be sure I was hearing right.

"Yea, just dropped she home," he bragged.

"You need another girlfriend," I said.

"Naw, Chandra is Alright," he said as he prepared to go to bed.

I had thought about telling him what I saw that day but, knowing Sunil, he would run straight to her and confront her. I could not afford that since Chandra was keeping my terrible secret about the fire. I had to find another way to pry my brother loose from this girl.

The next day in school we were over at the gardens during lunch break. There was nothing to see in the lovers section so we retired to the playground since the swings were all occupied.

"Guess who like you," Tillam said with a mischievous grin.

"Who?" I was hoping he would say Sharon Cambridge, a cute dougla girl I was starting to like. But she was in my class, not Tillam's.

"Carla Tahal," he said.

"Who's Carla Tahal?"

"She in my class. Look she over there," he said and indicated a girl standing at a vendor's stall. She was a thick-set fair skinned girl with her hair combed like Reena's usually was.

I drew my teeth in disapproval.

"Me ain't like no girl with more moustache than me," I sulked. Tillam burst out laughing.

"Don't worry man. In four, five years time you go catch up with she," he said and laughed heartily. I sucked my teeth again. "Look on the bright side. She father own a shop man."

"So why you don't take she as your girlfriend," I said.

"Is you she like, not me."

"Well me ain't like she."

"Is she sister I like," he said.

"Who's she sister?"

"She does go commercial school. She does come for she in the afternoons."

I did see the sister the following afternoon. She wasn't a bad looking girl; fair like Carla but slimmer and taller. She had a bit too much on the chest for a girl that thin. I began to hatch a plan.

That afternoon in the Yard I told Tillam to tell Carla that I liked her too. The next day, after midday, I saw her looking in my direction and smiling often. If only she looked anything close to Bucky I would have been in heaven. I panicked that morning break when I realized she would want me to go talk with her. Instead, I galloped over to the Gardens and over to Lover's lane since she might very well come over to the swings to look for me. There was a couple sitting on the bench near to where I was but they were doing so poorly that I found a group of ants struggling to transport a dead marabunta more interesting.

When the bell rang to end recess I waited another couple of minutes before going back over to school. I saw her going up in her line and she waved to me. I waved back to her. That afternoon her sister came for her as soon as school was dismissed and I was relieved to see her go.

The next morning she ambushed me just as I was sneaking off to lover's lane again. Tillam was in the background smiling. I supposed he was the one who told her where to cut me off from escaping.

"Hi Milo," she said and smiled brightly. I wanted to grimace but smiled instead. Close up she was better looking than first forecasted and the moustache wasn't exactly "combable." But Bucky had spoiled my taste where girls were concerned. I found myself comparing every girl's looks with Bucky's.

Carla extended a small bar of chocolate to me. I took it hesitantly.

"I'm Carla," she said in perfect English. "Roderick said you wanted to see me."

"Roderick?"

"Tillam."

I wanted to laugh. That was Tillam's real name? Roderick? No wonder he preferred to be called Tillam.

"Well, he told me you like me," I blurted out. "So…."

"Yes, I told him so," she said boldly. "Do you like me?"

I stared blankly at her for a few seconds. This chick was as blunt as the back side of an axe.

"Yea, yes," I blubbered.

"Then we can be boyfriend and girlfriend?"

"I guess so." Then I caught myself. "If…"

"If what?"

"Well, your sister have a boyfriend?"

"You like me or my sister?" she asked with dead eyes and folder her arms determinedly.

"You. I like you. But I was wondering since your sister nice like you if I can get her to be my brother' girlfriend," I said quickly.

"Oh!" She seemed delighted by this. " No, Cheryl don't have a boyfriend."

"You think we can get them to meet up?" I said.

"Sure we can. We can have double dates," she said.

"Wha' is a date?" I asked with furrowed brows.

"I like when you do that," she said in admiration.

"Do what?"

"Do that with your brows." I put my brows down.

"We can meet here Sundays. I does come here with Cheryl every Sunday afternoon," she said.

The school bell broke up our first meeting. She wasn't that bad when I did look at her. Just that she had the tact of a redneck in an opera house. I made a note to walk with an interpreter, maybe Tillam, next time we met. Her perfect English was slowing down my thought process.

I hoped this little scheme of mine worked. If it did I had no idea how Chandra would react to Sunil parting with her. Worse yet, what would she decide to do with our little secret if she found out that I was behind it. My only consolation was that if she spilled the beans on me some of that blame would spill back on her, if she didn't lie. And I had little reason to believe she wouldn't.

Chapter Fourteen

That Thursday afternoon I was sitting at Bucky's table doing some written work she had given me. It was the first time I saw her cooking. Whenever I came over the food was already cooked.

"How come you cooking today?" I asked.

"Lucky gone to Georgetown. He coming back 'till tomorrow," she said as she chopped up seasoning.

"Lucky can cook?" I said in surprise.

"And a very good cook too. I'll tell you a secret Milo. You better learn to cook too. I know a lot of boys don't cook but a girl really likes a boy that can cook."

I heard her but just didn't see myself skipping around a kitchen in a multiflowered apron and pot spoon in hand. I looked at her amidst the smoke swirling from the hot blackened frying pan on the two burner kerosene oil stove. She had on a badly creased dress, had her hair disheveled, and was sweating from the heat in the kitchen. But even at her worst she was still beautiful. She was cooking liver stew and it smelled good.

She threw in something from a tin then stirred it in. When she had added all that she needed to, she left the pan to simmer and came back to the table to see how I was doing. She corrected a couple of things then gave me some more work.

"Ah doing good?" I asked.

"Better than I thought you would at this point," she said.

"How long it go take me to read?"

"I depends on how hard you work and how often you read. But it comes slowly. You don't just wake up a morning and Bam! You can read," she said and knocked her forehead in an animated way. I laughed and she laughed with me.

223

Chapter Fourteen

"When did you learn to read?" I asked her.

"Boy that's a good question. Maybe about the same time I learned to swim," she said. From what I had heard about people who grew up in areas up the river, that could have been two days after she was born. For most of the people living where the river is the main route of transport, cannot remember when they learned to swim since their parents made sure they could as soon as they could walk, if not earlier.

She returned to the stove to attend to the cooking. I stared at her like I tended to do from time to time, whenever I was not sure she's not looking at me.

"Why you stare at me like that sometimes?" she said without looking in my direction.

I looked away and blushed. She came back to the table and sat across from me.

"No, seriously. Why?" she repeated and was smiling.

"Bucky, you don't know how beautiful you is?" I asked and was a bit puzzled, because sometimes I got the impression that she had no clue how her looks affected people.

Surprisingly, she wasn't flattered nor amused.

"If I wasn't a good looking girl would you still like me?" she said seriously. That took me by surprise. I thought for a moment.

"Yes, I still would like you," I said.

"Why?"

"Why?"

"Yes, why would you like me if I was just plain looking or even ugly?"

"Well, because you're a nice person."

"How?"

"How? Well, you care about people... me. You care about me when even my sister can't stand me sometimes," I admitted.

"So you're saying you like me because of the kind of person I am, right?"

"Well, yes."

"That's the important thing. Not what somebody look like, but what kind of person she is. Looks come and go," she said and leaned back. Then she continued reflectively. "That's what I wonder sometimes when people carry on about how beautiful they think I am. If I weren't, would they think I'm just another Buck girl come to town? Or would they see me for who I am, regardless of looks." She wiped sweat off her forehead with her a forearm. "But you too young to understand all this," she said with a smile.

"No, I understand," I said.

"You do?" she said with an eyebrow raised.

"Well, this girl in school like me..." I began.

"Milo!" she beamed and pulled up closer to the table like a disciple to a guru. "Tell me more."

"Well," I gushed. "She say she like me but she not all that beautiful. I mean, not like you..."

"What's she like as a person?"

"Well, she' clean."

"That's a good sign."

"She bring chocolate for me."

"That mean she's kind. You think she want something from you?"

"Want something? No. No, I don't think so," I said.

"But you don't like her all that much because she's not that good looking," she said.

"Yes, but now that you tell me all this it make me think about what I should look at to like somebody," I thought aloud.

"Ah hah! So you do understand," she said with a bright smile. "When you finish your work I'll show you something. But keep it a secret. Promise?"

"Promise," I said and smiled.

Chapter Fourteen

"B-A-T bat, C-A-T cat!" chorused some of the boys just outside Bucky's door, then they burst into laughter.

"Alyuh leave Milo alone before I empty me potty on you!" Bucky shouted at them from the door.

"They'd probably like that!" I thought and burst out laughing.

Bucky looked back at me with a smile.

"It's nice to see you can laugh at that," she said quietly.

When I finished my lessons with her that evening she showed me a photograph of herself when she was younger. It was a black and white photograph of a girl about eight years old, standing next to an Amerindian lady. She had an oval face with pronounced cheekbones, scared eyes and had her hair plait in two ponytails. It was hard to believe this was Bucky at that age. She said the lady was her mother. She showed me another black and white but more recent picture of herself in her work uniform. Standing beside her was what looked like her younger self again.

"How come you have a picture of you now with your younger self standing up next to you?" I asked.

"That's me in the uniform and my little sister next to me," she explained with a smile.

"What she name?"

"Yvette."

"Yvette? That's my mother' name," I marveled.

"She just wrote common entrance exam," said Bucky.

"Where she is now?"

"She's back home."

"Oh."

"I'll tell you a secret. But you have to keep it just between me and you."

"Alright." I felt delighted that she would confide in me.

"You know I have a boyfriend?" she said with a smile.

"You?" I said and wore my surprise on my face.

"And why I can't have a boyfriend?" she asked with mocked indignation.

"Well, nobody never see you with him," I said.

"That's because he's in England," she said.

" In England! He' white?"

"Now what color has to do with it. What if he was," she said with a smile. I had mixed feelings. Not because he was white but because of the fact that she did have a love of her life at all. She got up and went inside the bedroom. She soon emerged again. She placed another black and white photograph before me. It was a picture of a very dark fellow in a low afro, and with glasses. He looked more like an overjoyed black chemist than the boyfriend of a gem like Bucky.

"And yes, he's not white," she said.

"How did you know him if he live till in England?"

"He is from right here in New Amsterdam. We went to the same high school and we used to work together at the bank too," she said and I could see she had feelings for this lad.

"So you all were boyfriend and girlfriend since High School?"

"Naw, we were just friends. We only became boyfriend and girlfriend after we started working at the bank. Then he went to England on a scholarship."

"Why you like him?"

"I love him, not like him. It's a big difference." She said in a sing song manner, then picked up the photograph and took it back inside. She came back to the table and sat.

"I love him because he cares for me more than he cares for himself," she leaned back with a hand to her cheek and was reflective. "You know he never made a pass at me until after we were working together for two years?"

"Make a pass?"

"Well, you know, try to be my boyfriend," she explained. "He thought I already had a boyfriend tucked away somewhere and he was afraid I might turn him down. And that would've messed up our friendship."

She was smiling as she recalled all this. "The funny thing was, I already liked him because of his personality but was afraid he would turn me down if I made the first move. I thought he already had a girlfriend."

"What's his name?"

"Nathaniel. Mr. Nathaniel Hinckson," she said and I could see she even enjoyed the sound of the name rolling off her tongue. I consoled myself by concluding that, at least I was second banana.

"When you all plan to marry?"

"Sooner than you think," she said then put her fingers to her lips to communicate secrecy.

That evening Reena came in our room hurriedly and sat on my bed.

"Where the cards. Take them out quick," she said excitedly.

"Wha' happen?" I asked with my curiosity peeked. Sunil got the cards and began sharing them out.

"The boy came today and ask for See," Reena blurted out excitedly as soon as the cards were shared out and Sunil had peeped around the corner to see if the coast was clear.

"Wha' you mean ask for See?" I asked.

"To marry she, you fool."

"Which boy?" Sunil asked.

"Christopher came here? He mad?" I blurted out. I was stunned.

"Who's Christopher?" asked Sunil.

"He came here this afternoon after work," she said while making a great effort to keep her voice down and contain her excitement.

"Wha' Aunty Doogoo do?" I asked.

"Who is Christopher?" Sunil repeated louder.

"Shhh! Is See' boyfriend," Reena said.

"So what so big about that?" Sunil wanted to know.

"He's black," I said.

Once Upon A Time In Berbice

"Oh! Oh? Ouch!" He got the point. "You mean the same boy I did see she talking to the other day?"

"So wha' happen?" I asked.

According to Reena, Christopher was well dressed in a suit when he came. Aunty Doogoo thought he had come from the government or something, and got her glasses. But all this time See was in the kitchen as nervous as a long tailed cat in a room full of rocking chairs. When Christopher finally stated what he was there for, Doogoo's glasses slid off her face and she stared at him for a couple of seconds before catching herself. She could not have been more stunned if Christopher had opened the conversation with a string of cuss words. According to Reena, it got so still you could hear the tap dripping all the way across in the bathroom. Then Doogoo called See who was just short of peeing herself. Christopher, meanwhile, was oblivious to the reaction he was causing and was smiling lovingly at See. Doogoo asked See if she knew Christopher and See said she had seen him pass by a couple of times. Doogoo wanted to know pass by where and See said the house. Then Doogoo asked Christopher where his parents were. Christopher said they lived in Georgetown and that he was recently transferred to New Amsterdam. She asked him what he thought their reaction would be to him wanting to marry an Indian girl. He said they were fine with anyone he wanted to marry. Then Doogoo said that, in any case, See was already spoken for and was to get married by the end of the year. Now it was See and Christopher's turn to be shocked. Tears welled up in See's eyes while Christopher looked embarrassed that See did not mention any of this to him. Doogoo apologized for See and Christopher left shortly after.

"Jeese!" Sunil exclaimed and exhaled.

"Then wha' happen?" I asked.

"Well, See stay on the chair waiting for Doogoo to show Christopher out, knowing that she going to get cuss out when Doogoo came in back," Reena explained.

"She cuss her out?" Sunil asked.

"Nasty. Ah never see Aunty Doogoo so mad yet," Reena said with eyes wide open. "And that vein stand out on she forehead. And she call Lea and Indira down to hear the cussin' out. But Lea wasn't home yet."

"What she cuss her out and say?" Sunil asked.

"A whole set of things man. First she want to know how See see this boy a couple of times and the boy done reach home here to ask for she. And she carry on about how See sneaky and scampish. Then she start on how the black boy had the nerve to come in she house and ask for one of she daughters dem. Then she ask See if she want to end up having dougla children like Aunty Nalini. Then she start cuss out Aunty Nalini too. Was a whole lot of things. Then she say she going back up Corentyne and look a boy for See," Reena concluded breathlessly.

"What a thing!" Sunil remarked.

"What See do?" I asked.

"Wha' she go do. She sit down there and take it," Reena said. "Then after Aunty Doogoo finish she went upstairs to tell Nanny. And See run upstairs and cry to Mammy."

"To Mammy?" me and Sunil chorused.

"Yes."

"Wha' Mammy tell her?"

"I don't know. They lock the door. But she was crying a lot," Reena said. "She still up there."

"Up to now?" I asked in surprise.

It must have been about two in the morning when I felt someone waking me by tugging on one of my big toes.

"What happen?" I started to fret, thinking it was Sunil.

"Shhhh! Don't wake up Sunil," See said.

"See?" I said with genuine surprise.

"Come outside," she whispered as she stood up and went out of the room quietly. I got up and followed her out the front door then into the front of the yard.

"I got to see Christopher tonite," she whispered.

" See, you mad?" I protested.

"You go drop me with daddy' bicycle," she said and indicated the bicycle which was leaning against the front fence just inside the gate. She had already rolled it out from the house. I had on my short pants and tee-shirt while she had on the plaid dress I had seen her wear before.

"You running away with him?" I was still in shock.

"No, I just got to see him tonite. I go owe you a dollar for this," she said and sounded strained and stressed.

We walked out of the street with the bicycle to the Backdam then we mounted up. See directed me up the Backdam toward Stanleytown. She said nothing but from time to time I heard her sniffle. I could tell she was still crying. Periodically I noticed her body shiver, although it was not cold.

"You' cold See?" I asked her. She shook her head in the negative. I couldn't think of anything comforting to tell her so I kept my mouth shut. Following her directions we turned into Second Scheme then to the second house in the fourth street. They were all two storied houses that were constructed alike.

"Christopher!" she called loudly in the early morning stillness. "Christopher!" she shouted again.

It was obvious See didn't care who she woke up as long as she got to see Christopher. A light came on in the house and we could hear movement.

"Who's that?" came a drowsy voice.

"Christopher come downstairs and talk to me," See said.

"See, is you that?" It was Christopher's voice.

"Just come downstairs," See said firmly and went into the yard.

Chapter Fourteen

After a while Christopher came down dressed in short pants and white vest. See walked quickly into the yard and met him at the door.

"What the hell you mean by showing up at me house just like that," she stormed. I was flabbergasted at her rage and he was obviously taken aback too.

"It was the right thing to do See," he said, "But at least you coulda tell me she done had a husband waiting for you."

"Chris, why you think I went through all that and go out of my way to meet you. Why I risk so much just to see you if it was true I done plan to get marrid by year end," she said and sounded very hurt.

"What you mean?"

"She lied Cris. She was lying. She ain't got nobody waiting to marry me. At least not until now. She just say so to make an excuse," See said and broke down crying again. He put his arms around her and she collapsed against him. And then, to my surprise, he started crying too. What was wrong with these two.

"Oh gorsh See, and I fell for that. Ah sorry," he said in a broken voice. She caressed him around the middle and buried her head in his shoulder. "I shouldn't have gone without letting you know first See. Ah sorry."

They collapsed in each others arms at the foot of the steps and cried. I was becoming embarrassed standing there and seeing this display.

"It don't matter. I love you Chris. It don't matter," she said in tears and raised her face to his. They kissed passionately. I didn't know how long they were at it but I was suddenly aware of my leg falling asleep over the bar of the bicycle.

"And to think I lie down here thinking you were just playing with me if you know you were going to get marrid already," he said and sounded so vulnerable.

"Everything I ever tell you is true Chris," she said as she leaned against him while in his arms.

"See, I want we get marrid. I don't care how your mother feel about it," he said.

"I promise you Christopher, I'm not going anywhere, I swear. I'm not getting married to anybody else but you," she said determinedly. They exchanged a few more "I love you's" before I cleared my throat to remind them that there was a third party here.

"Is that you Milo?" he said and peered at me in the dim light from the lone naked street bulb at the head of the street.

"I go tell Milo to tell you where we could meet," See said as she got up and composed herself again. "I can sleep now."

They kissed again and he followed her out to where I was on the street.

"Ah glad you came," said Chris. "You take a big risk leaving your house to come here."

"You have no idea what I would do for you," See said sincerely. He kissed her again on the lips before she got on the bicycle.

"Well, that beat any love picture I ever see," came a female voice from the dark house next door, followed by laughter.

"Some people need to go to bed and mind their own damn business," Chris grumbled.

"Is who that," See said after recovering from her initial surprise. I rode off with See on the bar of the bicycle, into the cool morning air and headed for home.

That Saturday morning Uncle Inchan was admitted to the New Amsterdam hospital. But he checked himself out by late afternoon when Dixie's Bar was in full swing. He was butt in the backside by a bad cow owned by a man named Percy who lived in Smythfield.

Chapter Fourteen

From what I heard, Uncle Inchan and Rubberdog stopped by the latter's house for what they called an "eye opener." Rubberdog's yard was well fenced with pickets, like the yard of a stockade is fenced with lumber. His gate was also high; up to eye level. When they entered the yard and locked the gate, it was not until they were almost up to the house, which was a good twenty-five yards back from the front fence, that they detected Percy's ill tempered cow was locked in the yard with them. The cow, already in a foul mood and having been placed in a strange yard which must have reminded it of the dreaded abattoir - any cow worth her salt would have educated her calf about avoiding that last station in a cow's life, and this cow's mother was apparently, no exception – took it upon herself to charge the two intruders who she figured could very well have been butchers, and make short work of them. I later learned that Doogoo and her two business associates were bitterly disappointed to hear that Rubberdog took prompt evasive action and had nimbly hopped onto the nearby chicken coop, leaving Uncle Inchan to fend for himself. So, doing the best he could for a man of his age, he managed to dodge his way back to the gate and even got the latch off when disaster struck. The bovine, at full gallop, connected with one curly horn striking the stout gate and the other the right and center half of Uncle Inchan's left buttocks, four and a half inches north northwest of the blowhole. He went sailing across the street and skidded to a halt amongst the bisi bisi grass in the trench across said street. Here he moaned until help arrived. Eventually they coaxed the cow into a noose and hauled it out of the yard.

People were still wondering how Percy's cow got into a well protected yard like Rubberdog's who always had his gate closed.

Sunday morning See gave me the dollar she promised. I got another fifty cents from Tillam and Coco after I took them up in the loft. Indira was the unlucky one then. I did my timing depending on who bathed already and who didn't. I made sure it was when Mammy or Reena had already bathed or weren't home.

There was a lot of activity out on the Backdam about this time. The government was pitching the road there. Throughout that week the heavy machines rolled up and down the Backdam and the trucks came and went with bitumen. Through the influence of Mr. Abrams, they did our street with fine red bricks and rolled it.

The following Sunday Mr. Abrams turned down the street and revved his engine. Strangely, he wasn't making any effort to sneak past the rowdy children in the street. He seemed very much like the fabled Pied Piper, luring the children who came running to the back of his car. We watched from the Yard as he slowly accelerated down the street until the children were at full gallop behind his car. Mr. Abrams was smiling fiendishly. Suddenly he slammed on his brakes. There were several soft thumping sounds as the children ran into the back of the car. Some fell to the ground. A few of them began crying. The neighbors were appalled. Mr. Abrams was doubled over his staring wheel laughing his fat head off.

Some of the neighbors began telling him off and calling him a cruel ogre. Mr. Abrams retorted that it served them right and asked the neighbors where they were when he complained every Sunday morning about the children running behind and smudging up his car. However, the means seemed to have justified the ends, for after that Sunday the children never ran behind Mr. Abram's car again, not close enough to touch it anyway.

The Pinnies had found me trustworthy enough to run my credit up to about fifteen comic books. I was good for it, for I had a solid source of exchange in Spanner. Several times he wondered aloud what my source was but I kept that a secret at that end. Tillam knew I was taking about a dozen comics from the Pinnies but didn't know how I managed to keep clear of Big Pinny's cricket bat.

The scheme to get Sunil to like Carla's sister was not working out. I just couldn't get hold of Sunil on a Sunday to drag him to the Gardens.

That Wednesday midday when I came home for breakfast I sensed there was tension in the house. Doogoo had a visitor. He was a man in his late fifties beside whom sat a boy in his twenties who I supposed was his son, even though there was no resemblance. The man was wearing a kind of cloth hat and I concluded he was Muslim. Doogoo was trying her best to be polite but I could see the vein standing out on her forehead. Uncle Inchan was lying on the couch on his belly and apparently following the proceedings from there.

See was sitting there too with her hands in her lap and her head bowed respectfully. Reena and Lea moved around the kitchen nervously. I ate quietly then brushed my teeth and left for the Yard to pick up Tillam and Squingee before returning to school.

That evening I couldn't wait for Reena to come down to our room.

"Doogoo find a boy for See?" I asked anxiously as the Sunil shared the cards.

"Well wait nuh," Reena said and seemed to be taking her time to make herself comfortable. "This boy and he father turn up today to ask for See," she began.

"Another boy? He black?" Sunil asked.

"He dark skinned but he's Indian," Reena said.

"At least Doogoo go feel better about that," Sunil commented.

"Not really. He's Muslim."

Sunil gagged. Me and Reena laughed.

"Muslim! That worse," Sunil said.

"When it rain it pours," Reena commented.

"So how this boy know See?" I asked, for I didn't know where Christopher stood with this boy in the picture now.

"He father say he saw See and like her for his son," Reena said.

"What See say?" I asked.

"Nothing."

"So what Doogoo say?" Sunil asked.

"Well, she give him the same excuse about See done spoken for already and she getting marrid this year end. Then the man left with his son."

"But Indira prettier than See. How come she don't get boys pouring in here begging to marry she?" Sunil said.

"Because she more fair than See don't mean she prettier," Reena said and took offense to that.

"See nicer," I said.

"Yea, she got more personality," Reena pointed out.

That sounded exactly like what Bucky was trying to tell me a few evenings before.

"I just saying why no boy don't turn up here for Indira," Sunil said defensively.

"By the way, Doogoo had another meeting with Rubberdog and them," she said anxiously.

"Rubberdog show up?" Sunil asked.

"Yes, he come to apologize to Inchan for the cow butting he," she said and we giggled when we recalled the incident.

"Wha' Doogoo say?"

Reena explained that Doogoo wasn't as concerned about Inchan's injury as she was about the fact that Rubberdog squandered a golden opportunity to legitimately get himself a bed in the hospital. During the heated discussion she let slip how much she had to pay Percy to get him to put that cow in that yard. At this piece of information Uncle Inchan perked up and tried to get clarity on whether he had heard correctly about the deliberate placement of the cow in the yard. Doogoo brushed him aside claiming that it wasn't important and that there was a lot at stake. During all this Rubberdog kept his head down in shame.

Then they came to the point on what other steps they could take with Rubberdog to help him to get himself injured. Uncle Rohit suggested they should all take a ferry ride at the back of Torani where the big propellers spun. Rubberdog objected vigorously to this, wondering aloud if they were trying to hurt him or kill him. To this Uncle Rohit mumbled that the latter meant more money. The meeting ended with Rubberdog promising that something would happen by the end of the next week to which the others responded that it had better be so. Time was running out.

That Thursday afternoon See had me go with her on the Round-the-Town bus. We went all the way to the southern end of the town where we came off. She led me onto the river wall where Christopher was waiting for her. I left them and went farther up the wall where some children of my age group were catching fish with improvised hooks. See and Christopher leaned against the wall and talked while I watched the children fish. A man came up the wall past me. He seemed familiar but I thought no more about him. The man continued along the sea wall and stopped where See and Christopher were. They talked for a while then Christopher gave the man some money. The man pocketed the cash and came back up the sea wall. After he passed me I was finally able to place that face.

I didn't see Reena until the following afternoon when she, Mammy and I were doing our cleaning duties in school. After Mr. Anton finished his lessons and Mammy was finished with her cleaning the two of them sat to his table and played draughts like they did every afternoon when he was there. I pulled Reena aside in one of the benches by the door.

"You remember the Muslim man that did come for See?" I said secretively although no one was within earshot of us. Reena nodded.

"And he son?"

"Yes, yes I remember. What happen?" She said impatiently.

"I went out with See yesterday to meet Christpher…"

"She still seeing Christopher?" Reena said and was obviously surprised.

"Yea, but that's not it. I see the man meet with them and Chris give him some money," I said.

"Which man?"

"The man that did come with he son to ask for See the other day," I said.

"But that don't make sense," she said and leaned her head thoughtfully to one side. "Unless…"

"Unless what?"

"Oh me Mumma!" Reena exclaimed and jumped up wringing her hands in alarm, then clasped her hands to her face in horror. "Oh me gorsh!"

"What? Wha' happen?" I asked anxiously.

"See is so sneaky! You know what she did?" Rena finally settled down with this look of awe on her face as though See was a chess master worthy of admiration.

"She pay that man to go to Doogoo and drag some poor soul along to act as he son to ask for she."

"I don't get it. Why she go do that if she like Chris? And suppose Doogoo did agree for she to marrid this boy?"

"That's the whole point," Reena said with admiration. "Doogoo would never ever agree for she daughter to marrid a Muslim man. She would rather See marry a black boy before she agree to that. And Christopher is black, right?"

I saw her point.

"So now she go more agree for See to marrid Christopher than for her to marry this Muslim boy," I said.

"Right. Although I doubt that would happen. Doogoo go grab some Hindu boy even if he ain't got anything, now that she see so much people coming to ask for See," she said. She leaned back and sighed. "Boy, See ain't taking this easy. She fighting back."

"It have a girl that like Sunil," I began.

"Chandra?" she said then drew her teeth.

"Naw, a girl that does go Commercial school."

"She know about Chandra?"

"No. And he don't know about her either."

"So how you know?"

"She sister does come to this school."

"Alright." She said and seemed to be waiting to see where this conversation was going.

"Well, I was thinking if we can get him to like this girl then he won't worry with Chandra," I said.

"Oh." She said and leaned her head to one side as she looked at me. "What this girl name?"

"Cheryl Tahal."

"Alright, where she does be?"

"She does be in the Gardens over there on Sunday afternoons," I said.

"We go have to think about something," she said thoughtfully. We heard Mammy laughing in the back with Mr. Anton.

"You think Mammy like Mr. Anton?" I asked Reena.

"Not like that. Is just that they like playing draughts," she said and didn't seem bothered by them being together so often. If she wasn't worried about it I guess I shouldn't be.

With the Backdam road now being smooth with a pitched surface the boys down the street as well as those in the whole area, were preoccupied with making scooters. Suddenly pram wheels, ball-bearings and wood were in demand. I started spiriting pieces of wood out of the shed and sold each for twenty-five cents. I gave Spanner two pieces for free with the understanding that he was to make my scooter. I thought of asking Uncle Inchan if he could get ball bearings from the bauxite company at which he worked. But he was out of action. He had to ride daily to the hospital to get his dressing changed. These trips were made on his bicycle and he sat crookedly since he could only rest the left half of his buttocks on the seat.

Then an unusual source of ball-bearings accidentally surfaced. Actually the source was there but I did not recognize it until I stumbled on my favorite postman in Henry's mechanic workshop as I passed by one afternoon after dropping off clothes. I called out to Bertie. He cheerfully came out to the street to me. After a short conversation in which he tried his best to steer the topic to Reena, I eventually surmised that this lad's uncle worked in the shop and was on a first person basis with ball bearings. In exchange for a promise to deliver Reena in the Gardens on the coming Sunday, four well lubricated ball bearings were delivered to me by mid week.

I swapped one of them with Moppa for a pram wheel. Moppa had sabotaged his Aunt's pram and helped her to decide it was no good. Then he had salvaged the four wheels. In response to the "holier-than-thou" looks we shot him on hearing how he came by the wheels, Moppa exonerated himself by explaining that his niece was already walking and didn't need the pram anymore anyway. Another bearing was sold to a boy in the next street for fifty cents. The remaining two were for me and Spanner's scooters.

Every afternoon after lessons at Bucky I stopped at Spanner to inspect my scooter. He had finished the back part with the bearing in place, along with a little box section at the joint where the upright part that would connect to the front section. Tillam and Moppa already had theirs finished and were scooting up and down the Backdam in the vicinity of our street every afternoon until night fell.

That Thursday afternoon we were standing around in front of Spanner's shack and watching him work on both of our scooter fronts when Bucky came down the street looking immaculate as usual in her navy blue Barcleys Bank uniform. As was her custom she was saying her "hello's" to the neighbors as she came toward the Yard.

A woman who I had barely noticed earlier standing at the head of the street as though she was waiting for someone, moved quickly from that position and bolted down the street in Bucky's direction. She was a tall light skinned woman with her hair in curlers. She was heavyset with much bust on top.

"Hi Miss, are you Alice Williams?" the woman said as she rapidly approached Bucky.

"Yes?"

"Leave me blasted husband alone!" She shouted and with that announcement, she jumped on Bucky. All of us in the Yard as well as the neighbors were taken by surprise. Before we knew what was happening the woman had knocked Bucky unceremoniously to the ground and proceeded to jump on her. Bucky's handbag went flying in the dirt. Straddling her the woman grabbed at Buck's hair and tried to claw at her face. But Bucky held her "scratching" hand and was kicking and squirming.

Suddenly, Bucky brought her head up sharply and connected just below the woman's left eye with a butt. Then she wriggled free of the hurt woman, ran a few steps in the yard and kicked off her shoes. She quickly pealed off her stockings and discarded them while the woman shook her head and gathered her senses. Blood was trickling from a gash on her cheek bone below her left eye. Bucky lifted her dress to her waist to be more mobile, revealing her pale violet whole slip. Then she turned back

242

to the woman who had slowly got to her feet again. Bucky had her hands up like a boxer while she slowly approached the woman who was bigger in body and taller than Bucky. The woman growled and charged at Bucky again. Bucky took two steps back, grabbed the woman by her hair and pulled her head downward. With her momentum going forward the woman began falling and as her head went downward, Bucky stepped into her and sharply brought her right knee upward. We heard the crunching sound as her knee connected to the woman's face. The woman bellowed in pain and dropped to her knees with her hands to her face. Blood gushed between her fingers.

In a rage, Bucky belted her two close handed blows to the left side of the face and the wailing woman toppled over on her right side. Bucky was closing in for the kill when Lucky, who had just come out of his shack after being awakened by the commotion, and Kisskadee from the Yard, quickly intervened and held her back.

"You tell your blasted husband to keep the hell away from me!" Bucky screamed at her as she struggled to free herself from her restrainers. "Don't you ever put your hands on me again!" she warned the woman. "Alyuh loose me man." She said and wriggled free of Kisskadee, but Lucky still had his strong arms locked around her middle from behind. A few women in the yard approached the woman who was writhing on the ground with her hands and face now fully bloodied.

"Somebody call the ambulance," someone shouted as we all gathered around the fallen.

"Don't call no damn ambulance," Bucky shouted as she struggled to free herself from her brother's grasp. "She walk and come up here to fight so let she walk she way back to where she come from."

"The woman bleeding bad," Richie said. " Spanner, run over at Mr. Abrams and tell he telephone for a' ambulance." Spanner ran out of the Yard and headed for Mr. Abrams.

"Let she bleed!" Bucky shouted. "Lucky loose me."

"When you cool down I will loose you," Lucky said calmly.

"Ah say loose me Lucky," she threatened.

"Not until you cool down," Lucky said.

"Lucky loose she nuh," Spanner's mother said.

"Is my sister. I know how she can get," he explained.

"Every day this woman husband deh behind my tail at work and won't leave me alone," Bucky explained to some of the women around her. "Ah tell him I have a boyfriend already but he won't take no for an answer. Then you got the nerve to come down here to cut my tail for a no-good man like that?" I could tell she was still mad. "Don't ever come down here again. And when you see me on the road cross to the other side before I see you. Or is another burs' face for you."

Eventually somebody got a hire car to come down the street to take the woman to the hospital. The ambulance never came until an hour and a half later. The women from the Yard attended to a slowly simmering Bucky in her shack that evening. She had a cut above her hairline and a bruise on her forehead where she had connected with the butt. Her wrists were sore and a finger on her right hand was sprained. Her stockings were ruined and one shoe heel was broken off. Mammy took her uniform to wash it and have it ready by morning.

As the crowd dispersed one woman remarked, "With so much woman comin' down here and getting they tail cut, you would think the rest of them would take a hint and stop coming."

Chapter Fifteen

Chapter Fifteen

Those of us who didn't know this side of Bucky had something else to respect her for other than her beauty. The older tenants in the Yard were not surprised that she was capable of defending herself, which was probably why they weren't in a hurry to intervene when the woman first attacked her. Their attitude was to leave them alone and the woman would get what she was looking for.

That Sunday, we went in to work at Mr. Anton's place just after ten o'clock. His sister Rhonda was parked outside in the verandah and her attitude made it quite plain we were not welcomed. Mammy greeted her and ignored her snide remarks. Mr. Anton apologized again for his sister's behavior and led us into one bedroom on which we had to work.

After cleaning up and scrubbing the floor for half an hour we heard someone come through the gate. I peeped through the wooden louvers in front and saw a handsome dougla man come up the stairs and greet Rhonda. She looked at him suspiciously.

"Where you been whole night. You were supposed to come last night," she said in a low but angry tone.

"Well, you know how it is with this work," he said and laughed, displaying two gold teeth in front of his mouth. He sat next to her in a battered basket chair.

"No, I don't know how it is. Spell it out," she demanded.

"I had to work overtime. I ain't come off 'till five this morning," the man said.

"So why you didn't come straight here?" she asked.

"I got to get me rest, Rhonda. I got to go back in to work just now again," he said as he kicked off his shoes.

"Prettyboy, if I hear you ain't been where you say you been, ah ain't go take it so you know," she warned.

"Take it how ah give you. Is just so it happen," he said nonchalantly.

"You want we go inside now? I could make some breakfast for you after," she said confidentially.

"Naw man, I tired and want sleep. Like ah say, I got to go back to work just now," he said. She looked away and looked hurt.

"You never used to make excuse before," she said. "Since diabetes eat out me one leg is all kinda excuse you making."

"Come on doux doux, you know that ain' true," he coaxed. "Is just that ah tired. Ah go make it up to you next week."

"Next week! Every damn week is next week," she said angrily.

"Prettyboy!" called a thick red girl as she rode by on a bicycle. "Ah hear you proper wine up yourself at Penguin last night."

"Me? I ain't been there girl," he said aloud and laughed uneasily.

Rhonda looked away and I could see the muscles in her jaw bone tighten.

"Is joke the girl joking Rhonda. I been working last night," he pleaded with her.

"Put on back your shoes," she said quietly.

"But Rhonda…" he said but reached for his shoes.

She got up with some effort and balanced herself on her left leg. For the first time I noticed there was no right leg. As he bent to put on his shoes she smoothly picked up the aluminum leg that was under her and, holding the leg by the foot, used it like a club. The first blow came from below when she swung the leg like one would swing a golf club. It hit Pretty somewhere in the face with a metallic clang, causing him to straighten up and flop back violently against the outside wall.

"Mammy look they fighting!" I screamed.

Chapter Fifteen

"Is which woman you been wining on last night," she said and swung again, this time downward. The leg caught him on the left shoulder and Pretty squealed and grabbed his shoulder. He dropped in agony to one knee and Rhonda did the golf swing with the leg again. This time she swung into his stomach. Pretty doubled over bawling. Rhonda hopped on her good leg into position then swung up again. The blow caught Pretty on the chin with a sharp crack and he pitched backward off the veranda, breaking the rails and falling heavily onto his back in the front yard..

"No wonder you too blasted tired to do anything this morning. Don't come back here again, or ah go kill you," she said and pointed threateningly to him with the leg.

The neighbors were now gathering around. Pretty moved his head slowly from side to side and moaned while still prostrate on his back.

"Alyuh haul he lying behind out me yard!" she shouted to the gathering crowd and hopped back into the house with the leg in hand. Mammy, Reena and Mr. Anton had come outside by then. Mr. Anton rushed to Pretty who put a testing hand to his bloody mouth. One gold tooth was loose.

"Ah go bring police on you tail!" he gargled.

"Pretty, why you don't clear out the yard before she change she mind and come out back swinging," one of the men in the crowd said.

We spent the next two hours cleaning, with Rhonda inside fretting about Mammy being there so often and referring to Mammy as the "coolie woman." Reena was getting angrier by the minute on hearing Rhonda throwing these insults Mammy's way while Mammy totally ignored Rhonda. Mammy didn't appear to be afraid of her. Mr. Anton kept apologizing for his sister's behavior while he moved around the house helping Mammy move things to get the place cleaned up. I had the impression he was a lot younger than Rhonda and she was accustomed doing what she liked.

By the time we left Reena was so angry she was close to tears.

"Mammy, why you didn't leave she house since she was being so nasty to you?" Reena asked angrily as soon as we were out of the yard.

"Because I'm sorry for her," Mammy said.

"Sorry for her! For what?" Reena wanted to know.

"Well, you can see she once was a good looking woman who probably used to get whatever she want. Now she got diabetes, lost a leg, can't hold on to she man, and we got to come and do cleaning she used to be able to do for herself," Mammy explained.

"That ain't no reason for you to stay there and take all them insults," Reena complained.

"Then if we leave because of how she getting on, she woulda get her own way again, because that's exactly what she want," Mammy said.

"Well I ent going back there again if that's how she go treat you."

"She probably won't do it again now that she see that won't affect me," Mammy said.

That afternoon I don't know what Reena told Sunil but he came with us on his bicycle to the Gardens. But disaster struck when we were on our way there. I didn't know whether Chandra was going in or coming out of Coburg street but she saw us. Reena and Sunil didn't see her and she didn't call to us. As we walked on I kept looking back to see what she would do. To my dismay, she started coming our way.

The Gardens was full with screaming, playing children when we got there. All the play equipment were occupied. I looked around and after a while I saw Carla's sister but not Carla. She was dressed in a pink and white checkered dress with a bando of the same color holding her hair in place. She looked nice. I pointed her out to Reena

Reena and Bertie Bhagwandin

who took Sunil over there and the three of them began talking. I headed for the occupied swings to await my turn. Just then I heard the distinct sound of a certain postman's motorbike, then Bertie entered the gardens.

Apparently Reena heard it too. She immediately abandoned the Sunil-Cheryl project and went to meet him. They sat on one of the seats nearby and began chatting their heads off. Then Chandra came into the gardens. She surveyed the crowd and like a bloodhound, sniffed out Sunil's location in a second. She walked straight across to where Sunil and Cheryl were. Sunil immediately became apologetic and she led him away from Cheryl who seemed amused. They went toward the lover's section of the gardens.

I left the swings and headed after them. Reena had not noticed a thing, having all her attention on tall, clumsy Bertie Bhagwandin who was nervously plaiting and unplaiting his legs like he needed a manual to show him how it was done. I saw Sunil and Chandra settle on one of the benches. I snuck around behind them, then under the neighboring hedge.

I must have missed something because, instead of being mad at him, she was all nice and loving, and had her hands all over him. And he was as happy as a drunk at Opening Time. This was making me sick. She actually put one of his arms around her waist and another on some part of her person that was making him delirious.

"You love me?" she purred.

"Yea, you?" he said and was trying to sound like a Casanova, but his voice broke.

"You know I love you. Yuh want see how much?"

He nodded his head so vigorously that I thought I heard his little brain rattling in there.

"My great-aunt not home now. Want to come keep me company 'till she come?"

He nodded vigorously again. She got up and straightened her skirt. They left the gardens on his bicycle. When I went back to the play area of the gardens Reena was still enthralled by Bertie.

"Alyuh come on. I have to use the toilet," I said to them.

"Why you can't go in the bush here?" Reena asked and seemed annoyed that I had disturbed them.

"I got to use the latrine now," I insisted. I was mad at her for the way things turned out with Sunil.

"Well, let me drop him home and come back," Bertie volunteered. "We won't stay long."

Chapter Fifteen

"You wanna bet?" I thought.

When we got on his bike I told him to ride up Waterside.

"Why I riding up Waterside and is Backdam you living?" he protested.

"Look, you go do what I ask you or you don't want Reena coming back in the gardens? I can arrange for that to stop you know."

Up the Waterside we rode. We hadn't gone far before I spotted Sunil gingerly towing Chandra up the road.

"Slow down, slow down!" I ordered Bertie. "We following them but I don't want them know that."

"You sneaky li'l so-and-so! You don't want to use no laterine," he exclaimed and pulled on his brakes.

"Temper, Temper. I feel like you wasn't enjoying yourself in the gardens with me sister," I said.

"Well yea, but..."

"The faster we follow them and see where they going the faster you will get back to me Reena."

"Well, alright. But you pull a stunt like this again and...and..."

He pulled off again. Sunil was making rapid progress up the road, considering this was not a box of groceries he had in there but a fully grown heifer. Past the empty market we went and farther along Water Street. When we got to Pilot street they turned down the street so fast I thought Sunil would've run in the drain. He turned into a yard with a small wooden cottage which appeared to be closed. He quickly parked the bicycle after she got off and hurried up the steps behind her. They went in the house and the door closed. I considered going up to the house to peep in but changed my mind. That might be pushing Bertie too far.

When we got back to the Gardens Reena was gone. Bertie was mad at me, so I promised him she will be there the following Sunday. This promise seemed to pacify him a bit. He dropped me home but Reena didn't come out to meet him. I guessed she was mad at him leaving for so long. Besides that, Doogoo was home and she wouldn't have appreciated seeing Bertie there with no letters in hand.

That night we got bad news from across the river. Our former neighbor Mr. Ramnauth, Chandra Ramnauth's father- from the village across the river, had died. He had been in a coma since the accident at Blairmont and was in Georgetown hospital where he eventually died. The funeral was to be held on Tuesday morning, so Mammy was taking me and Reena over the river. She said we were going to spend Monday and Tuesday over there.

That night I went up to Mammy's room to watch them pack some clothes and other things to take with us. I lay on the bed and was between sleep and wake when Reena started talking about what had happened at Mr. Anton again. Apparently she had been deeply affected by Rhonda's racial attitude toward Mammy and could not understand Mammy's non reaction.

"Mammy, why you think Rhonda hate coolie people?"

"She hate coolie people or just me?"

"It look like she hate all coolie people."

"Then how come she wasn't telling you anything?"

"I don't know."

"Maybe she think me and her brother getting too close and since he's the only one taking care of her she feel threatened," Mammy said.

"I don't like her. I hate her."

"You hate her or you hate black people?" Mammy asked and peeping between my fingers covering my face, I could see she was smiling mischievously.

"Just her. I have black friends and cousins."

"Then it got nothing to do with race then."

"If it got nothing to do with race then why she talking so much about 'coolie this and coolie that,'" Reena said heatedly.

"Because she think that's the best way to get under my skin."

Chapter Fifteen

"So how come it didn't. It got me mad."

"In the first place," Mammy said and stopped packing. "I don't see myself as coolie. I am Indian and I'm Guyanese, and I'm West Indian and damn proud of it. My great grandfather was a coolie but I'm not."

"I don't understand."

"A coolie is a person who came as a worker to this part of the world. You got Chinese people who were coolie. And if black people did come over here like that then they woulda been coolie too. You know when you go to England or America they call all O' we blacks? Whether you're Indian, black or dougla they call you 'colored.' Is only home here we does play the ass about race."

"How you know all this?"

"I went to school you know," she said and continued packing. "So when people call me that I don't let that bother me."

Reena was thoughtful for a while.

"Why some people racial?" she asked.

"Different reasons. Maybe they just listen to the bad things they hear about another set of people and live by that. Most times they don't even know much about the people they hate."

"How come you and Aunty Doogoo grow up same place and you don't see black people like how she see them?"

"I don't know."

"How come you don't hate black people?"

"In the first place, it take too much energy to hate anybody."

"And?"

"Well, I had black friends when I was growing up. And I had a good teacher name Mrs. Rich. She's the one that made me understand that most racial people are like that because they don't know or care to know about the group they' racial against."

Mammy stopped packing again. "She told me culture more powerful than race."

"I don't understand."

"Well, would you be more comfortable marrying a black or Amerindian man from this country, or an Indian man from India?"

"I dunno."

"With the man from here you eat the same food, accustom to the same things, talk the same way, so you'd be more comfortable than with a man of the same race that accustom to different things. Is more about differences in the way you live than in race. And I see that is true ever since then. So looking at people by race seem very shallow to me."

"You like Mr. Anton?" she asked.

"Why you ask that?" she looked warily at Reena.

"I just want to know."

"We have a lot in common and yes, I like him. But that don't mean anything."

"I ent saying so. Just asking. What you like about him?"

She looked over to me to make sure I was sleeping. I pretended to be deader than an Egyptian mummy. She put a finger to her lips.

"The first thing is, he never treat me like I'm just the cleaning lady in the school and don't know anything. He treat me like a person," she said thoughtfully. "And he make me feel like somebody, you know, like a woman again …. Is kinda hard to explain."

"He like you? Or just like you playing draughts with you?" Reena asked.

"What you think," Mammy said with a hand to her hips. Then she leaned forward and whispered, " He did want carry me cinema the other night. And he wasn't going bring his draughts board with him."

"What you tell him?" Reena sounded disappointed.

"I tell him it too early," She said and was reading Reena.

"Oh."

"Reena, if Mr. Anton was Indian would you be happy about him wanting to carry me cinema?"

"No, is not that," she said with her head down.

"Then what?"

"Well, if people start seeing you all going out together they go say things and it go get back to Aunty Doogoo. Then she mightn't want we stay here no more."

"Reena, I'm not See and Lea. I'm a big woman and Doogoo don't run my life," Mammy said smartly.

"Besides, you won't find much time for we no more," Reena said.

"Ohh, so is that," Mammy said and raised her head thoughtfully as she eyed Reena. "Reena, you know I could make the same complain about you since you talking with this Bertie," she said and smiled.

"I still spend time with you," Reena said defensively.

"Not as much as you used to," Mammy complained. "But you're getting bigger and that is to be expected. Is Milo I'm worried about."

"Milo? Why?"

"I don't help him with his school work and spend as much time with him as I should," she said and looked in my direction. "I shoulda been doing what Alice is doing for him."

"Mammy, apart from the reading I don't think you should be worrying about Milo. He know a whole lot more about what going on than you think," Reena said.

"Milo?"

"Yes. Sometimes I think he smarter than Sunil who can't tell he nose from he behind when he around that Chandra."

I was enjoying this. My sister Reena was actually saying something nice about me.

"This is Milo pants?" Mammy said and had turned her back to me. "Is how he got two dollars in he pocket?"

I jumped up without thinking.

"Where?" I said.

"Go in your bed and stop pretending you sleeping," Mammy said with a smirk. Reena's mouth dropped open.

"Where the two dollars?" I asked as I got off the bed.

"It ain't have no two dollars. She just want know if you sleeping and you just fail that test," Reena said.

"I thought you said he getting smart," Mammy said and laughed. I sulkily left them and went downstairs.

Chapter Fifteen

Sunil never came in until after midnight that night. I pretended to be asleep. He tip-toed into the room then turned on the light. He had this stupid grin on his face that made me wonder what he was doing. He located his sleeping shorts then turned off the light. Through the semi darkness I saw him take off his pants and bucta then pull on his sleeping pants halfway. He had his back to me. He was examining something in front of him then I heard him wince like I would have if I had touched a sore spot. He carefully pulled on his pants then lay down. I heard him sigh contentedly then he lapsed into a deep snore in minutes.

Monday morning we caught "Second Boat" which was the six-ten ferry across the river. Sunil was not interested in coming, claiming he had to work. We got on a short drop bus which stopped all the way along the coast. By the time we got to our village the sun was already up and people were going about their morning chores. The bus pulled up before our old house. We got out and I could smell the old familiar crab grass in the brisk morning air. I looked at our old shack. It looked smaller than I remembered it. The bedroom window was open and had blinds on it. Someone was living there. I looked across to Majeed's house but no one was stirring.

We crossed the road and went into the Ramnauth's. They were already up. Chandra's mother wiped her hands on her apron and greeted us. There were two other women in the kitchen preparing meals for the people who would be coming in later that day. Chandra was nowhere in sight. I hung out to the front of the house until school children started coming out on the road to wait for transportation. I ran inside and asked Mammy if I could visit my old school one last time. She told Reena to look for my red school shirt and let me dress in uniform. Then she gave me bus passage and lunch money.

Once Upon A Time In Berbice

By the time I came out I spotted Majeed racing out of his house to catch the bus which was just pulling up by his gap. The bus had pulled off before I could get to it. I had to wait another half hour until the next bus came by. By then I knew I was late. But then I was just a visitor.

When the bus pulled up at the village with the Police Station Dracula came aboard. It seemed he had not changed a thing since I last laid eyes on him; not even his clothes, by the look of them. He just gave me the once over and pretended I wasn't there.

The bus pulled up in front of the school and I made my way in with the other children. When we got to the gate Spanky was on duty again. The latecomers were going to get it. I felt sorry for the poor souls since I was no longer a student here.

"Ah, Mr. Teekasingh. Late at last. Long time no see," Spanky said and flexed his cane as my turn came in the line. "What's the excuse this morning?"

"Sir, I don't come to this school no more," I said and beamed at him.

Spanky threw his head back and laughed heartily.

"Now that's a good one," he said and laughed some more. "You're no longer a student here. Since when?"

"Since... well, since my stepfather died," I said and swallowed deeply. I now saw the possibility of getting whipped although I was no longer attending the school.

"Anyone in Teekasingh' class out here?" he asked.

Dracula raised a paw. I swallowed again. I was doomed.

"When last this boy came to school?" Spanky asked.

"Friday Sir," Dracula declared.

"Bend Teekasingh," Spanky ordered.

I was fuming, to say the least, that I had got a flogging and I was merely visiting the school. I composed myself before heading for the classroom. I soon forgot my recent disaster when I entered the class and was welcomed like a hero. Mala was goggling at me with admiration. Even Mrs. Seepersaud was happy to see me.

"Well, well, well! Look who's here with us this morning," she said and beamed at me.

"Morning Ms. Seepersaud," I said sheepishly.

"Good morning Milo. Came to visit us?" she said pleasantly.

"Yes Miss," I answered and sneaked Mala another look. She was looking at me like a fan staring at a film star.

"Miss, Mr. Defraitus just beat he at the gate for coming late," someone announced from the class.

"Mr. Defraitus beat you for…" Mrs. Seepersaud started saying with concern then began laughing. I didn't find it funny. "You are visiting and you got licks for coming late?" she repeated and was hysterical. "Why didn't you tell him you don't come to this school anymore?" she asked while still laughing.

"I tell he," I said soberly. " He didn't believe me."

"And nobody from the class was out there to tell him that was the truth?" she asked.

"Yes Miss," I said and pointed out Dracula.

"Mr. Jainarinesing, why didn't you let Mr. Defraitus know Milo don't come to school here anymore?" she asked Dracula.

"I thought I did see he here Friday, Miss," he mumbled. Mrs. Seepersaud went into another spate of laughter.

"That was so terrible. Alright Milo, go take your usual seat," she said when she calmed down.

I went to my old seat at the back. Majeed and the boys were all smiles there, except for Dracula. Hector was not in school that morning. The boys said he was in school up to Friday.

By the morning break I was swamped. The boys wanted to keep close to me while Sunil's friends, including Dolly Shivnarine, wanted to know how Sunil was. They seemed very impressed when I told them Sunil didn't come because he had to go to work. I didn't specify what kind of work he did. Dolly was impressed until I told her he had a girlfriend.

Reena's friends wanted to know how she was doing too. Harry Kissoon slipped me a note to give to her. I pocketed it, intending to get rid of it as soon as possible. I told them that, although she didn't come with me to school, she was at Chandra's house.

That morning Mrs. Seepersaud pulled me aside. She wanted to know what I had done to do so well in the common entrance exam. I had passed for a secondary school. I told her I studied, but I couldn't remember what I did since it was some time ago. Inside, I was elated. I was going to go to a Secondary School, something neither Sunil nor Reena was able to do.

By midday I learned from the boys that Arnold no longer attended the school since the Common Entrance results came out. His parents had pulled him out since they were disappointed that he barely made it to one of the lesser Secondary Schools.

Just when I was going off to the lunch stands to buy a snack, a girl told me Mala wanted to see me. I told her to tell Mala to meet me on the other side of the ball field. I had seen how enthralled she was by me so I was going to play a little hard to get.

After spending more than ten minutes with the boys telling them about life in New Amsterdam and about the cinema, I went across to the other side of the field where I had seen Mala waiting.

"Milo, so you turn big shot since you gone and live New Amsterdam," she said as I came and sat next to her in the grass.

"Not really. Is just that I so glad to see everybody again," I said and looked at her. She was still pretty but the Bucky factor had already kicked in and I was seeing her through different lenses.

"How school in New Amsterdam?" she asked.

"It Alright," I said.

"The girls them there nicer than the girls them over here?" she asked with a smile.

"Some of them." That took the smile off her face.

"Then you get girlfriend already then," she said.

"No, I still like you," I said and looked her in the eyes. She was smiling again and seemed pleased.

"I say you gone New Amsterdam and forget everything about me."

"No, not really. You have a boyfriend?"

"No. You want to be me boyfriend?"

"It depends." She stopped smiling again.

"Depend on what?"

"Well, if I is your boyfriend what we go do together?"

"What you mean?" she asked and I could see from her expression she had no idea what I was talking about.

"Well, I see what people in the pictures does do…"

"You went to pictures?" she gasped and was wide eyed with excitement. "Tell me about it."

I spent the next ten minutes describing to her what the cinema was like and embellished events by telling her that my uncle took sick and left me to operate the projector during one show. By the time I was finished she was so impressed that I felt she would do anything I asked of her.

"You going to Chandra' father wake tonite?" I asked.

"If me father going I will come," she said.

"I can see you after school before you go home?"

"I wait for you last time and you went home and leave me here," she said and pouted. She looked prettier like that. Not in Bucky's range, but still pretty.

"A teacher hold me up," I lied. "I saw when you was waiting and when you catch the bus. But that won't happen this afternoon if you wait for me." I took a chance and held one of her hands in mine. She did not pull it away.

"Alright?"

"Alright. I see you pass Common Entrance too," she said.

"Yea, I going High School September. You?"

"I pass for high school too," she said and seemed very pleased with herself.

That afternoon after dismissal I told Mala to wait for me in school, that I was just running over at Hector and come right back. She wasn't pleased about it but agreed. Majeed went with me up the dam to Hector's house. We didn't have to call to him. He was filling a drum with water he was carrying in a plastic bucket from the stand pipe in front of the yard.

Hector grinned widely when he saw me and dropped the bucket. He walked briskly to meet us in front of the house and wiped his hands on the seat of his pants as he approached.

"Milo!" he exclaimed with genuine joy. "When you come?"

"This morning," I said and found myself laughing with him. It was good to see him again. Without warning he grabbed me in a bear hug and I did the same. Majeed stood there grinning.

"You all moving back this side?" he said when he had me at arms length again.

"Naw, we just come for Chandra' father funeral."

"Oh." He said and seemed disappointed. "Sunil and Reena come too?"

"Only Reena. So how come you not in school today man?"

"Mammy sick, so I stay home to help she," he said.

"She sick bad?"

"Naw, just throwing up and thing."

"So you coming funeral tomorrow?"

"Naw, I ain't got passage man,." he said apologetically.

"He talk with Mala today," Majeed announced.

"You talk with Mala?" Hector marveled.

"And hold she hand too," I bragged.

"You lie!" both of them said.

"Is not a big thing though."

"Is a big thing for we," Majeed said wide eyed.

"I got to go back. She waiting for me in school," I said. Their jaws dropped.

"Mala waiting for you?" Hector said incredulously.

"Is nothing big. We just go talk," I said.

"But she waiting on you though," Majeed said.

"When we go see you again?" Hector asked and I could see the smile fading from his dark face.

"I don't know," I said sadly.

"When somebody else dead," Majeed said.

We laughed uneasily.

"Whenever I come over this side I will always come and see you man," I said and punched him playfully on the arm. He liked that.

"Alright Milo," he said. " I go still be here."

We left Hector standing on the dam watching us go. Even when we were all the way back to the school entrance he was still standing on the dam with his hands on his hips looking in our direction. He seemed so sad and lonely. I stopped and waved. He waved back to me but still stood there. I was beginning to feel depressed.

"Wha' happen to Hector mother?" I asked Majeed.

"I don't know. She just sick like he say," Majeed said with a shrug.

"She dying or anything?"

"Hector mother? Naw man. Maybe she just get upset stomach or something."

"Then why he so sad?"

"He been like that since you all went away."

I made a decision then and there that the next time I came across on that ferry to this side of the river I was going to come see Hector.

"I can come?" Majeed asked when I turned into the school entrance.

"Naw man. Mala won't like that."

"Right. Right, she won't like that," he said. " Well, see you over at Chandra them tonite."

"Alright."

I walked back into school. Mala came out of the girl's toilet and intercepted me. The two women who swept the school were here and would have wondered what she was doing in school alone since there were no afterschool lessons. She held my hand and led me onto the stairs to the upper flat where we could hear if anyone was coming without being seen.

"So you does think about me when you in New Amsterdam?" she said.

"Uh huh."

"You lie."

"Why you think I come over for the funeral when I coulda been over there instead?"

"To see you friends them."

"No, to see you. If you was absent like Hector today I woulda gone long time." She seemed pleased by this.

"You does still draw?"

"Yes."

"You draw anything for me?"

" I didn't bring me book."

"The sweeper coming!" she announced and we could hear footsteps coming our way. "Let we go."

I helped her pick up her books and we scampered down the stairs as quietly as we could. When we ran down the main steps and out toward the entrance there were three girls from the upper Forms hurrying out before us. We got

Chapter Fifteen

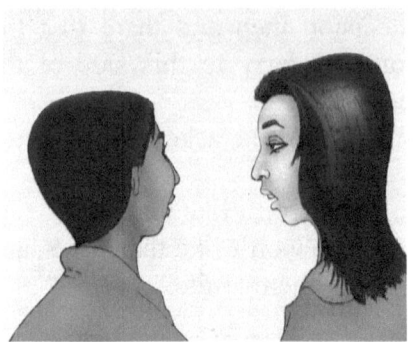

Me and Mala

to the public road and waited for transportation.

"I will come tonite," Mala whispered to me.

"Alright," I said.

When the bus came three boys from the upper forms raced out of school to catch it. The girls were giggling.

That night the Ramnauth's yard was crowded with neighbors and other sympathizers coming to pay their respects to Chandra's family. Mrs. Ramnauth didn't seem so distressed. Mammy later explained that maybe it was because she was already prepared for her husband dying, with him being in a coma for so long.

Tables were set up under the house and there were several games of domino, draughts and cards in progress. There was a car parked in front with its trunk open. From there the bottles of liquor flowed.

Mammy was playing draughts with the men on one of the tables while two other men behind her were making jackasses of themselves, trying to sweet talk Mammy. Reena was helping in the kitchen earlier but when her friends from school came she was out on the front steps with them. Harry Kissoon showed up again, well dressed in silky red shirt, blue gabardine pants and pointed tipped shoes. I don't know whether or not Reena really didn't remember him but she did a good job of giving that impression. Harry then lapsed into a moody silence and withdrew to one of the game tables.

Majeed came over and from my old class, Goofy and Charlie Valentine showed up. Over a couple bottles of Icee sweet drinks I told them about the fights in the Yard across from us, and about Coco taking a dump in the drain during a blackout. They found that hilarious. Charlie wanted to know if I played any cricket and I told him about what had happened that first day with Mr. Christian and the fence. I mentioned Lucky's ability to turn the ball both ways and Charlie told me I got to use my feet and reach the ball where it was pitched. That way, where it turned wouldn't matter much. That made sense.

"You got to do that with every ball?" I asked.

"Unless you can read where the ball go turn," he said.

I had a hard time ditching them to get to Mala's side. When I did she was vex because I had spent so much time with the boys. Her father was over at a table playing dominoes and drinking. She complained that it was too noisy that she wanted some fresh air.

We went out to the dark street where the liquor car was parked. They weren't paying attention to us, for people were coming and going out of the yard.

For some reason I wasn't as excited to be with Mala as I thought I would be. I didn't know if it was because I was disappointed in the fact that she was so attentive to me now that I was a "town boy" and she had been so indifferent to me before I left. From our recent conversation I learned that she knew all the time that I had liked her. But yet, she had shown absolutely no interest in me before.

"Let we go across to your old yard," she said and took me by the hand and led me across the dark public road and into the yard.

"Who living here now?" I asked.

"I don't know," she said.

Chapter Fifteen

We stood uneasily in the yard and I was so grateful that it was dark so she couldn't see any sign of the awkwardness I felt. She was still holding my right hand. I felt her hold my left hand then felt her chest graze against me. I knew she was standing right up to me now. I peered through the darkness at her face. I felt her breath against my chin as she brought her face closer to mine. Our lips met and our teeth clashed. We giggled uneasily as we pulled back our heads. Then we tried again. It took us some four tries before we were able to take our teeth out of the equation.

We remained in my old yard practicing kissing until a vehicle came up the road and stopped in front of the yard. We instinctively stooped down to be more inconspicuous. Mala kept her face close to mine and I resumed kissing her. When the vehicle pulled off we stood up and continued kissing with Mala being more adventurous, putting her arms around my neck.

Then we heard a bottle burst and an uproar began under the house as a fight was in progress. That put an end to my first intimate moment with a girl. And that girl happened to be my old love and it happened in my old yard.

The following morning after bathing and eating we gathered for the funeral. The dead, lying in a polished wooden coffin, was brought home and Chandra cried her heart out for her daddy. Her mother did not cry much. The man I saw lying there looked smaller and darker than the man I remembered as Chandra's father. There was a good turn out, considering it was a work day as well as a school day, and it was a morning funeral.

We followed the funeral procession the short distance to the same small village burial ground where we had buried Haroon. I noticed Mammy stayed on the road and did not go into the ground.

As they were shoveling dirt into the grave after lowering the coffin, I saw Reena go over to a grave with a wooden marker. I went over and stood with her.

"Haroon bury here," she said quietly.

"You think worms eat he already?" I asked.

Reena looked at me with distaste and started to walk away.

"You're one nasty-minded li'l boy," she said sourly.

We went to the road where Mammy was. Mala was sitting in the cabin of her daddy's truck and beside him. He was leaned halfway out of the driver's window talking with another man. Mala waved at me then blew me a kiss.

"Milo got a girlfriend," Reena whispered in awe then laughed.

By midday we were back on the ferry and by one O'clock we were back home. Mammy and Reena went upstairs to press and fold clothes. See got us some food while Doogoo went over to the Yard to attend to some complaints about repairs to one or two of the shacks.

I went to sleep since there was nothing else to do. Reena woke me sometime around four thirty that afternoon. She had a box of clothes for me to deliver in Cooper's Lane. Sunil wasn't home yet. So I couldn't get him to drop me.

I headed up the Backdam with the box on my head. As I turned down the street I noticed the burnt out rubble that was once the shoemaker shop, was still untouched. I stopped at the gate of Rosanne's house and called "inside" once before I heard someone "sush" me.

I looked up to see Rosanne in the verandah. She signaled me to wait. She came downstairs and opened the gate quietly. I went into the yard and to the front step with the box of clean clothes.

"Where Celeste?" I asked.

"She sleeping."

"So who go pay for the clothes?" I said and indicated the box I had put down at the foot of the steps.

"I go wake she just now," Rosanne said.

"Why you don't wake she up now?"

Chapter Fifteen

"I got something to tell you."

I sat down with her on the step.

"I think the man that used to live over there burn down the place because he ain't want we picking he cherry," she said confidentially. It was the silliest thing I'd ever heard but I didn't let on that I thought so.

"Why you think he would burn down the whole house to kill a tree?"

"Then why else he go burn down the house?" she asked.

"He coulda just chop the tree down if was that," I pointed out.

"So why he burn down his house then?" she asked.

"What make you think he burn down the house?"

"Because I saw him do it."

"See he do what?" I asked. I was getting tired of this girl and her tall tales.

"I see he throwing kerosene oil around the house late the night before," she said quietly.

"What?"

"He was throwing kerosene oil…"

"How you know was kerosene oil?"

"Well, at first I thought he was watering plants or something. But he got a hose. So it look strange that he was sprinkling the back of the house with this thing from a can. And way past midnight."

"It still coulda been water."

"Well, I did still think that. But next thing I know, voosh! One big blaze, and he out on the road bawling fire fire."

"And wha' happen to the can?"

"He throw it in the gutter behind we house."

"You sure about that?" I asked with squinted eyes. This girl had lied to me before and I found it hard to believe this tale.

"I know what I saw."

"You tell anybody?"

"No, because whunuh wouldn't believe me."

" 'Whunuh?'"

"Alyuh. Well, maybe only you."

"I don't know."

Me and Rosanne

"Is the truth."

"Rosanne?" Celeste called from upstairs.

"Celeste, the boy come with the clothes," Rosanne called and got up with the box in hand.

Celeste came to the top of the steps as Rosanne went up with the box of clothes. Rosanne brought down the money and gave it to me.

"I swear what I just tell you is the truth," she whispered, then went back up the stairs.

I left Coopers Lane with heavy thoughts on my mind. What if Rosanne was telling the truth. That meant that the fire wasn't me and Chandra's fault at all. I was excited by this possibility. But what if this was just another one of her fabrications.

Chapter Fifteen

Chapter Sixteen

When I returned to school the following day I nearly tasted the cricket bat of the Pinnies. It was Wednesday and I had forgotten about the Tuesday deadline. However, probably because I was a valued customer, I was given until the following day to come in with the books.

That afternoon after school I was over in the lover's section in the gardens under the hedge. Lea was in the gardens again and her boyfriend was late again. I could see she was upset. When he did arrive he seemed more annoyed than she was.

"I had to leave early and come down here you know," he said impatiently as he sat next to her. There were no kisses exchanged this time.

"It important," she said and looked at him with as serious an expression as I'd ever seen on her.

" What so important that you had to drag me all the way here?"

"Ah pregnant," she said quietly.

"Oh me mumma!" he said and turned away with a hand to his forehead. He sat there massaging his forehead for a minute.

"How Lea?" he said in anguish.

"What you mean 'how' Suresh. How a woman does get pregnant." she said in anger.

"I mean, ent we does always use them things?"

"Not always. Remember? Right here?"

"Me Momma!" he said and looked away again.

"And stop with the 'Me Momma' all the damn time. Your mumma didn't put this here!" she snapped and indicated her lower belly.

"When this boy plan to marry you?" he said.

"You pig!" she exclaimed and stood up abruptly. "You had no intention of leaving she at all!"

"Is a bad time Lea."

"'Bad time' me backside! I go always be outside looking in. I was always just a side thing for you," she stormed.

"Lea, don't be like that," he pleaded.

"Suresh, you go marrid me or not?"

"I can't do that now Lea."

"From now on don't talk to me. And don't come near me again," she said and threatened him with a stiff index finger.

"What you go do with it?"

"Same damn thing I had to do last time. And you go pay for it too," she retorted.

"I ain't got no money for that now Lea."

"You had money to go over the river at hotel and restaurant, but for this you ain't got," she said scornfully.

"I just ain't paying for that again," he said.

"You know what? Don't bother no more."

" What you go do?"

"That is my damn business," she spat at him and stalked off. Suresh remained seated for a while then sucked his teeth, got on his bicycle and rode off in the opposite direction.

When we began sweeping that afternoon a woman in office uniform came in the school yard in a hurry on a bicycle. She ran up the front stairs and asked for Mr. Anton. We directed her to where he was. She went back there to him then he came hurrying out and stopped at Mammy.

"Yvette, keep an eye on the children for me. I got to run home for an emergency," he said then he rushed out and went up the road on his bicycle riding beside the lady. Mammy sent Reena to see what the children were doing. They were quiet back there but after Reena went she didn't come back in a hurry. After a time curiosity got the better of me and I went back there to see what was going on.

Reena was at the chalkboard showing three girls and a boy something in mathematics. Although she was good at math I hoped she knew what she was doing.

It was nearly an hour later when Mr. Anton returned. He was sweating and looked exhausted. He thanked Mammy then went back to his class. After lessons were over Mammy told him that maybe it was best if they put off draughts for that evening. He still wanted to talk with her.

"Was Rhonda. She in the hospital. She had a setback and the neighbors had to rush her down there. It's her sugar," he said.

"She go be Alright?" Mammy asked.

"Yes, she's Alright now. But I don't know. They might have to remove the other leg too."

"Ah sorry to hear that. It must be hard for you," Mammy said and seemed very concerned.

"Imagine that. After the terrible way she treat you you still sorry for her," he said and shook his head.

"I kinda understand what she going through," Mammy said. "How long she's going to be in there?"

"Last time was three days. If they have to remove the leg it will be longer," he said.

"You go be Alright?"

"Yes. Yea, I'll be fine I guess," he said and sighed.

"You' sure?" she said. "I'll come over and clean up her room before she come out of hospital."

"Thanks Yvette," he said and sighed again.

He turned to his desk to get his things together to leave.

"Yvette," he said thoughtfully. "Why you didn't sent Reena back to school?"

Mammy looked at him blankly.

"I know is not my business…" he continued.

"No, is alright. Probably because she's not learning much at school, so I'm saving to send her to commercial school."

"I saw some math she did on the board for the children this afternoon. She's pretty good at it," he said indicating the board filled with algebra Reena had done.

"Her father was good at math," Mammy said. "But what can she do with it without passing exams."

"I know somebody working at Wrefords who told me they wanted a cashier, someone good at math. You think she would be interested?"

"Cashier? I don't know," Mammy said. "Reena!" she called.

"Would you be interested in a cashier job at Wrefords?" he asked when she arrived. Reena looked stunned like someone had knocked her on the head.

"Me!" she said in amazement.

"They want someone who's good at math," he explained. "And thanks for the work this afternoon. You're very good at it."

"Well, yes. Yes thanks. I would like a job like that," she gushed.

"Okay. Let me talk to the person then I'll let you know by Friday," he said.

"Thanks. Thank you Mr. Anton," she said excitedly then went back in front to finish up with the cleaning.

"I think she said 'yes,'" he said to Mammy with a smile. Mammy mouthed 'thank you' to him.

Sunil came in just after ten that night.

"Chandra came by here?" he asked.

"No," I said. "I thought that's where you been whole night."

He didn't comment. He changed his clothes slowly and was thoughtful. Mammy came by and stuck her head in our door.

"Milo? You didn't tell me you passed Common Entrance," she said and I could see she was all smiles.

Sunil looked around wide eyed and open-mouthed at me.

"Who tell you that?" he asked Mammy.

"His name on the list in the newspapers," she said proudly. "He going Secondary School come September."

Sunil was speechless. Mammy came in the room and hugged me tightly.

"I have to buy something special for you," she said and tussled my hair.

"How's the work?" she asked Sunil.

"It going alright," he said.

"How is Chandra?" she asked.

Sunil tried to read her expression but there was nothing to read there. He looked at me then back to her.

"She Alright," he said.

"Alright," she said then went back upstairs.

Reena came down shortly after, all excited about the day's happening.

"Guess what!" she began and jumped on my bed. " Milo you keep your trap shut," she warned as I was about to open my mouth. "I getting a job soon," she announced.

"Getting a job where?" Sunil asked.

"At Wrefords as a cashier," she said joyfully.

"She ain't even sure she getting it. He say 'might,'" I said.

"I sure ah getting it," she said.

"Who is 'he' that getting the work for you?" Sunil asked suspiciously.

"Mr. Anton from the school Mammy does work at," Reena said.

"He black?" Sunil asked.

"What that got to do with anything?" Reena wanted to know.

"What you doing for him to find job for you?"

"Is wha' does wrong with you. If he was Indian you woulda think the same way?" She was getting angry.

"Why not. Which man go get a job for a good looking girl and nothing in it for he."

Chapter Sixteen

"Oh? So I good looking now," Reena said. "You sound just like Aunty Doogoo," she hissed.

"You wait and see if he don't ask for li'l bit," Sunil said and laughed.

"You mean if you were in his position that's the kinda man you woulda be," She said. Sunil sucked-his-teeth.

He seemed to have other things on his mind tonite.
I was glad for Reena. She wore her old red school uniform skirt and a big yellow jersey with the word "pele" written on it. It was kind of chilly tonite and I wished I had a jersey like that to put on. I wondered how much pocket-piece I was going to get from her. So far Sunil was yet to give me a cent.

"Ah go need some money to buy my uniform for work," Reena said.

"When you sure you get the work," Sunil said.

"Alright. So, you pass Common Entrance," she said gaily to me.

I shrugged.

"I got to buy you something with my first salary."

"How them people in the village?" asked Sunil.

"Same way," Reena said. "I saw a couple of them."

"Who you saw?" he asked. Reena called a couple of names.

"You see Dolly Shivnarine?" he asked.

"Yea, I saw her," I answered.

"How she look?"

"How you mean how she look. She still got two foot and she didn't grow another eye," I said.

"She get thicker or what," he said.

Reena drew her teeth in disgust.

"She ask for you," I said.

"She ask for me?" he said and beamed. "What you tell she?"

"I tell she you working that's why you couldn't come."

"And wha' she say?"

"Nothing." He seemed pleased by this. "Then ah tell she you got a girlfriend name Chandra." He stopped smiling and Reena burst out laughing.

"What the hell you tell she that for?" he said.

"I thought you didn't like she," I said.

Sunil looked at Reena who shrugged.

"I only saw who came to the funeral house. I didn't go in school. He went," she said.

"I see all of them," I bragged.

"And guess who get he tail cut for going to school late," Reena said and burst out laughing again as she pointed at me. Sunil found that funny.

"Spanky beat you? Why you ain't tell the man you don't go to school there no more?" Sunil said between laughter.

"He ent believe me."

"That's because you lie too damn much," Sunil concluded.

"You ain't tell he you see you' girlfriend Mala?" Reena said while smiling at me.

"That li'l girl he did like in he class?" Sunil asked.

"Same one. And what you all did doing across the road in the dark?" she said. I opened my mouth in surprise.

"Close you' mouth before fly go in. You think I didn't see you?" Reena said and laughed.

"Wha' that girl in the Gardens did name?" Sunil wondered aloud.

"Which girl in which gardens?" Reena asked.

"The two ayo shut up," I said sulkily. "I going to bed." After that display in the gardens the other day these two had the nerve to bring that up now.

The next day the Pinnies were absent. It was unheard of but there it was. It might have been a good thing because I had forgotten to check in with Spanner to make the swap. It rained for most of that day. That evening it was wet and

279

miserable. Even the boys were not stirring much outdoors. I got bored in my room and settled for going through a comic book in the loft of the wood shed. I had taken to hiding out there when I did not want anyone bothering me.

When I was about to leave Lea came out to the bathroom to bathe. I went to my position at the wall overlooking the bathroom. After she undressed she had the pipe running to keep the bucket full. She poured water over her head and let it soak her hair and run over her body. After she did that a few times I thought I saw her shiver, then I realized she was crying. She had her hands on her stomach which looked very much the same as always to me and she was sobbing quietly. Then she slid down in a fetal position in a corner by the bucket and just cried bitterly but quietly with her hands across her lower belly. She let the water run noisily in the bucket to drown the sound of her crying.

I didn't know how long she was at it but she eventually stood up, dried herself without bathing, blew her nose a couple of times, then began working on drying her hair. After a while she got dressed and left the bathroom.

I sneaked out of the shed and went to the front of the yard. Nobody was outside in the Yard. I looked up the street and considered going by the cinema. Mr. Abrams was shining his car which was parked under his house. He seemed quite contented now that he had got rid of the problem of the children smudging up his car.

When it got darker and he was attending to something else in the car I ran around to the next street, St. Ann Street and stood where I could see the back of his house. Using some choice stones I aimed and let loose on the roof of his house. I heard four of the stones land with resounding bangs on the zinc roof of his house. Then I quickly ran around back into our street from the Main Road side by the cinema. As I approached Mr. Abram's house he was standing by his gate looking up at the roof of his house.

"Blasted wicked people!" he exclaimed quietly.

Once Upon A Time In Berbice

"Good night, Mr. Abrams," I said cheerfully. "What happen Mr. Abrams?"

"These blasted wicked boys pelting on me house top," he complained.

"Is the boys in the next street, Mr. Abrams," I said.

"In the next street?" he said.

"Yes, Sometimes they does pelt to see who go pelt the highest," I explained.

"Blasted ragamuffins!"

"I see them do it already," I continued.

I spent the next ten minutes feeding Mr. Abrams information on the origins of the stoning of his roof while he used some pretty colorful language, short of cursing, to describe the boys in the next street and their lineage. Sometime after he declared I was one of the good boys down the street, I took my leave and Mr. Abrams went into his house. I made a note to resume the stoning the following night.

The Pinnies were back in school on Thursday and I was in trouble. I had forgot to exchange the books with Spanner and promised to get them by afternoon. But it rained heavily all morning. A boy named Tilly in Tillam's class got a seizure. The teachers put something in his mouth to prevent him from chewing up his tongue while he bucked violently and was in spasms on the floor. He must have been at it for about a full minute but it seemed longer. When he came out of it he looked dazed. They put him to lie down on a bench at the back of one of the classrooms across from us. He dropped asleep there for the rest of the morning.

The rain was still falling heavily at lunch time so the headmaster decided we would have double-session. This involved school continuing without a lunch break and dismissing for the day at one O'clock instead of the usual three. We whooped it up, for we were all delighted. Big

Chapter Sixteen

Pinny asked me how they were going to get their books. I told him I would bring them for him the next day.

Tilly had awakened and was watching the little children in the class in which he was put to rest.

When school was dismissed at one we ran through the rain to go home. Tilly ran through the rain along with the rest of us. When I got home I told Mammy we had double session and school was done for the day. Reena thought we should go and sweep the school early and get that over with, but Mammy said we'll go later when the rain stopped. Mammy asked if all the teachers had left and I told her yes. She said she had to go out and that she will be back by four. Then she dressed and went out in the rain with an umbrella.

I looked over in the Yard where the other boys had also run home through the rain from their schools. It looked like we weren't the only ones who got double-session. But the rain continued pouring, forming large poodles of water in the Yard and in our backyard. The day seemed to have got darker. The sun was nowhere in sight and the sky was generally dark gray. The frogs, toads and insects were loud and put me in the mood for being in bed instead of outdoors.

I forgot about Mr. Abrams that night and went to my bed. I wanted to run over to Spanner with the comic books but it was still raining and I didn't want them to get wet. More importantly, I didn't want to get myself wet. I dropped to sleep with the soothing, droning sound of the rain beating down on the zinc roof.

Reena was sitting on my bed when I awoke and Sunil was drying his hair, having just come in. It was still raining. I could hear the night creatures outside and the dogs were howling.

"What time it is?" I asked drowsily.

"Why, you going to work?" Sunil asked.

I sucked-my-teeth.

"We ain't going to clean the school today?" I asked.

"School done clean already," Reena said. She was eating a sapodilla.

"Ah see they start make preparation for Lea and Indira' wedding," Sunil said.

"Oh yea, they buy a set of food stuff for the preparation," said Reena while eating.

"I go need clothes for the wedding," I said. "You go buy my clothes for me Sunil?"

"I ain't your father. Besides, me boots burst and ah got to find a shoemaker," he said.

"I hear the shoemaker buy a place out on the Waterside," Reena said.

"Who, Sooklall?" I asked.

"Yea. Borrow ah set of money and buy a bigger place," she said.

"Where it is?" asked Sunil.

"Somewhere by Kissoon furniture store on the waterside," Reena said.

I was lost in thought, for I recalled what Rosanne had told me about him setting the fire. Suppose he did set the fire and somehow ended up gaining money for it, then what she said she saw made sense.

We continued talking until sometime after nine in the night. I knew the time because Doogoo had the radio on and the death announcement program was coming over.

"Shhhhh!" Reena said.

"What?" I said.

"I think somebody calling you," she said.

We listened and sure enough, amidst the drone of the rain falling, someone was calling me from the street. I went out to the front door. It was Tillam.

"Come nuh. I ain't coming out in the rain," I called to him.

Chapter Sixteen

Tillam was holding a big plastic over his head like a tent and wore long rubber boots. He came splashing through the poodles up to the door.

"You hear wha' happen?" he said wide-eyed. "Tilly dead."

"Tilly?"

"The boy that did catch fits in school today."

"Tilly dead? How?" I asked and was truly shocked.

"He mother just find he dead. He was sleeping after he went home and he never wake up. I hear they try to wake he for he dinner and they couldn't get he up."

"They sure he dead?"

"Ambulance just carry he away," Tillam confirmed.

"Jeesum! And is just today he been lying down looking at them children in that class!" I exclaimed in awe.

"Yup. Stone dead," Tillam said and shook his head sadly.

"Ah wonder what kill he?"

"I don't know. He must be get another fits or something. Ah wonder how Mary go feel when she hear," he said.

"Which Mary? Who's Mary?"

"Mary Lindy. A girl he did like. Up to yesterday he did troubling she and she was ignoring he. Now he dead."

"But that is not she fault," I pointed out.

"Yea, but... you know, if she was nice to he he might'a dead happy. You ain't think so?" Tillam said.

"Maybe," I said. I didn't know what Tillam was thinking, but I suppose he was very shaken up by this news.

"Where Tilly live?"

"He from Smithfield," he said. "I think them and Spanner them related in some way."

"Spanner know he dead?"

"I don't think so. They gone up Canje Creek for another funeral. I think he grandmother on he father side dead," Tillam said.

"Oh! Alright."

"Well, see you tomorrow," he said and turned away.

"Wait! Hold on! You say Spanner gone where?" I said after it suddenly occurred to me that the death of Spanner's grandmother miles away could have implications on my life.

"He gone up Canje Creek… Barakara, I think the place name," he said as he stood there in the rain.

"When he coming back?"

"I don't know. Must be after the funeral done," he said.

"When is that?"

"How I go know that," he said. "See you tomorrow."

Tillam walked out into the darkness with his Wellingtons making soggy sloshing sounds in the mud.

"Wha' happen?" Reena asked when I got back in the room.

"A boy from school dead," I said and sat down with my thoughts racing.

"He drown?" Sunil asked.

"Naw, he just dead so."

"I know he?" Reena asked.

"No, he don't be there after school."

"So how he dead? He just stay just so and dead?" she asked.

"Yea," I said and was deep in thought.

"He lie," Sunil said.

"He had fits in school today but he look Alright after," I said with my thoughts far away.

"Oh. Some people can dead from that," Reena said.

They continued talking but I wasn't with them mentally. I couldn't get over the fact that the boy was active that day and dead that night. Then I got to thinking why that could not happen to Fat Pinny. I remembered the picture Reena had showed me in a book of a skeleton in a black cloak with a large grass-cutter she called a scythe. She said he was Mr. Death and he went around choosing who was going to die. I knew that Fat Pinny lived in Smithfield area too. Lord knew his heart had enough trouble getting blood through all that fat, why didn't it just give up. And there was slim, trim Tilly catching fits and dying in one day. This Mr. Death had to be cockeyed.

The following day in school everyone was depressed and saddened by the news of Tilly's death. During the morning break most of us hung around in the building since it was still raining. A few brave or greedy souls braved it outside to the vendors. Tillam pointed out Mary Lindy, a pretty fair skinned girl who was in one of the upper forms. She was crying along with a group of girls in her class. For most of the day we did not do much since the teachers too were upset by the news of Tilly's death.

The Pinnies, however, took advantage of this situation to get in some comic book reading and let me know they expected their books by afternoon. I guessed my status as a valued customer had expired. I planned to make a dash for home as soon as school was dismissed and hide in the loft so I won't have to return with Mammy to sweep after school. But Li'l Pinny was a lot faster than I was.

At dismissal that afternoon a stroke of luck ran my way. Li'l Pinny was detained by Ms. Halls for interfering with a girl in the dismissal line. That left Big Pinny to do the footwork in uncollected books. I made a dash for it through the drizzling rain. When I got home I bathed and changed into dry clothes. Mammy was sleeping and Reena wasn't home. See gave me some lunch to eat. As I was about to sneak away I saw Doogoo talking secretively with a "part time madman" they called Whiskey. Whiskey got that moniker because of his fondness for liquor and, although quite sane, was in that category of "mad men" who were sane enough to roam the streets of New Amsterdam. Doogoo had just given him a bottle of liquor and I don't know what they were talking about. I sneaked away to my loft above the wood shed.

I thought of getting in contact with Chinee Roy but he had not come around since the rainy season began. That had put an end to the cricket season.

After a while I heard Mammy calling me but I didn't answer. I guessed it was time to go to the school but I wasn't going anywhere near there. I thought of what I could do to avoid going to school until Spanner returned.

I came down from the loft just when it began getting dark. I went out to the head of the street by the cinema. I got wet from the drizzle that was still falling. I decided against going into the cinema since I didn't want to sit in there in my wet clothes. As I turned down the street to head back home, I froze. The Pinnies were at the head of the street at the other end by the Backdam. They were milling about as though unsure about where exactly I lived.

I turned and went back by the cinema before peeping down the street again. These boys were sadists. They were willing to stalk me even in the rain for their comic books. Now I understood what Tillam was trying to tell me.

I was getting soaked. I needed to kill some time until they got tired and went away. The cinema would have been ideal had I not been so wet. Then I thought of a possible place of refuge and began running up the road to Wapping Lane.

When I got to Mr. Anton's house there was no Rhonda standing guard there since she was still in the hospital. The rain had come down heavier and sounded as though it was trying to bore holes in the zinc roofs. I knocked on the door. There was a light inside but he did not come to the door. I didn't see his bicycle either and I figured he was still at the hospital visiting his sister. I lifted the third flowerpot by the broken rail of the verandah and located the key. I opened the door and went inside. I was dripping wet. I took off my shirt and went back outside to wring some of the water out of it. I went back inside and tied the wet shirt around me to prevent my wet pants from dripping all over the floor. There was already a poodle of water by the door.

As I was heading to the kitchen to get the floor cloth to dry the floor I heard a sound from inside one of the bedrooms. I thought it was the radio but when I stood still I could not hear anything else above the noise of the rain on the roof. I looked in the kitchen again and I could see Mr. Anton's bicycle was in there. I was about to move again when I definitely heard something. It was a feminine voice, and more like a moan. A pale yellow light was coming from Mr. Anton's room. I tip toed over and peeped through the crack by the hinge of the door. Reena's yellow "Pele" jersey hung on the head of the bed and, although I couldn' t see much, Mr. Anton was doing something in a slow rhythm with her on the bed. I could see her bare legs wrapped around him although, from my vantage point, I couldn't see their faces. Neither of them appeared to have on clothes.

I tip toed back to the door and out of the house and headed up the street in the rain, oblivious to the fact that I was getting soaked.

What the hell was Reena thinking? Sunil was right about Mr. Anton having a motive for getting the job for Reena. But how could Reena do this, and with a man more than twice her age? I felt so betrayed and mad at Mr. Anton. And to think I was beginning to like him. I felt even madder at Reena. She came into our room every night and talked with us. I never felt as close to her as I did since we had moved to New Amsterdam. I felt I could have trusted her, more than I could have trusted Sunil. It made her seem so cheap to have to do this with Mr. Anton, just because she wanted a job.

It was only when I was almost out to the Backdam that I caught myself. I was too busy trying to process what I had seen. The Pinnies would be coming this way up the Backdam after they left my street. I did an about turn and was about to walk back down the street when I decided I did not want to pass that house again. I walked up the Backdam to the next street, King Street. I walked back to the Main road then back up to the cinema by my street.

As I did I got to thinking what Mammy would say if she found out. Reena knew Mammy spent a lot of time with him, yet she went behind Mammy's back to do this. And where did that leave poor Bertie Bhagwandin. As much as I liked to torment him, I liked the lad and my money was on him to come through by a nose as a future brother-in-law. And if Reena thought I would keep this a secret from Mammy she didn't know me too well.

I turned down the street and headed home, walking through the poodles instead of around them. I didn't care if the Pinnies were still waiting for me.

"Milo! What you doing walking in the rain boy? You want to catch a cold?" Bucky said behind me in alarm. She was apparently coming in from work and held a dark umbrella over her head which was wrapped in some improvised plastic head tie. She came up and held the umbrella partly over me although I was soaking wet. She put an arm around my wet shoulder and that triggered off something in me.

I started crying silently and in rage. My chest was heaving.

"Milo! What happen?" Bucky asked with concern. But I just cried hysterically, but not with much sound.

"Alright, Okay. Get out of the rain first," she said as she patted my shoulders soothingly. Instead of leading me home she took me over to her shack in the Yard. She had to remove her shoes before coming into the yard. Apparently she had already removed her stockings when leaving work.

Chapter Sixteen

When we went in she took off my shirt and gave me a towel. She didn't ask me what happened again. She made some hot chocolate and gave it to me.

"Wha' happen?" Lucky said as he came from in the bedroom and stood by the doorway.

"I don't know. Something happen to upset him," she said.

"You alright Milo?" he said. But I just looked at him while my chest heaved and I sniffled. He went back inside.

By the time I was done drinking the chocolate I had calmed down considerably. Bucky was eating and eyeing me with concern.

"Is Reena," I said eventually.

"What happen to Reena?" she asked with concern.

"I went over at Mr. Anton…"

"The teacher at your school?"

"Yes… and she and he was on the bed naked," I started to shiver again but made an effort not to get all teary eyed again.

Bucky opened her mouth in surprise then ran her tongue around the floor of her mouth in thought.

"You sure?"

I nodded.

"Why would she want to do that?" she asked rhetorically with a frown.

"He promise to get a job for her at Wrefords," I said.

Bucky leaned back and put a hand to her mouth.

"You talking about your sister Reena here, right?"

"Yes."

"Jeese, this is shocking," she said. "No wonder you so upset. You going to tell your mother?"

"I go have to tell her," I said determinedly.

I must have been at Bucky's for about fifteen minutes before I ran across the road and to my house. I quickly changed my wet clothes, put on my warm, dry home clothes, and ran upstairs to Mammy. I knocked on the door and went in.

Reena was sleeping on the bed in what looked like her night clothes. My coming in apparently awoke her. She seemed drowsy but then I could have pulled off that "I was just sleeping" stunt too, although I didn't know Reena to be deceptive. But after what I saw earlier I felt like I hardly knew her at all.

"What time it is?" she asked drowsily. I stared at her and didn't answer. Something didn't seem right. She could not have dressed and got back over here, and in bed so quickly.

"How long you been sleeping?" I asked suspiciously.

"Since I come home this afternoon," she said. "Mammy come in yet?"

"I don' t know," I said, still trying to figure out this puzzle.

"You eat already?" she said and got up to a seated position.

I went across to her and put a hand in her hair. It was bone dry.

"Wha' wrong with you boy," she said and knocked my hand away.

"You saw Mr. Anton today?" I asked and looked for any guilty reaction.

"No, he ain't had lessons today," she said and pulled down her dress as she swung her legs to the side of the bed and got up. "Wha' happen to you?" she said and eyed me distrustfully. She adjusted her brassiere under her dress as she walked away from me to the door. "I going and eat." She headed downstairs to the kitchen.

I decided I would confront her with what I had seen when she came back up and see what her reaction would be. I went back down to my room. I settled down on my bed with a Daredevil comic. Someone came in. It was Mammy, for I could hear her voice. I thought quickly

291

about whether I should tell her or wait until I confronted Reena. Just then she came to my doorway.

"Milo? You eat already?" she asked. I lay there staring at her. Her hair was partly wet and she was wearing Reena's yellow "Pele" jersey.

Chapter Seventeen

Wednesday arrived and promised to be a bright day with the sun at last putting in an appearance at sunrise. But it was soon blotted out by inky clouds swelling up and spreading from the north. Monday and Tuesday had been holidays and it had rained continuously. I went to school and stayed clear of the Pinnies and Mr. Anton. I no longer felt so bad about what I had seen that evening, although I was still upset that he knew Mammy that way. At first I was disappointed in Mammy. But then I thought about how lonely she must be, having lost two husbands. She was working at three jobs just to get by. What little she got went back to us, the children. The only time she was ever happy was during the little time she had with us. And when she was with Mr. Anton. First it was playing draughts, and then this.

The Pinnies stalked me at every turn. I had explained to Li'l Pinny that my contact had gone away for a couple of days. But it seemed it was the cricket bat for me until I could come up with the books.

Tilly's funeral was to be held on the following Saturday. There were plans for the school children to turn out in uniform in a show of support.

By afternoon I found Mr. Anton to be my only refuge from the Pinnies and I sat by his desk talking until the Pinnies got tired of waiting and went away. Mammy came by alone for us to clean that afternoon. She said Reena had to go by Wrefords to begin learning what she had to do.

That afternoon I went home with Mammy who said she had to stop by Mr. Anton for something. I went over to Bucky after I had changed my clothes.

"Remember what I tell you the other day?" I asked her. She nodded.

"Wasn't Reena I saw," I said and she looked relieved.

"Somehow I just don't think Reena would do that," she said with a smile.

"It was Mammy," I said quietly.

"Okay," she said and didn't seem surprised.

"You' not surprised?" I asked wide eyed.

"Not really. Your mother is a widow…"

"What is a widow?"

"A woman whose husband is dead."

"Oh."

"She's still a woman and, well, big people do certain things when they're in love," she said. My heart began thumping as a realization hit me.

"You mean… you and Nathaniel do that too?" I asked incredulously.

"No," she said and laughed. "Not yet. But we will when we get marrid."

"So is alright for them to do that?"

"I guess so. He's not married either, right?"

"So he go marry Mammy?"

"You will have to ask her that," she said then brightened up. "By the way, I don't have them printed yet, but I'm telling you first. I'm getting married next month."

"Alright," I said and beamed. I was glad for her.

"And I want you to attend… you know, come with me up the alter when I go up," she said.

"Me?" I said incredulously.

"Yes, you," she said and laughed while playing with my mop of uncombed hair.

"Alright," I said and really felt special.

Reena came in my room when I was about to go to bed that night. I had no idea when she had come in from work but she already had on her night dress.

"Where Sunil?" she asked.

"I don't know. He out late these days."

"Is he and that Chandra again," she said. "What that girl name again that we meet in the gardens?"

"Cheryl? Alyuh don't bother," I said moodily. "Last time, as soon as long nose Bertie show up, you forget everything about what we plan."

She blushed and laughed uneasily.

"But I did already introduce them. What more you want," she said.

" So why you asking me about Cheryl then."

"Because we got to rescue we brother from that girl."

"I think he does do thing with her," I said.

"Do what thing?" she asked with concern.

"You know…" I showed her the finger in the hole action signifying copulation.

Instead of looking shocked, she got up and peered around outside the doorway then came back and sat closer to where I was lying on the bed.

"What you know about that?" she asked quietly.

"How you mean?"

She looked uncomfortable like she didn't know how to ask what she wanted to know.

"Well, why you think he doing that with her?" she eventually managed to ask.

I told her about the time I saw her take him to the house in Pilot Street.

"That's where she live with she great-aunt," Reena said.

"Well nobody was home and they went in there," I said.

"That don't mean they were doing … thing."

I then described what I had observed when he did come in late that night. She seemed embarrassed and looked away.

"Satisfied?" I asked. She nodded.

I took a deep breath then asked, "You think Mammy doing that with Mr. Anton?"

Again, I was surprised she wasn't shocked.

Chapter Seventeen

"Why you ask that?" she asked slowly and turned squarely to look at me.

"I think they doing thing together," I said.

"Why you say that?" she asked slowly again.

"I know. I can tell," I said, trying to throw her off from the truth.

She looked at me like she was trying to figure me out.

"You can keep a secret?" she said.

"Yes," I promised.

"Don't tell anybody; especially Sunil."

"Alright."

"Yes she is," she said, looking me straight in the eye.

"Yes she is what?"

"You know, doing thing. Is something big people do when they in love or care about one another."

"How you know?"

"She tell me."

"How long ago was that?"

"For a while. Couple weeks I think."

We were both silent for a while.

"By the way, Bertie carrying all o' we to Cricket this Sunday," she announced.

"Oh yea? Where? Who playing?" I asked excitedly.

"Guyana playing Combined Islands at Welfare Center."

"Where that is?"

"I don't know. He say in Canje."

"Alright." Good ol' Bertie. "You doing thing with Bertie?"

"Milo!" she exclaimed. Again, the reaction was the opposite from what I expected. A quiet "no" would have been sufficient. Instead she was genuinely horrified and taken by surprise. She hopped off the bed.

"I just want to know," I explained.

"Just shut up!" she said angrily and went back upstairs.

I smiled to myself. This was the Reena I knew and it was nice to see she had not changed on me.

Once Upon A Time In Berbice

Saturday morning began with a drizzle. I thought about going to the funeral but it wasn't worth getting beat up by the Pinnies. It rained heavily that morning and by afternoon it had petered out to a thin drizzle.

I was surprised to learn that the boys in the yard were heading up that way to see the funeral. Tillam's mother made him go in uniform like the other students who were attending. I took the risk and went with the boys, figuring I would be more inconspicuous not being in uniform.

When we got up there Scott's church yard, which was right next to the school, was full to overflowing. The coffin stood in the church while the mother and siblings were in tears. There were three to four rows of our school children in uniform. The Pinnies were there and in uniform. I was glad about this since they had to remain in formation for the duration of the funeral and, being in uniform, I could spot them a mile off.

After the service was over, the procession lined up in the street behind the big black hearse into which the coffin was slid. Behind the coffin were two cars, one of which transported Tilly's family, then came the red uniformed school children with Mary Lindy leading out with the school banner held out smartly on a pole. Behind the school children were a group of about twenty mourners walking and pushing their bicycles. Following this group were the inquisitive like me and the boys. Up the Main road we went with onlookers standing in groups at the head of each street as we went south toward the burial ground in Stanleytown.

When we got to the ground the hearse and cars stopped and the crowd filtered down the second entrance on the right where the grave diggers were waiting beside the empty grave. Me and the boys hurried into the cemetery to get a good vantage point. Some men took the coffin out of the hearse and brought it into the ground. The majority of the crowd followed them to the grave.

As the priest did the final reading for Tilly the mother got hysterical and somehow, she began blaming Tilly's brother for everything. Tillam let me know that that brother was a wayward thief. He could not be more than a year younger or older than Tilly was. She cursed this brother and began asking God why He didn't take that brother instead of Tilly. The siblings were already bawling. On hearing this divine request, other people around, especially women, began sympathizing with the boy and told the mother that she shouldn't say things like that. Mary Lindy was standing on the main dam crying her eyes out.

After the funeral we headed back up Main road toward Theater Alley. Two of the boys were shooting sling shots at things in the drain as we walked slowly. It eventually turned into a game with the rest of us taking turns at the two slingshots. One of us would point out what the target was and the shooter had to hit it. When one person missed then it was someone else's turn. Each hit was worth ten points. First person to a hundred was the champion.

By the time we got to Pitt street I had thirty, Squingee fifty, Dillip had sixty, and Tillam had cheated his way to seventy. It was Dillip's turn to shoot and Coco's call.

"Hit that can there," Coco said and pointed up a flooded drain that ran behind the houses in two streets.

"Where?" Dillip asked.

Coco pointed to what looked like an old kerosene oil can that was half submerged in the weed choked drain overflowing with the excess water from the recent rains. Dillip loaded up the sling shot with a suitable pebble, pulled the rubber taut and took aim.

"Miss by a mile!" Tillam predicted.

The rubber snapped violently and there was a loud "pang" as the pebble connected to its target.

Once Upon A Time In Berbice

We continued up the road and I noticed the next street was Pitt Street. Realizing I had just passed Cooper's Lane, I went back and peered down the street, hoping I would see Rosanne but it was getting dark and with it being wet and rainy, there was hardly anybody on the street. As I thought about what she had told me, the reality of what had just occurred hit me, making the "skin crawl."

I took off my slippers and went down by the main drain. Some of the boys had started coming back to see what I was up to. I jumped over the flooded Main road drain and carefully made my way beside the drain which ran at the back of the houses in Cooper's Lane and Pitt Street. I fished the can out of the dirty drain and carefully emptied the water that was trapped in it

"You want a kerosene oil can so bad boy?" Dillip said.

"You coulda ask me. I got six empty ones home," Squingee said.

"Six cans? Alyuh does drink out of them or what," said Coco.

Dillip examined the can and admired his marksmanship. It was a Castrol can and I could see the handle at the top was once painted with red paint. I took the can with me. When we got down the street I asked Tillam to hide the can and keep it for me. He objected at first until he heard there was twenty-five cents in it for him.

When I got home that evening Mammy and Reena were not home. See said they had gone to the dressmaker. Sunil was not home again. That night I asked Dil if I could come and watch him work. I sat in balcony and watched an exciting movie named "Dirty Dozen" after they showed another war movie named "Play Dirty."

Sunil still wasn't at home when I came home that night. I went to bed.

Chapter Seventeen

That Sunday just after ten o'clock Bertie came by on his motorcycle. He was going to leave it at us while we all traveled by bus to Welfare Center in Canje. I was all excited and overjoyed. Mammy told Bertie he had to come back with Reena early since she had to go to the dressmaker before night fell. Bertie invited Mammy to come with us but she said she would come later.

That morning me, Sunil, Reena and Bertie stepped lively up the road to the Market where we climbed aboard one of the blue Canje buses. It was crowded with other passengers going up to the cricket match. The bus took us all the way to the northern end of the town, past the Mad House, then over the Canje swing bridge under which flowed the wide and dangerous, dark waters of Canje Creek. We traveled another quarter mile before the bus turned right into Canje. Bertie told us the road continuing straight was to Corentyne. It wasn't a long drive to the ground.

When we got there, there were colorfully dressed spectators crowding the entrance. The ground seemed full inside. We forced our way to the ticket booth where Bertie bought tickets for all of us. We entered the ground and made our way to a stand near the main pavilion. We made an agreement that, should anyone get lost we would meet at a certain post by the player's side of the pavilion. We did our best to stick together.

Bertie seemed to be an avid cricket fan and knew all the players by sight. Some of them I knew by name only. He showed me Roy Fredericks and I looked at this dark ordinary man in awe, finding it hard to believe this was the same Roy Fredericks I used to hear about on Ms. Seepersaud's radio at my old school. Bertie also pointed out Rex Ramnarace, Rohan Kanhai, Lance Gibbs, and Basil Butcher.

When the match started Combined Islands went in to bat. We watched the match and responded with the crowd as the day wore on. Bertie bought cane juice and other refreshments for us during the day. By midday Combined Islands had lost three wickets which included the prized wicket of Jim Allen. He was a batsman who everyone said was bound for the West Indies team. But there was. a young batsman no one seemed to have heard about named Vivian Richards who was banging the bowlers to all parts of the ground.

It was just after the lunch break when this Richards fellow played a shot that brought people to their feet. He picked up a ball that was outside off stump and not too short of a length and pulled it effortlessly over the heads of the leg side fielders. The ball sailed high over the boundary for six. It connected to one of the uprights in that stand and flew into the crowd, skimming off the head of a chap in bright orange overalls. The fellow fell backward and toppled over the back of the stand. Surprisingly the man fell off the stand and on to the grassy ground below. The crowd roared in appreciation of the shot even though it was off our bowler.

I looked over at where the fellow fell and there was a little crowd running to him. He didn't move. The crowd remained there for another few overs then we heard the ambulance siren as it made its way through an emergency entrance to the ground in the vicinity of that stand.

I left my seat and ran down the steps then pushed my way through the curious crowd and as near as I could get to the ambulance. People in that stand were leaning over and looking down at the medical workers attending to the chap in bright orange. As I surveyed the stand to see the best place to get to so I could see down to where the man was, I saw Mammy. She wore a full length loose fitting yellow dress and a big straw hat. She looked young and very attractive. She was looking onto the cricket ground where the match had resumed. Mr. Anton stood next to her in slacks and a very colorful shirt. He had sunglasses pushed back on the top of his head. I waved to them but they didn't notice me.

I climbed up the side of the stand where I could see over the heads of the adults.

They had the fellow on a stretcher and had immobilized him with splints and bandages. They were all over him and I couldn't see his face.

"He dead?" one female spectator asked.

"Look like he got broken limbs and he's out cold," said a policeman standing nearer to the injured.

When they brought him past me as they headed for the ambulance, I had a better view of him. Rubberdog was out cold, as the policeman had said, and seemed to have more broken limbs than he had teeth.

Then, as they were just a few steps from the open back of the ambulance we heard a cry, not unlike the scream of a samurai before dicing someone with one of those two-yard blades. Whiskey came charging in with a piece of lumber. It took everyone by surprise and there was a scramble to get out of the way. He slammed down the wood with tremendous force on the stretcher in the vicinity of Rubberdog's legs but the aluminum upright for the stretcher absorbed the blow. Before Whiskey could get in another blow policemen were all over him.

"What the hell he trying to do?" one spectator wondered aloud.

"I don't know why they don't keep them people lock up in the mad house," someone else commented. They took Whiskey away in handcuffs while Rubberdog was driven away in the ambulance, presumably to New Amsterdam Hospital.

After the match there was a mad scramble for transportation to get home. Except for the people who lived farther in Canje, everyone else was headed west toward the Canje turn junction where some would head up the

Corentyne, while most were headed for New Amsterdam, with some having to cross on the ferry to get to other destinations over there, including Georgetown.

Bertie decided that we should walk down to the junction with the Corentyne highway where we could catch one of the Corentyne buses headed for New Amsterdam. We began the half mile walk to that turn and noticed many people had decided to do the same. When we were almost out to the turn Bertie saw the cream Morris Oxford driven by a man we called "For A Few Dollars More," passing by in the opposite direction, most likely heading for passengers at the cricket ground. Dollars, as he was called for short, was so named because of his penchant for money which resulted in him driving to the end of the world to get a passenger.

"Dollars!" Bertie called and stopped him. Bertie told him something and Dollars turned the car around. We piled in and so did other passengers who knew him. Reena sat in Bertie's lap in front and I was squeezed in somewhere at the back with Sunil. In all, twelve people came down to New Amsterdam in that car.

When we reached home I was exhausted. But we had enjoyed the day. As soon as I got home I ran over to the Yard where the boys were sitting on Spanner's step talking excitedly. Spanner was back at last. I ran over there and joined them. I was all set to tell them about the exciting match, only to learn that, except for Spanner, Squingee, Chinee Roy and Moppa, everyone else was there at the match.

"So why you ain't go Moppa?" I asked when there was a lull in the conversation.

"I was too tired man," he said.

"He lie. He broke," said Coco.

"You more broke than me," Moppa shot back.

"Yea, but I still make it up there though," Coco said.

"Why Chinee Roy didn't go? They got money," I said.

Chapter Seventeen

"Chinee people don't play cricket boy. You ever see a Chinee man' picture on a cricket card?" said Spanner.

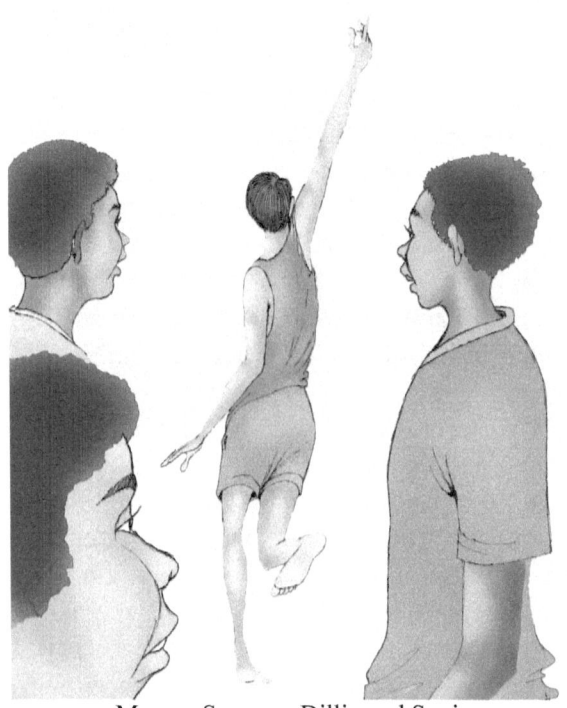

Moppa, Spanner, Dillip and Squingee

"Chinee people does play cricket yea," said Dillip.

"You ever hear West Indies play China? Is only England, Australia, New Zealand, Pakistan and India," said Spanner.

"And West Indies," I added.

"We know that , you idiot," said Squingee.

"Then how it have a type of ball you bowl name 'Chinaman' if chinee people don't play cricket?" argued Dillip.

"What chinaman ball? What you talking about?" asked Coco.

"Yea, a chinaman is the kinda ball you bowl like a' off break but it turn the other way," said Dillip.

"You stupid or what boy," said Moppa. "It ain't got nothing go like that."

"Yes man. Is a ball you bowl so," Dillip said and took two steps, hopped, then did an overhand delivery of an imaginary ball and turned his wrist.

"Is with the left hand," said Lucky who was listening from his step nearby where he was in conversation with Spanner's sister and Kisskadee.

"What?" several of us said.

"Chinaman you does bowl with the left hand," he repeated.

"Only left handers can bowl it?" asked Coco.

"Yea," said Lucky. "It look like a leg break when it leave you' hand but it turn like an off-break."

"Ah tell you! Ah tell ayo skites!" Dillip announced triumphantly. "Wha' ayo know about cricket."

"If you know so damn much, how come you can't last more than four balls in this yard without getting you wicket knock upsided down," said Spanner. We laughed at that.

As we continued talking I heard Chandra call for Sunil. She was standing by our gate. I left and went over to her before Doogoo confronted her. I had already heard Doogoo saying that Chandra was a "stray" girl, that she didn't have any mother and father to keep her home.

"Ah think Sunil gone to look for you. He ain't home," I said as I walked up to her.

"You too blasted lie," she said angrily. That took me by surprise since I didn't say anything to get her mad. "You think I ain't know you all trying to fix he up with that skinny girl in the gardens?"

"How you know that?" I blurted out.

"Sunil done tell me already," she said. "Sunil!" she called to the house.

"Sunil ain't deh home," See answered from within.

Chapter Seventeen

"You come here," she said and before I could say otherwise she grabbed my tee-shirt at the neck and was dragging me up the street toward the cinema. "If I only hear you trying to get Sunil fixed up with another girl again I done keep secret for you, you hear?"

"What secret." I retorted.

"If you want everybody know you burn down that place you just go ahead and... look he there. And is who he with?" she said and released me. I looked around and saw Sunil with his back to us, sitting on his bicycle at the head of the street with a girl on the bar. He was talking to someone standing in front of the cinema by a vendor. Chandra walked faster toward him.

"Sunil!" she bellowed. "Is who..." She stopped talking, for Sunil and the girl had turned around and were looking in our direction. It was Reena. Sunil was all smiles while Reena shot him an ugly look.

"I been looking for you whole day," Chandra said. "Hi Reena." Reena nodded.

"Ah tell you ah going Cricket today," he explained and turned the bicycle around after Reena slipped off it.

"Why you going on like you's he mother?" Reena said and seemed agitated.

"Look, ah done know ayo trying to split up me and your brother but that ain't go work. So ayo better give up on that," she said angrily.

"I have my own reason why I don't want him with you," Reena shot back.

"You ain't he mother," said Chandra.

"She don't like him with you either."

"I don't care. Just stay out of we business," Chandra snapped.

"Chandra, is wha' wrong with you girl. Is just Cricket ah went," Sunil said and tried to laugh it off.

"You ain't got to explain nothing to she. She is your boss?" Reena said heatedly.

306

"You better shut your mouth if you know what good for you," Chandra threatened.

"Girls, come on," Sunil said and tried to lead Chandra back down the street and away from where people were.

"Don't calm me down. She ain't no damn good for you, so I might as well say it," Reena said angrily.

I hoped they didn't come to blows because I knew Reena couldn't fight to save her life. And this girl Chandra seemed like a good knock-about. You never know what she could be capable of. Maybe living near the Yard made Reena think she was from there.

"Tell your sister shut up if you know what good for you," Chandra snapped at me.

"To hell with you! You tell she yourself," I retorted. That stopped her in her tracks. She didn't expect that from me.

"What? Ah say tell she shut up before I let me tongue go," she threatened. "You want you' nasty little secret out on the street?"

"Oh that? I ain't burn down nowhere. The man light the fire he self. Somebody see he," I said. We were standing by the high zinc fence by the cinema with not very much light coming from the street light by the cinema. But in the dim light I could see Chandra's eyes threaten to pop out of their sockets.

"What?" she said in a voice higher pitched than her usual low husky tone.

"Sooklall burn down he place he self," I repeated. "So to hell with your secret."

"What ayo talking about?" Reena asked with a puzzled frown. Sunil was looking open mouthed at us and was no more enlightened than Reena was.

"Is a long story," I said.

"You lie!" Chandra said. "You lying to get yourself out of this."

Chapter Seventeen

"I ain't no lying. And ah find the kerosene oil can he was using to do it too," I said.

"Milo, what you talking about fire?" Reena asked.

"Is you're the one lying," I said to Chandra and was getting really mad at her.

"I should slap you li'l lying tail," she said savagely.

"You know what she used to be doing at the shoemaker shop so steady?" I asked Sunil who still had that puzzled look. "She and Sooklall does be doing thing in there," I lied.

"What?" Reena said. Sunil looked angrily at me.

"This blasted liar!" shrieked Chandra.

"I see for meself," I went on quickly seeing I was losing both Sunil and Reena from my corner.

"You see what?" Reena asked doubtfully.

"A' afternoon when I stop over there, I hear she and Sooklall talking then when I peep they were in the backroom with she on top of him naked," I said.

"What we were talking about?" she asked.

"That is my damn business," I said.

"He lying Sunil!" Chandra shrieked.

"It ain't no lie. She got too big cut here, high up on she batty," I rattled on and indicated the approximate location on my own left buttocks.

I heard a yelp and saw Chandra with her eyes bulged even wider. Her hands flew up to her mouth. There was raw shock in her face instead of anger.

"Milo…" Reena began and I could see she was disappointed in me.

"What the cut look like?" Sunil asked with eyes slitted with suspicion.

"It like a' eleven about this long," I said and indicated the length on an index finger.

"How the hell he know that Chandra?" Sunil asked, turning slowly to her. Chandra was still bug eyed and fumbling for words.

" He lie...he..I.. well, is a lucky guess," she said and tried to laugh it off.

"It got to be true or he can't know that," Sunil said as though trying to convince himself.

"Look, it only happen one time, alright?" she said suddenly. Now it was Reena's turn to do the eye popping exercise. I was stunned but I didn't show it.

"I see them more than once," I lied.

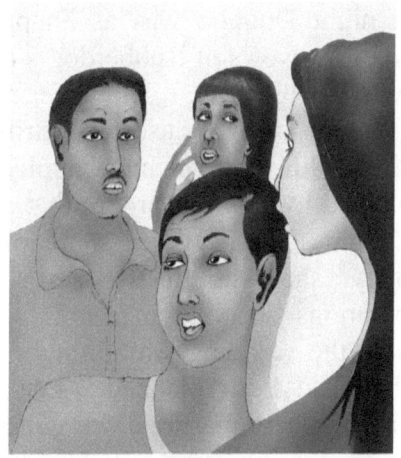

"Alright! Alright. Is two times it happen but that's all," Chandra confessed. "Sunil, ah sorry. But is he make me do it."

"Sooklall?" Sunil said in disbelief.

"Sunil, let we go home," Reena said in disgust.

"Sooklall Chandra?" he repeated in disbelief.

"He force me Sunil. I didn't want to do that," she pleaded with Sunil and reached out to him. Sunil pulled his arms away from her.

"He force you all two times?" he said scornfully.

"Is the truth Sunil," she pleaded with him.

"Milo, let we go home and leave Sunil with this mess," Reena said and put her arms around my shoulder and led me away. Sunil remained at the head of the street arguing with Chandra. I hoped that would be the last I was seeing of those two together after what just happened.

Sunil came home very late that Sunday night after the argument with Chandra. When he came in he was not in a mood to talk even though Reena came down and tried to pry his tongue loose. We did decide that he definitely had beer on his breath, something he never drank before. For the rest of the week he went to work and came straight home. And slept. He didn't talk much that week.

Earlier that night Doogoo was as happy as a carrion crow on a dead cow. News of Rubberdog's misfortune was common knowledge by now. The other two associates gathered that evening at the house for a drink to celebrate Rubberdog's ill health, with Inchan happily participating. As Reena explained to me in our room that night, now that Doogoo was about to collect her share of Rubberdog's insurance money, she was free to go ahead with the wedding preparations she had in mind. Apparently, at Lea's insistence, the wedding was brought up to a much earlier date than had been planned. Lea seemed to be resigned to her fate where marriage was concerned. In fact, she seemed eager for the event. Indira didn't complain. She never complained.

See hadn't asked me to "go for a walk" since that early morning sneak to Christopher's house. I knew she was still seeing him but those plans excluded me recently. The house was suddenly busy with various people coming in to Doogoo as they were involved in some stage of the wedding preparation. During that week Doogoo took Lea and Indira to Georgetown to buy their wedding dresses after complaining that she could not find anything suitable in town nor in Rose Hall on the Corentyne.

Meanwhile I had come to a standoff with the Pinnies. With Spanner being back I was able to swap the books with him. But when I delivered the lot to the Pinnies they "froze my account," taking the books and not allowing me to get any more until further notice. I then hatched a plan to get one up on them. I knew they collected on Tuesdays and had their stash of books in school on that day. I knew where they hid them too.

I got Tillam to write a note stating where the stash was hidden and left it in a conspicuous location on Mrs. Halls' desk. Sure enough, during the day, she made the swoop and seized the whole lot. The Pinnies were flabbergasted. They had no idea I was behind the haul. I kept an eye on where Mrs. Halls put the seized books. When we came to sweep that afternoon I looked behind the rows of hard cover books in her cupboard and discovered close to fifty comics in storage there. I took ten of them per day for three days. Then I started my own lending program to rival the Pinnies. Of course they were not too pleased that I was rivaling them but they couldn't do anything about it but try to reestablish my credit with them.

After a time I was down to fifteen books because the fellows who borrowed books from me realized that I had no enforcer nor cricket bat to back me up if books were not returned. Eventually I was back in with the Pinnies except that I was trading even with them. Instead of owing them, I was simply trading my fifteen for another fifteen.

I still talked with Carla Tahal even though the Sunil-Cheryl project was shelved. At one time she had pointed out a pretty dark skinned girl who was wearing the white and brown checkered blouse and brown skirt uniform of Overwinning Secondary school. She said the girl's name was Ruby Tahal and they were cousins. The girl looked more negro than mixed, and I couldn't help reflecting that I had the same situation with my cousin Alicia.

Reena started work that week. I was so proud to see her coming home in her dark gray skirt and cream blouse. See had done her hair and had it pinned up in a bun at the back. She looked like a woman when she went to work. One afternoon, I think it was a Thursday, she was coming down the street from work with Bucky. They got compliments on their looks all the way up the street until they got home. Even Mr. Abrams paid them a compliment.

The downside of Reena starting out to work was that I had more work to do with Mammy in school in the afternoon and had to sweep as well as do the garbage. In addition, when Reena came home she was so tired she had no time to come gossip with us in our room.

Once Upon A Time In Berbice

Chapter Eighteen

Rubberdog came out of his "coma" on Saturday morning and Doogoo and the gang scooted down to the hospital with bouquets of flowers and a bag of oranges in hand. I was not present but heard what had transpired from Mammy who had heard it from Mr. Anton who, in turn, heard it from a nurse who worked on the ward in which Rubberdog was laid up.

According to her, the trio marched in there Saturday afternoon with Inchan limping in tow. They were all smiles. They exchanged pleasantries and Doogoo pulled up the lone chair available while the other three stood lining the bed. The first sign of trouble was the way Rubberdog seemed not to remember them as being close buddies of his. He sat up in bed with his head still heavily bandaged and his limbs in plaster of paris. They asked him how he felt and he said he had no pain unless he moved. Uncle Rohit promised to sneak in a "quarter" – referring to a quarter bottle of rum - for him. Then Doogoo leaned forward and asked him confidentially if he had heard from the insurance people.

Rubberdog wanted to know which insurance people she was talking about. Doogoo told him the people from Mutual Life Insurance and reminded him about the accident insurance with a wink. Rubberdog said he did have an insurance policy but did not know how that was her business. Doogoo looked at him for a few seconds then leaned forward and reminded him of their scheme. Rubberdog looked shocked and told Doogoo that was against the law. He went on to stress again that his insurance was his business and he didn't see why that should be her concern.

It was at this point, I was told, that Uncle Rohit charged at Rubberdog with the bed pan in hand and had to be restrained by Uncle Inchan and the fourth person there.

Chapter Eighteen

Doogoo was having a very hard time restraining herself from doing the same thing. I imagined her face had that fierce expression one would usually find on the face of a Viking when he was at the top of the forward swing of a heavy battle axe, having all intentions of lopping off the head of the fellow before him. They thought she would have got a heart attack.

Inchan thought it best for them to leave since Rubberdog obviously had not yet got back his memory. Doogoo threatened to help him get it back by knocking him in the head hard enough to jog loose whatever it was that was preventing him from recalling their plan and agreement. Then she voiced her regret that she had not given Whiskey two bottles to do Rubberdog in all together. At this bit of revelation Rubberdog became very agitated and vocal, calling Doogoo a Hindu assassin. Apparently he had heard about Whiskey's late charge at his legs and, until then, he could not figure for sure what the motive was.

Eventually they left with Doogoo dragging her flowers away. She took the oranges too.

That Sunday morning I woke up to what I thought was a row of some kind going on over in the Yard. I jumped up quickly, for I thought there was a fight in progress. I ran out to the gate in only my short pants. There was a car parked there and most of the tenants of the Yard were outside and noisily celebrating something. I went around the car and my mouth dropped open. Bucky was in her sleeping gown draped all over a tall dark fellow dressed in a suit. She had her arms around him as though she had to hang on for her life. And she was in tears. I supposed that must be the Nathaniel she had told me about. He had to be very tall, for she was standing on the last round of her step while he was on the ground and he was still taller than she was. Bucky must have been about five feet six. Lucky stood leaning against the doorway smiling.

Once Upon A Time In Berbice

After a while she disentangled herself from Nathaniel who then went up the short steps and into the house, bending as he passed the doorway. Bucky wiped her eyes but was smiling at the neighbors now. She said something to Spanner's mother then went in the house behind Lucky.

Meanwhile, preparations for Indira and Lea's weddings were becoming hectic. Doogoo was in a foul mood all week since her encounter with Rubberdog. The wedding dresses were already bought and there was to be a rehearsal on Thursday evening. Meanwhile, a truckload of bamboo and coconut tree branches was brought in and put in the backyard between the house and the latrine. During the week workmen came in and they began building a big bamboo tent extending from the house all the way by the latrine. Then they covered the top with the coconut branches. Most of the backyard, excluding the bathroom and latrine, was covered by the tent.

When I went over to Spanner that evening he told me that Bucky had told them she was getting married the following Saturday. I didn't let on to him that I already knew. He said Nathaniel was staying with his mother in Stanleytown until they got married.

I noticed Sunil was looking for something all day. I had asked him what it was and he did not say. He seemed to be looking outdoor, around the yard. I supposed it was a piece of rubber to patch his bicycle or some such thing. Later in the day, from what I heard him ask Reena, he was looking for a can to put in kerosene oil. At the time I didn't think of why.

Reena spent most of Sunday evening preparing her clothes for work on Monday. Sunil had promised to give her some money for her to start Commercial School in the evening. That evening Sunil dressed and went out. He never came back until nearly day break on Monday morning. I had no idea where he went. What I did notice after that was that he and Chandra were back together again.

On Monday afternoon I was hungry when school was dismissed. So I went home with Tillam. It was while eating the lunch See gave me that a car pulled up outside. A well-dressed, heavyset light skinned man about Inchan's age emerged and came into the yard. Doogoo was not home but Inchan was. He ran out and greeted this man so enthusiastically that I thought the fellow was a long lost brother.

After they hugged and commented on each other's health Inchan eagerly ushered him into the living room and called to See to meet him. See came from the kitchen after taking off her apron and greeted the man respectfully. Inchan then had the man sit and was gushing all over the fellow. I ate slower as I was curious as to who this apparent "royalty" was. So far, from what Inchan told See, this was the man responsible for putting them on their feet. Apparently, they used to be neighbors when Inchan had first got married and lived in their first house at Rose Hall on the Corentyne. I gathered his name was Sammy Ramkissoon and he was in the rice and also the sawmill business. He now lived in Georgetown and had been living in Demerara for the last decade or two. I was getting bored and was about to go upstairs to locate Mammy for us to go back to our evening job when the conversation turned to the reason the man had come.

It seemed that Sammy was never married and had been sowing whatever oats he had here and there. One such sprinkling resulted in a son he had left behind on the Corentyne. He and the boy's mother were seldom in contact unless she needed something for the boy. Every year or two she used to send the boy for a week or so to spend time with him during the August holidays. But Sammy and the mother had a serious falling out about seven years ago and she stopped sending the child. His pleas to her by letter to remain a part of the boy's life remained unheeded. Sammy then resorted to providing for the boy through a third party in the area, unknown to the mother. Now Sammy was told by this third party that the mother had arranged a   marriage for him.   Using his considerable resources, Sammy found out that the bride-to-be was the daughter of an old neighbor and friend of his, Inchan. He was delighted and wanted to be a part of the wedding.

Inchan was so excited by this news that he forgot and painfully sat on the wrong half of his buttocks.   This elicited a painful response from him and he then had to explain to Sammy how this misfortune had befallen him.

That afternoon I went with Mammy to the school to clean. When I was finished I left her playing draughts with Mr. Anton. I went over to the Gardens to see if there was anything erotic to be seen in Lovers section.   Having noticed there were nothing but ambitious men and unwilling women over there I retired to the swings. When I got tired of swinging I went back over to the school. Mr. Anton and Mammy were just finishing up playing. For some reason their lips were wet. We locked the building and the three of us walked toward home. Again, Mammy said she had to stop to tidy up Rhonda's room since she will be getting out of hospital the following day, minus another leg.

I had intended going home then trotting over to the Yard. Spanner was supposed to put the finishing touches on my scooter. But as soon as I got in the yard I could sense there was something wrong. See was all wild eyed and nervous and Lea was in tears with Indira trying to calm her down. Doogoo was very mad about something. Sammy had apparently left.   Inchan was quiet while Doogoo carried on with whatever she was objecting to with the term "over my dead body" being thrown about pretty liberally.

Chapter Eighteen

"Pssssp!" Someone called from the stairs. It was Reena. She put a finger to her lips then motioned for me to come up with her.

When we got to Reena and Mammy's room she closed the door quietly behind her then led me to the bed.

"Big trouble downstairs," she whispered.

"Wha' happen now?"

"The wedding is off."

"What?"

"Shhhhhh! The wedding is off, at least for Lea," she said.

"How? Wha' happen?"

"The boy' father been here today."

"Yes, I saw him. And he and Inchan was happy about the wedding."

"Well, the man did gone by the time Doogoo come home. And when Inchan tell she the man was here she was glad and everything."

"So wha' wrong?"

"Wait nuh. When Inchan tell she the man will be taking part in the wedding she was happy still."

"So?"

"Is when he tell Doogoo that the man is the boy' father that Doogoo hit the roof. She get white white like she see a ghost."

"Just because he's the boy father?"

"It look so. She don't want Lea marrid the boy no more."

"But why?"

"Same thing Uncle Inchan ask she and she can't say why."

"The man meet Lea?"

"Yes, Lea and Indira came in just before he left."

"So wha' is the problem?"

"I don't know. All I know is Aunty Doogoo say Lea not to marry the boy."

318

Reena lay back on the bed with her hands behind her head and looked up at the roof. She still had on her work clothes.

"You know what the funny thing is? She tell Uncle Inchan she would probably let See marrid the boy instead of Lea, seeing she and Indira are twins."

I didn't know what to make of that. It just didn't make sense to me. I looked at Reena lying there and was thoughtful for a while. I leaned closer to her.

"Reena, Lea pregnant," I whispered.

Reena's eyes swiveled to mine. I could see them widening.

"What?"

I didn't repeat it because I knew she heard me. She rose slowly back to a seated position.

"What you say just now?" she asked and looked at me with disbelief.

"Lea getting baby," I whispered.

"How you know that?" she said.

"Shhhh! If they hear that they go kill she," I said.

"How you know all that?" she whispered with her head closer to mine.

"I hear she and she boyfriend arguing about it in the gardens," I explained.

"You sure is that they were talking about?" she said.

"I know was that yes. They does go to the gardens steady. One time they left there to go over the river at a hotel."

"What!" Reena said and put her hands to her mouth. We were quiet for a while as Reena digested all this new information.

"But she just meet this boy to arrange a wedding and she couldn't wait?"

"What?"

"She coulda at least wait 'till she marrid to go running off with he to hotel."

Chapter Eighteen

"That ain't the man she does be in the gardens with," I said.

"Oh me Momma!" Reena exclaimed as she jumped to her feet and wrung her right hand. Then she put her hands to her mouth again. "Ohhh me Momma!" She sat down then got right back up again and did some more hand wringing.

"You can't tell Mammy this you know," I said.

She stood up there with her hands to her mouth and her eyes darting from me to the floor, to the door and then back to me.

"Ohh me momma!" She stomped a leg on the floor then abruptly sat down on the bed.

"Is another man she pregnant for?" Reena whispered in awe as though there was something bitter in her mouth.

"Yes. And he' marrid," I added.

This time she leaned her head to the side and looked at me with a touch of anger in her expression.

"Milo! You making this up?"

" Nooo! No, every word I say is true," I swore. "If you don't believe me ask Tillam."

"Tillam? Why Tillam?"

"At first is the two of we see them first in the Gardens," I explained.

"How long this going on?"

"How long what going on?"

"Lea and this man."

"I don't know. Must be long. Because when they were arguing about what to do about she getting pregnant, he say she could do the same thing they do last time. So must be a long time."

"Me Momma!" Reena moaned and was rocking back and forth with her hands clasped together and pressed against her mouth. Her eyes shifted to me and remained there. I could see she believed me and was trying to process everything.

"No wonder she was so happy to get marrid quick," she said thoughtfully. She was quiet for a while.

"But that still don't explain why Doogoo don't want her to marrid this boy," I said.

"No wonder she so upset. If she don't marry him what she go do now that she pregnant already. That go be one big scandal for Aunty Doogoo," she said in awe.

When Mammy came home later that night Reena just told her what had happened downstairs but mentioned nothing about what I had disclosed to her. Mammy left and went downstairs to talk with Doogoo. Reena promised to bring me up to date if Mammy found out anything.

I lay on my bed thinking about what Lea and her boyfriend were going to do, now that the wedding was off. I waited for Reena to come down with any news but she never did. Just when I was going to drop off to sleep Sunil came in. I pretended to be asleep. He came in and changed into his short pants and tee-shirt in which he slept. He sat on the bed after turning off the light. Then a match was struck. Before it went out I could see the glow in the dark then I smelled the tobacco smoke. My brother Sunil had started to smoke.

I didn't know how long I was asleep before I felt someone tugging at my big toe. It was See again. In ten minutes we were riding down the Backdam on Uncle Inchan's bicycle. It was drizzling. See didn't say anything and seemed calm under the circumstances. Instead of directing me into Stanleytown where we had gone the last time, I followed her directions and turned left heading toward BEI high School and into Vryheid. We had to turn on the headlight of the bicycle since the streetlights ended by the school and we were riding into pitch darkness. I was beginning to wonder if all of this was worth the dollar she promised me when she told me to slow down. We stopped not too far after the school and on the right.

Chapter Eighteen

See slipped off the bar of the bicycle and walked across a wooden bridge consisting of two planks across a narrow trench. Through the darkness I could see a small cottage which was dark. She went up to the door and knocked.

"Christopher, open," she called. A light came on inside and the door was soon opened. He looked out at me and waved. Then they both went into the house.

They came out again after ten minutes and I headed back home with See through a heavy drizzle. She still was not saying anything. I supposed See was alarmed by Doogoo mentioning switching Lea for her for the wedding. She and Christopher must have planned something, for she was calm and not panicked like she was the last time she made the midnight run to him.

We rode right up to the gate. She helped me take the bicycle in the dark back in the dining room. Just as we had secured the bicycle the dining room lights came on. Doogoo was standing in the doorway to the living room and Inchan was sitting in the dark back there. I immediately abandoned See and scooted to my room. I changed my clothes and dived into bed, putting the pillow over my head as though that would conceal me if Doogoo came hunting for me.

Their voices were low but intense. Doogoo was telling See what a snake she was and that she's not spending another night under her roof. Then I heard crying from the steps and saw Indira come downstairs and join them in the living room. I got up and peeped around the corner. Doogoo was standing over See who stood there dripping wet and with her head bowed in shame. Indira was crying and trying to hug See but was apparently under instruction not to touch See. Inchan was sitting on the couch holding his head and shaking it sadly.

Eventually Doogoo told See to go get her clothes and get out. And to let the "li'l" boy drop her wherever she had come in from. Indira began sobbing loudly and was on the floor at her mother's feet begging her not to send See away. See passed by me in tears and headed upstairs for her things. I changed back into my wet clothes but did not go outside yet. I did not want to face Aunty Doogoo.

After what seemed like an hour but must have been a shorter time I heard See at the top of the stairs. Reena was crying and hugging her. Mammy hugged her and asked her if she would be safe and she nodded. Then See came downstairs with a heavy grip. Inchan brought out his bicycle and called me. I went out with my head bowed and took the bicycle from him. I saw him daub at his eyes as See tearfully left the yard.

We headed once again up the Backdam. This time See cried all the way back into Vryheid.

The next day was a holiday and I woke up late. It was evident there was a change of atmosphere in the home with See being absent. Sunil hadn't a clue what transpired earlier that morning and wanted to know if See was sick. Strangely, Raj and Dil were indifferent to their mother putting out See. Indira was puffy eyed and was still crying that morning. Lea stayed in bed most of the time since her wedding was off. Aunty Doogoo didn't tell me anything which made it even worse for me. I would have preferred she cussed me out and be done with it. But she said absolutely nothing to me about helping See.

I spent most of the morning over in the Yard. My scooter was done and I had taken two trial spins on the Backdam. It ran smoothly but it needed painting like the other scooters were. Chinee Roy said he had some paint home and went home to get them. While waiting in the Yard I learned that Bucky and Lucky had gone to Georgetown with Nathaniel to shop for the wedding.

"How he sound?" I asked.

"Wha' you mean 'how he sound,'" fretted Dillip.

"He talking funny?" I asked.

"Naw, he sound normal," said Moppa.

"I ain't think he went away that long you know. Just a year or two," said Coco.

"That ain't mean nothing," said Tillam. "I know Smithy from scheme went away for seventeen days and when he come back you had to get translator to tell you what he saying."

"That is true. Some people does just put on," Dillip said.

"Where Roy with this paint man?" I asked impatiently.

"If Roy say he bringing paint he bringing it. Just hold on man," said Moppa.

"Squingee you go lend me your brush them?" I asked.

"Wha' you think, I ain't no brush library," he said.

"Lend the man you brush them. You too blasted stingy," Tillam said.

"Is joke ah making man," Squingee grinned at me and headed home for his brushes.

By midday I had painted my scooter and took it to the back of my yard to dry. I had painted it light blue and painted two guns and a socket in the front then painted in red, "Duck, You Sucker." Doogoo was on the prowl again and I retired to the loft where I went through some comic books I had stashed there. I must have dozed off for I was awakened by the bathroom door slamming shut. I got up and crept to my usual spot. It was Lea. And she wasn't singing.

Lea took off her clothes and let the water run in the bucket. She had extra clothes with her including a rag. She threw water over her body twice then she took a wire clothes hanger and bent and twisted it into some sort of shape. I had no idea what she was doing. After she seemed satisfied with the shape of the wire she squatted with her legs apart. She was backing me and I couldn't see exactly where she was putting the hanger, but it was somewhere between her legs. Her hands were trembling and I could hear her crying and making straining noises as though in pain. She stopped suddenly and was sobbing with short breaths while the water ran in the bucket to prevent whatever sound she was making from reaching the house.

To my horror, when she threw the wire away from her, there was blood on it and blood on her hands. It wasn't much, but I could see the bright red. She sat with her knees pulled up to her chest like she had done before. She had a hand to her face as she cried and her shoulders jerked spasmodically. I felt so sorry for her and the mess she had got herself into.

After a while she got up and threw water on her head again and began bathing. She spent an unusual amount of time washing between her legs. I didn't see any more blood so I supposed she had only bled a little. She stopped crying and composed herself before leaving the bathroom. When she came out she went behind the bathroom and threw the wire hanger over the high back fence and into the drain behind there. Just when she came around the bathroom to head back to the house I heard someone come into the shed. I froze. I peered down between the rough flooring and saw Sunil looking around down there for something. After a while he went back out and into the house. That was a little too close for me. I would have to think of something to stop Sunil from prowling around.

After thinking about the reason behind Sunil's need for a kerosene can, I was able to put two and two together since he was obviously back with Chandra and I had mentioned having a kerosene oil can that night when we had the argument. I supposed Chandra wanted to know if I was lying about the kerosene oil can. Maybe if Sunil found the can for her she would know that she really was in the clear where starting that fire was concerned.

That afternoon I asked Squingee for one of the dozen kerosene oil cans he claimed he had. I got a Castrol can just like the one I had picked up from the drain. I smuggled it into the house and put it under my bed. If Sunil wanted a can so badly he was going to get one.

Now that See wasn't there Mammy, Doogoo, Lea and Indira took turns in the kitchen. Late that afternoon Lea called me from the Yard. She was at the gate.

"You know where Ganpatsingh Drug Store is?" she asked. I nodded.

"I want you run down there and buy a couple things for me," she said.

She told me what to buy and gave me the money. She told me to bring them right back to her and not to tell anyone. She would give me a dollar if I did that.

I took my scooter from the back of the yard and stopped over at the Yard for Spanner. We scooted up the Backdam on our scooters then down Pitt Street, across the Main Road and all the way out to the Waterside. The drug store was across the street from the big JP Santos store and the market.

Spanner did not want to go in the store since he was afraid of the lady who owned the store and worked there. We could not take the scooter in the store anyway so he kept them outside while he waited for me.

It was a big drug store with a long counter and what seemed like thousands of bottles and medical looking things in cases behind the counter. There were two doorways leading back there and I could see more of the same stuff back there but in bigger bottles. There was a girl in her teens and the woman Spanner was afraid of, attending to people who were lined up at the counter. The woman was probably in her forties and was dressed in pants and shirt like a man. She was fair, had her hair cut short and combed back, and had a cigarette bobbing from the edges of her lips. All her mannerisms were masculine, even her speech.

"You go just stand up there staring or you want to buy something," she said to me when it was my turn. She stood there squinting at me through the cigarette smoke as I recalled what Lea wanted.

"Yes Mam. A pack of cotton wool, a small bottle of essence and a bottle of malathion," I said.

She disappeared briefly behind the cloud of smoke she exhaled then, as she turned away she said, "Somebody trying to kill they self?"

"She ask you anything?" Spanner asked when he got back outside.

"Who?"

"The man-lady."

"Just what I did want. Boy, she does smoke like a chimney."

"Yea. I think she's a man with breasts. You get what you want?"

"Yes," I said and took the things out of the paper bag to show him.

"Malathion? People does use that to kill grass or kill they self," he said. "Alyuh ain't got no grass."

We had just moved off and I stopped in my tracks.

"To kill they self?"

"Yea. Is a poison. They does drink it and kill they self."

I didn't say anything else. I was deep in thought. I took out the bottle again and looked at it. It was a dark yellow liquid.

When I got home Lea wanted to know why I took so long. I told her there was a crowd at the drug store. I gave her the things and she gave me the dollar she had promised, then smuggled the things upstairs with her. I put up my scooter in the shed. I went over to the yard to see if Bucky was there but she had not come back yet.

Chapter Eighteen

That evening Mammy took Indira to the cinema, I supposed to get her mind off See for a while. She had invited Lea too but Lea said she wasn't feeling good. Reena went with Mammy and Indira.

After they left I was lying on my bed, reading one of my comics when Sammy Ramkissoon came back to visit. He came with the boy's mother this time. From what I heard, Doogoo was adamant that Lea was not ready for this marriage and that it was off. The mother could not understand and Doogoo was not giving her any satisfaction as to why the wedding was off. The mother asked about the other girl and I knew she was referring to See. Doogoo made some excuse but didn't tell her the truth. Inchan was very apologetic throughout the whole preceding.

Shortly after they left I saw Lea heading out to the bathroom with her towel and a little too much clothing. She had been crying. She had her hair combed up like she was going out. I quickly sneaked around to the loft of the woodshed.

I climbed the ladder then fumbled my way in the semi darkness to my usual spot. The light from the kitchen splashed out into the yard and made inside of the bathroom bright enough for me to see everything. Lea closed the door behind her. She started to cry again and took off her dress. Under the dress she had on her Commercial school uniform. She made sure her hair was in place. Then she unwrapped her towel and I could see she had what looked like the bottle of malathion hidden in there. She unscrewed the cork and looked at the bottle for a while. She whispered something religious, then took a deep breath, leaned her head backward and drank.

Chapter Nineteen

I remembered the first time I had watched something die. We were living in the village then. It was when we saw Mammy kill a fowl for the first time. I must have been three or four years old at the time. Mammy had taken the protesting bird and placed its neck on a tree stump. Then she had swung down hard with the big kitchen knife. The head flew off and bright red blood spurted from the neck. The feet kept kicking up until the life and blood drained from the bird. It was an ugly sight.

There was no blood this time. I had never watched a person die and had no intention of doing so after that first unpleasant experience of watching the chicken die.

I backed away from the wall and took my time climbing down the ladder. I was mad at this Suresh fellow who had put Lea in a situation where she found it necessary to take her own life. I took my time climbing down the ladder from the loft. I could hear Lea gagging in the bathroom. I came out of the shed. There was no one in the kitchen. The gagging suddenly stopped.

I walked cautiously to the bathroom door.

" Lea?" I called. There was no answer. "Open the door Lea. Is me, Milo," I called. There was still no response. I reached into the crease between the door and the upright and flipped the wooden latch. I opened the door quickly, slipped inside, then closed the door behind me. She was lying on the wet floor with the half full malathion bottle lying on its side on the floor.

"Lea?" I called.

"Ah dying Milo," she moaned. She seemed scared but somewhat relieved at the same time.

"You not dying Lea. Is not malathion," I said.

She blinked a few times and turned her eyes to me. She moved her fingers then arms, then she slowly sat up, probably realizing that they all functioned like they usually did.

"You didn't buy the malathion?"

"Yes, but I empty it out," I said. She picked up the half empty bottle and smelled it.

"Then is what I drink?"

"Cooking oil and healing oil," I said.

"Cooking oil and healing oil!" she exclaimed. I turned on the pipe and let it run in the bucket. She was getting loud and definitely wouldn't like the other ingredient I had added to the brew.

"And a li'l dirty water," I confessed.

"And dirty water!"

"The cooking oil wasn't enough and the smell was too strong. You woulda know."

Lea leaned forward and spat several times.

"At least that won't kill you," I said.

She spat on the concrete a couple more times then she began crying again.

"What's the use. I can't even kill meself properly," she lamented.

"Lea, where people does go when they don't want to be pregnant no more?" I asked.

She stopped crying and looked at me strangely.

"Why you ask that?" she asked guardedly.

"Lea, it ain't worth killing you'self over Suresh," I said and kneeled before her. This time she reacted as though I had spat in her face.

"You... you know about Suresh? Who tell you?" she asked and looked like she was going to get rambunctious with me like she had done that evening when she had come in late from her clandestine trip with him across the river.

"I know you' pregnant for Suresh already," I said quietly.

Lea's eyes were wide open now.

"Who else know?" she asked in awe.

"Only me," I lied.

"Omigorsh!" she exclaimed. "How … how you know all this?"

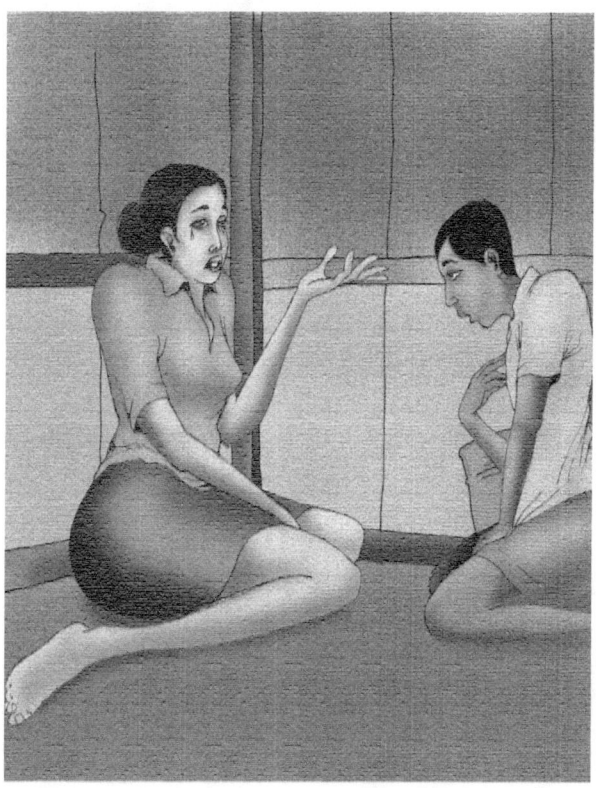

"It ain't matter. You is me cousin and you' not going to kill yourself. We go figure out how to fix this, right?"

She leaned her head to the side like Reena did and looked at me in disbelief.

"How old you is Milo?"

"It don't matter. Lea, if I know all this you ain't think I could fix a li'l problem like this?"

"A li'l problem! How?" she said.

"You got to promise not to try kill yourself first. I ain't going through all this just to see you turn around and kill you'self," I said in a business-like manner.

"What?"

"I could get you out of this but you got to stop trying to kill yourself."

"Alright, what you go do?" she said doubtfully.

"The good thing is that only me and you know about this, right?"

She nodded.

"And it go stay so. How you did stop getting baby the last time?" I asked.

Lea's eyes opened even wider.

"You know... how you know..."

"Yes, I know that too."

Lea folded her arms and leaned back against the zinc wall of the bathroom. I could see she did not know what to make of me.

"What else you know?" she asked in awe.

"I know Suresh is married too," I said softly.

Her mouth opened and closed like she wanted to say something but couldn't.

"Who are you?" she managed to ask with a frown.

"Wha' you mean?"

"How the hell you know all this?"

I had a mischievous compulsion to tell her I was the reincarnation of *Ganesh*. In her state of mind she probably would have believed me. But I let it go.

"The same way I know all this the same way I can get you out of all this," I said.

"Alright," she said and had probably reasoned that if I knew all this I probably knew what I was talking about.

"But if I see you anywhere near a bottle of malathion or gramazone I done with you and you on your own," I said.

"Alright," she said and nodded slowly.

"And don't go buying no rope neither."

"Alright."

"And don't go cutting your hand them..."

"Alright! If you get me out of this then I have no reason to do that," she said without emotion.

"Alright. Where you went last time to stop get baby?"

"A lady in Islington. But she dead now. There is another lady somewhere in Vryheid but I hear she expensive," she said.

"Alright. Find out how much it is and you go go to she," I said. I heard Reena calling toward the Yard for me.

"You can get money for that too?" she asked skeptically.

"No, Suresh go pay for it," I said. She was disappointed. "I done know he say he not paying but I will make he pay for it."

"You? How?" she asked.

"Leave that to me," I said. "I getting call. I got to go," I said and got up.

Lea got to her feet still staring at me.

"Why you doing this Milo?" she asked and still seemed to be in a daze.

"What?"

"Why you doing this for me and I don't even be nice to you," she said and was crying again.

"You is me cousin Lea..." Before I could finish she had me in a bear hug and was crying all over me.

"You save my life tonite," she cried. I wanted to cry too. I just couldn't understand her wanting to take her life over this.

After a while she released me.

"You going to get out of this and next year this time you won't even remember what you were so sad about," I said cheerfully. She managed a smile even though she was still crying.

"Dry your eyes. We got to go," I said and picked up the malathion bottle. Then I took the bucket of water and threw it on the floor to wash away whatever liquid was there.

"You go first," I said. "I ain't want nobody think I been peeping at you."

Lea smiled. She put on her dress over her wet school uniform, then kissed me on my forehead before leaving with her things. I waited a couple minutes then came out of the bathroom and threw the malathion bottle over the high fence.

Reena had wanted me to go to the shop for Mammy who was cooking. She needed me to buy cubes but sent Sunil instead. I went to my room, removed the kerosene oil can I had got from Squingee and put it under Sunil's bed. I hid it not too far under the bed and right behind his empty grip. I settled down to do some drawing.

When Sunil came in I pretended to be sleepy and turned over to sleep. After he turned off the light and settled down to sleep I came out of bed and removed the can from under his bed and put it under mine. I made sure he heard the clanging sound of the can. He didn't move and pretended to be asleep. Then I went back to bed and after a few minutes, pretended to be asleep. I knew he wasn't sleeping.

I breathed deeply so that he could suppose I was asleep. Sure enough, Sunil came out of his bed quietly and removed the can from under my bed. I heard him go outside and I peeped to see where he was going. He headed to the shed with the can. I jumped back into bed and faked a deep sleep. My brother could be such a sucker sometimes.

The following morning before I left for school Reena asked me if I would go with her to the Commercial School for her to register. She didn't explain why she wanted me with her but I realized that, since we began talking regularly, she had this confidence in me being perceptive.

I'm not so sure if she thought I was intelligent or just plain devious.

That midday when me, Tillam and Squingee came back early from lunch and were in the Gardens we struck silver in the lover's section of the Gardens. Squingee would have gotten a finder's fee if he had thought about it. He led us around the hedges to a spot we hardly frequented. To my surprise it was Lea's lover. He was all over this girl who wore the Commercial School uniform. She seemed rather unwilling and was determined to keep her knees together despite his wrestling moves. Eventually he gave up, lit up a cigarette then looked at his watch. The girl smoothed out her clothes and wanted to know if he was vex or disappointed. He said he was both and that they wasted their time coming up there. After looking at his watch a couple of times he said they had to be getting back. The girl wanted to stay a while longer.

"Lea know about this?" Tillam asked when we were heading back to school. Squingee was still back there hoping the girl changed her mind.

"I don't know," I said.

"You go tell she?" he said.

"Naw, let she find out for she'self. And you don't tell she nothing either."

"When I could get to peep Lea again?" he asked with a grin.

"You have twenty-five cents?" I asked.

"I go owe you."

"When you get it let me know," I said. I was beginning to have second thoughts about selling peeping spots for Lea, being so sorry for her and the situation she was in.

"If ah ask you something you go vex?" Tillam said.

"What?"

"Just between me and you."

"What nuh?"

"I would pay you a whole dollar to see Reena," he said sheepishly.

"What?"

"Ah know you woulda vex," he said.

"You ain't got twenty-five cents but you could pay a whole dollar?" I said but was getting upset that he had asked to see my sister naked.

"I could borrow it," he said.

"No! A hundred dollars wouldn't make me do that," I said.

"How about one-fifty?" he said and laughed.

I was feeling badly that he would pay to see Reena. When I did think about it, Reena seemed to have more curves and would be more interesting to look at than one would at Lea. And he had seen Lea already anyway. But this was my sister he was talking about. What would come next, five dollars to see Mammy? I realized then that I had opened this door and should not have been surprised where it led. I decided there and then that peep shows were no longer available.

That afternoon I left school and headed straight up the waterside toward Wrefords where Reena worked. As I passed Globe cinema I noticed a huge poster for "Duck You Sucker" outside. It looked like it was opening that weekend. I made a mental note of it.

When I got to Wrefords Reena was one of three cashiers at work. I felt so proud to see her sitting there confidently working the cash register and counting money. I watched her for a few minutes before letting her know I was there. She said she would be with me in fifteen minutes. Barkley's Bank was across the street. I walked across there but it was closed to customers. When I looked through the glass door I could see employees in there attending to their work. I didn't see Bucky.

Once Upon A Time In Berbice

Reena came out from Wrefords and signaled to me that she was ready. We walked farther down Water Street and eventually turned down Nicolay Street. The school was an ordinary looking residence with a shop looking entrance downstairs.

We went in and Reena spoke to a lady in glasses at a counter. I supposed she was the secretary. She talked with Reena for a while then got some forms and sat down with her. There were half a dozen girls in uniform standing around while others were preparing for dismissal. I was tempted to go explore the school while Reena attended to her business. I decided to stay put since Reena did ask me to come with her. There were teachers coming in and out of the office. Some were female and at least one elderly male.

"Mr. Rai, you ain't attend to me yet you know," a girl said as a younger male teacher brushed passed me and went to a cabinet in the office.

"Give me a second and I'll be there," he said.

His voice sounded familiar. He had his back to me and I kept my eyes on him. Even without seeing his face I started thinking of Suresh from the Gardens. When he turned around, sure enough, it was he. He looked in our direction and smiled. His eyes had slid past me to Reena who was still with the secretary.

"Hello. We getting a new student?" he said with what he thought was a syrupy smile and walked over to us.

"This is Mr. Rai," said the secretary. " He will be one of your teachers."

"Hi," Reena said with a smile.

"Hello, I'm Suresh Rai," he said and extended a hand.

"Reena Teekasingh," Reena said with a smile and got up half way.

"No no, sit down and finish up. We'll see more of each other soon I hope," he said and smiled slyly, looking her straight in the eye. I could feel my skin crawl. Reena nodded and sat back down to attend to her applications.

"Mr. Rai?" the girl called from the door again. I watched him slither out of the office and to her. Then I realized this was the same girl I had seen with him in the gardens that midday. They went back into a classroom with some other students. I went to the door to see where they were. When I turned to go back in the office I saw Lea. She was standing with a small crowd by the gate looking toward where he and the girl had disappeared in the classroom. She didn't notice me.

I didn't know who this Suresh Rai thought he was. He got my cousin Lea pregnant twice and had now pushed her to the point where she was trying to kill herself. Then he had the nerves to start working on another of his students while he had my cousin pregnant. And he was flirting with this girl in front of Lea like she meant nothing to him. Now he had the testicular fortitude to have designs on my sister Reena? I was never so ticked-off since Tillam offered me a dollar to peep at Reena. This Suresh Rai had to be dealt with. I had to get busy fixing his business where Lea was concerned and then attend to him to make sure he didn't touch Reena again; not even a handshake.

"When you supposed to start at the Commercial school?" I asked Reena as we walked home that afternoon.

"Next Monday after work," she said and was pleased with herself.

"When it finishing?"

"They say eight o'clock."

"Who bringing you home?"

"I'm a big girl you know. I could walk home myself," she said and smiled. I could see she appreciated me being concerned about her. "I go ask Bertie to pick me up."

"You know who Mr. Rai is?" I asked.

"He does teach something at the school. He look like a nice person," she said.

"He is Lea' boyfriend that get she pregnant," I said.

Reena stopped abruptly.

"Mr. Rai!" she exclaimed and I could see her face contort in distaste.

"He same one," I confirmed.

"He's the one that get Lea in trouble?"

"Yes. So you better be careful around him," I said.

She started walking slowly again. Then she looked at her right hand and wiped it on the side of her skirt as though she had slime on it.

"You can get a typewriter to type a letter for me?" I asked her.

"Type a letter for what?" she asked suspiciously.

"A letter to Mr. Suresh Rai," I said.

"What you want me do that for?" she asked with concern.

"Just between me and you, right?"

"Alright."

"He got to pay to take care of Lea," I said.

"Take care of... You mean what I think you mean?" she said with narrowed eyes.

"Yes."

She stopped again and shook her head.

"Milo, how you know about all of that?" she asked.

"How *you* know about that?" I countered.

"Girls talk about things like that. Don't tell me Tillam and Coco and your li'l friends over at the Yard does be talking about that too," she said and was smiling.

"Only sometimes," I said and laughed.

"What you want me to type?" she asked.

"When you get a typewriter I go tell you," I said.

"Where I go get a typewriter from?"

"Mr. Anton has one on his desk in school. You can use that one," I said.

"I got to go class in the evening. When I go do that?"

"You can do it this week before you start class next week."

"This week when?"

"You got to tell me."

"Maybe this Thursday." She seemed amused by something and looked at me with a frown.

"What?" I said innocently.

"I remember that letter you did send to me that was supposed to be from Harry Kissoon," she said.

"Which letter?" I said and pretended to have amnesia.

"Don't get stupid now and play you can't remember. Is something like that you plan to do right?"

"Something like that," I said and laughed.

That evening I whispered to Lea to meet me by the wood shed at the back.

"I saw you in school today," I said.

"What?"

"I saw you at your school today."

"What you been doing there? Don't tell me you went there to see him."

"I did see him. But that's not why I was there. I went with Reena. She registering to do evening class there."

"Oh me gosh!"

"What?"

"He might want... never mind."

"What that girl name that was running behind him when school dismiss?"

"You saw that too?" she said. Then she looked away for a few seconds. I could see her eyes were wet again.

"What that girl name?" I asked again.

"Rita Mahobir," she said quietly.

"Must write it on a piece of paper and give me," I said.

"Alright." She seemed resigned to letting me handle things for her.

That Thursday afternoon Reena turned up at the school when we were cleaning. She asked Mr. Anton to use the typewriter on his desk, claiming she had to do some practice before she started evening classes the following Monday. That was partly true. At her request he brought the typewriter to the table of the Standard Two classroom.

"Alright. I can't type so I go take me time," she said and operated a couple of things to familiarize herself with the machine. After a few minutes she was ready.

"My dear Mr. Rai..." I dictated and Reena began pecking on the keyboard with two fingers.

By the time Mammy and Mr. Anton were through with their draughts we were done. On our way home Reena stopped at the corner shop and bought some plain envelopes.

That evening there was a big rehearsal at the house for Indira's wedding. It was crowded and noisy in the house and under the tent. I sought refuge in the Yard. Most of the boys wanted to hang out by our gate and peep at the proceedings in our house.

"You know what I see today in the market?" Tillam said as he steered me toward the Backdam culvert and away from the others.

"No, what?"

"I been in the market to buy shrimps for me mother late this afternoon. When I coming back through the main market and them vendors were packing up I see Lea' boyfriend," he said.

"So?"

"He was at a stall with this lady that was packing up. She had two li'l children with she. He was hugging and kissing them up," he said.

"That is he wife?" I asked wide eyed.

"It look so."

"I see." I was beginning to think how I could use this. I wished I knew this before we typed the letter.

"Where this stall is?" I asked.

"You know Ms. Dookram stall? Everybody in the market know she," he said.

"No."

"Just ask for she. This lady stall is right across from Ms. Dookram. She does sell rice and peas and things like that."

"What she look like?"

"She fair and kinda tall and skinny. Got she head in a head tie and wear glasses."

The next day I got Lea to drop one letter on Mr. Rai's desk without him knowing it was she who delivered it. I later learned that she watched him in the sly when he did get to it. He read it, smiled slyly and spruced up his moustache, combed his hair and began humming a love song. He looked at his watch.

The letter actually stated that the writer was a new student who had briefly met him and had fallen in love with him. And that she knew he would be her teacher but she would like to know if he liked her too. If he was interested she would meet him privately at Harvey's snackette that midday. She was shy about it and would not come into Harvey's if he was not there. If he did not turn up she would understand that he was not interested and she would never write another letter nor try to befriend him again. At the bottom was typed "Secret Admirer."

Lea later told me that that midday Mr. Rai left early like he used to when he was meeting her. At the same time and across town, I walked quickly from school with Tillam down to Harvey's at Church Street.

"You're Mr. Rai? A policeman just stop outside and tell me to give you this," Tillam said and delivered the second letter to him. He looked puzzled and opened the letter cautiously and with a frown. Tillam was gone by the time he opened the one page letter.

From across the street I saw him crumple up the letter after he had read it, and look around suspiciously. Then he smoothed out the letter again and read it a second time.

Basically I had Reena write that this letter was from the same "Secret Admirer" who had sent the first letter and that "we" had been watching him for the past few months. "We" wanted him to get this letter privately since, if it fell into the wrong hands it would be very scandalous and he would probably lose his job. "We" knew he had already got one student pregnant, and "we" believed he was having sex or trying to have sex with another student, Rita Mohabir. "We" were not sure who the pregnant student was but we knew he had taken her to a hotel across the river at Rosignol and "we" were in the process of finding out her name. As soon as we did find out who the student was "we" will contact her family as well as his wife.

Mr. Rai left Harvey's in a hurry. Although it was not a hot day he was sweating.

That night the wedding festivities began. The house was crowded downstairs and the kitchen was bustling with activities. The odor of spicy foods and baked delicacies floated through the house. In the midst of all the confusion Lea signaled me to meet her at the shed.

"What you did?" she asked with concern.

"What you mean?" I asked cautiously, for I had no idea what Mr. Rai did after he left.

"He gave me the money," she said.

"What? He gave you already?"

"This afternoon. Said he wanted to see me. Then ask me how much it is. He gave me twenty dollars extra. What did you tell him?"

"Nothing. Just the letter I give you to give him."

"But he look happy when he get that letter. Is what happen afterward that must be frighten him," she said.

"I can't tell you that. Is better if you don't know."

She was silent for a while. As she stared at me I could see she was trying to figure out what I had done.

"So what now?" I asked.

"I go need a drop in Vryheid."

"You find out is where?" She nodded. "When?"

"Now."

In fifteen minutes I was riding up the Backdam and heading for Vryheid with Lea on the bar. I had borrowed Uncle Inchan's bicycle under the guise of having to go on an errand. With everybody busy or getting drunk nobody questioned me. We rode into the darkness past BEI High school and past the little house where Christopher and See now lived. The light was on inside. I told Lea that's where See lived and I wanted to stop. Although she wanted to see her sister she said it would not be a good idea since See might guess why she was in this area at night.

At Lea's directions we crossed a bridge and turned down a dam. We had to walk since part of the dam was muddy and it was difficult to see with there being no street lights. We walked across the little bridge of the third house on the left and into the small flooded yard.

In response to Lea's knock a woman opened the door and let us in. Lea left her shoes at the door. I expected an old woman but this was a dougla lady in her mid forties. She was very businesslike. She asked Lea how far and Lea said five weeks. She then asked Lea if she had one before and Lea nodded. The lady went into her kitchen where there was a large pot with something boiling in it. She had some white towels in a pile on a table.

Lea was fidgeting with her hands nervously. The woman came back to Lea and asked for the money. Lea gave her several twenty dollar notes. She counted them and put them away in the pocket of her blouse. Then she went back in the kitchen, washed her hands with soap, then, to my surprise, took out some metal implements from the pot. She put them in one of the towels and wrapped them up. She went into the second of two bedrooms. Then she came back to the doorway which was concealed with a thin cloth curtain. She motioned for Lea to come. Lea got up, smiled at me uncomfortably then went into the bedroom behind the curtain.

I didn't know how long it took. The muffled screaming had started about five minutes after Lea went in there. She sounded like she had something stuffed in her mouth to prevent her from screaming loudly. The screaming and crying continued with the woman trying to assure her it was alright. After a while curiosity got the better of me. I got up and poked a crease to one end of the curtain and looked in.

Lea was lying with her head to the end of the bed closer to me. It was a single bed. She held a white rag that was in her mouth with both hands. She had her dress pulled up on her chest. There were white towels on her stomach. Her legs were wide apart with each resting on a wooden contraption and secured there with what looked like cloth belts. The woman was sitting on a chair and bent forward between Lea's legs at the edge of the bed. She had one of the metal implements she had put in the towel and everything in that vicinity appeared to be bloody. I could not see anything else but Lea's head, bundled dress on her chest, white partly bloodied towel below, her naked spread legs on the wooden stands, and the woman sitting there manipulating something between Lea's legs.

I went back and sat in the chair and put my hands to my ears. After a while the screaming stopped and she was just crying. The lady came out a couple of times to go to the kitchen. The last time she took in a glass of brownish liquid for her to drink.

Chapter Nineteen

Eventually, when Lea came out she walked slowly and with short steps. The lady told her she was going to be alright. We walked slowly in the dark out to Vryheid road.

"How you feeling?" I asked since she wasn't going to say anything.

"Very sore. I get cramps," she said quietly.

She got on the bar and told me to ride slowly, which I did.

When we got back to the house it was still busy and noisy. Lea went in quietly and lay down on my bed. If anyone was looking for her she could always say she wasn't feeling well and had laid down downstairs which was why they couldn't find her.

I went milling about the crowd that had spilled onto the street in front of our gate. Some of the boys were still up. Spanner, Dillip and Tillam wanted me to go get some food for them from the kitchen. When I went back there Mammy and about four ladies I did not know were in there. I got two plates of food and came back out to the gate. On each plate was rice, bounjal curry with chicken, channa and a roti.

It was while we were eating outside by the gate that it happened. I knew Inchan, his brother, his friend Sammy Ramkissoon, and some other men were drinking heavily and were all drunk and noisy. Mr. Jacobs had come down the street drunk and had sniffed out the free liquor flowing across the street at our house. So he waltzed in there as though on special invitation and joined the party of drunks. Word got to his wife that he was partaking in the drinking frenzy going on over there. She went across the street to get him. Mr. Jacobs was reluctant to leave that which he had paid for earlier at Dixie's bar, but was now getting free of charge. A row between the two ensued. Sammy Ramkissoon took it upon himself to intervene and broker a compromise between husband and wife. The row spilled onto the street with Mrs. Jacobs dragging a reluctant husband and Sammy mouthing off between the two.

Mrs. Jacobs was a well proportioned and good looking dougla woman. The home dress that clung to her buxom figure enhanced this property about her. In his drunken state Sammy fell into some of his old habits, one of which was his tendency to believe he was Cupid and capable of charming any woman into bed. He made several physical passes at Mrs. Jacobs who was stunned by his audacity and flattered at first, until Mr. Jacobs noticed what was going on.

What resulted was a drunken brawl between Sammy Ramkissoon and Mr. Jacobs that began in the street. Inchan and several others, all drunk, tried to part the fight and caused more harm than good.

By the time the unliquored men did get around to separating the combatants, Sammy Ramkissoon had a black eye and his shirt and part of his pants torn off, while Mr. Jacobs was nursing a split lip. They brought a blubbering and half naked Sammy back into the house.

It was then that we saw it. Against the background of his fair skin and in the middle of his chest was a large red birthmark, the size of a big closed fist.

Chapter Twenty

Chapter Twenty

With the attention of most of the people who were present at the occasion being on the disturbance, there weren't many people who didn't notice them bringing Sammy Ramkissoon into the yard. And only the blind could have escaped noticing that large birthmark on his chest. It was as conspicuous as the tall telecoms metal tower was in the middle of the town. But to most, it was nothing but an ugly, unsightly birthmark. However, to me, Tillam, Doogoo, Indira, Mammy, and Lea, it stimulated different reactions.

At first sighting I was just surprised by the thing, like I was when I first saw Lea naked. Then it dawned on me that it was coincidental that both she and this man had the same mark. I didn't think much else about it but was surprised by Tillam's wide eyed, open-mouthed expression, and the few expletives that escaped his lips. He looked wide-eyed at me but didn't say anything else. I was then distracted by Lea screaming from the doorway where she had been standing after having been awakened by the ruckus outdoor. She kept screaming and wouldn't stop even though Mammy and some other women ran to her side to console her. Her attention was riveted on Sammy Ramkissoon's chest. I couldn't help wondering why she was so appalled by his birthmark when she had one just a bit smaller than his.

Indira just stood there crying and staring at her mother with this bewildered look on her face. Doogoo stood by the living room door and kept her eyes cast downward. Other than that there was no reaction from her. Mammy, with this general expression of disbelief, shot Doogoo angry glances from time to time as she and the women tried consoling Lea who had collapsed to the floor in a faint. They had to make room around her and some of them were fanning her. Inchan was too drunk to know what was going on. Reena was standing in the kitchen and not quite sure what to make of all this. They took Sammy Ramkissoon to the bathroom at the back to clean him up.

After they revived Lea they took her up to her room. Mammy appeared to be very angry and upset. She came back downstairs and said something angrily to Doogoo who went back upstairs with her. They closed the door and I had no idea what they were talking about. Reena went up there shortly after but could not get in the room. However she stayed up there.

The fight had apparently broken up the festivities and in an hour or two the house was cleared of visitors and most of us began settling down for the night.

Reena came downstairs and slipped into my room. Sunil was not home yet.

"Mammy and Aunty Doogoo got big argument upstairs," Reena began with eyes opened in alarm.

"What they arguing about?"

"I ain't sure. Something about Doogoo doing something terrible when they used to live on the Corentyne."

"Wha' she did?"

"I don't know. Mammy was asking how she could do that and Aunty Doogoo said that Mammy didn't know what she had to go through to get where she is."

I had no clue what that was about and it must have shown in my face.

"It look like Doogoo did something bad back then and she was arguing with Mammy that if she didn't do that that she woulda end up with nothing like Mammy. Then Mammy say at least she didn't have to do something like that. And Doogoo mention something about Mammy and the black teacher boy."

"Mr. Anton?"

"I think that's who she mean. Then all kinda things they bring up. Mammy talk about Doogoo putting out See instead of letting the girl get marrid, and Doogoo ask she if she want See to end up like Aunty Nalini. And Mammy say that ain't a bad way to end up. Then Aunty Doogoo said she not surprised Mammy said that, seeing Mammy doing the same thing. Mammy ask she if she even knew where See was staying and if See wouldn't ah been better off if Doogoo did let the girl get married to Christopher. Is a whole lot of stuff came up."

"Like what so?"

"Well," Reena sighed and seemed tired by all this drama in the house. "They bring up things about when they did growing up and how Nanny used to treat Mammy like she was an unwanted pregnancy and Doogoo wasn't any better. Then Mammy bring up Lea and how this going to affect her. I don't know why all this come up because of a fight Mr. Ramkissoon had."

"I don't know. Except that Lea and Mr. Ramkissoon have the same red birthmark on their chest," I said. "I wonder where Sunil is?"

"What you just say?" Reena said and in such a way I wondered if I had just cursed without noticing it.

"What?"

"What you just say about Lea and Mr. Ramkissoon?"

"Nothing."

"About a birthmark…"

"Oh, they have the same red birthmark on their chest. It shape like a fist and is right here," I had taken my eyes of Reena to show her on my chest where the mark was, and didn't notice how this was affecting her.

"Oh me-lawd-O!" she exclaimed and jumped off the bed wringing her hands. He eyes were bulged open and staring at me.

"What?"

Reena reacted worse than she did that night when I had told her that Lea was pregnant. After about two full minutes of hopping around and hand wringing, she finally sat down closer to me with her hands to her mouth.

"Mr. Ramkissoon is Lea' father," she said.

"Because they have the same birthmark?"

"You can be so smart and so stupid sometimes," she said without malice. "He is Lea' real father. That is why all this coming out tonite. Everybody that know Lea have that same birthmark realize what going on."

It made sense. Which is probably why Tillam, Doogoo, Mammy and Lea reacted that way.

"You think Uncle Inchan know?"

"I don't know," she said and got up again. "No wonder Doogoo didn't want Lea marrid that boy. She woulda been marrying she brother."

I was finally putting the pieces together and couldn't understand why I didn't make that link before.

"And Lea know that now. Jeese!" she said and sat down again. "Poor Lea. What she go do now?"

"Nothing. She Alright now," I said.

"What?"

"She ain't pregnant no more," I whispered.

Reena pulled back and looked at me with narrowed eyes.

"He give she the money?"

"All of it."

"And she... she went already?"

"Tonite."

"Oh me Momma! Poor Lea," she said. We sat there quietly for a while. "Where she went?"

"Why you ask that?" I asked and pretended to be suspicious.

"What you looking at me for. I ain't want.... I should slap you," she said angrily when she realized what I was implying.

"I not telling you. When your time come I will carry you," I said.

"When my time come? That go never happen to me boy," she said adamantly. There was another lull in conversation then she said, "You saw what she had to do?"

I nodded sadly.

"What it was like?" she asked and seemed embarrassed to be asking; I'm not sure whether it was because of the topic itself, or the fact that she had to ask her little brother about it.

"It terrible. She was hollering most of the time and there was a lot of blood," I said. Reena's face contorted into an expression of scorn and she closed her legs with her hands between them as she cringed.

"They let you watch?" she said in surprise.

"I peeped."

"I shouda know that already."

That Saturday morning, the day before the wedding, things more or less went back to normal. Mammy was still angry but she held her peace. Sunil had come in close to four O'clock that morning. We were all supposed to bathe early since people would be in decorating the place by ten O'clock. Eight O'clock that morning there was major concern when Lea locked herself in the bathroom and threatened to cut her wrist with a kitchen knife she claimed to have. They tried to reason with her but that did not work. Then Doogoo tried talking to her, but she didn't want to hear from Doogoo. Uncle Inchan tried begging but to no avail. Mammy tried reasoning with her again but nothing doing. Then she told Mammy that she wanted to talk with me.

All eyes turned on me as though I had some sort of power of which they were now becoming aware. Lea wanted no one anywhere near the bathroom. She opened the door and let me in, then locked it behind her.

She had on her sleeping dress and was seated on the bucket which she had turned upside down. She had a kitchen knife in her right hand.

"Don't worry. I only fooling them about the knife," she said. I smiled and squatted before her.

"How you feeling now?"

"Ah li'l crampy but I Alright now," she said. Her eyes were swollen from crying too much and she looked like she didn't sleep much. "You know what happened?"

"Yes."

"About my father?"

"Yes."

"My real father?"

I nodded.

"No wonder that bitch didn't want me marry the boy," she spat. I winced at the fact that she had called her mother a "bitch."

"I always wonder how come I'm the only one in the family with this ugly birthmark," she said and rubbed her chest between her breasts with a hand.

"You know, in a way, I'm sorry I went and do that thing last night. It woulda serve me mother right if I did just wait till couple months then surprise her; just like she shock me with this," she said angrily.

"You think so?"

"I feel so sometimes. You know how it feel to find out all of a sudden your daddy ain't your father?" she said and started to cry. She seemed like a little girl again.

"Well, at least you have a rich father," I said and tried to look on the bright side.

"That don't matter. I wonder if he even know he's my father," she said. I never thought of that.

She used her dress to dry her eyes then said, "Anyway, I ain't going to no wedding."

"Why?"

"To hell with them. Mommy ain't care about me or she wouldn't ah do this," she said, still daubing at her eyes.

"Is not Aunty Doogoo getting marrid you know."

"What you mean?"

"It not fair to Indira. She done missing she twin sister and now you not going to go," I said. She looked away and I could see she realized I was right.

"So what you think I should do?" she said and really seemed like she needed my advice.

"Right now you can tell them what you want," I said.

"Yea, that's true," she said with a smile.

"And Doogoo know you know about Mr. Ramkissoon so she won't want to get you mad and make you tell everybody. Right now only a few people know."

"Who know?" she asked and I could see she had not thought about that before.

"Well, Mammy know, Reena and Indira," I said. "I don't know if Uncle Inchan know. And Raj and Dil weren't home."

"Imagine that. Poor Daddy ain't even know I'm not his daughter," she said and was getting angry again.

"Is no sense getting mad. Just think of what you want or what Indira would want to make her happy tomorrow."

"I only doing this because of Indira. She don't deserve being unhappy on she wedding day," she said determinedly. "What to tell them I want?"

"Why you don't let Indira decide that since is she getting marrid," I said.

"Alright," she said. Then cracked the door open and told the crowd of family members at the back door that she wanted to talk to Indira.

Indira came through the crowd and to the bathroom.

"Lea, you alright?" she asked with genuine concern as she came up to the door.

"Come inside quick," Lea said and let her in. She locked the door behind her.

Indira immediately hugged her and started to cry.

"Indira, don't cry. Is alright. Don't cry," Lea said.

She held Indira at arms length then said, "Tomorrow is your wedding day and it going to be a happy day for you. Dry your eyes."

"You go be alright?" Indira asked and brightened up.

"Yes," Lea said and smiled. "Right now they going to do what I tell them to do. I want you to tell me what you want."

Indira looked at me and was probably wondering why I was even there at all.

"Milo know everything," Lea said.

"I want you to be at the wedding Lea," she said.

"What about See?"

"I want her to be there too but Mommy..."

"Mommy got to do what I say," Lea said determinedly.

"She go let See come?"

"She ain't got no choice," I said.

"He' right. She will have to, if I say so and you say so," Lea said.

"Alright," Indira said and brightened up.

"What about we cousins?" I asked.

"Yes, what about that," Lea marveled. "I never thought about that before because of Mammy. What you want Indira?"

"You think they would want to come though?" she said doubtfully.

"Is only because of Mammy they don't come around," Lea said.

"Alright."

"How we go do this?" Lea said to me.

"Let Indira tell them," I said. Indira looked at me, surprised that I was the one calling the shots.

Indira stepped out of the bathroom.

"Aunty Yvette, everything not going to be alright unless Mommy and Daddy agree with what I want for my wedding," she said.

Chapter Twenty

Mammy stepped in front of the gathering and on to the passage way to the bathroom.

"What you want Indira?" she said.

"I want See to come to my wedding," Indira said.

Mammy turned and called for Inchan and Doogoo. The latter reluctantly stepped forward. She looked tired and didn't seem to have had much sleep either.

"Mommy, I know you put See out but unless she will be here Lea say she not coming to the wedding. And I'm not getting married without Lea there," Indira said with much effort. Mammy was looking intensely at Doogoo who was fidgeting uncomfortably. Inchan looked at her pleadingly to agree which she reluctantly did.

"And I want Aunty Nalini and my cousins Alicia and Juanita here too," Indira said quickly. Doogoo sucked her teeth and attempted to turn back into the house, but Mammy held her firmly by the arm.

"Doogoo!" she snapped. Doogoo turned back and glared at Indira while Inchan begged her to agree, even if it was just to make Indira happy for her wedding. After a nervous pause and to everyone's relief, Doogoo reluctantly agreed. She turned and went back inside.

Indira looked back at us in the bathroom and smiled broadly.

"She shoulda ask for a million dollars," I said to Lea who laughed. It was good to hear her laugh.

"Lea, you coming out?" Mammy called to her.

"Ah got to bathe first," she shouted. " Alyuh move let me bathe."

By ten o'clock I was riding Uncle Inchan's bicycle up the Backdam heading for See's place in Vryheid. It was good to be riding in there in broad daylight for a change and on an official errand. When I got there Christopher and See were at the back of the house. They were surprised to see me. See was washing some clothes and Christopher was putting up wire clothes lines from the house to a tree nearby.

They sat on the back steps as I brought them up to date with what had been happening at the house. Then I got to the part with the fight.

"Uncle Sammy and Mr. Jacobs had a fight? Over what?" See asked in alarm. Christopher was sitting on the step just above the one she sat on. He had his arms around her middle and she held an arm.

"Mr. Jacobs say Uncle Sammy was getting fresh with he wife."

"I ain't surprise," she said.

"Why you' not surprised?" Christopher asked.

"When I was small I see he do something fresh with Mommy before and she pass it off like was a joke," See said. "So what happen after that?"

"Well when they part the fight nearly all of Sammy clothes get tear off and he had this big red birthmark on he chest," I said and looked for her reaction.

"What birthmark?" See said slowly.

"It big and red like a fist."

"Where it is?"

"Here," I said and showed her by placing my clenched fist in the middle of my chest.

"Oh me Momma!" See exclaimed and looked around at Christopher.

"What?" he said.

"Lea have a birthmark exactly like that in the middle of her chest," See said in awe. "And Uncle Sammy used to live next to Mommy them just after she marrid."

"Oh shucks! You think…" Christopher was wide eyed.

"And I always wonder how Lea get this big ugly birthmark there and nobody else in the family get it," she said in deep thought. "You know what that mean? That boy she was to marry to is she brother. No wonder

Chapter Twenty

Mommy was so much against the marriage as soon as she know who the boy father was."

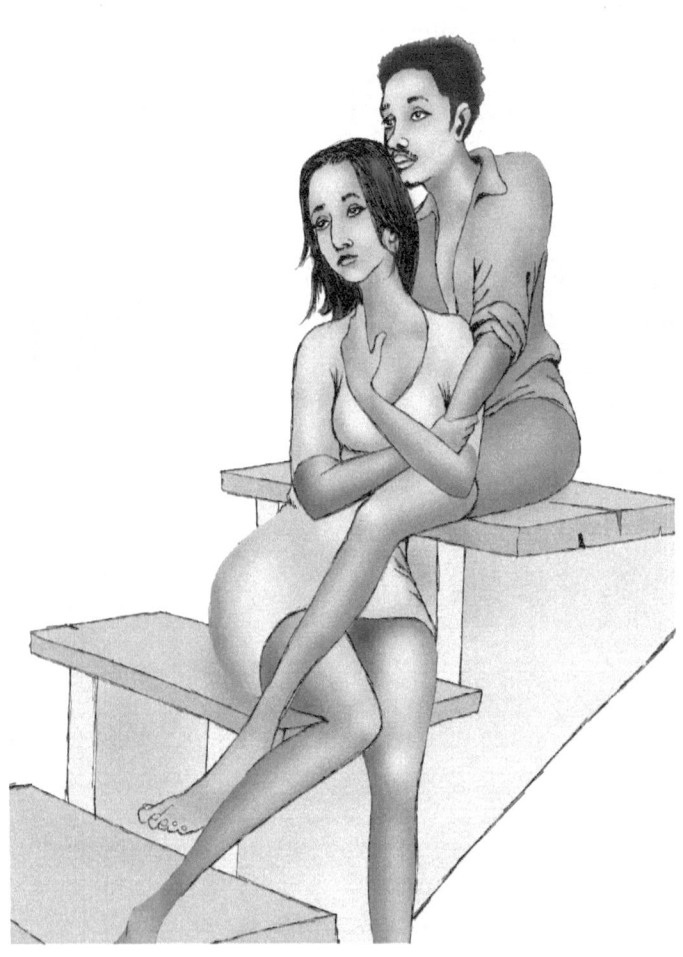

"You think the two O' we have the same father too and that's why she don't want we get marrid?" Christopher leaned forward and said confidentially to her.

"Christopher! This is serious man," she fretted.

"Alright, Alright!" he said and pretended to be serious.

"How Lea take all this?" See asked.

"Not too good at first," I said.

"She nuh must. She must be now know why Mommy didn't want she get marrid to that boy."

"She tried to cut her wrist this morning," I said.

"What!" See was shocked. Christopher looked at me in alarm.

"She try to kill herself?" he asked.

"She wasn't serious though," I said.

"How you know?" asked See.

"She was in the bathroom and I went in to talk to her. She tell me she wasn't going to do anything like that. Then she call in Indira. And they make your mother and father agree that they not going to go to the wedding tomorrow if you weren't there."

See didn't say anything. She just sat there in Christopher's arms and stared at me.

"Indira say that if her twin sister can't be there on she wedding day then they ain't go have no wedding," I continued. "Then she say is her wedding and she want Aunty Nalini and Alicia and Juanita there too. And she make Uncle Inchan and Aunty Doogoo agree to that."

See continued to stare at me but there were now tears streaming down her face. Christopher hugged her tighter and pressed his cheeks to hers.

"They agreed to that?" See asked quietly.

"They had to. Lea still had the knife in she hand."

"And what go stop Mommy from changing she mind after Lea put down the knife?" See asked.

"Mammy make them promise and we other relatives was there."

She continued crying silently for a while with Christopher hugging and consoling her.

"You going to come?" I asked her.

"Is me twin sister. If she want me to come I will come," See said quietly.

Chapter Twenty

"You got to get your dress today then," Christopher said.

"Let me finish washing off them clothes quick then we going down Pitt Street to look for one," See said and slipped off the step where she was seated by Christopher's lap. "Tell Indira she go see me tomorrow."

When I got back home Mammy was still at Aunty Nalini. That afternoon she and Reena were going to go over to Mr. Anton to work since the following day was the wedding and everybody would be busy. I had hidden myself away in the loft so they won't find me. " Duck You Sucker" was opening at the Globe that afternoon and I wasn't going to miss it. All the boys said they were going.

After Mammy and Reena got tired of calling me and left for Mr. Anton I slipped into the bathroom, bathed and changed my clothes. Tillam and Coco were calling for me by then. Everybody else in the house was too busy doing wedding preparation chores.

I got fifty cents from what I had saved up and put it in my pocket then headed out with the boys. They all were there except for Moppa, for that day was his church day. We hurried out of the street and up St. Ann Street to the waterside and to the Globe. There was a huge crowd in front of the cinema with many people spilling onto the street. They were trying to get into House and Balcony. We went around the side of the cinema by the street to the stelling where the entrance to Pitt was located. My heart dropped.

There was an even bigger and noisier crowd there. They were all rowdy and were pushing and shoving. Many of them had their shirts off in the battle to get tickets. These were big strong grown men and I didn't see how we were going to get in there for tickets. I watched in amazement as one fellow in his late teens and dressed in a lime green shirt and jeans fiercely pushed his way into the crowd. He was at it for some time before he was expelled on the other side of the crowd and back to where he had started, except his shirt was now ripped and the buttons were gone.

A big fellow without shirt emerged from the crowd smiling toothily and holding aloft a string of five or six tickets triumphantly. He began distributing them to people he had bought them for.

"Bengay! Bengay!" shouted Squingee and waved to the fellow. The fellow came over to us smiling.

"You know he?" Whispered Coco.

"Is me cousin," Squingee said.

"Alyuh going in?" he asked." Is how much alyuh?"

"Is seven o' we," Squingee said.

"Alright. This is what we go do. Alyuh take off ayo shirt them. When I push and go in alyuh stay right up under me, understand?" he said. "Because even if I buy the ticket alyuh still got to push to pass in. So when we reach in there just buy you ticket and go in."

As soon as we had taken off our shirts Bengay roared, "Watch it deh! Ah coming through!" and bulled his way through the crowd. We squeezed in behind him like a Morris minor slipstreaming behind a big truck. Bengay waded through the crowd with us wriggling right up under him. It was hot and sweaty under that lot and one could hardly breathe. The next thing we knew we were through the major part of the crowd and into the narrow passage way with the ticket hole in the wall.

When we got in the windows were still open and, unlike the last time, we could see where there were still seats. After we settled down somewhere at the back the boys began talking about other movies they had seen. We could still hear the noise of the crowd outside above the music being played in the cinema. Then a man walked down the side of pit and reached up to push a wood bar that was attached to three windows. The windows slammed shut. As the other windows were closed the cinema got darker.

Chapter Twenty

He walked up a step and through a little gate to House and continued. It had got pitch black. The music stopped and they started showing trailers.

When I got back home the house was still busy. The odor of various spicy dishes filled the house. Again Sunil was not home. I got some food from the kitchen and ate in my room. Then I went over to the Yard. The boys were on Spanner's steps talking about the movie we had just seen. I could hear Bucky's voice next door. I knocked and went in. She was glad to see me. She was fussing with Lucky about a beige suit that was hung up by the door to his room. Then she told me that I had to come to the wedding rehearsal on Wednesday at Mrs. Munroe's house. She was the music teacher who lived at the head of the street. I made a mental note of this and went back out to the boys since Bucky was preoccupied with preparing for her wedding.

I borrowed the page with the "Duck You Sucker" poster in the Sunday newspaper that Spanner had kept. Then I went back to my room and began drawing it. Reena came in shortly after.

"I ain't going back to Mr. Anton no more," she declared.

"What happen this time?" I asked.

"That woman getting more and more miserable," Reena fretted.

"Who?"

"His sister nuh. You think she was nasty to Mammy before, she get worse now that she ain't got no legs at all."

"Wha' she say?"

"Ah whole lot of nasty things, that how Mr. Anton letting this coolie woman come in and take over the house. And if she think she go come and take away she house that go happen over she dead body," Reena said miserably.

"And wha' Mammy say?"

"Mammy ask she how much the house worth and that she didn't think about it before, but since she brought it up was not a bad idea."

"Mammy say so?" I asked and laughed.

"That's not funny. People trying to help you and you got nothing but nasty things to tell them? Ah wonder if she know the wheelchair she sitting in is Mammy get it for she. She come home from hospital and meet wheelchair at home, she ain't ask where it come from."

"Where Mammy get it from?"

"That man we does wash for down Coburg street. He wife dead long time and leave it, so Mammy ask he for it and Mr. Anton pick it up."

"She just mad because she can't walk no more," I said.

"That ain't give she the right to be so nasty and mean."

"You still got your two legs and you used to be nasty and mean to me," I said without looking up from my drawing.

"I should slap you for that," she said.

"You see? You still mean and nasty."

"Anyway, she might be going back in hospital soon."

"Going back in for what. She ain't got nothing else to cut off."

"She got diabetes and she not supposed to eat or drink certain things and she still doing it."

"Well, she is a big woman. She can do what she want."

"Yea, but she sick. Mammy say sometimes she think she trying not to live no more."

I looked at Reena but didn't say anything. She came in here mad at the woman and at the same time she seemed sorry for her.

"See coming tomorrow?" she asked me.

"Yes. She say is she twin sister and if Indira want she to come she will come."

"Christopher coming?"

"I don't know. What about Aunty Nalini?"

Chapter Twenty

"Mammy say they left right away and went up Rosehall to look for dress. It go be nice to be with my cousins again."

That night everybody was up late into the night as men came in and decorated under the tent and had flowers strung all over the place. They had brought in a large jukebox with two speakers and were setting them up in the drawing room and under the tent. Then they wired them to amplifier and the turntable set up in the dining room. I had tried sleeping earlier but the hammering and noise in the yard kept me awake. Eventually, I gave up and went back outside. Most of the boys in the Yard were up. Many of them had parents who were over at Doogoo helping out in one way or the other.

I went over to where the boys were sitting on Spanner's steps. Bucky's shack was well lit with many people busying themselves in there. Lucky was sitting on their steps talking to an old Amerindian man who was smoking a pipe. Standing in the doorway was an Amerindian girl about my age and height. Her face was round and, although she wore a loose fitting dress a size too big for her, I could see she was more on the stocky side. She was eating something and watching us without expression.

"Is who that stand up there by Bucky' door?" I asked Spanner.

"Is Bucky' sister," he said with barely a glance over his shoulder. I gave her a second look, trying to identify her with the girl I had seen in the picture Bucky had shown me.

"She look strong man," I commented.

"She must be does paddle canoe whole day up the river. Maybe is she paddle the whole family down from up river," Spanner said softly and laughed. "But don't make dem joke around she. She done slap-up Dillip for dat."

"What?" I gasped.

Once Upon A Time In Berbice

"He make some joke about Buck people and she put one slap on he," Spanner said.

"Wha' Dillip do?" I asked, keeping a curious eye on the girl.

"He go to slap she back and he get another one by the time he raise he hand," Spanner said.

I was flabbergasted. I looked at her standing there, coolly chomping away on some fruit. It was hard to believe that this girl would blossom into a beauty like Bucky when she grew up, but that was the investment I was willing to make. I was going to try befriending this girl who, by the look of it, had a better left hook than any of us down the street. But then again, chances were that she might turn out looking like the grandfather instead. I would have to play it by ear and see how it went with her.

Sunday morning, the day of the wedding, began as a warm sunny day with a mild wind coming from the north. Mammy got us to bathe early and ordered Sunil not to leave home. She wanted him to be at the wedding. Mammy brought down a brand new brown pants and white terelene shirt for me to wear. She had me wear a pair of black shoes that were too tight for Sunil and was now mine to inherit. For Sunil she got this long cream gown and spread it on his bed for him to wear. By nine O'clock everybody had had something to eat and I was well dressed and mingling amongst the people beneath the tent where the ceremony was due to take place.

The pandit arrived, clothed in just ordinary pants and shirt but with a suitcase. Dil took his bicycle and parked it in the wood shed at the back. Inchan led him upstairs where he changed into his religious outfit for presiding over the ceremony. Most of the women were either in the kitchen preparing meals or upstairs fussing over Indira's preparation. There was a crowd outside peering over the fence and through the gate to get a glimpse of the

365

proceedings. The **Dulaha** or bridegroom had not yet arrived but already the air was humming with excitement and gaiety. The musicians were in place in the main part of the house. They were equipped with many instruments of which only the tassa and sitar I knew.

Most of the people here I did not know. I did recognize Aunty Nalini who came with Sondra and her daughters Alicia and Juanita. Sondra stuck her tongue out at me when she saw me but made no move to come in my direction. They were all well dressed in loose fitting gowns and even Sondra had her hair done. It was the first time I was seeing my cousin Juanita. She was darker than Alicia, a little shorter but looked more Indian than anything else. She was prettier than Alicia but appeared to be less jovial. Their father was not with them. They spoke briefly with Mammy and she lifted up Sondra who seemed overjoyed at seeing her. They spoke briefly, with Mammy admiring her nieces. Then she ushered them under the tent to their seats.

Sunil was slow in getting dressed and I had no idea where Reena was. I did not know when See had arrived but I saw her attired in a lime green sari and busying herself in the kitchen with the other ladies there. I had not seen Doogoo for the morning.

I sauntered out through the overcrowded house and to the entrance where the curious onlookers were gathered. The boys were gawking and making faces and eyes at me from the fence. Even Yvette was there grinning in my direction.

Eventually everyone was urged to gather under the tent. It wasn't long after when the Dulaha arrived with his people in several cars that had their horns blasting, announcing the wedding. The whole street seemed to be onlookers to this affair. The party came in the yard through the crowd and the musicians began a lively piece with lots of drumming to which the Dulaha and his people danced. I was excited.

Once Upon A Time In Berbice

The dulaha was dressed in a long white gown down to his ankles with a long burgundy sash over the shoulders and down the front of the gown. He wore a kind of cloth hat with burgundy stripes. He was clean shaved and looked very presentable. After the little dance they went under the tent to the pooja area which was a little flat platform area where the ceremony was to take place. I followed them in with their sweet scented perfume assaulting my nose.

It wasn't long after when Inchan came downstairs, dressed in a cream gown and walking proudly without a limp nor hint of his recent accident. Soon after a dozen or so ladies came down the stairs with Indira in their midst. She was dressed in a white sari and veil which did not completely cover her face. Her dress and the long veil were speckled with shiny floral decorations. Her hair was parted in the middle and combed in a bun at the back. There were gold jewelry in her hair, around her neck and many gold bangles on both wrists. Her hands, feet and face were covered with mensa paintings which consisted mostly of little dark orange flowers in various patterns.

When the Dulaha and Dulahin, or the bride, were brought together in the pooja area the pandit had them stand facing each other. The other people up there included his mother and Uncle Sammy, along with Nanny, Doogoo, Inchan, Lea, See and Dil. I had seen Raj earlier but he was nowhere in sight now. Doogoo was solemn and showed no emotion. Inchan seemed happy.

The pandit was attired in a simple white gown and a little orange cloth cap with no peak. He now wore glasses and had an orange scarf wrapped partly around his neck.

"Sisters and Brothers, this morning we're here to witness the marriage ceremony between Ganesh and Indira," he began in a moderate and steady tone. He held up two large garlands consisting of white and red flowers then said, "Ganesh and Indira, these flowers are tokens of your love and affection for each other. They are put together by these strings. Even though the flowers may wither, the strings that keep these flowers together will bind you for lifelong friendship. Let us all pray."

We all bowed our heads as the pandit, still holding up the two garlands, began praying in Hindi in a sing-song manner. After two minutes he stopped and switched to English again.

"Oh Lord, protect Indira and Ganesh and enable them to help and serve each other with love. May they enjoy the sweet fruits of this earth and your other blessings together. Through your grace may their knowledge make their lives glorious and gorgeous. And may they never bear any ill will towards each other. Let peace and harmony ever be in their lives."

Then he said something in Hindi as he placed one garland around Ganesh's neck, then the other around Indira's. Then he had both Indira and Ganesh sit with Indira on the right of Ganesh. Most of what followed involved the pandit telling them what to do or say and he explained to them and the platform party whatever he said in Hindi.

I lost interest somewhere at the beginning of this long session. With all of them up there and Aunty Nalini, Mammy and Reena all seated up front, there was nobody to make sure I remained under the tent.

I got up and sneaked out through the crowd of other members of the wedding party on the fringes of the tent and out to the front of the yard and on the street. The boys had migrated to the yard again after realizing nothing exciting was going to happen until the religious ceremony was over. They were playing cricket over there. I took off my shoes and socks and left them on Spanner's steps then joined the game.

"Boy, ent you suppose to be in the wedding?" asked Kisskadee who was seated on his steps watching the game.

"Is not me getting marrid," I said defensively. He found this funny and laughed with his frilly lips spreading across his narrow face.

"Boy, you go mess up your clothes," Tillam said when I joined him in the slips position.

"So, if it mess up I go just go home and change it," I said nonchalantly.

"You go get a good cut tail," Dillip commented.

"Nobody don't get licks on wedding day boy," I explained.

"Is not your wedding day. Is not you getting marrid," Spanner pointed out.

After several boys were out and I thought it was my turn I walked up to the wicket to pick up the bat but Yvette got to it first.

"Where she come from?" I said, half turned to the boys.

"I in the game before you," she said and held the bat away from me.

"She playing at all?" I asked the boys. Dillip and Squingee shrugged.

"She was fielding out by the road," said Coco.

"Ain't nobody knocking ball out by the road where the crowd is," I said.

"How much balls you field for the morning?" she asked with the bat still held away from me.

"More than you," I said.

"Milo, let she bat man. We only wasting time," Spanner said impatiently.

"Is only because you is a girl ah go let you bat first," I said sulkily and withdrew to the slips position again.

She drew her teeth and brushed her thick black hair back from her broad forehead then settled down to bat.

Chinee Roy came in and bowled the first ball to her and she did that bat and foot stroke that girls do when playing cricket. We were hilarious at first but it got very frustrating when we realized that it was pretty hard getting the ball past both the bat and the leg she carried beside the bat, to get to the wicket. I was all for wading in there and beating her up, were it not for the fact that she had a win in the beat-up column against Dillip. This girl had the kind of arms Hercules must have worn in his day and was obviously no push over when it came to fighting. Besides, she was Bucky's sister and I didn't think Bucky would have thought well of me if I beat up her little sister. In addition, it would be hard applying for boyfriend status later on when she turned out to be the swan Bucky was.

Eventually we got her out when Coco got a ball to bounce up suddenly and it came off the bat and into the safe hands of Tillam. We all rejoiced while she retreated back to her original fielding position without comment.

I took up the bat and stroked the first ball beautifully along the ground past Tillam and across the street amongst the crowd. Fifteen minutes later I was still at bat and playing stroke after stroke. Even Kisskadee had to comment positively from where he sat on the steps.

"The boy batting like Kanhai man," he said when I glanced one off the legs and under one of the shacks. Tillam retrieved the ball from the muddy water under the shacks and came in to bowl without even squeezing the water from it. The ball came zinging up to me with water spilling all the way. They found it hilarious and I laughed along with them because I was batting so well and loving it.

It was only after I was finished batting, having carelessly played over a yorker, and Yvette made a comment about my dirty shirt that I realized the spilled water had speckled the whole front of my shirt with muddy sprays. Even my pants were a mess. I continued playing since I was already dirty and changing now wouldn't make a difference.

After another half hour of play the music started up again. The onlookers at the fence crowded closer. The cricket game broke up as everyone raced away to the fence to see what was happening over there. I ran with them then

370

into the yard amongst the crowd. Indira and Ganesh were now sitting in two large white basket chairs in the drawing room of the house. They had two smaller additional garlands around their necks and flower petals were all over them.

The music died down and the people were coming up and giving small envelopes to the couple. The speech followed by the surrendering of each envelope was beginning to sedate me. I caught sight of Reena. She wore a long yellow gown and looked as womanly as Lea did. Now I saw what long nosed Bertie saw in her. She was with Aunty Nalini and Alicia. Aunty Nalini caught sight of me and looked like she was going to pass out, then she rolled her eyes to the ceiling. Only then did I remember the mud splattered state I was in and withdrew hastily to my room to change.

I had no more "good" clothes to put on so I pulled on a Tee-shirt and short pants before melting back into the crowd of onlookers. They were giving speeches and drinking from tall thin glasses and paper cups every time someone was finished talking. I went out on the street to look for the boys but they were all plastered against the fence, peering through the windows at the wedding inside. Amongst the crowd gathered outside along the fence I noticed Rubberdog sheepishly hobbling on crutches behind a section of the crowd. I supposed he was awaiting the liquor segment of the wedding. He had better not let Doogoo see him around here.

I poked my way through the crowd and to the fence where the boys were. I found myself standing next to Yvette. Seeing her from this close and in broad daylight for the first time she looked a more imposing specimen. Her calves were stouter than mine and her copper colored arms looked the kind ambitious wrestlers aspired to achieve. In short, this chick was one hefty heifer. Again I rethought my theory of her blossoming into a beautiful flower like her elder sister Bucky.

"Is not your sister getting marrid?" she asked.

"That ain't me sister, girl. That is me cousin," I said.

"So how come you look so and she so pretty," she said.

"I is a boy. How I go be pretty. Only girls does be pretty," I explained.

"I thought Alice say you have a sister," she said.

"The one in the yellow dress is me sister," I said and pointed out Reena sitting next to Aunty Nalini.

"That is your sister?" she said in disbelief.

"Yes, and I have another smaller sister name Sondra."

"I like your eyes," she said abruptly. That floored me.

"What?"

"You got nice eyes," she repeated.

"You have...ah... nice muscles," I said after fishing around for something complimentary to say. She looked at me blankly for a while and, just for a second, I wondered if sending me a right hook was being considered by her. She smiled and brought one arm up to show her muscles.

"Yes, and you better remember that before ah use it on you," she said in a half mocking, threatening way. This girl really had muscles. I wondered if Bucky had muscles like those when she was Yvette's age.

"Man, nothing ain't going on in there. They only talking, talking all the time," she said and turned away from the fence. I followed her out to the head of the street at the Backdam.

"Why your family them like talk so much," she commented.

" Them is not me family girl. Half them people there me ent know," I admitted.

"Then they just come to eat out the food?"

"Maybe is the boy family them."

"Where this road lead to?"

"It gone all the way to Stanleytown down so and to Winkle up so."

"What it have after Stanleytown?"

"I don't know. The bauxite company?"

"Is you living here. Me ain't from here."

"Where you from?"

"Ebini."

"Where is that?"

"Up Berbice river."

"How far up?"

"A hundred miles."

I looked at her expressionless face and wondered if she was like Rosanne where contorting the truth was concerned. The music at the wedding started up again but this time it was not the band but the jukebox playing an Indian song with a racy rhythm.

We rushed back to get a space at the crowded fence. A lady in a red gown was in the middle of the floor dancing for the audience. I supposed they hired her to dance, for she looked like a professional dancer with all the hand and hip movements. Both the invited and uninvited portion of the crowd seemed to be enjoying it. After the dance everyone cheered with a few of the pre-liquored men shouting for more. More speeches followed but mercifully, they were much shorter.

The jukebox cranked up again with another Indian song and people were invited to join the dulaha and dulahin on the floor. By the time the song was half way through there was hardly any room in there for one more couple to join them.

The food and liquor began flowing, the latter from an open van parked in front of the house. Yvette urged me to go in and get her some food and drinks. I made my way through the surging crowd to the kitchen. See was aghast to see me in home clothes and asked me what happed to the nice clothes she had seen me in earlier. I told her somebody vomited on it and I had to change. The look she gave me told me she didn't buy my story. She loaded me up with food and two bottles of Juicee soft drinks. I went back outside to Yvette. We took it across the street and sat on her steps where we ate and talked. The boys were over at the kitchen getting food for themselves by begging the ladies in the kitchen.

For the rest of the afternoon and into the night we were back and forth between the yard and the kitchen getting food and drinks and coming back over to the Yard to eat and play. The music was loud and people were dancing in the house as well as under the tent where they had cleared some of the chairs. We had our own dancing over in the yard where we tried to outdo each other dancing to Indian music, then to the calypso they were playing.

It must have been after nine that evening when the dulaha and his people left with Indira and Aunty Droopatie, Inchan's sister. As Reena later explained to me, Aunty Droopatie was going as the **Lucknee**; the older woman who slept between the dulaha and dulahin on the wedding night to make sure they keep apart, for they were not allowed to get together as yet. According to Reena, when the choosing of the Lucknee was discussed, Indira had suggested Mammy. But the ladies said Mammy was too attractive to be Lucknee. She had to be someone that would discourage sex, not encourage it.

The music, drinking, dancing and eating continued late into the night. It must have been midnight when I left the boys on Spanner's steps. Most of them were still outdoor since their parents were over at the wedding making the most of the free food and liquor. Even after I retired to bed the music was still playing.

The next morning I woke up with a headache. It was a school day but when I did not prepare for school Mammy didn't object. Both Reena and Sunil had gone off to work leaving me to sleep as late as I wanted. Mammy was helping Lea, Doogoo, and two other ladies to clean up the house now that the guest had departed, leaving debris in their wake. The Yard was quiet with the boys and other children off to school. I went back to sleep.

When I awoke it was drizzling outside. It was just approaching two O'clock and I was hungry. I went into the kitchen where Mammy and two other ladies were cleaning up. Mammy gave me some left over roti and curry to eat with some sorrel drink. After I ate I was bored and didn't feel like drawing, so I went out to the head of the street. The cinema was quiet and empty since there was no twelve thirty show. I headed up the waterside and toward Wrefords where Reena worked.

When I got there Reena was on her break. She was standing by the main door in front of the store talking with Bucky who was not dressed in her bank uniform but in a pale yellow jump suit. She had two parcels under an arm and a big handbag over the other shoulder.

"I ain't know what I do she," Reena was saying.

"She just walk up to you just so and say she want fight you?" Bucky asked and looked across to J.P. Santos store next door.

"She say something about me taking away Bertie from she, but Bertie tell me he and she finish long time now," Reena said and looked worried.

"Is which one, the one with the long hair?" Bucky asked.

"No, the other one with the pony tail and uniform," Reena said.

"She? Is not Selma D'aguiar that? Don't let she bother you. She full O' talk," Bucky said. "If she tell you anything else tell she come down Theater Alley if she want fight."

"Wha' happen to your forehead?" Reena asked.

"Is Lucky playing the fool last night and make ah bump me forehead," Bucky said while putting a testing finger on the Band-Aid on her forehead over her left eye. "Ah hope it go down before weekend. I can't turn up at me wedding with bungie over me eye. People might think is Nathaniel give me," she said and both she and Reena laughed.

"Milo? Wha' you doing here?" Reena said when she noticed me standing there.

"Eh eh. I thought you went to school Milo," Bucky said.

"I tired from the wedding so ah stay home," I said.

"Tired?" Bucky said and laughed. "You going on like is you get marrid last night."

She turned back to Reena and they continued talking with the conversation going back to this girl that wanted to beat up Reena. I left them and strolled over to where this girl was talking animatedly with another girl by the metal rails in front of J.P. Santos store.

I stopped just next to them by the rails. This Selma character was taller than Reena and full bodied. She had light complexioned pock-marked skin and she seemed pretty soft but was angry as she talked to the other girl who was encouraging her.

"She know Bucky?" the girl was asking her.

"I ain't know. It look so," said Selma.

"You sure you want fool around Bucky?" the girl asked ominously.

"I ent got no fight with Bucky," said Selma. "I go wait till she come off from work when Bucky done gone. Maybe Bucky don't even know she so good to want fight either."

" 'Cause you know Bucky ent deh down here. I hear she beat up Telma Braithwaite last week," the girl said.

"Yea, I hear about that. Me ent got nothing against Bucky," said Selma.

"Alyuh talking about dat new girl that does work at Wrefords?" I said to them.

They both turned around and looked me up and down.

"You know she?" asked the other girl.

Once Upon A Time In Berbice

"I know she and Bucky had a fight yesterday but now they best of friends," I said.

"She and Bucky fight yesterday? Who win?" asked the girl. I could see Selma's eyes widening as she gazed over there at Reena.

"How you think Bucky get that cut over she eye. And you see any mark on the other girl?" I said indifferently.

Selma swallowed deeply and I could see the fight seeping out of her.

"Selma, you try there. You on your own. I won't go near dat girl if she beating Bucky," the girl said gloomily.

"She and Bucky live down the same street and Bucky just bring a pants for she to put on for the fight she getting this afternoon," I said.

"Selma, you on your own. I gone. I go hear about you all tomorrow," the girl said and was obviously distancing herself from Selma for fear of Reena coming after her too. Selma swallowed again and seemed incapable of taking her eyes off Reena and Bucky over at Wrefords.

"Oh, before I forget, the girl send me over here to tell you wait for she five O' clock after she come off work. She say if you want fight she here or if you want reach she over by Children Property because she ain't want them people at work see she and make she lose the work she just get," I said in a carefree manner. " Wha' to tell she?"

All of a sudden Selma wasn't looking too healthy. Small droplets of sweat had popped out on her forehead and she was looking wild eyed over at Wrefords. I looked over there and Bucky was just finished talking to Reena and was heading across the street to the bank. Reena started coming in our direction.

"Maybe she want fight right now," I said anxiously. The girl started backing away and toward the store. Just before she turned and fled back into J.P. Santos I noticed her left shoe was now wet from liquid snaking down the inner part of her left leg.

Chapter Twenty

I turned and walked quickly to intercept Reena before she reached over here. I wondered why she was coming to meet this girl she was scared of. I steered her back toward Wrefords when I met her.

"Where that girl gone?" she asked as she let me guide her away.

"Wha' you coming over here to she for?" I asked.

"Bucky say lemme tell she I don't want no fight and if she still want fight Bucky go come over here and talk to she," Reena said.

"She ain't want fight no more," I said.

"What you tell she?" Reena said and pulled her arm away from me, giving me one of her suspicious looks she reserved for me.

I told her what I had told the girl.

"And she believe you?" she said in disbelief but I could see she was relieved.

"If she ain't believe me why she run back inside?" I asked.

"Jeese, she real stupidy," Reena said and shook her head in disbelief.

"I think she pee she self," I said and laughed. Reena laughed uneasily.

"I got to go back to work now," she said as we got back to Wrefords.

"I go come back for your five O'clock in case she change she mind," I said.

It was the closest I had seen my sister look at me with grateful, adoring eyes.

I strolled past Wrefords farther south along Water Street. Coco had told me they were building a new cinema just up the road by Lad Lane. It was just a few streets down. When I got there it was just the foundation work that was done and it did not quite look like it was shaping up to be a cinema. The only indication that it was was the large area it took up between two stores.

Once Upon A Time In Berbice

I retraced my steps up Water Street and past Wrefords and J.P. Santos and on an impulse turned into the main entrance of the big New Amsterdam market. It was very busy given that time of day. I walked right up the center isle with well constructed stalls all but covered with clothing and household goods. All the stalls were well lit with electric bulbs. As I continued walking through, the indoor part with the high roof gave way to another section with a much lower roof. The stalls in this area were mostly wooden stands and products on sale in this section were mostly rice, provision, barrels of salt beef and generally, dry goods. The rice was stacked in neat heaps with the price written on a piece of cardboard stuck in the middle of each mini hill. There were no walls in this section of the market and I could see the side of J.P. Santos next door. A girl in J.P. Santos work uniform was ducking under the wire link fence. I wondered if she was getting away from work without her supervisor knowing about it. She quickly climbed over the low fence and scooted into the market. When she turned I could see the pony tail and I immediately recognized Selma.

I followed her as she quickly made her way through one aisle then another as she worked her way to the front of the market. She stopped by the main entrance and peered out in the direction of Wrefords. Then she scrambled into the Round-The-Town bus parked before the market and sat in the middle and away from the windows. She was leaning forward to remain out of sight. The bus pulled off shortly after. I didn't think I would bother coming back for Reena that afternoon.

I continued up Water Street to the Globe cinema to see what was showing. The only movies of interest posted there were a war named "Salt in the Wound" and a western named "Bury Them Deep."

By then school children were appearing on the street. I guessed it must have been after three. I left the Globe and turned down Charlotte Street to head for home. While passing Persaud's Funeral Parlor on my left I saw Chandra talking with a tall middle aged man who I knew worked there. She had her back to me and did not see me. Just as I was about to slip away unnoticed I saw the man slip to her a small green bottle which she palmed quickly and sneaked it into the right pocket of her dress. As I continued up the street I wondered what she was doing there. She seemed to be turning up at these strange places for some reason. If she was looking for a job that would be the last place she would want to work.

I headed home, hoping the boys were gathered in the Yard.

Chapter Twenty-One

"Milo, what you know about that fire over at the shoemaker shop?" Mammy asked me as soon as I got home.

"Me? Nothing Mammy," I said with my mind racing.

"Sunil say some policeman was here saying that he hear you had some information about how it start," she said and eyed me curiously.

"I did just telling Chandra that to fool her," I said.

"You see what does happen when you run your mouth? Now somebody must be hear you say that and gone and tell the police you know who set the fire," Mammy fretted. "You go explain that to the policeman if he come back."

"When he been here?" I asked.

"He say this afternoon. And is where you been whole afternoon?"

"I been by Reena at she workplace."

"What you doing over there. Don't go hanging around Reena when she working before you do something stupid and make the girl lose she job."

"Yes Mammy."

I went outside by the entrance by our gate and looked across the street into the Yard. Spanner, Tillam and Dillip were standing by the steps to Spanner's shack. I headed over there while wondering what kind of trouble I could get into with this inquiring policeman.

"Wha you'all doing," I said as I joined the group.

"Shhhh," said Spanner. "We going and swim."

"Where, Backdam trench?" I said quietly.

"You mad! You won't catch me swimming in no Backdam trench," Tillam said and they laughed. "That too nasty boy."

"Naw, we going Canje Creek, behind Winkle," Dillip said. "You can swim?"

Chapter Twenty-One

"Like a fish," I lied.

"Same thing Markie used to say before he drown," Tillam commented.

"Where he drown?" I asked.

"Cane field trench," said Tillam.

"Cane field trench don't deep," I said and laughed. They looked at me like I had a few mental screws plus a bolt missing.

"Is wha' wrong with this man," said Spanner. "You ever find sounding in them canfield trench that punt does haul cane in?"

"Them trench bottomless boy," observed Tillam.

"So wha' you'all waiting for?" I asked.

"Moppa, Coco and Chinee Roy say they coming," said Spanner.

"Wha' happen to Squingee?" I asked.

"He can't swim," said Dillip.

"He frighten water," Spanner said.

"He don't bathe; he does just dust off," explained Tillam. We found that funny.

We turned as one as we heard a slurping sound from Bucky's steps. Her sister Yvette was standing there eating a mango. She eyed us without expression. She wore an orange pedal pusher pants and cream blouse. She had her long hair combed back from her broad forehead and tied in a pony tail. The boys lapsed into silence on seeing her there.

"Bucky deh home?" I asked to start a conversation.

"Why you want to know that. You is she husband?" she said as she detached her lips from the yellow flesh of the ripe mango.

The boys found that funny and giggled. I smiled at her.

"You is Yvette, right?" I said.

"How you know that," she said and seemed mildly surprised.

"How you know that Milo?" Dillip asked.

"Yea, how you know that," Tillam said.

"I is a detective," I said and grinned.

"You name Tinnin?" she asked.

"What?" I said.

"You name Milo Tinin?"

The boys giggled again.

"You want come swim with we?" I asked her.

"Shhhhh! You want me mother hear and start carrying on?" Spanner said with concern.

"Where alyo going and swim?" Yvette asked.

"Canje Creek," said Spanner.

"Where is that?" she asked.

"Behind so," Spanner said and indicated a general northern direction.

"No, I ain't coming," she said. "Besides, alyo can't swim good."

"I could swim better than you," ventured Tillam.

The boys turned and looked at him like he had lost it mentally.

"What! I could swim better than she," Tillam said again.

"Is only last year you learn to swim boy," Spanner pointed out. "She been swimming since she born."

An argument broke out about who was the better swimmer between Yvette and Tillam. Even though we knew Tillam better than we knew this girl, most of us were of the opinion that she was the better swimmer; just based on the fact that she was Amerindian and that she grew up on the river.

Eventually Coco and Chinee Roy came into the Yard and we decided to leave without Moppa.

As we turned out of the yard to head up the Backdam I saw Reena coming in from the Main Road.

"I thought you was coming back for me Four O' clock," she said moodily.

"That girl frighten you like a cat," I told her.

Chapter Twenty-One

"How you know that. Suppose she did decide you were lying to her," Reena said.

"She left work early and run home before you could see she again," I said.

"What?"

"I see she duck under J.P. Santo fence and dash through the market to run in a Round-the-Town bus. She was hiding from you," I said.

"Jeese! She is one coward," Reena said shaking her head as she headed into our yard. "And to think I did frighten she jump on me."

I headed behind the boys and caught up with them at the head of the street on the Backdam road. Tillam brought his scooter with him which made me regret forgetting mine at home.

We walked north up the Backdam until we got to the junction with the Smythfield road. We were about to continue north into Winkle when someone called me from somewhere behind and by Essex Street.

"Is who that?" I asked as I looked around.

"Is you' brother' girlfriend," said Tillam.

Then I saw her. Chandra was pushing a bicycle out of the shop at the head of Essex Street. She wore a fluffy brown and yellow flowered skirt and a cream shirt with the long sleeves rolled up to the elbows. The boys slowed to a stop. She jumped on the bicycle and rode slowly to where we stood.

"I got some news for you," she said.

"What?" I said and was reluctant to entertain her.

"Come nuh boy. I ain't want everybody in me business," she said. I left the boys and went to her reluctantly.

"What?" I said when I got to her.

"A policeman went by you all today?" she asked.

"Who tell you that?" I asked.

"Sunil," she said. I should've known he would go straight to her and report that. "Wha' he ask you?"

Once Upon A Time In Berbice

"I wasn't there. I didn't see him."

"I'll give you ten dollars if you keep your mouth shut about the fire. It ain't matter what you say but it go cause trouble for other people. So is better if you don't say nothing."

I was still gasping silently at the prospect of owning ten whole dollars just to keep my mouth shut.

"Where the ten dollars?"

"I have to go get it now."

"Then go get it and then come back and we go talk," I said and pretended to be shoving off.

"Where you all going?" she asked.

"We going Canje Creek go swim," I said.

The boys had started walking up the road again hoping I'd catch up with them.

"Come with me and I go give you now," she said.

"Come with you where?"

"Sooklall have forty dollars pay for me and I going and collect it now," she said.

"I want twenty dollars," I said. "Or when the police come again I go tell he all that I know."

Chandra frowned and looked at me through slitted eyes. She turned her head slightly to the left while still staring poisonously at me. Somehow that little gesture seemed very strange and sinister to me.

"Alright," she said. " But not a penny more."

"How we getting there?" I asked.

"Jump on and ah go tow you," she said.

"Aye Tillam, ah coming and reach you all later," I shouted to the boys. Two of them waved to me and continued up the road.

She had a ladies bicycle with a carrier at the back. I had no idea whose bicycle she had borrowed. She smoothed her knee length skirt under her then sat on the saddle. I straddled the carrier and after a shaky start she rode off.

385

Chapter Twenty-One

We went up the continuation of Backdam where it ran west to Main Road by the Gardens then straight over to Water Street. Then she turned left up Water Street past the big Kissoon furniture store on the right. She said nothing while we rode and I remained silent. Twenty dollars was the most money I would ever have had, should she live up to her promise. We passed the big noisy sawmill on the right then she turned across the street to a little shop sandwiched between two stores just after the saw mill. Sooklall's Shoe Maker sign was out there but the shop appeared to be closed.

She got off the bicycle and so did I. I followed her into the sawdust covered front yard where she pushed the bicycle right up to the store front. I wondered if she was pulling a fast one on me about Sooklall having money for her. In any case, I felt I was in a winning position since she very well knew that if she didn't give me the money I could certainly get her and whoever else in trouble.

I stood up in the yard and looked up the street toward the police station and the stelling. A green bus named " Prince Charles" was coming up the road full with passengers.

"Come nuh boy," Chandra called as she pushed the bicycle around the side of the shop and to the back. I hesitated, for I had looked around and thought I saw Sunil peering at us from the head of King Street across the road. He was standing straddling his grocery bicycle. I wondered if it really was him and what he was up to.

We went around to the back of the building. I was still thinking about Sunil and why he was spying on Chandra. For someone who ran and told her every single thing that happened, why would he be keeping an eye on her. I guess he still did not trust her around Sooklall. That meant that, regardless of what she told him to make herself look good in his eyes again, he still believed what I had said that night when she and I had words by the cinema.

Once Upon A Time In Berbice

The back of the shop was relatively quiet. The saw mill was still busy but apart from that, the back of the buildings on this side was pretty lonely. The saw mill extended some fifty meters back west and toward the Berbice River which was about four hundred meters farther in that direction. Behind there was just a larger area of swampy savanna and bush. There was a grassy trail from the house leading away to the river which was not visible from here because of the dense growth of bush and trees in that direction.

It smelled dank back here and apart from the traffic on the street in front, the dominant sound was the buzzing of the big saw over at the mill as it bit through tough lumber.

Chandra parked the bicycle by the back door and rapped. At least that was a good sign. That meant Sooklall was in there and so was my soon to be acquired twenty dollars. Imagine that. Twenty dollars. I don't think Reena nor Sunil had that much right then.

Sooklall opened the door quietly and walked back inside. Chandra stepped in and motioned for me to come in.

I stepped into the poorly lit room. The windows were of the wooden louvered type and with them closed, most of the light was shut out. Only one low watt bulb was on and was the only significant source of light in the room. The shop might have been opened just a couple weeks ago but already it was littered with shoes, although not as many as he had over in the old building before the fire. There was a faint sweet smell like some kind of chemical but I figured it was something Sooklall must have been using when working on his shoes.

He had his back to me and was attending to something on a little dinner table against the wall by a little room. There were two wooden chairs to the table. There was half eaten food in a plate on the table. Maybe Sooklall was eating when we came in but he had not returned to the meal. Whatever he was doing did not involve going for money and Chandra was not saying anything. For a minute I wondered if she was afraid of him for some reason, although I had never had that impression before. But she did seem tense and uncertain.

I caught her attention and motioned her to ask him about her money. She looked at him and cleared her throat.

"Sooklall, ah come for the money you owe me," she said stiffly.

"You sure you don't have it already?" he said but remained with his back to us. Something on the table caught my eyes. It was a little green bottle and it was open. I couldn't be sure but, although I got but a glimpse of it earlier when it was slipped to Chandra by the fellow at the Funeral Parlor, it did seem to be the very same bottle. Why would that bottle be here and it seemed like it was being used. What kind of liquid did they use in funeral parlors? Maybe it was a poison. Why would she need a poison? Was it for Sunil? Why would she want to poison Sunil? That didn't make any sense.

"No, I didn't get it," Chandra said uncertainly.

"Yes, and you put it in a purse in your skirt," he said.

Were these two playing games to rob me of my twenty dollars? I looked from him to Chandra and got the feeling that my twenty dollars was slipping away.

"Oh yes, I forget ah put it away under me skirt for safe keeping," she said and laughed nervously as she reached under her skirt. My eyes were riveted there for she was not too careful in lifting her skirt. She did so with both hands and lifted it high enough to reveal most of her thick shapely legs. I sensed some movement behind me but my attention was too focused on Chandra's exposed legs.

Suddenly I was grabbed around the neck from behind and my mouth and nose were covered with some kind of wet cloth in a strong hand. In a panic I grabbed at the hand as I struggled to breathe. The hand with the cloth eased up just enough for me to breath in the now very strong odor of that sweet chemical scent I had detected earlier. I bucked violently as I attempted to free myself. I glared at Chandra beseechingly with bulging eyes as I felt myself getting woozy and faint.

"Hold he, hold he tight!" Chandra urged Sooklall and I could see the anxiety and excitement in her now bright eyes. He was way too strong for me and although I knew I would eventually pass out I held my breath and pretended I had fainted. After a few seconds he eased his hand with the cloth from my face and let my limp body slump to the dirty floor. I was barely conscious and could hear Chandra talking fast and angrily.

"He dead?" she said anxiously.

"Naw, he just unconscious," Sooklall said.

"Kill the bastard!" she said harshly and I felt a vicious kick to the thigh. I was barely conscious and did not respond.

"Why you didn't do it one time and done," she said angrily to Sooklall.

"Not here," he said.

"Don't back out of it now man. We come too far for this li'l so-and-so to spoil everything," she said.

"You sure he ain't tell the police nothing?" Sooklall said.

"No, I had to promise he ten dollars to get he here and you know the li'l bastard trying to dig twenty out of me?" she said and dropped me another kick, this time in the buttocks. Even though it was painful I remained motionless. I was in shock and terrified that they were talking about killing.

"You sure nobody know he come here? Once we do it we can't turn back," he said.

"Look, you get rid of your wife and she father, so why you have a problem with this li'l runt," she said bitterly.

" Is not a problem. Just that we got to be smart about it. You sure nobody know he deh here?"

Chapter Twenty-One

"He been with he friends and they were going and bathe in Canje Creek," she said.

"So they see he go with you then," he said with concern.

"So what. I could just tell them I drop he off somewhere and that's the last I see of him."

"It better if it look like an accident so nobody go suspect," he said.

"What accident. You go throw he in front a bus?"

"No, carry him up the Creek with Wahid' boat. He ent coming back 'till tomorrow night so we can use it, come back and clean it out before he go fishing again."

"That make sense yes. Carry he about a mile past the bridge so when they find the body they go think he went and bathe after the boys left and he drown," she said and seemed satisfied with that plan. I kept my eyes closed so that the tears won't spill over the lids. I had to play deader than an opossum and make a run for it when I got the chance.

"You got to get rid of the rest of the chloroform and any trace of anything he come in here with," said Sooklall. He was standing somewhere in the vicinity of my head and I could feel him staring down at me.

"But is how this li'l so-and-so see when I start that fire and he living till at Theater Alley?" he wondered aloud.

"I don't have a clue. Just like how he know about we screwing together in the backroom. I don't know what the li'l bastard don't know. That's why you got to make sure we get rid of him," she said in a commanding tone.

" I know what I got to do girl. Take it easy," he said and moved toward her.

"You sure he pass out? How you know the li'l bastard ain't playing he faint," she said and kicked me in the thigh again.

Again I sensed Sooklall stoop before me. I smelled the strong sweet smell again then felt the damp cloth pressed to my nose and mouth again. I held my breath again but he kept the cloth there and eventually I had to breath in. I coughed and he held my head with a strong hand again as I tried to pull my face away from the cloth. I passed out.

When I gradually came to I had a slight headache. I was conscious of being moved in something that was rolling on bumpy ground. I opened my eyes to find I was wrapped in some kind of netting that had a strong fish scent. I tried to move but my hands and feet were tied. I slowly became aware of my surroundings.

The sun was lower in the afternoon sky. I must have been out for at least an hour for it to be this late in the afternoon. I was lying in a wheel barrow, tied up and wrapped in a cast net. My legs were over the side of the wheel barrow and Sooklall, still in the same clothes but minus his shoemaker apron, was pushing the barrow. He had a cigarette dangling from one side of his lips and had no expression on his face. Chandra was not with us. I guessed she had stayed behind at the shop to clean up any evidence of my presence there.

I could see the back of the houses and the saw mill through the tall grass and figured he was pushing me down the grassy trail I had seen earlier that ran toward the river.

I tried wriggling but couldn't do much with my hands and feet tied. I began to cry aloud but Sooklall seemed not too worried about anyone hearing me.

After a while the ground got softer as we got to the stand of trees before the side of the river. He put the barrow to rest on its stand and walked ahead toward the trees. I tried working my hands free but they seemed to be tied firmly behind my back.

Sooklall soon returned and he picked me up without much effort and carried me toward the trees. He walked up the narrow now muddy track between the trees. I could see the mudflat ahead and the brown waters of the wide Berbice river beyond. There was a small fishing boat tied to one of the trees. It had no engine nor paddle. The little white crabs scampered to and disappeared into their holes as he carried me across the mudflat and to the little fifteen foot fishing boat. He put me to lie to the front of the boat where there were other nets lying about. There was a stronger scent of fish in the boat. He went back to the trees by the mud flat. He moved away a clump of bushes and I could see the grey outboard motor hidden beneath.

While he struggled to transport the engine from its place of concealment to the boat, I struggled with the cord that tied my hands together. I couldn't even get my fingers to where the chord was knotted. I tried wriggling my hands free.

Sooklall got the engine onto the back of the boat and began yanking at a cord at an attempt to start it. I looked out across the river, hoping someone would pass by in a boat and rescue me. But there was not a vessel to be seen on the light brown choppy waters of the river. Futility began to set in.

I started thinking about things to come where I was concerned. He would take me up Canje Creek, probably hold me over the side by my feet until I was drowned. Then he would loosen the chords from my feet and hands and leave my body in the creek for it to be discovered days later when it floated down by the Canje Bridge.

I wondered how long it would take them at the house to realize I was missing. Reena would probably be the one to miss me first. Then the boys would tell them that I had gone off with Chandra. I guess they would have to go find her but then she'd just tell them she dropped me off somewhere. So that would be a dead end until they found my body. I wondered what my funeral would look like. I supposed all the boys would be there and those at the house. I didn't suppose Dil would take time off from the cinema to come, nor would Raj if he had a football match on that day. I wondered if Hector and Majeed would come from across the river. Would Mala come?

I started crying hysterically and resorted to begging Sooklall to spare my life, promising him I would tell no one about the fire if he gave me five dollars instead of twenty. Sooklall's response to this request was to sardonic smile, take the cigarette from his lips and flick it away into the water.

"You still want money, eh?" he said and seemed amused.

He yanked the cord on the engine again and the engine roared to life. He loosed the rope from the tree and climbed into the back of the boat. He sat half turned so he can manipulate the handle which steered the engine. He revved it and the boat started moving away from the mud flat and toward the middle of the river.

I continued pleading for my life between sobs and thought it better not to put money as a condition for my silence. My promise to keep quiet about everything for free did not seem to impress Sooklall as he maneuvered the boat about fifty yards away from the shoreline then straightened up and headed north toward the mouth of the river.

"How you know about the kerosene oil?" he shouted above the noise of the engine.

"Is a girl tell me," I said hopefully.

"A girl. Where she live?"

"She living next door to where the fire was. She name Rosanne," I sang. "She is the one that say she see you pouring kerosene oil around the shop."

"Rosanne, eh? And she live next door?" he said thoughtfully.

"Yes. She father does work at the hospital. You go let me go now?"

"Naw, you know too much."

I continued bawling with all my might above the noise of the engine but no one was around to hear me. Sooklall left the engine and carefully stepped forward in a stooping manner toward me. He pulled more of the fish netting in my vicinity over me to conceal me then went back to the engine.

On our right the wide tributary of the Canje Creek came up and he turned the boat in that direction. I stopped bawling, figuring I'd have to pass by the bridge where there would be people around there. As we progressed into the mouth of the creek up its dark brown waters I could see the big buildings of the Mental hospital behind the trees on our right. I knew the swing bridge across this waterway was not too far after. I kept working my hands behind my back, keeping my fingers straight and together in a bunch to make my hands narrower. I felt the cord had a little room by my wrist and kept working to get a wrist free.

The boat continued upstream and I could see Crab Island come to an end on our left and coconut trees appearing. We were approaching the back of Sheet Anchor village which was the first village across the bridge.

Suddenly I felt my left hand come free of the cord. I stopped and looked at Sooklall who had his attention on whatever was ahead. I supposed he was nervous that someone might see us as we approached the bridge. Once he passed the bridge and the ship building area and got around the first bend in the Creek he would be home free.

I used the now free left hand and worked on freeing the other. The loud blast of a ship's horn filled the air. Sooklall looked concerned and started steering the boat closer to the shore on the right of the two hundred yard wide creek. I turned and raised my head to try to see ahead. The bridge was open with the center span turned across facing the direction of the creek so that the ship could pass on one side. The ship was coming through the side of the middle span on our right and Sooklall was steering toward that same side of the river. Then I noticed other smaller boats on the left and figured he didn't want to pass near them for fear of me starting to bawl for help. For they would certainly hear.

With the bridge open, vehicular traffic on both sides of the bridge came to a halt. People were standing around watching the ship pass through. Sooklall didn't seem happy about this. As we got nearer and we approached the left side of the ship's bow I threw the netting off me and attempted to free my feet. Sooklall's eyes bulged and he scrambled forward to get to me but by then the huge swells from the ship had reached us and rocked our little boat violently. He fell back and grabbed at the throttle of the engine as he tried to stabilize the boat.

I jumped up and bawled for help, waving my arms crazily. Sooklall was terrified. He attempted to get up again but the boat was rocking too much. He sped up and passed the boat where larger swells kicked up by the propellers awaited us. I kept screaming and waving and could see I had the attention of some of the people standing at the New Amsterdam side of the bridge.

As we sped through the gap over which the closed bridge would have been, we ran right into the large swells kicked up by the big ship. Our little boat lifted violently and I was momentarily airborne. The boat fell with a loud bash onto another swell and I landed hard on the side, bruising my right hip in the process. As I screamed out in pain the boat bucked and twisted violently to the right, throwing me clear of it and into the turbulent waters of the creek. I went under the cool dark brown waters of the creek and could feel a strong undercurrent. I opened my mouth to breathe but took in water instead. Suddenly I was thrust to the surface where I gurgled and splashed about with my freed arms. My feet were still tied.

The current was taking me in a wide circle as if in a whirlpool. While I bawled for help I noticed the boat had capsized and Sooklall was in the same predicament as me. Someone at the ship building site plunged into the water and started heading out for me. Then I was pulled under by the currents again. I flailed my arms desperately, not knowing how deep this current would take me. I closed my mouth and tried not to take in water. Just when I felt I couldn't hold my breath anymore I broke the surface again. I gasped, coughed and sputtered. I must have been facing the Sheet Anchor side of the creek for I couldn't see the ship building site. Just as I was about to be sucked under again I felt someone grab me around the neck from behind. I held on to the strong brown arm for dear life.

The current was taking us in a wide circle but the person holding me was taking his time and not fighting against the current. I got a glimpse of a wild eyed Sooklall some twenty yards away fighting desperately against the current then saw him get sucked under the surface.

"Hold around my neck," my rescuer said. Despite my aching side I turned and grabbed around his neck. He swam powerfully with me in tow as we headed back to the ship building site from which he had come. I could see the people on the bridge with their attention on us. Some were clapping while others were pointing in the vicinity of the water where Sooklall had disappeared.

There were many hands there to pull us out of the water when we got to the ship building site. Two more men were in the water heading out to where Sooklall was last sighted.

I lay on the wooden landing and coughed violently. One man turned me on my stomach and massaged my back. I coughed and choked as I vomited the water I had swallowed.

"You Alright Milo?" a familiar voice asked. I looked up and saw it was Lucky. It was he who had pulled me from a watery grave. I cried like a baby as I clung around his neck.

Once Upon A Time In Berbice

Chapter Twenty-Two

They only kept me for one day in the hospital. I was kind of sorry it wasn't longer. Of the eight children on my ward I was like royalty. The boys all came and, for the most part, made fun of me. Lea came with See and Christopher. Aunty Nalini and her two daughters came with Sondra and Reena came for most of the day with Mammy. Even Mr. Anton and Bertie came by at different times. Bucky came for half an hour with fruits that midday and brought along tall Nathaniel with her.

My surprise visitor was Rosanne. She came by when Reena and Mommy were there with me. We didn't have a chance to talk privately for long. She couldn't help giving me the "I told you so" treatment about her being right about Sooklall deliberately setting fire to his shop and killing his father-in-law. She said she had come to the hospital by herself but I figured she probably came to her father's workplace at the dispensary on the ground floor and had sneaked up to see me. However, I was still glad to see her, although I felt a little guilty about selling her out to Sooklall in an attempt to save my own skin.

Later that day I learned from Reena that Sunil had actually seen me go in to Sooklall's place and was waiting for me to come out. When he saw Chandra leave shortly after and I didn't, he headed for the police station. When he went back to the shop with two policemen Chandra had returned and they arrested her when she claimed to know nothing of my whereabouts. When they threatened to lock her up she revealed Sooklall had taken me in a boat up the creek. They then raced around to the bridge to intercept us but it was too late by then.

They locked up Chandra who was claiming that Sooklall cooked up the whole scheme and threatened her to go along with it. They were yet to find Sooklall's body. Sunil never came to see me that day. Neither did Doogoo who, I supposed, was wary of hospitals since her last visit there was very much unpleasant. They sent me home that afternoon.

Later that evening Sunil came in looking very haggard. I could smell alcohol on his breath. He didn't say anything to me and I could see he had been crying. Reena told me afterward that he had taken food to the prison for Chandra.

The next day was the day before the last day of school. The teachers, frustrated and preoccupied with the task of balancing their registers, let us out for recess for most of the day. We ran over to the gardens and played most of the time. By midday the celebrity status I had enjoyed over the incident at the bridge had blown over. As I went home for lunch that midday Mammy reminded me that I had to go over to Ms. Munroe at the head of the street for Bucky's wedding rehearsal that evening. I was looking forward to a very busy and exciting afternoon and weekend.

When I went back to school with Squingee and Tillam they got bogged down in a marble game under the school. I slipped over to the gardens and to the Lover's section. As I surveyed the terrain I noticed my friend Mr. Rai was back in his old hunting grounds. He had his back turned to me and arms around a girl who had her head buried on a shoulder of his.

I scooted under the hedges and nearer to that location. As I peered through the bushes I could see they were kissing. Then she hoisted herself onto his lap and straddled him as she continued to kiss him. Only then could I actually see her face.

"No Lea, No!" I heard myself screaming aloud.

END

Epilogue

Unknown to me and several streets away, in a little wooden house in the middle of Cooper's Lane, ten year old Everard Harding was about to get a beating from his irate mother because he could not find the Castrol can she usually had him take to the shop to buy kerosene oil. He had lost the last one a month ago and she had got another and even painted the metal handle red to avoid him misplacing it again. He knew he was in for it this time because, in a panic, he had thrown it over the back fence and into the gutter in the alley behind there some weeks earlier. He and a friend had been playing bush cook in the backyard when his mother had come home earlier than expected. He had figured that, had she seen the can back there with them, she would have figured out what they were doing. So in his haste to get rid of it, he had thoughtlessly tossed it over the back fence. Since then she had left money for him to buy kerosene and he had borrowed a can to do so. He made sure he had filled the glass reservoir of the two burner kerosene stove so that she would not have to get the can herself. He had made an attempt to find the can after but supposed the drain cleaners must have swept it away. So he had given up after just one try.

Now his mother wanted the can and had gone inside for the leather strop she used to keep him on the "straight and narrow." He prepared himself for a tanning, for his mother was one who staunchly believed that if something was to be done it was to be done right. He just hoped his crying wasn't loud enough to be heard by the girl he was recently liking; the Bajan girl living in the house right behind and on the other side of the drain in the alley.

Once Upon A Time In Berbice

Acknowledgements

The following people were instrumental in providing background information or contributing in some way in making this book possible:

Aubrey Henry
Belinda Smith
Bertie Henry
Bibi Mohamed
Brent Rose
Camille *Ann Marie* Mohamed
Charles Krishnlall
Clairmont "Tait"
Colridge Moore
Compton Cole
Crystal Hawkins
Dennis Mitchell
Desmond Henry
Eustace Aaron
Everad Harding
Fitzroy Lewis
Frank Samaroo
Gafton "Twiddle" Williams
Gary Sulker
Glendon Franco
Gordon "Gilly" Jordon
Harry Rose
Ivor "Ounces" Williams
Joe Samuels
June Mackennan
Junior Lewis
Kelvin Cole
Leslie Mayers
Lincoln Earl
Linden Jones
Linden Casey
Lindon "Bird" Hinckson

Liza Inshanally
Lorry Hinckson
Michael "Dada" Henry
Monty Samuels
Morris Henry
Ms. G. Maraj
Neville "Scarro" Williams
Nitaasha Singh
Oral "Fat Man" Trellis
Oral "Tanker" Samuels
Orin "Slabber" Rollins
Orin "Jabbar" Hazel
Owen Collins
Owen Lewis
Paris Cole
Paul "Pablo" Larose
Peter Chesney
Phillip Carington
PinkyWeatherspoon
Preston Franco
Preston Phillips
Prince Jordon
Rhonda Carrington
Roy Franco
Rudy Henry
Savi Fredericks
Seelochanie Mathura
Sherry Larose
Tony Franco
Troy Steele
Wesley "Scoodameese" Rose
Winston Henry

Glossary

Bisi-bisi	long tube-like grass that usually grow in swampy areas
Breakfast	The large midday meal
Bucta	male underpants
Crapaud	toad
Cussing out	Verbally abusing someone
Dhoti	Indian garment worn like a pants and fits like an oversized baby napkin; worn mostly by old Indian men with a strong cultural links with India.
Dougla	Mixed person of Indian and black parents
Doungs	Small yellow-green plum-sized fruit that grows on a not too tall tree.
Eye-opener	drinking of liquor early in the day
Flambo	Homemade lamp made with a drink bottle with a makeshift wick dipping in fuel, usually kerosene oil.
Foreshore	The side of the road closer to the sea
Fullerman	Local name for a Muslim
Ganesh	one of the most popular of the deities in the Hindu religion
Jamoon	Purple fruit like a plum which is very sweet and juicy.
Kisskadee	A small local bird which is black in color with yellow on the head; named after the sound of its whistle.
Koka	sluice, a large gate sliding up and down to control water in a canal. With the coast of Guyana being below sea level, these sluices are numerous and necessary.
Lunch	Light afternoon meal children eat after coming home from school in the afternoon.

Once Upon A Time In Berbice

Marabunta	Wasp
Mehbooba	hindi for "my love" or "my beloved"
Meri	
Pandit	Hindu religious leader who usually presides over Hindu marriage ceremony.
Punt	small metal flat-bottomed barge used to transport sugarcane
Scampish	Dishonest
Senna	(senna pod) is a powerful laxative used locally.
Sitar	long necked guitar used in Indian music
Stelling	Landing where boats or ferry come in to dock.
Suck Teeth	"Stewpsing" sound made with the lips to register disgust or disapproval; mostly done by West Indians and Africans. Also called "kiss teeth" (Jamaican).
Tassa	two sets of drums
Tea	Light morning meal
Velosolex	looks more like a small bicycle with a huge engine over the front wheel.

Other books by this author

Now Available

Now Available

West Indian Humor is a cartoon collection by Mal who has done political and humorous cartoons for the Gleaner Company and the Jamaica Observer in Jamaica, Trinidad Express in Trinidad, Nassau Guardian in Bahamas, The Carib News company, and The Caribbean Impact

newspapers in New York.

Roll Over

Step into the lives of Ruby Tahal, Fenton Little and Maxwell Richardson, and rediscover the joy, dreams, and frustration of growing up in the West Indies.

Malcolm Alves

Now Available

Available in 2009

Previews and samples for
all books can be found at

www.unitedstatesofthewestindies.com

Once Upon A Time In Berbice

www.ingramcontent.com/pod-product-compliance
Lightning Source LLC
Chambersburg PA
CBHW020833030726
47496CB00001B/216